SPRINGWATER
REUNION

by

J. Alan Hitchens

ISBN: 978-0-692-71495-9
Library of Congress Control Number: 2016908278

FIRST EDITION

Not-So-Fast Press
P.O. Box 64
Elk, WA 99009

DEDICATION

*To Christian for
His inspiration . . .*

*With gratitude to my
family and friends for
their encouragement
and their patience.*

PART ONE

RETURN TO SPRINGWATER

CHAPTER ONE

Just before you die your whole life catches up to you...

Noah Conklin had always heard this and as he sat on his horse in the middle of an open prairie he wondered if he should be getting ready to die. Parts of his life were coming back to him in the visions of his memory – a piece here and a piece there. Images trapped forever in his mind's eye.

He thought of the dead Mexican laying naked and bloated on the parched earth with his wrists tied across his chest. He'd been gut-shot and had been stretched out in the full sun for a couple of days. Even in death the Mexican's face bore an angry scowl. Close by was a peon wearing a bandanna for a mask to help ward off the stench of the putrefying corpse while he dug a shallow grave. The flies were thick and their buzzing was the only sound in the still air on that hot lazy day – the constant buzz of the flies and the sporadic clank of the shovel as it pecked away at the hard ground.

Then another time, one spring day, there was the Apache sprawled face down in the tan water of the Yaqui River. His long black hair floated on the water and he was engulfed in a cloud of rust colored blood as the last moments of mortal life seeped from his body. There were still times in the darkest hours of the night when memories of the Apache tormented Noah's dreams. And he could still picture the two dead Indians dangling side-by-side from the limb of a cottonwood. One was an old man and the other was only a boy, their necks broken and distorted from the hangman's noose. Their ears had been cut off and the yellow jackets fought over their rotting flesh. To Noah, that entire incident had been an abomination – and it angered him every time he thought of it.

The clarity of the images made Noah shudder like a cold wind had swept over him. Other memories from bygone times began to whirl in his head and he felt as though he was riding back into the part of his life that haunted him the most. He tried to put it all out of his mind as he touched his spurs to the horse's flanks.

It was late in the summer as Noah loped his dappled gelding across the floor of the Snake River valley in the Idaho Territory. In the distance was a small farm nestled at the base of the foothills. It was a simple farm with a log barn and a small frame house and a few fruit trees. There was a chicken coop and a tool shed, and on the hillside beyond the barn was a mortared stone springhouse. A small creek ran through the barnyard and off into the cattails and cottonwoods.

There was a knot of anxiety in Noah's gut that twisted even tighter when he saw the figure of a woman cross the yard and watch him from behind a clothesline full of bright swaying bed sheets. She remained motionless, mostly hidden, and he felt like the whole world was frozen in time watching him and he was the only thing that was still moving. He looked all around and behind him at the open spaces and there wasn't another soul in sight. The silence was broken only by the sound of him riding and he could smell the tired and sweaty horse beneath him. He felt a fear as though something was trying to tell him that he was riding smack dab into a bad time. It was the same feeling he got when he knew that where he was going more than likely someone would shoot at him. Surely the woman hidden behind her wash wouldn't want to shoot him. He began to wonder about her husband. Where was her man?

In the shade of the cottonwoods a half dozen milk cows stood up from chewing their cud to watch him pass by. Noah slowed his horse to a walk before crossing the creek and as he drew closer he could plainly see it was her. It was Rose. It was the woman he wished would have gotten out of this place years ago. His mouth was dry and he thought of the pint bottle of whiskey in his saddlebags. He cursed himself under his breath for not having braced himself better for this meeting. He had come all this way to see her – all the while hoping she would be long gone.

He rode across the barnyard and reined up so he was looking down on her over the bed sheets. She was holding onto the clothesline with both hands and staring at him with an intensity that was hard to read. He couldn't tell if she was scared or mad, but the way her eyes scoured him just added to his discomfort.

"Is your husband around?" he asked, crossing his wrists over the horse's withers. He watched the house to see if there were any faces in the windows. She didn't answer. Instead she walked around and stood at the end of the clothesline in order to get a better look at him.

The elements and the years had worn creases in his face and dusted his black hair with white at the temples, and he kept his whiskers scraped off the best he could. At nearly forty years old, there was still a hunger for adventure in Noah Conklin's gray eyes and he was lean like a man half his age. His wiry torso was a direct result of the restless life he led – combined with a somewhat miserable diet. He sat in a tooled Mexican saddle trimmed with silver and he wore silver conchas on his pants and jacket. His hatband was made from the skin of a coral snake, and ornate Spanish spurs adorned his boots. He carried with him an air of confidence that other men either respected, or feared. Her gaze fixed on his holster with the loose hammer thong and the leather strap cinched tight on his thigh – and the pistol, worn to a dull shine from handling.

"You're not welcome around here anymore," she finally said, matter-of-factly, and walked past him toward the chicken coop as if she was looking for a place to hide out for awhile.

"I didn't think I would be." He rode along behind her until she reached the henhouse door, then slid down out of the saddle. "I'll leave, but first I need to talk to you, Rose," he called out as she ducked inside.

Leading his horse over to the creek, he took off his hat and slapped some of the trail dust from his pants. He dropped the reins on the ground leaving the animal to drink, and headed back to the chicken coop to try to conclude his business so he could be on his way. And right then he had no idea which direction that might be.

He looked around the little farm and saw it had been well kept. There were lace curtains in the windows of the house and beneath the windows rose bushes were blooming and daisies and other flowers lit up the place with reds and yellows and purples. The flowers along with the scrubbed clean sheets hanging in the sun were a dead giveaway that there was a woman around. But there was something else, too. There were fresh split cedar fence posts stuck in the ground holding up shiny new barbed wire and a new cedar shake roof over the henhouse. The work of a man. There were signs of a man all over the place. His eyes finally settled on the patches of pale-green lichen growing on the north face of the log barn. The years were taking their toll. The gray weathered logs brought a deep sigh from him.

When he went inside the henhouse, Rose had a basket and was gathering eggs. It was a cozy structure and only a few feet separated them as the heat of the day sharpened the stale air. A soft and gentle light was cast over her through the dusty windows and he watched as she focused on the task at hand – pilfering the nest boxes. An iridescent rooster came strutting in from the coop with a couple of hens cackling after him. Rose shooed at the chickens and they skittered back outside.

She looked younger than her years and the gentle lines in her face showed signs of contentment, but her hands told of the hardships. The sparkle in her green eyes had dimmed, and the strawberry curls that once danced on her shoulders were twisted into a tight bun on top of her head. She had changed over the years from the pretty little girl he remembered into a strong, elegant woman.

Noah spotted an egg and when he reached down to pick it up Rose noticed for the first time that he wore his hair long and braided down the back of his neck. "You look like some fancy trail slicker," she commented, "or some kind of darn gunman. Why in heavens name have you come back here?"

"You do have a husband, don't you?" He walked over and held the egg out for her.

"He ran out on me a long time ago," she answered flatly, taking the egg. "What do you want?"

"Nothing," Noah shrugged. "I guess I really didn't expect to find you still here after all these years. All the way I kept thinking over and over again that I didn't want to cause you any problems. I mean, if you have a husband I don't want to cause any trouble for you in that way."

"You weren't too worried...here you are," Rose said as she quickly brushed past him going outside for a breath of fresh air.

"If you got a man around here I guess I ought to talk to him, too," he followed her.

"Talk about what?" Rose turned back to face him. "Right now I'm trying to think what there is that's worth talking about anymore, and I can't think of anything so if you have something you want to say, go ahead and say it. I have things that need tending to."

"Tell you the truth, Rose," he said, "my tongue is stuck to the inside of my mouth right now. I need to go get a drink of water first."

"I'm sure you remember where the spring pipe is," she looked at him, doubtfully. "But I don't think you have anything to say that I want to listen to."

"How do you know that?" he reasoned. "You don't know what it is that brought me back to this country."

Shaking her head slightly, Rose gave him a troubled stare, then walked away from him toward the house. Noah remembered back over the years and could recall her always shaking her head like that when she was upset over something. The memories made the years melt away.

Almost seventeen years had passed since the last time Noah had seen Rose. At that time she was nothing more than a young bride – his. Together they had traveled the Oregon Trail ending up here on this remote piece of land. It seemed so long ago when she had loved and trusted him. But there was more to it than that. She had put her faith in him and he had failed her in the worst way. Noah had brought Rose to this forlorn little crease in the earth only to abandon her. He took a deep breath and began shaking his own head wondering how it was he ended up right back where he started.

CHAPTER TWO

There was a wagon trail that ran alongside the barn and followed the small creek. Noah took the trail and after walking for about a minute came to where it ended at the base of a steep hill. He found the iron pipe that had been driven into the hillside where a steady stream of water as big around as his thumb flowed out the end of it onto a flat stone and splattered away. A drinking ladle hung from the pipe. The water coming from beneath the ground was cold enough to cause the rusty pipe to sweat.

As he drank the cold sweet water his gaze settled on the springhouse that stood a few yards up the hillside above the spring pipe. It was built of mortared stone and he could remember hauling the rocks up there one at a time and cementing them together – and at that moment the sight of it reminded him of the reason why he had gone off on his own.

In the beginning he had thought up all kinds of senseless reasons for cutting out on Rose, to try to justify it in his own mind. Ultimately, he realized it was the spirit of adventure that had stole him away. This is the West after all, the new frontier, never ending landscapes filled with excitement and hope on one side of the coin and misfortune and suffering on the other. When he was a younger man he had yearned to experience the adventure of it all – and he found it at every bend in the trail. But along the way somewhere he had grown weary of the adventure and now all he yearned for was a little peace in his life. When he had cried out for adventure it always came rumbling in, and now that he cried out for some peace it seemed to elude him. And now he wondered if perhaps it wasn't his comeuppance for leaving Rose out here all alone way back when.

Having browsed its way up the little stream, his tall gray horse stood nearby cropping the lush green clumps of grass growing along the bank. Noah took his canteen from the saddle and refilled it with the cold spring water. When he returned to the horse he stowed away the canteen and dug the pint of whiskey out of his saddle bag. He stooped down behind the horse to block the view from the house and took a generous swig. The smell and taste of the whiskey had a calming effect on him as it burned its way into his stomach. There was no going back in time to set things straight with Rose. The only time that mattered now lay ahead of him. He put the cork back and tucked the bottle away.

"Where in hell do I go from here?" he asked the horse as he grabbed the reins and led it back down the creek. Along the way, he reminded himself of the reason he had ridden to this end of the valley to begin with. There was still the business at hand. He walked slowly back past the barn and past the laundry hanging on the clothesline. He figured Rose must be inside the house watching him from behind her lace curtains and he hoped she would come out to talk, but she didn't. And Noah kept going down the creek leading his horse.

He passed a couple of plum trees that were loaded down with the dull red fruit, and just the sight of all those ripe plums made his stomach growl. In a nearby pasture the handful of dairy cows were up grazing on the blue-green blotches of clover and farther downstream Noah could see the roof of a barn. The barn seemed out of place to him as a crow flew overhead calling out to unseen allies.

Noah took a moment to stop and look around, hoping in vain that Rose had come back outside. It was a peaceful sight, the whitewashed house surrounded by a yard full of bright colored flowers and the clean sheets flapping in the breeze. And there were fruit trees scattered about. He could see the ambitions that were once his because Rose had carried them forward. The land he had settled and worked many years ago was well cared for – and he figured she couldn't have done it all by herself. Something wasn't right. She was still a beautiful woman. So where was her man?

A footpath split off from the wagon tracks so as to follow the meandering creek more closely. Noah took the path and soon came to a small stand of locust trees. In a clearing was a wooden bench and nearby was a rope swing that dangled from a branch and the ground beneath the plank seat of the swing was worn smooth.

He hitched his horse to a tree at the edge of the clearing in hopes of letting it have the flies and gnats all to itself. And he had barely sat down on the bench when he spotted Rose coming down the path toward him. She had a teacup in her hand and he could tell by her stern look that she had something weighing down her mind – and she was about to lighten her load.

"If you came here to say something, then say it," she told him bluntly as she approached. "I have chores to tend to. Say what it is you came here for, and then I wish you'd ride out of here and go back to wherever it was you came from. Just please leave me be."

"I can see this was a bad idea, stopping by here." Noah got up from the bench and as he strolled past her, added, "I thought maybe I could help out, but I suppose you don't want any help from me." He stood at the edge of the creek and looked back over his shoulder at her.

"I got all the help I can afford," she scoffed.

"I'm not looking for that kind of a job," he said. "I have a job if I want one."

Everything he had come to tell her was running through his head, if only he could find a place to begin. He doubted she would understand even if he could come up with the right words to say. What could she possibly know about such things?

"Noah, if you must know," Rose offered before he had a chance to speak, "there is a man that helps out around here. On down this path a short ways is a little two chicken farm. It's Mixy Alexander's place."

"Mixy Alexander," Noah said, with a certain amount of disbelief. "Is that old darkie still kicking?"

"Yes he is, and he's a Negro," Rose responded sharply. "If you were from Kansas instead of Missouri you'd know the difference. And I don't know if I'd even made it here without his help. He helped you a lot, too, before you went off. That man can build or fix anything that needs to be built or fixed."

"I didn't mean any disrespect," Noah assured her. It made sense to him, that after all this time it would turn out to be Mixy Alexander keeping Rose's farm all fixed up and running. "I can remember what all Mixy did for me."

"There were times over the years," Rose said, "that I could only think back on you with hate." This had been on her mind far too long. "I grew to hate you. There were other times that I wondered about you – if you were alive or dead. Most of the time, though, when I thought of you, I just got plain confused from wondering what in heaven's name it was I did wrong."

"You didn't do anything wrong," Noah assured her.

"Then you did," Rose declared.

There was a long moment of silence where all that could be heard was the little creek gurgling at their feet and the birds chirping among the tree branches. Glancing upstream at the old log barn, Noah thought back in time as he spoke. "I built that barn and I built that house, along with Mixy's help," he said, pointing around. "I plowed the field over there and I harvested the corn and potatoes. I put up hay for the animals and laid in wood for the winter. I knew that the next year I would be doing the same thing all over again. And the year after that, too. I could see my whole life laid right out there in front of me in that piece of dirt."

"And what you saw didn't please you?" Rose moseyed over and sat down in the swing.

"No, it didn't," he concluded, turning to her. "And I still don't know if it would please me or not. I can tell you this, though, it wasn't all I wanted to know. I've always had the feeling that there has to be more than what there is. I needed to find out for myself."

Rose gazed at the house and barn, then out at the cows. It was difficult for her to understand what he meant. The way she saw it, she had a roof over her head, a good store of food in the root cellar, and the dairy herd for a little hard currency. "To me, more would be a new Chinese silk scarf," she said, thinking aloud as she pushed herself in the swing. "So, what did you find out?"

"Lots of things," Noah informed her. "I learned that it feels like the years are getting shorter, but life keeps getting longer."

"What's that supposed to mean?" Rose asked.

"I don't know what it's supposed to mean," Noah shrugged. He stared into the crisp, clear water as it flowed by. "I learned that there are men out there who are happy to kill each other over water...or money, or grass. Even less."

"And what does any of that have to do with you?" Rose felt lost in the conversation.

"That's what I've been doing for the past few years," Noah explained. "I've worked on some big ranches. I've worked for men who owned spreads bigger than this whole valley. Most of them had a lot of trouble with Indians, or Mexican rustlers. And white rustlers, too. But then there was times it was nothing more than two stubborn men wanting each other's grass and water."

Rose pushed herself around in the swing, staring through the locust trees at a point known only to her. She appeared to be truly concerned about something. He studied her as she lazed a moment, bathed in the beams of sunlight breaking through the branches above her. How could he have forgotten how lovely she was?

"Rose, I can't hardly believe a good-looking woman like you doesn't have a man around," Noah restated.

"I haven't been looking for one," she told him.

"Seems to me they would have found you by now," he suggested.

"Like I said," Rose looked past him toward her farm, "I had one once. He went away and left me with this place. I had a house and a barn, and a hundred and sixty acres."

"And good water," Noah added.

"That's one thing I have to admit," she looked at him, "this place has always had the best water." And for the first time since he arrived that day he could detect a little smile in her eyes. She tossed out the last of her tea and let herself sway back and forth in the swing.

"They named this valley Springwater, after all those springs you found up there on that hillside behind the house." As she thought about it, she realized how strange it was the way some things came to be, and it made her sigh. "It seems they built a town down there overlooking the river, Noah, and all because of your nose for clean tasting water," she conceded.

"I always did like the taste of good water," Noah reminded her. "I still do.

"Are we still married?" The question just popped into his head and before he knew it had just popped out of his mouth.

The smile had vanished from her piercing green eyes. After a long moment, she replied, "I suppose according to the fancy scrap of paper buried somewhere in my hope chest. But I'd say not in the eyes of God...or mine."

When brought to light, the painful memories awakened the anger and it flared up in Rose. The unresolved events of a time long ago still troubled and upset her. She glanced up at the sun like she was looking at a clock, then down the valley toward the Snake River.

"I have things to get done," Rose said, standing up from the swing and starting for the house without waiting for him to speak another word.

He unhitched his horse and stepped up into the saddle and trailed along behind her. When Rose reached the wagon tracks he reined in beside her. She took another survey of him as they walked along in silence and she shook her head a bit. Besides a pair of bulging saddlebags, his bedroll and a frayed carpetbag were tied on behind the cantle.

"So," she quizzed, "is that your whole outfit?"

"Every last thing," he admitted to her. "I haven't gathered much over the years that you can see. But even though I'm poor of possessions, I'm rich in experience. And if it wouldn't be too much to ask, I'd pick a few of those plums to take with me." As they approached the tree, the smell set Noah's stomach to gurgling with hunger pangs. It had been awhile since his last good sit-down meal.

"I guess I don't mind," she offered, and watched as he picked a half dozen plums and tucked them away inside his shirt. A gust of warm wind swept past them causing the clean sheets on the line to make a popping sound. The commotion spooked Noah's horse slightly and it danced about.

"That's a fine looking gelding," she commented. "He's a thoroughbred, isn't he?"

"Yes he is," Noah replied, patting the horse's neck. "This here's Pecos, 'cause he came from down along the Pecos River. I've been riding him for about four years now. He's a damn good saddle horse, and he's due for a rest. An Apache Indian had him. Hated to give him up, too."

"Should I dare ask how you ended up with him?"

"The Indian was an outlaw and a murderer," Noah explained to her. "He was killed in a gunfight, so he didn't need the horse anymore. You seem to know horses a lot better than before."

"Do you know Jared Sowers?" She asked bluntly.

Noah wrestled with her question for a moment. He thought it strange Rose even considered it possible that they might know the same person after all this time. "No, I can honestly say that I've never met the man," he finally answered. "Who is he?"

"He has a big ranch on the east rim over there." Rose stared off across the faded-green landscape. "He raises and grazes beef cattle. He's a bitter little man and most everyone around here figures it's his ambition to have most of this whole valley all to himself. I guess if that's the case, it's to make up for some of his other shortcomings."

"Such as?" Noah urged her to continue.

"He's another one of those unhappy, greedy men, Noah, who are never satisfied with what they have," Rose stated, bending down to pick up a plum that had fallen from the tree. "Thinks he deserves anything he wants because he has money. Even what he never can have."

"Sounds like you know him pretty well," Noah said.

"Everybody around here knows about him," Rose stated. She fixed a curious gaze on him as she stuffed the plum into her apron pocket.

"I don't imagine I'll be staying around here long," Noah told her. "I want to see what Oregon has to offer that Idaho don't. Have you been to Oregon?"

"No, I haven't," she responded, and grabbed hold of one of the reins. "Noah, Mixy Alexander is over seventy years old now. He traveled down to Tennessee a few years ago and brought himself back a wife. Her name was Sarla and the poor thing was always sickly. She's been dead two years now. Mixy has done so much for me, I gave him a piece of ground to live on, down where the creek runs off my property. He's made it real nice down there. He's a sweet and gentle old man and all he wants on this earth is live out his days on that little farm."

"It's good he found a place to stay," Noah sighed.

He thanked her for the plums as he buttoned his shirt. She let go of the rein and he tipped a finger to the brim of his hat and bid her goodbye.

There was much more he wanted to say to her, but figured it might be best to let it rest awhile – give time a chance to do its work. He'd let the dust settle and come back in a couple of days. The mention of Jared Sowers had caught him off guard. Now it was time he tended to his own business.

As he rode out of the yard, he turned in the saddle and Rose was standing among her flowers with an arm up to shade the sun as she watched him, her long skirt blowing in the breeze.

CHAPTER THREE

From Rose's farm at the head of the valley, the wagon road ran to the south. He soon passed by where it split off to Mixy Alexander's place, but there was a sharp bend that kept him from seeing anything. Noah stayed on the main road that wound down along the creek toward the Snake River and the newly founded village of Springwater. He aimed his tired horse along the strip of grass that grew between the ruts and let his eyes and mind wander over the land – and he ate plums.

Farther down the valley, another set of parallel lines worn in the earth by the wheels of wagons streaked across the rolling prairie and merged with the road he was following. At one place he coaxed his horse to ford the creek where a rock bottom had been laid for wagons. The road became more traveled and he crossed over a bridge built from logs and planks. He stopped at the crossing to wash the sticky nectar from his hands.

Along the way Noah passed by a scattering of poor dirt farms that were unfamiliar to him. At one of the farms, a stout chestnut-colored mule pulled a plow across a field while a flock of white gulls followed the plowshare, crying sharply at one another as they gleaned grubs and earthworms from the freshly turned furrow. The man walking behind the plow didn't have time to look up as Noah rode past. Off in the distance on a low rise was a simple frame building that was bright with whitewash. It appeared somewhat desolate sitting out in the middle of the vast prairie. Noah thought it had to be either a church or a school – or maybe even a grange hall. Cattle were here and there along the creek most of the way.

An hour after Noah left the head of the valley, he gazed down upon the Snake River. In the near distance was a clutter of a dozen or so buildings. There was a church steeple among them. The little village was perched on the basalt bluffs overlooking the blue-green water. The main street that ran through the middle of Springwater was part of the Oregon Trail.

To avoid the town, Noah reined Pecos away from the creek and across open land where he passed by a cemetery. He soon struck the main trail again and rode upriver to a ferry crossing called Rocky Bar where a new hotel had been built above the flood plain of the Snake. Before reaching the hotel he turned onto a lesser traveled wagon road that forked off up a draw into the hills.

Following the wagon path, he rode into a narrow hollow bordered by towering cottonwoods. A breeze stirred through the treetops making the leaves rattle and glisten silver and green in the afternoon sun. In the meadow stood a building with a sign over the door that read, Eddies Saloon-Oysters. A barn and corral were out behind the saloon and two one-room cabins stood to the side near the tree line. All the structures were built from logs, and the whole operation was fairly run-down. Foul smoke from a nearby burn pile hung in the air.

Years before, when Noah first came to this country with Rose, the place was the main stopover for travelers along the trail. He remembered the image of the man who used to own it – a huge man who was more blacksmith than innkeeper. Tethered in the shade of a cottonwood, an old roan mare stood hitched to a wagon. The mare nickered as Noah rode up to the saloon and his gelding snorted back. Noah recognized one of the horses hitched to the rail in front of the saloon. It was a lanky bay that belonged to a man named Lester Dunlavy. He tied Pecos beside the bay and went inside.

The voices of the men in the saloon died down as their heads swiveled around to see who had walked in. The barkeep was a scrawny old man with fuzzy white hair named Eddie Button. He hopped up from a low stool behind the bar the instant Noah came through the door.

"Glass of whiskey," Noah said, slapping a coin down on the bar.

"I got some beans cooked up if you're hungry," Eddie said when he sat the drink down and picked up the money.

"Not just now," Noah said with a shake of his head.

The barkeep went back over and sat on the stool where he kept an eye on his customers. At the far end of the bar was a robust young man dressed in farmer's overalls. The tan-faced boy had coal black hair and the most unusual eyes – they were the color of a turtledove. He was hanging onto a mug of beer and tipped it as a gesture of greeting when Noah looked his way. He guessed the boy to be no more than fourteen or fifteen years old.

Three other men played cards at a table near the only window in the saloon. One of them was staring and grinning at Noah. In his early thirties, Lester Dunlavy wore his sideburns full down his cheeks and his light brown hair grew out long from under his stiff-brimmed Stetson. Under the hat he was bald. Noah attributed the untimely hair loss to the fact that Dunlavy had spent most of his life around men and situations that scared him. Besides being skilled at gathering information, Dunlavy seemed to possess a natural ability to stir up trouble. Noah had once used the term *instigator* to describe him. The description seemed to please Dunlavy more than what others called him...they simply referred to him as a busybody.

"Excuse me, gents," Dunlavy said. He folded his card hand and came over to stand at the bar between Noah and the farm boy.

"Noah," Dunlavy greeted, "I heard that you came across on the ferry this morning."

"You heard right, Dunlavy." Noah swallowed the whiskey and set the empty glass on the bar. "How did you know it was me?"

"The description I got from the ferry master," Dunlavy said, motioning for Eddie to get Noah another drink.

"You'll never learn to tend to your own knittin', will you?" Noah challenged. The big farm kid at the end of the bar set the mug down with a loud clunk as silence fell over the room. Eddie was slow to get up off his bench and moved about with uncertainty.

"Well, I reckon not," Dunlavy replied, forcing a smile. "You know me, Noah."

"Don't blame yourself, Dunlavy," Noah said, putting his hand on the man's shoulder. "Some men are just born that way."

"Eddie, give me a pint," Dunlavy said, digging in his pocket for silver. "I heard you were still riding that tall gray horse." He spoke softly to Noah, "Let's go outdoors and have a look at him."

As they stepped outside Dunlavy uncorked the bottle and handed it to Noah.

"You seem kind of surprised to see me," Noah said, before taking a drink.

"Pecos is looking a little gaunt," Dunlavy noted, rubbing the hind end of Noah's horse.

"He's covered a lot of ground the last few days," Noah stated, handing the bottle back to Dunlavy. "When did you get here?"

"Couple weeks ago," Dunlavy informed him. "You know Burt Perry is hiring on."

"Has he showed up yet?" Noah asked.

"I haven't seen him," Dunlavy said. He tipped the bottle and took a sip of whiskey. "But Niles has already hired on. I really didn't expect for you to show up. This isn't going to be the kind of job you like. How do you put it, 'not your game'?"

"Jobs are getting scarce these days," Noah said, loosening Pecos's belly cinch.

"Burt swore the next time he saw you he'd shoot you on sight," Dunlavy said with a troubled look.

"Dunlavy, you don't know what the hell you're talking about," Noah said, taking the bottle for another snort. "It was me that swore I'd shoot him on sight. Anyway, it was whiskey talk."

Over the years, Noah had on more than one occasion worked with Lester Dunlavy. When it came to the killing part, Dunlavy was one of those men who had a talent for keeping out of sight – for a good reason, too – he was fairly poor with a gun and would shoot only if it meant saving his own hide. He was no match for most of the men he lived and worked with, not even the likes of Niles Whitehead. And when he was around men of Noah Conklin's or Burt Perry's abilities, Dunlavy made it a point to be very careful.

"Did you hear about that job in California?" Dunlavy asked. "I heard the pay is supposed to be good. The story I got was that there's a couple of ranchers around Bakersfield having a hell of a time with Mexican vaqueros rustling their whiteface cows. Have you ever been to California?"

"No, I haven't, Dunlavy," Noah replied. "Have you?"

"Nope," Dunlavy shook his head.

"How come you're not down there then, if the pay's good and you've never seen it?" Noah insisted. "I hear them Mexican vaqueros ride and shoot about like the Comanche."

Noah made the comparison between the Mexicans and Comanche so he could watch Dunlavy's reaction. A few years back Dunlavy had a run-in with a small Comanche war party. He escaped an agonizing death by accidentally riding his horse off a sandstone cliff into a river. The fall broke the horse's neck and Dunlavy nearly drowned, but he survived to talk about it – as he often did.

"I know," Dunlavy said, quivering at the thought. "That's what I hear, too. Anyway, this job was a lot closer."

"And safer," Noah added.

"I wouldn't exactly consider being caught in a cross fire between you and Burt a safe place to be," Dunlavy scoffed, taking another gulp of whiskey.

"And I don't suppose this rancher that's hiring men is having trouble with rustlers?" Noah asked.

"He's a sheep-hater," Dunlavy said. "He's got us sitting up there at that big ranch of his trying to act busy. We've moved some cows around from one prairie to another, but that's about it."

"What about Niles Whitehead?" Noah pursued. "How's he spend his time? I know he doesn't like to work."

"He's keeping his eye on a couple sheepherders that are grazing their critters in the wrong direction," Dunlavy answered. "And he shows up down here ever-so-often to get drunk and..." He stopped talking and squinted at Noah. "Goddamn it. I just figured out what you're doing up in this part of the country."

"I'm looking it over, Dunlavy," Noah told him bluntly.

"You came up here to kill Burt, didn't you?" Dunlavy seemed pleased with himself for solving some mystery. "I know you well enough to know that there's no way in hell you would ever work for a buzzard like Jared Sowers."

"What's he like?" Noah solicited.

"Wait till you meet him," Dunlavy said, grinning. "He's a strange old buffalo."

Noah talked with Dunlavy awhile longer and watched him ride out. He looked over the small cabins by the cottonwoods before going back into the saloon.

"Are you Eddie?" Noah asked, leaning on the bar and looking at the bean-pole of a man poised on his stool.

"Yes sir," Eddie answered, getting up from his seat. "Eddie Button."

"Either one of those cabins vacant?" Noah asked.

"Both empty and for rent," Eddie said. "Six-bits a day. Take your pick."

"Six-bits," Noah groaned. He wondered if that was too much as he surveyed his surroundings.

"That includes meals," Eddie explained. "At least two a day if you want them."

"Well, if it includes meals," Noah said, digging in his pocket and smiling at the boy down the bar. He laid a ten dollar gold piece on the bar. "Let me know if that runs out. I'll stay in the furthest one down. And better give me one of those pints, too."

While Noah was stripping his gear from Pecos in front of the cabin, the boy came out of the saloon and walked over to the wagon. Farm work had given the lad broad shoulders and muscular arms, and his movement was fluid like that of a cougar. He watched Noah closely for a moment, started toward him, then changed his mind returning to the wagon.

"If you have something to say, boy, say it," Noah called out to him. There was something about him that Noah found almost disturbing. It was a certain familiarity like he'd met him somewhere before though he knew he never had.

"I was just wondering..." the boy said slowly, coming over to watch Noah.

"Wondering what?" Noah asked when the boy failed to state what was on his mind.

"I wondered if sometime...maybe...you would show me some tricks to shooting?" he asked hesitantly, then quickly added, "I have my own pistol and cartridges."

"Huh," Noah grunted with amusement. It was usually the cocky young cowboys who wanted a shooting lesson. Here was a soft-spoken, somewhat bashful, peach-fuzzed farm boy wearing bibbed overalls and work boots. "What's your name?"

"Everyone hereabouts calls me Tater," the boy told him flatly.

"Tater?" Noah declared, as he pulled his saddle off of Pecos.

"I used to grow lots of potatoes to sell to the settlers heading for Oregon," Tater explained. "The name just kind of stuck to me."

"I'll tell you what, Tater," Noah said with a shake of his head, "there are no tricks to shooting that I know of. But let's say you come around here tomorrow in the afternoon with your gun and we'll break a few bottles."

"Yes sir, Mister Noah," Tater nodded with excitement.

As the boy hurried off in the wagon, Noah put his saddle inside the cabin door and went back to the saloon.

He had a supper of stewed rabbit and beans and then walked up into the hills behind the corral – taking the pint of whiskey with him. The terrain proved steeper than it looked and the climb was more than he bargained for, but worth the effort in the end. He soon found himself perched on a barren hilltop that stood sentinel over the river valley.

From his vantage point he gazed down on miles of the Snake River and the jagged canyon that its endless waters had carved into the immense plain. Sagebrush and bunchgrass stretched south to the distant skyline creating a mottled green and gray and brown landscape. Smoke from the town of Springwater was visible two or three miles down river in the pale blue sky to the west.

From there, the Springwater Valley ran north into the foothills that eventually became the Sawtooth Mountains. The tree-lined creek meandered like a dark green serpent through the valley that was speckled with small homesteads, plowed fields, grazing pastures and vast amounts of open range. At the uppermost end of the valley a hump in the earth hid Rose's land from his view.

The screech of a hawk overhead caught his attention. A small black bird dove menacingly at the hawk as it flew through the sky. Sipping the whiskey, Noah realized he could never have imagined that seeing Rose again would be so pleasing to him – and it troubled him. Perhaps she was right, maybe it would be best if he just kept on riding.

When the sun touched the horizon, turning the sky gold, he hiked back down the trail to his cabin. He thought about the boy called Tater having his own gun and wanting to learn the tricks of shooting – and most likely sneaking beers behind his folks' backs. The innocence and simple honesty of the boy, and his quest for an adventure, brought back memories to Noah of his own youth.

CHAPTER FOUR

Rose could see Mixy coming up the road as she finished loading a crate of eggs onto the wagon for the trip to Springwater. The old Negro strode briskly beside his small donkey that pulled a two wheeled cart.

"Mornin', Mizz Rose," Mixy greeted as he drew near. Halting the donkey beside the wagon, he mopped his brow with a shirtsleeve.

"Morning, Mixy," Rose said. She noticed a squadron of flies buzzing around muslin-wrapped sides of meat in the cart. "What do you have in those butcher sacks?"

"Why that was my last pig, Mizz Rose," Mixy said. "Couldn't you hear him squealin' just after sunrise?"

"I thought for a minute that it might be some mutton," Rose said, teasing. She knew Mixy had acquired fine breeding stock and prized the sheep he raised.

"No, Mizzy, I'm workin' hard to keep them sheep livin'," Mixy said, grinning. "Someday I'm gonna have them runnin' all around here."

"Cattle ain't all there is, Mixy," Rose said.

"No, Mizz Rose, there's enough room out here for all God's things," Mixy agreed, then added, "Includin' us."

"Who gets the pig?" Rose wondered aloud.

"The cook at the new hotel," Mixy told her as he transferred the butcher sacks from the cart onto the wagon behind the eggs. "Mizz Rose, do you believe in hain'ts?" he asked solemnly, mopping his brow again.

"Ghosts?" Rose was amused. "Why do you ask that?"

"'Cause of yesterday. Just past my dinner I wandered over to sit by the creek, and when I look up I see the spirit of Master Noah come ridin' this way across that prairie." Mixy's eyes widened. "I had to put my hands up over my eyes, Mizzy."

Mixy Alexander was a former slave. After the war, and freedom, he had fled as far as possible from the South. He was a tall, slender, God fearing, gentle man who had wandered into the valley about the time it was being settled. He helped the homesteaders build their houses and barnyards for a living, helped put up the crops as a neighbor – and raised or made most everything he needed to live. Though his hair was the color of salt and pepper, he was brimming with energy and forever smiling.

"Your eyes weren't playing tricks on you," Rose said, shaking her head. "That was Noah. Rode straight in here after seventeen years like some old rooster returning to the coop. I was wondering whether to tell you, or not. Why...I woke up out of a sound sleep last night and had to convince myself it really did happen before I could doze off again."

"I suppose bein' I seen him, too, it must be true," Mixy reasoned. "How's he been, Mizzy?"

"You should have seen him close up," Rose said. She fixed her gaze on the springhouse that was cut into the hillside above the barn. "On the outside he looks like a hard man, but his eyes haven't changed. I could still see a trace of the same young man I fell in love with when I was a girl. Rambunctious as all Hades." Looking back to yesterday, Rose couldn't help thinking Noah was still the most handsome man she'd ever laid eyes on. She gazed back at Mixy with uncertainty. "However, I have to be honest and say that I don't think he's been up to any good."

The springhouse door swung open and Tater came out with a dairy can in each hand.

"What did he think about the boy?" Mixy asked.

"Mixy, you be quiet now," Rose hushed him sternly. "I don't know what I'd have done if Tater had been here when Noah showed up. I wouldn't know what to say. I didn't tell him and I don't want you to speak a word to anyone."

"No, Mizzy, I won't," Mixy looked down at the ground. "But that is his boy."

They stopped talking as Tater approached.

"Where are the eggs going, mom?" Tater asked. The crate of eggs was an unwelcome sight, as it meant a delay in his shooting lesson. He tied the milk cans against the sides of the wagon to keep them from tipping over.

"Anybody who needs them," Rose answered. "You might see if Mister Vanlew can use any at the mercantile. If not, sell them to the travelers."

"That might take some time," Tater stated, climbing up into the wagon box. He saw that the oilcloth bundle containing his pistol had not been disturbed. It was tucked in among the tether rope and a rain slicker. A basket lunch that had been packed for him sat on the seat, and he could smell the fried chicken.

"You be home by supper, regardless," Rose instructed him. "Don't be dawdling, there's milking to get done."

"How much for the pig, Mixy?" Tater asked, picking up the reins and kicking off the brake.

"Six dollars in silver," Mixy said firmly. "Don't take no greenbacks, and you keep four-bits for yourself."

"Thank you," Tater nodded at Mixy with a grin. He jiggled the reins and clucked the old mare forward. "I'll be home to do the milking." He assured his mother as he drove away.

"Do you even know where that pig is going?" Rose called out after him.

"To Mister Schwarting at the new hotel," Tater yelled back as the horse broke into a smooth gait.

CHAPTER FIVE

Tater convinced the owner of the mercantile to take half the eggs, then hurried on to the newly constructed Rocky Bar Hotel. The hotel sat on a terrace above the Snake River, overlooking the ferry crossing. A flat-bottomed barge used for transporting passengers and their belongings was pulled across the water by a team of oxen. The barge had just pulled up to the near shore and was off loading a large family of immigrants with their prairie schooner. As Tater drove around to the back of the hotel he wondered if they were headed for Oregon, or maybe even Washington. He halted the wagon at the kitchen door.

The hotel cook stood in the doorway. Schwarting was a squatty little man with a big belly and flabby jowls. He wore a smudged apron and held a ladle with which he waved a welcome to Tater.

"Afternoon, Mister Schwarting," Tater hailed him, locking up the brake. "Can you take some extra eggs today?"

"I have so many eggs right now, I'd like to be able to hatch some of them," Schwarting remarked, peering into the wagon. "Is that the pig from Mixy?"

"Yep," Tater nodded.

"So how much do I owe?" Schwarting asked, testing the weight of one side of pork by lifting it.

"Let's see," Tater concentrated a moment, "six dollars for the pig and two dollars for the milk. That's eight dollars even."

"That's right." Schwarting finally agreed after counting on his fingers. "You go ahead and put it all in the root cellar. I'll go get your money."

While Tater was unloading the wagon, a bell rang out from the far side of the river. It was the signal that someone wanted to come across on the ferry. Schwarting was in the habit of seeing who or what was coming from the other shore and walked over to his spot beside the hotel where he could gaze out across the river.

"Looks like a couple squaws over there," Schwarting commented as he met Tater back at the wagon. He began to lay out eight silver dollars on the wagon bed. "They're different from those who live around here. I'd say they was Pawnee or Cheyenne from way south toward Colorado. I once lived where there were lots of Indians. Mostly Cheyenne."

"Good, all silver," Tater said, counting the money before picking it up.

"I've dealt with Mixy enough to know he won't take paper currency," Schwarting grumbled. Bewildered over a reason why, he shook his jowls. "Doesn't trust in it."

"Did you ever kill any Indians?" Tater asked, climbing up in the wagon.

"No, I never had the opportunity," Schwarting admitted, moving back over to observe the ferry crossing. "And I really can't say I'm sorry for it. Better men than me went under fighting with them."

Tater drove down to the landing for a closer look at the Indian women when they came across.

CHAPTER SIX

The Indians were a Pawnee mother and her daughter who looked to be a couple of years younger than Tater. With them was a mountain of a man holding the reins of a tall black mule. Two Cayuse ponies, one loaded down with supplies, were attended by the girl. They waited to take their place on the flat-bottom barge as a team of Percherons pulling a freight wagon was driven aboard.

The ferryman oversaw the loading operation as the barge ebbed into the river under the teamster's load. When he was satisfied with the position of the wagon and team of horses he motioned the others to come on.

The teamster chocked the rear wheel of the wagon and joined the ferryman at the bow of the barge. They watched curiously as the big man and Indians led their animals on behind the wagon. Soon the drag line to the opposite shore snapped taut and the barge eased out from the shore into the slow current of the deep blue-green water.

The large man scowled at the ferryman and teamster when they looked his way again. The curious pair moved over to conceal themselves behind the team of draft horses.

At well over six feet tall and weighing nearly three hundred pounds, Burt Perry was a menacing sight. He was dressed in greasy buckskin pants and a mangy wolf skin vest, and had the demeanor of a buffalo hunter. Stringy brown hair dangled out from under a well worn bowler. He wore his beard full and it was wild and streaked with white. His face was well-tanned, or dirty, with large brown eyes bulging out from under thick, bushy eyebrows that grew together over a bulbous nose. A big bore rifle hung in the crook of his arm and on his hip was a bone-handled Colt pistol.

After hitching the reins of the mule to the rear wheel of the wagon, Perry dug a twist of tobacco out of his saddlebags. He took a chew that filled one cheek. The Indian woman let it be known she wanted a share so he held the twist out and she bit a piece off. The girl's eyes followed their every move. Perry offered her a chew, but she shook her head.

Spitting into the river, Perry leaned back against the wagon. Within a couple of minutes he casually lifted the tarp covering the wagon's cargo. The shipment was barbed wire – rolls and rolls of barbed wire. Perry's brow wrinkled with disgust.

Going over to the girl, Perry bent down and whispered something to her. He untied his mule from the wheel and gave the reins to the older woman, then headed forward.

"Morning," Perry said as he approached the men. "Which direction would the Springwater Valley be?"

"Down river about two miles," the ferryman said, pointing to the west.

"Have either of you heard of a man named Jared Sowers?" Perry asked.

"I sure have," the ferryman responded. "He lives in the Springwater Valley."

"How would I find him?" Perry pursued.

While Perry held the attention of the ferryman and teamster up front, the girl slipped silently beneath the wagon and unhooked the traces from the whiffletrees. She performed the task with such quickness and stealth even the horses were unaware that they were loose.

"He has a ranch on the east slope, almost halfway up the valley." The ferryman appeared reluctant to be giving out the information. "There are two big white barns, you can't miss it."

"Much obliged," Perry said, starting back to join the women.

The barge glided slowly over the water, the waves slapping at the bow. Perry peered into the water and determined they were near the middle of the river. It was deep and he was barely able to make out the bottom.

Resting his arms on the side of the wagon, Perry nonchalantly kicked the front chock away from the wheel. Nothing happened. The two Indians gave him a bewildered stare. The barge drew closer to the shore. He kicked the rear chock but it was firm. He kicked it again only harder and this time it shot out from under the wheel. The wagon rolled backward forcing the women and horses to the sides of the barge in a clamor.

"Hey?" Perry bellowed, attracting the attention of the men at the bow.

The ferryman and teamster spun around just in time to see the wagon roll off the barge into the water. At the same time the reins to the Percherons jerked free, spooking the team. They bolted off the bow into the river dragging the teamster, who had grabbed the reins at the last moment, with them. The barbed wire laden wagon sank swiftly to the bottom as the horses swam toward the shore side-by-side in their harness.

Coughing up water, the teamster clung desperately to the barge as the ferryman tried to get him out of the river. Perry trudged over, grabbed the man by the collar, and lifted him straight up onto the deck.

"What the hell happened?" Perry gave them an ornery grin. "I've never seen anything like that in my life. Hope it didn't upset my goddamn mule too bad." He walked back to take the reins from the woman. The Indians were stone-faced.

A few people who had been in the hotel began to assemble at the landing anxious to hear about the mishap. The tired, wet Percherons stood patiently at the river's edge waiting for someone to catch them.

Perry and the Indians wasted no time in mounting up once they were on land. As they rode past Tater, the girl noticed him and smiled. Tater thought she was as pretty as any girl he had ever seen and smiled back. Her eyes and smile excited him until he found himself staring into the cold, cruel eyes of Perry. It had the same effect on Tater as if someone had drenched him with a bucket of cold water. He wanted to hang around to find out how they were going to get the wagon up from the bottom of the river, but hurried on to meet with Noah.

CHAPTER SEVEN

Gunnysack in hand, Noah poked around the burn pile of the saloon for whiskey bottles to be used as targets. He paused at his task and glanced up as Tater drove the wagon in beside the saloon. The boy jumped down from the seat and waved to Noah before scurrying inside. Noah dropped a couple more bottles in the sack and decided that he had gathered enough. He started out behind the corral to find a place to shoot.

"I'll be right with you," Tater yelled as he hurried back out to the wagon. Before Noah had a chance to respond, Tater grabbed the crate containing the eggs and disappeared back inside the saloon. A moment later he came out, hopped up on the wagon and drove over to where Noah was standing with the gunnysack of empty bottles.

"I guess I'm ready to go, Mister Noah," Tater said, eagerly.

"Where are you going?" Noah was perplexed.

"I thought you were going to show me how to shoot," Tater reminded him, wondering if Noah had forgotten.

"Did you bring your gun?" Noah asked.

"It's in here under my feet," Tater assured Noah, looking down between his knees. "I didn't want to wear it with these overalls. It looks stupid. One of my neighbors who was in the war wears his old Navy Colt with bib overalls and I think it looks sort of funny."

"We don't have to go anywhere," Noah proposed. "I figured we could practice out here behind the barn. I don't think anyone would mind a little racket."

Gazing out toward the barn, then at the saloon, Tater appeared somewhat nervous. The prospect of being seen shooting with Noah made him uneasy. If the word got back to his mother and she found out he owned a pistol, she would most likely yank one of his ears off.

"I kind of have my own place down along the river where I practice," Tater explained. "There are a couple targets set up already. I might be more relaxed there."

Noah had hoped to give Pecos the day to rest up, and now contemplated the thought of having to put a saddle on him. He never found much comfort on the seat of a wagon. "There's a real nice sand eddy. It's a good place to take a bath," Tater urged Noah further.

"How far is this swimming hole?" Noah asked, thinking that he understood the boy's reluctance to shoot targets in front of any audience that might assemble.

"A mile at the most," Tater told him. "I know an easy trail."

"I'll go catch my horse," Noah said, giving in. The bottles in the gunnysack rang out as he laid them in the back of Tater's wagon. "I imagine he can stand a little exercise – and I could use a bath."

A trail led out through the cottonwoods that was traveled so infrequently that unless a person knew it was there they wouldn't have found it. Noah followed a short distance behind the wagon as Tater negotiated his way through the trees and bushes. They soon broke out of the woods onto a rocky knoll that sloped off gently toward the banks of the Snake River. The trail down the hillside was two dusty ruts with loose footing between. Noah dropped back a little way to stay out of the tan cloud of dust the wagon kicked up.

Tater stopped the wagon along the edge of a switchback that looked out over the river and waited for Noah to catch up to him. "I bet they're trying to decide how to get that wagon off the bottom of the river," Tater commented.

A short distance below them was the ferry crossing and hotel. The reflection of the midday sun created a bright ribbon of silver sparkles along the rippling water. In the middle of the river, silhouetted by the glare, was the flat-bottomed ferry barge loaded with men peering into the river. A couple of the men were even down on their hands and knees for a closer look.

"What are they doing?" Noah wondered.

"A wagon rolled off the ferry into the river," Tater informed him, "and I saw it happen. Sank like a rock, too. It was quite a sight the way it went under. I've seen the immigrants drive their prairie schooners across the river when they couldn't afford to pay. They float pretty good. I think this here wagon would float a little, but not that one – it rolled off and was just gone." Tater shook his head, thinking back on it.

"Maybe it was loaded with gold," Noah suggested.

"I reckon not or those Indians would have probably stolen it," Tater reasoned.

"What Indians?" Noah asked.

"Two Indians came across on the very same ferry that lost the wagon," Tater stated. "Two squaws. Well, one of them was barely a squaw. I know darn well she was younger than me. The cook at the hotel thought they might have been Pawnees."

Noah was glad Tater was too busy watching the events taking place below to notice the look of concern that must have been on his face. "Was anyone traveling with the Indians?"

"A great big old grisly looking fellow." Tater turned to face Noah. He could sense something wrong in Noah's tone. "Do you know who he is?"

"Was he mean and dirty looking?" Noah tried to smile.

"Filthy," Tater uttered with disgust.

"I might know him," Noah said, somberly.

"Is there going to be trouble for you?" Tater asked. He could see that the thought of this man bothered Noah.

"I'm not sure," Noah told him. He caught Tater's eye. "But if it's who I think it is, there could be trouble around. The problem with that man is that he's just plain mean. Like a rabid wolf. He likes to kill."

"What's it like to kill a man?" Tater asked bluntly.

"Well..." Noah thought, "that's a good question. I reckon that some are easier than others."

"You mean they're not as fast?" Tater pursued. "Or they're not a good shot?"

"Nope," Noah reasoned, "I mean some deserve it more than others."

"If it's the man you're thinking of, what's his name?" Tater wanted to know in case he ever heard about him.

"His name's Burt Perry. He's an old buffalo hunter and he owns that Indian woman," Noah said, turning to scan the horizon of the hill above him.

"Does he own the girl, too?" Tater asked, and for some reason hoped that was not the case.

"That's the squaw's daughter. She's too young to be on her own so she runs with them," Noah replied.

The salvage operation on the river was not making much progress, though one more man was down on his hands and knees with his nose nearly touching the water. Noah and Tater watched a few more minutes before futility set in causing them to continue along their way.

Taking the lead, Noah was the first to make it down the hillside and strike the old trail running along the Snake. They headed up river in a direction away from Springwater. The tracks in the road they followed were those of Perry's mule and the two Indian ponies. Noah recognized the imprints made by the mule – he had followed them before. The big mule was shod for crossing rocks and the tracks were deeper than usual from hauling Perry's bulk. No other riders or wagons had been on the road since Perry and the Indians. It made their tracks easy to follow.

They traveled the road without speaking. Noah's thoughts were on Burt Perry who was out ahead of him somewhere. After awhile Tater turned off onto a rough trail that wound down into a shallow ravine.

"Mister Noah, this is the way to the river," Tater informed him. "There's a little blind gully that runs out flat to the water's edge."

"You go ahead on down and set up a few of those bottles," Noah instructed him. "I'm going to ride on up the road a piece and come right straight back. I'll be able to find you."

"Want me to go with you?" Tater offered.

"No, you go on down and wait for me," Noah was firm.

Noah rode out easy and looked back once to make sure Tater was doing as instructed. He was. As soon as Tater was out of his sight, Noah put the spurs to Pecos. The horse broke into a smooth, effortless lope. Even at this pace it was an easy chore to keep an eye on Perry's trail.

As Noah topped each rise and rounded each curve, he tried to anticipate coming up on Perry. It crossed his mind that if they heard him coming, Perry might even try to bushwack him. The thought made Noah rein Pecos to the side of the road, using the sparse grass to muffle the rhythmic drumming of the big gelding's hooves.

The road swept up away from the river along a rim that ran above a series of coulees, each of which had a trail running down into it. The Snake River was plainly visible at the end of most of the coulees. Noah followed their trail to a brushy ravine where the river was not visible from the main road. Perry and the Indians had made an effort to conceal their tracks by riding off the road through a patch of sagebrush.

After a moment of deliberation, Noah decided not to go any further into the coulee. It was senseless for him to risk being discovered when he was sure Perry was holed up along the river below. It was pure luck that led him there in the first place and he didn't want to push it. Turning Pecos around and urging him into a lope, Noah headed back to find Tater.

CHAPTER EIGHT

Pecos was dark gray with sweat by the time Noah rode down into the ravine where Tater had taken the wagon. Noah would have to grain him up good when they got back to the corral.

A shot echoed out of the ravine causing Noah to flinch. Knowing Perry was in the area made him jumpy. He soon realized it was only Tater warming up on a cast iron stove lid that hung by a wire from a giant tree stump that had floated in during high water. Noah hitched Pecos to the wagon. Though he had seen it before, Tater was right about how a man looked wearing a gun belt with bibbed overalls.

"Did you hit it?" Noah called out as he wandered over to the edge of the river. A tangle of driftwood left by spring floods lined the bank, and beyond was a nice sand beach where the water swirled into an eddy.

"Sure," Tater announced, re-holstering his pistol. "Would you like to see?"

"You bet." Noah walked over to stand beside him. "That's probably the most important trick to shooting. Hitting what you aim at."

Noah watched intently as the boy squared off to the stove lid. Tater fixed his eye on the target, licked his lower lip, drew and fired. There was a dull clink of the slug hitting cast iron simultaneously with the blast of the pistol. Tater was not real fast, but every move was deliberate and he hit what he aimed at. He was better than Noah would have ever imagined.

"I hit it," Tater boasted. He looked at Noah for approval. "That's what I've been practicing."

"That's the main trick," Noah assured him, nodding his head. "Now set a couple of those bottles up on that stump and I'll show you another trick."

Finding a long straight stick, Noah stuck it in the ground and placed the neck of a bottle upside-down over it. He situated this target so that when he faced the bottles on the stump, the bottle on the stick would be a few yards behind him.

"Best come over here and stand beside me," Noah suggested as he took up a position facing the bottles Tater had set up.

"What do you want me to do?" Tater questioned, walking over to join Noah. "Want me to crack `em?"

"Tater, I want you to be quiet for a second and watch," Noah replied. He looked over his shoulder at the bottle behind him a moment before concentrating on the ones perched upon the tree stump. Then he asked softly, "Do you read?"

"Yep, I do," Tater answered.

In a heartbeat, Noah slid his pistol from its holster and began fanning the hammer with his left hand. He shattered both bottles on the stump, swiveled the gun past Tater's belly and fired a third shot at the bottle to the rear. It splintered to the ground around the stick. Tater took a quick step backwards and nearly sat down from surprise.

The roar of gunfire echoed across the river. As the smoke cleared, Tater stared wide-eyed, his mouth gaped open. "The man in the moon!" he roared, going over for a closer look at the bottle shot off the stick. "That's like magic. How long does it take to learn to shoot like that?"

"About twenty years," Noah stated, reloading his gun. "Always try to shoot from the left to right. It's not really a trick, it's the natural way your eyes are used to moving."

"I'll remember that, Mister Noah," Tater said, letting out a deep sigh. He gave Noah a disheartened look. "But how did you hit the bottle behind you so quick?"

"I knew where it was," Noah explained. "I had a picture of it in the back of my mind. Tell me why it is that you want to learn to shoot like this?"

"'Cause there's a man about that thinks he owns this whole country," Tater declared as he reloaded his pistol. "If and when he shows up at my place he's gonna have a fight on his hands."

"Does this man have a name?" Noah asked, though he was able to guess who Tater was talking about.

"His name's Mister Sowers," Tater responded, as he prepared to face the stove lid once more. Noah did not know if it was the way Tater tightened his jaw, or the glint in his eyes, but there was little doubt to his determination. "It's no secret. Everyone in the valley knows something funny's going on. I need to practice being faster."

Tater made an attempt at quick-drawing and nearly blew a hole in his foot – the slug tore up the ground less than two feet in front of him.

"Whoa there!" Noah took a step back. "The first rule of gun fighting is to keep a cool head."

"Sorry," Tater said. He avoided making any eye contact with Noah as a flush of red crept into his cheeks. "I'll never get good enough."

"What does your Pa have to say about all this?" Noah wondered aloud.

"My father is dead," Tater answered, expressing no emotion. "I never knew him. He drowned trying to cross this river when I was a little baby."

If it came down to a fight, Noah knew Tater did not stand a chance against the men Sowers was hiring. As good as he was the boy could not even take Dunlavy – who in Noah's opinion was the most inept gunman he had ever known that was still living. Fortunately, it was unlikely even Tater would be able to force Lester Dunlavy into a showdown.

"Tater," Noah pondered a moment, giving the boy time to look at him. "I'm going to tell you something and I hope you heed my words. Right now you can handle a gun and shoot good enough to get yourself into trouble, but not near good enough to get yourself back out of it."

Shuffling his foot in the dirt, Tater stared a hole in the ground. He tightened his jaw in silence.

"You do me a favor. Don't go out looking for trouble. Wait for it to come to you," Noah implored. Before Tater could say a word, he added, "That's probably the best trick for you."

Changing his mood at once, Noah started toward the river. With his back to Tater he asked in a loud voice, "Just how cold is this water?"

CHAPTER NINE

The campsite met with Perry's approval. It was off the beaten path, but still within an easy ride of the valley where Sowers lived. The canyon was small enough to provide privacy, big enough to graze their stock, and there was plenty of water handy. It was Perry's first trip into the Snake River country and thus far he found it to his liking.

While the women worked at setting up camp, Perry sat back against the silvery smooth trunk of a fallen cottonwood. He pulled the cork on his favorite earthenware jug filled with rum, and shook the contents to try to determine if any was missing. Alice, the older Indian woman, had developed quite a taste for rum. As far as he could tell none was gone.

Taking a pull from the jug, Perry saw Alice start toward him. "Now, just get on back to what you're doing," Perry ordered sharply. She had been stringing a piece of tarpaulin between two trees, lean-to fashion. "I ain't giving you no rum, you old sow."

Alice did as she was told but grumbled under her breath while her daughter, Little One, scampered about the close-by rocks and bushes looking for rattlesnakes.

Perry hated snakes and it was a ritual when setting up a new camp for Little One to rid the site of snakes. She was an expert at it, and he watched her for a few minutes as he swallowed more rum.

"Bring me my carpet," Perry bellowed at Alice as she organized the supplies under the lean-to. She exchanged a quick glance with Little One as she picked up the small roll of carpet.

"Here's one," Little One called to Perry as the buzz of the snake's tail signaled its warning. The girl pointed into a pile of rocks she was near.

"How big is he?" Perry inquired, rising to his feet. He could hear the rattler but was unable to see it. Alice tossed the carpet down where Perry had been sitting and rolled it out for him to lay on.

"Not big, Perry," Little One answered, shaking her head. "Do you want to kill it?"

"No, you go ahead," Perry mumbled as he lowered himself back to the ground. He took a drink of rum as Little One smashed the rattlesnake with a rock. Alice held out a hand and Perry handed her the jug. "One drink," Perry offered, "then you go away."

Taking a big swallow, Alice sat the jug beside Perry and went back to the lean-to. When Little One was certain the snake was dead she dug it out of the rocks and held it up for Perry to see. It was a small rattler, not worth eating, but the skin would make a nice hatband.

"Give that to your ma to skin out," Perry said, stretching out on the carpet. "Then come help me with my boots."

Little One handed the limp rattler to her mother and walked over to Perry. He undid his pants as the girl took his boots off. He motioned her to pull his pants off, which she did leaving him naked from his waist down except for a pair of raggedy socks.

"Now, shuck off that dress and sit down here on me," Perry instructed Little One. She looked at her mother who nodded for her to do as she was told. Little One slipped out of the long buckskin skirt, straddled him, and slowly squatted down on his lap. Perry was ready for her. Alice turned her back on the whole affair and focused her attention on skinning the snake.

Ever since Little One first showed signs of womanhood Perry started taking his liberties with both of them. Anymore, he only humped Alice when she started chomping at the bit and he feared if he did not calm her down she might carve him up in his sleep. He humped Little One, who was much more lively, as often as he could.

"Now, go build a fire and cook up the meat," Perry told Little One as soon as he was finished. He pulled his pants and boots on, and set to cleaning the dust of their long ride from his pistol.

The remainder of the antelope Perry had shot a couple of days earlier was boiled as tender as it would ever get. Alice cut off a hearty chunk and carried it over to Perry on the end of a stick.

"What did you think of that wagon business? It was a sweet trick, wasn't it," Perry boasted with his mouth full of the stringy meat. "It was quick thinking, that's what it was. When I seen it was a load of barbed wire, the idea to sink it just came into my head. You got to keep a sharp wit about you, or you'll go under in this country."

The women sat under the lean-to slicing chunks of meat off a bone and chewing incessantly. They paid little or no attention to Perry as he rambled on.

"That's how you take care of goddamned business," Perry continued, taking another bite. "If there's business to be done, you got to goddamn take care of it now. There's work needs to be done hereabouts."

"You get meat, Perry," Alice said bluntly, as she came over and tossed him the bone from the meal. "We all out. No more." She waved her hands around in half-hearted sign language as she spoke.

Wandering down to the river with the bone, Perry gnawed the last morsels of meat from it, cracked it open and sucked out the marrow. He threw the remains into the water to keep the scavengers from sniffing around.

"Little One," Perry called out as he walked back up from the river, "fetch the mule for me. I need to take a ride and bring back some fresh meat. I couldn't stand no more antelope, anyway, it's too rangy tasting." As the girl went for the mule, Perry untied his old Sharps buffalo gun from the saddle. He would not need to take it along on this trip.

Perry rode out of the coulee leaving the Indian women to tend the camp. Crossing the main road that ran alongside the Snake River, he followed a game trail up onto a low plateau of low rolling hills. Beyond the horizon of the ridge to the west lay the Springwater Valley. The long, persistent legs of his mule covered the ground quickly, and soon he was looking down onto the fertile graze land, or farmland, however a man wanted to see it.

Scattered on the floor of the valley were barns and farms – and herds of cattle here and there. He tried to figure if one of the ranches might belong to Jared Sowers. Most of the places looked too poor. He continued along the crest of the valley until he spotted the two huge white-washed barns the ferryman spoke of. Ribbons of white fence ran out from the barns in all directions. Perry knew at once the ranch was Sowers'. Oftentimes, ranchers who wanted to keep others from putting up fences were the first to build their own. The thought caused him to grunt a little.

Dropping down off the ridge he passed a cattail marsh and followed a trickle of a creek toward the ranch. The banks of the creek were home to a few bright green frogs that let out shrill cries as they sprang into the water. Perry had to skirt all the wooden fences to reach the front of the house. It was a square two-story structure built of river rock with a wide porch that wrapped around all four sides. The doors of one of the barns stood open and he could see the shadows of men watching him from within.

Perry sat patiently on his mule in front of the house and stared at the entrance. The door soon opened and an odd little man stepped out. He was the color of charcoal with a snow-white rim of hair above his ears, but his skin was smooth and Perry found it impossible to guess the man's age.

"Who are you?" Perry uttered, as he watched the faint images of those in the barn fade out of sight.

"I'm Jules, sir," his deep raspy voice explained. "I'm Master Jared's manservant."

"Well good, I'm here to see Mister Sowers," Perry informed him.

"Yes sir, I'll tell him you're here," Jules said. "Can I tell him who's come calling, sir?"

"I'm Burt Perry," he snapped.

"Yes sir, I'll tell him you're here," Jules said, hurrying back inside.

After a minute Jared Sowers came out of the house holding two fat cigars. He was a large-framed man in his early fifties with an unruly shock of greying, reddish hair and muttonchops that pointed to a bushy red mustache. He had a ruddy complexion and piercing turquoise eyes. Sowers wore a silk smoking jacket that was shiny red with golden dragons embroidered on the lapels. Perry thought Sowers looked like a real dandy.

"Welcome to Idaho, Mister Perry," Sowers greeted, looking around. "I heard you were bringing two squaws with you."

"My women are camped," Perry said taking off his hat to scratch his scalp. "I just rode by to let you know I've hired on and I'll be needing some things."

"Would you like to come in and have a peach brandy?" Sowers offered. "Talk over the situation here."

"When's the last time you butchered?" Perry asked.

"Two days ago," Sowers answered automatically, not stopping to wonder why the question was put to him.

"I'll take some beef with me now," Perry screwed the bowler back on his head. "Get me a couple gallons of good rum and take it out of my wages. I'll be back to fetch it." Perry twisted in his saddle toward the lower valley. "How much of this valley do you want to own?" he asked casually.

A slow smile spread over Sowers' face. "All I can, Mister Perry," he admitted callously. He came off the porch and handed Perry a cigar. "Jules," Sowers yelled back at the house.

"Yes, Master Jared," Jules answered, sticking his head out the door.

"Find Niles Whitehead and have him get twenty pounds, no make that thirty pounds of beef from the cook, and bring it out here," Sowers barked the orders.

"Yes, sir," Jules quickly disappeared back inside.

"I understand you know Mister Whitehead," Sowers continued his conversation with Perry.

"I've worked with him before," Perry grunted. He had been sniffing the sweet rum smell of the fine cigar. As far as he was concerned Whitehead was not worth his room and board. "I hear Noah Conklin might be around."

"That's what I hear, too, but he hasn't come to see me yet," Sowers announced, having been informed of Dunlavy's meeting with Noah. "I've been told he probably won't come to work for me. Makes a man wonder why he rode all this way."

"I hope he's looking for a place to die," Perry said, raking his fingers through his beard. "In case you don't know, I don't get along with that sons a bitch."

Sowers didn't quite know how to respond to Perry and at that moment was glad to see Whitehead coming around the house with a hunk of meat that had been wrapped in a piece of linen. Whitehead was bowlegged and lanky and wore wide leather chaps.

"Burt," Whitehead greeted. He didn't make eye contact with Perry as he approached him. "I guess this must be for you." He handed the beef up to the big man sitting on the mule.

"Howdy, Niles," Perry said, laying the meat across his lap. "Much obliged, Mister Sowers, I'll be back in a day or so for the rum." As he rode out he smiled, calling back, "Niles, I guess you heard that Noah's around." Perry knew that for some strange reason Noah Conklin intimidated the hell out of Whitehead.

CHAPTER TEN

Only after Perry was out of earshot, Sowers commented, "Mister Whitehead, that is a very unique individual."

Whitehead remained silent because he was not sure exactly what Sowers meant – and because he did not want to make any remark that might find its way back to Perry.

"Where is Percy McRull grazing his sheep?" Sowers inquired.

"He's still in that little draw about four miles to the north," Whitehead reported.

"I want you to go run him out of there," Sowers said, starting for the house. "Tell him that grass is meant for beef cattle, not sheep."

"What if he doesn't want to go?" Whitehead asked. "Should I do whatever's necessary?"

"Do whatever you have done in the past," Sowers ordered, turning back to face Whitehead, "and take that kid who calls himself Mississippi with you."

Whitehead found Mississippi and it was not long before the two of them rode out. It was late afternoon by the time they reached the narrow strip of prairie where the sheep were grazing. A gentle breeze swept in silent waves over the grasses and the sun neared the horizon casting a red glow over the sky and the land – and the sheep.

A pair of barking Shelties alerted Percy McRull of their presence. The young Irishman stood up from a fire near his tent. A large flock of sheep nibbled at the grass surrounding the camp.

It would have been as easy to ride around the cluster of grazing sheep, but Whitehead aimed his horse into them and Mississippi quickly followed. The flock scattered off to the sides in noisy protest, flowing back together as the horses ambled through them. McRull whistled his dogs in to him and settled them down.

"Come on in," McRull called out in a heavy brogue. It was obvious to him they already had every intention of doing just that. "I can heat up the coffee if you want to sit a spell," he offered as they held up their horses across the flames from him.

"You can pour your coffee in the fire," Whitehead suggested, after seeing the man was not wearing a gun. He spun around in his saddle and jabbed his thumb toward the nervous flock. "These stinking woolybacks shouldn't be in here on this grass."

"But this is open graze land," McRull declared.

"Put your fire out and get out," Mississippi interjected so abruptly he startled Whitehead.

"Let me handle this." Whitehead glared at the younger man. From the little time Whitehead had spent with Mississippi he had him figured to be a hothead, and a braggart. "I know how to go about this. You ought to watch and try to learn something. This type of thing requires a certain amount of diplomacy." Whitehead leaned forward in his saddle toward McRull. "Now this here is prime grassland meant for beeves, it ain't here for those miserable louse-bags of yours. The problem is that beeves won't come graze here after them critters leave that mutton smell. No self-respecting cow wants to follow sheep around."

"They're smarter than some of the men in this valley," Mississippi blurted out.

"That's plain to see," Whitehead agreed, smirking as he sat up straight in his saddle. "Now we want to run beef in here and don't want the grass spoiled."

"Sheep don't hurt nothing," McRull explained. "They move on and the grass comes back quick behind them." He paused a moment and looked at his carbine leaning on the tent, then asked, "Are you suggesting that I move my sheep off of land that is open for grazing?"

"That's what I'm telling you." Whitehead hauled out his pistol and aimed it at McRull. "They ain't worth fighting for. Now sit on the ground by your fire and cross your legs injun style," Whitehead ordered pointing with his gun to a spot on the ground. Mississippi suddenly jerked out his own six-shooter and held it on the Irish sheepherder. Whitehead looked disparagingly at the younger man and shook his head.

"You work for Mister Sowers, don't you?" McRull queried as he sat down in front of his campfire.

"You just stay put until we're out of sight," Whitehead warned. "You ought to move these stinking critters up in the hills where they can't damage good range. Be the best thing to do, and soon." Whitehead reined his horse around and started off, but he kept his gun in hand and an eye on McRull. The herder sat motionless by the fire, and Mississippi followed Whitehead back into the flock.

The sheep scrambled out of the way and bleated at the horses as they rode through. McRull called out to one of the Shelties that ran barking after them. Every now and again a single sheep would dart across in front of the horses. When the flock thinned out and open ground lay close ahead, Whitehead spotted a lamb starting to make its move from one side of the flock to the other. He drew a quick bead on the helpless lamb and fired, wounding it and causing it to lunge forward into the front legs of his horse. Whitehead felt a splatter of warm blood hit him. "Whoa," he cried out, calming his spooked horse. "I must have got him in the heart."

Laughing, Mississippi shot another sheep that fell to the ground and laid struggling. Whitehead randomly fired twice more into the flock, not knowing or caring if he hit anything. The frenzied sheep set the dog to nipping loudly at the horses' heels. Without warning, Mississippi shot the dog, sending it yelping back toward the herder's camp.

"Goddamn you!" Whitehead bellowed out as he spurred his horse to get away. "Why in the hell would you shoot a dog?"

CHAPTER ELEVEN

Having spent the afternoon at the river shooting and swimming, Noah and Tater arrived back at Eddie Button's. Tater didn't have much to say, but scrutinized every move Noah made. While Noah stripped the saddle from Pecos, the boy followed him around like a puppy.

He turned the horse loose in a corral and they walked over to the saloon. It was deserted except for Eddie who was hunched over a twenty gallon crock near the cook stove. The place reeked of vinegar. Eddie had spent the afternoon boiling and pickling eggs. He served a whiskey to Noah and a beer to Tater before spooning a couple eggs out of the crock for them to sample.

"I never really did develop a taste for these kind of eggs," Noah commented as he licked the egg and dipped it in a saucer of salt before taking a bite. "I don't mind them as bad when they're pickled this fresh 'cause they aren't bitter yet." Then he quickly added, "But I'll eat the old ones, too, when everybody else is. You never want to be around someone who's been washing down pickled eggs with beer and whiskey without eating some yourself."

"Why is that?" Tater asked innocently. His egg was gone in two bites along with half his mug of beer.

"Because you never want to be around someone who's farts stink worse than your own," Noah said, grinning. Tater and Eddie both chuckled. The young man flushed a little red as he sucked down the rest of his beer.

"I have milking chores that need doing," Tater said, picking up the empty egg crate. Before going out the door he stopped and turned back. "Thank you, Mister Noah. I hope I get to see you again."

With a simple nod, Noah let the boy know he was welcome. After a few moments he heard the rattling sounds of the wagon driving away.

"That's a nice boy," Eddie remarked. "He's too young to be drinking beer, but he never seems to lose his head." He grabbed a ladle and stirred the contents of a large black kettle heating on a wood range beside the back door of the saloon. "I cooked up some pork ribs with the beans today for supper."

"That sounds pretty good, but I need to tend to my horse a bit more before I eat," Noah said. He took a fresh pint of whiskey out to the corral.

Noah gave the weary gelding a generous ration of oats while he brushed him to a shine. He turned Pecos out in the pasture and swore to the horse that the next day would be a holiday. Pecos seemed to understand, nodding and snorting his approval. The horse then toppled over on his side and began rolling in the dirt with his legs thrashing the air like a dying bug.

By the time Noah washed up for supper his stomach was growling and the pint was half empty. The saloon was busy for the evening meal and the vinegar odor that still lingered in the air was the main topic of conversation among the patrons. There were only two tables in the place – one by the window where men were playing cards and one in the corner closest to the door where a man sat eating. Two other men stood at the bar spooning down plates of beans.

The moment Noah bellied up to the bar Eddie slid a heaping plate of beans in front of him. "There's plenty more," Eddie announced, "so eat up."

"That's quite a helping," Noah stated as beans dripped off the lip of the plate onto the bar.

"I just wanted to let you know that as long as you're staying here, you get to eat all you can when I'm serving meals," Eddie said. "That's one of my house rules."

"This looks plenty right now," Noah said, trying to keep the plate as level as possible while he picked it up. "Any house rule against eating outside?"

"None I can think of," Eddie said as he spotted a customer with an empty glass and took off down the bar.

Noah walked over and sat on the stoop of his cabin to eat. A man rode in on a Morgan that drug its feet from having pulled a plow all day. Hitching his horse with the others, the farmer went inside, studying Noah for a moment as he did.

The saloon was always busy this time of day. Eddie Button was a good cook and he fussed like an old woman over the men he fed. Eddie's Saloon was the gathering place for many of the single men in the valley. They were able to get a hot meal served at the end of a hard day and drown the misery of their loneliness in whiskey. It was a place where they got together to tell tales of the loneliness and of the backbreaking labors they performed daily – and find a way to laugh over them.

Finishing the plate of beans, Noah was full and he stretched out on the cot in his cabin with the door open. From where he lay, he was able to keep an eye on the comings and goings at the saloon.

A farmer stepped out the door of the saloon and took a deep breath of fresh air. As a result of eating too many beans the man's belt hung open and he'd undone the top button of his pants. For a moment he appeared to be content, almost smiling, but the moment faded and the man looked around sadly as he mounted his horse. Noah suspected that the reality of the lonely night ahead and the thought of endless toil settled in on the poor soul.

The farmer's face haunted Noah as he began to doze off. He remembered how the man's expression changed from a look of near joy to one of despair. He wondered how Sowers and Perry and some of the other men that were starting to gather in the valley would affect the farmer's life. Noah found himself wondering how it might affect Rose's life.

A loud banging intruded into Noah's consciousness. It took him a few seconds to wake up and realize where he was, and that Dunlavy was standing in the doorway. Noah had been dreaming of Rose swaying in her rope swing in the locust grove beside the creek. The visions of his dream lingered fresh in his memory.

"Want to get up and eat with me?" Dunlavy asked a second time, not getting a response at first. "The sun's going down soon. Aren't you hungry?"

"I already ate," Noah groaned, rolling off of the cot. "In fact I had such a helping it put me to sleep. Why don't you have supper with the boys? Mister Sowers feeds you, doesn't he? Come to think of it, maybe I could eat a little bit more. It sure had a good flavor." Noah put his hat on and grabbed the empty plate. "Thought you should know that Burt showed up," Dunlavy stated bluntly. "He was out talking to Mister Sowers, and he's already been given a chunk of meat." They both knew that meant Perry had hired on. A devilish grin spread over Dunlavy's face. "Whitehead had to take this beef loin out to him. He even had to hand it to Burt. I was watching, and was about to piss my pants laughing."

"I would have liked to have seen that myself," Noah chuckled, shaking his head as he imagined the scene between Perry and Whitehead. He knew how scared Whitehead was of Perry. Noah didn't let on that he already knew Perry was around.

"It was a good one," Dunlavy assured him.

"And what did you talk to Burt about?" Noah bantered. Whitehead was just slightly less scared of Perry than Dunlavy was.

"I try not to talk to him, and you know it," Dunlavy responded sharply.

"I've always thought that the two of you would really get along," Noah continued in jest as he closed the cabin door and strolled toward the saloon. "I can't understand why you aren't better friends with him."

"I don't even like being around when he's around," Dunlavy admitted, falling in beside Noah. "I'm sure you can understand that. Sowers didn't know that Perry's squaws won't live around white people. I think he was expecting Burt to stay at the ranch."

"I bet after meeting him, Sowers was glad he didn't stay," Noah surmised.

"At times I get the feeling Mister Sowers isn't exactly sure himself what's going on," Dunlavy said. "He sent Whitehead out this afternoon with a new man who calls himself Mississippi."

"Never heard of him," Noah admitted.

"Just a youngster," Dunlavy said. "You'll know him when you see him. He's got lots of hair and a droopy mustache that hangs in his soup when he drinks it. He's always licking it like there's food stored in there. He's got a real quick tongue and that old South drawl."

"Wonder how he came by that name?" Noah smiled. There was a brief time in his youth when he considered going by an alias – they contained an element of mystery. But he could never settle on one that didn't sound stupid and finally outgrew the notion.

"I asked him the same question," Dunlavy said, stepping back to follow Noah through the door of the saloon. "He told me he gave it to himself. You'd think he'd at least make up some kind of a lie about it."

The sky had turned a dull red and the light of day was rapidly fading into dusk. As Noah and Dunlavy came inside Eddie struck a match to light an oil lamp that hung over the bar. Another lamp was already casting it's faint yellow glow from the card table where two men drank beer and played three-card monte. The two gents at the bar, who earlier had been scooping up beans, were now working on a bottle of whiskey. They all stopped briefly to gaze with watchful eyes as Noah and Dunlavy stepped up to the bar.

"How about a plate of grub," Dunlavy said, sniffing the air around him. "What the hell is that smell?"

"It could either be vinegar or farts, depending on who you're standing next to," Eddie replied smirking.

He noticed the way Noah was hanging onto his plate. "Do you want another helping of beans, too?"

"Just a few more, and one little piece of rib meat," Noah said, smiling at Eddie's wit.

Dunlavy had no idea what Eddie was getting at and stood mute for a moment before changing the subject. "What was all the commotion down at the ferry this afternoon? I heard there was some kind of accident."

"I understand a wagon rolled off in the river and sank," Noah said. He also suspected that he knew how it happened but kept quiet about it. Perry being on the same barge was too much of a coincidence.

"It was loaded with barbed wire," Eddie added. "That's the reason it sank. That wire was sold to Mister Vanlew at the mercantile right there in Springwater. With all the freight coming across the river, what's the chances of that happening to that particular wagon?" He seemed to ponder over the odds while he dished up the plates of beans from the big black kettle.

A man with graying hair who was shuffling cards in the corner offered his knowledge of the mishap, spoke out, "I heard it was Jared Sowers walking on stilts and dressed up like a buffalo hunter that hired them injuns to do it."

An immediate silence came over the room. It dawned on the saloon patrons who lived in the valley that the two outsiders standing at the bar most likely worked for Sowers. Eddie served the plates of food and went over and sat down on his stool. The others went back to drinking and playing cards, quietly minding their own business.

"I didn't hear about all that," Dunlavy said in a muffled tone. He questioned Noah with his eyes as he dug a spoon into the beans.

"Probably just a coincidence," Noah assured Dunlavy.

"Well, I suppose so," Eddie agreed, not knowing what he was agreeing to. He was still contemplating the odds of a wagon load of barbed wire destined for Springwater ending up at the bottom of the river. "But it will be interesting to see how they get it out of there. I was told the freight company has a man from the Sandwich Islands working for them that can hold his breath under water as long as he wants to. They sent for him over the telegraph to come here to swim down and get it."

"Whitehead was right," Dunlavy commented to Noah, with a mouthful of beans. "Burt keeps getting meaner and meaner. And crazier. You shouldn't have come up here."

"I don't see why not," Noah considered.

"Whitehead says..." Dunlavy started.

"I don't care to hear what Whitehead has to say," Noah cut him off. "The man is dumber than a mud fencepost, and you can tell him I said so."

"Dumber than a mud fencepost?" Dunlavy quit spooning beans in his mouth long enough to chuckle. "Should I tell him anything else?"

"Sure, while you're at it," Noah insisted, "you can tell him he's slower on the draw than a Kansas river in the summertime. That's one reason he turns yellow every time he gets around Burt."

"You'd think that after all the years you've known Niles you'd have learned to tolerate him by now," Dunlavy said. "I can remember a time when you didn't mind riding with him."

"That was before I got to know him," Noah said. "He's nothing but a nuisance to me and everybody else."

"When are you going to ride out of here?" Dunlavy asked. He stopped eating and leaned in closer to Noah.

"You sure are in a hurry to get rid of me," Noah said, glaring. He tossed down his spoon and pushed the plate away. Eddie got up to clean off the counter. "Eddie, get me a fresh pint while you're up and about."

"I might want to go along when you leave," Dunlavy revealed. "That is if you could stand a little company for few days."

"What makes you so sure I'm leaving in the first place," Noah rebuffed, drinking down the last bit of whiskey in his glass.

"Because there's going to be nothing but trouble here," Dunlavy spoke in a whisper. He pulled a pouch of cut tobacco from his vest pocket and began rolling a cigarette. "I know you and me are alike when it comes to riding away from what trouble we can. The only difference between us is, I ride away sooner and faster."

"I don't blame you, as poorly as you can take care of yourself." Noah needled Dunlavy, then admitted, "I don't honestly know what I'm going to do yet, Dunlavy. The cot in that cabin feels good for a change, and the grub here is better than average. And there seems to be no shortage of whiskey." Noah reached out and took the fresh pint as Eddie handed it to him. "I'm tired. I want to relax for a few days. Besides that, I have some unfinished business around here to take care of."

"Some business is better left unfinished," Dunlavy stated. He pushed the tobacco fixings down the bar for Noah to use.

"Some business is best if you keep your nose out of it, too," Noah contended. He poured a couple of shots of whiskey into Dunlavy's glass. "Have a whiskey and relax. Can't you just be happy that right now you ain't out beating your ass against a saddle, chasing after some ignorant sons a bitches who don't mind shooting at you?"

"I guess you have it right," Dunlavy gave in at once. "We need to drink some whiskey and try to figure out how to locate some virtueless maidens out here in the middle of all this prairie."

"I don't hear anybody else complaining right now," Noah stated. He looked around through the amber glow of the oil lamps. The men around him played cards and drank whiskey – and they talked peaceably amongst themselves.

"You're right, goddamn, it is pretty quiet around here," Dunlavy agreed, and took a swallow of whiskey.

What seemed to Noah to be a long period of silence fell over the room. He rolled a cigarette and drew long breaths of smoke from it. The night grew familiar to him. He had lost track of the times he sat out the night in a sallow-lit, smoke-filled haunt full of lonely men – and at times angry men.

CHAPTER TWELVE

The stillness was broken by the sound of horses loping up to the saloon. In the last hope of daylight the dark shadows of two horsemen stopped at the rail outside the front door. All motion inside the saloon was suspended while everyone had their necks craned toward the door to see who had arrived.

A few moments later Niles Whitehead tromped in. He came to such an abrupt halt when he saw Noah staring at him that Mississippi ran into his back. Niles automatically threw an elbow at the younger man.

"Well, looky who's showed up now," Noah stated. He tipped his glass toward Whitehead, who was obviously surprised to see him.

"I forgot to tell him you were staying here," Dunlavy said maliciously.

"That must have been hard for you, Dunlavy," Noah acknowledged. He looked down at the blood splatters on Whitehead's chaps. Whitehead knew at once what Noah was looking at and tried in vain for a second to brush them away like they were dust.

"It was," Dunlavy admitted. He turned around to rest his elbows on the bar, adding softly, "But it was worth it to see that look on his face."

"What in the world have you been in to?" Noah inquired of Whitehead. The sight of fresh blood roused his curiosity. "Have you been helping the cook pluck chickens?" Mississippi poked his head around Whitehead to look at Noah.

Whitehead's eyes darted around the room, taking in the faces of the men looking at him. After a moment he relaxed a bit and began nodding his head. "You might put it that way," Whitehead stated.

"Why don't you come on in, you're letting in the mosquitoes," Noah beckoned. "Have a beer Niles, you look thirsty." He turned away from the pair in the doorway.

Whitehead rambled in and took a place at the far end of the bar. Mississippi looked around at the door wondering if he should close it or not. He decided to leave it as they found it and quickly joined Whitehead. Both of the latecomers ordered beers from Eddie who was waiting to serve them.

Noah looked down the length of the bar past Dunlavy and the two local men at Whitehead and Mississippi as the pair gulped down their beers. Whitehead made it a point to focus on his mug, while Mississippi was brazen enough to return Noah's stare. His moustache was full of foam and his tongue darted out to lick at it.

"I have to go find a tree," Dunlavy said. He laid money on the bar for another shot of whiskey before stumbling out the door.

"Seriously now," Noah spoke up, getting Whitehead's attention, "what have you cowboys been up to?" He was still curious as to where the blood came from. Whitehead looked at Noah, groping for the right answer, while Mississippi guzzled down the rest of his beer.

"I'd say that's not your business," Mississippi answered as he set his mug down.

"You'd better let me handle this," Whitehead sternly warned his young partner.

With a swift flick of his thumb, Noah slipped the thong off the hammer of his revolver. He grabbed the pint bottle of whiskey in his left hand and started down the bar toward Mississippi. The two men drinking at the counter squeezed together a little tighter. The three-card monte game stopped as a player's glass thunked down hard on the table. Mississippi turned to face Noah, but kept his gun hand on the empty beer mug. He tried to puff out his chest against the uncertainty of the situation.

"When you don't know who you're talking to," Noah suggested, looking Mississippi straight in the eyes, "you shouldn't be so quick to speak." Noah stepped in beside the young gunman and poured a shot of whiskey into his mug. Then he added, "Sonny."

As Noah returned to his spot at the bar he instructed Eddie to pour another beer for Whitehead. Mississippi defiantly drank down the shot of foamy swill from the bottom of his mug. Whitehead took a survey of the other men around him. They were all unarmed settlers.

"If you got to know, Noah," Whitehead disclosed in a braggarts tone of voice, "we've been moving a few sheep around for Mister Sowers."

"I wasn't aware Mister Sowers raised sheep," Noah quipped.

"That's a good one," blurted out the gray-haired man at the card table. No one else made a sound.

"I think everybody in these parts knows how Mister Sowers feels about sheep," Whitehead groaned. It was easy for him to get worked up. The raid on Percy McRull's camp and flock was fresh in his memory. "He feels like any good rancher should. The range is meant for beeves to graze, not a bunch of goddamned smelly sheep, or them goddamn smelly mutton eaters that live with them."

One of the men at the counter drank up and made a hasty retreat for the door. On his way out he ran into Dunlavy who was coming back inside. The determination of the man to get out of the saloon caught Dunlavy off guard. He stood at the door a moment sensing that something was wrong, but was unable to figure out what. Noah was also perplexed by the man's sudden departure.

"The gentleman that just left was one of our local sheep ranchers," Eddie Button informed everyone as Dunlavy stepped back up to the bar.

"Sheep rancher," Whitehead cried out, grimacing. He slugged down half a mug of beer and cleared his throat. "Barkeep, you never call a farmer who raises sheep a rancher."

"I'll try not to forget that," Eddie said. He gave Whitehead a nod of assurance.

"Stinking sheep," Whitehead ranted on over his beer. "Mister Sowers has no use for sheep, what-so-ever."

"Especially, not like you, huh, Ni-i-i-i-iles," Noah teased, bleating out his name.

An uncontrolled burst of laughter was cut short by Whitehead slamming the beer mug down on the counter like a gavel. Fire shot into his eyes and he stepped out in the middle of the room to face Noah. Dunlavy and the other man at the bar cleared out of the way and went over to stand closer to the door. Noah continued to lean on the bar. He knew Whitehead did not have enough alcohol in his guts to do anything more drastic than throw a temper fit.

"Would anybody like to have a pickled egg," Eddie said suddenly. He went to the crock and started fishing around for eggs with a big spoon. No one made a move to take him up on his offer. "They're free if you want one."

"It was just a joke, Niles," Noah proposed. "Why don't you calm down and have a free egg. I had one earlier this afternoon. They're kind of tasty."

The anger on Whitehead's face faded away leaving him standing in the center of the room appearing lost and confused. He glanced over to see if he could depend on Mississippi to back him up. Mississippi was watching Eddie lift a pickled egg out of the crock.

"I'll take one of those eggs," Mississippi requested. He shrugged at Whitehead. "What the hell, they're free. Aren't you going to have one, Niles?"

"I'm headed out to take a piss," Whitehead grumbled. "Maybe when I get back." He brushed past Dunlavy and disappeared out the door.

"I guess I'll have one, too," Dunlavy said. He returned to the counter where his whiskey sat and held out his hand for an egg. Eddie spooned out another egg for Dunlavy. Everyone in the saloon soon got in on the handout. Noah watched as Eddie located the pale white spheres drifting around in the murky liquid, distributing them one by one. When everyone except Noah had a pickled egg, Eddie held one out for him.

"Oh, what the hell, I reckon I'd better," Noah said, with a certain amount of disgust. He took the egg from the spoon and dipped it in the salt.

"These are tasty," Dunlavy said as he chewed.

"Eat some more in a couple of months and tell me what you think about 'em then," Noah said. He watched the door out the corner of his eye for Whitehead to return.

"The older the better," Dunlavy commented, smacking his lips.

"You ought to have a chat with Niles when he comes back in," Noah urged Dunlavy. "Whatever he's been up to lately has got him on edge. See if you can calm him down some. Tell him we're all just drinking a little snake poison here and having a good time. Did you see that fresh blood he's wearing? Maybe he got himself into some trouble this evening. I asked him about it and he won't tell me."

Whitehead returned and immediately commenced drinking his beer. Dunlavy's eyes had followed Whitehead from the time he heard him come in. "That might be a good idea," Dunlavy agreed as he poured a ration of whiskey from Noah's pint. "He is fairly hot tonight. Perhaps he's still upset about seeing Burt." Dunlavy picked up his glass and shuffled down the bar to stand next to Whitehead. The old fellow in the corner had given up on winning at cards and started playing a sad and mournful song on his mouth harp. The men were mostly silent, listening.

The pint in front of Noah stood nearly empty, but he had left a noticeable swallow in the bottom of his glass to keep Eddie from pestering him. He was worn-out and thought of turning in for the night, but doubted that he would be able to sleep with Whitehead getting drunk only a few yards away from his cabin.

A melancholy mood seemed to settle in over the room, brought on by the woeful notes flowing from the harmonica. He was convinced that any information Dunlavy was able to extract from Whitehead about the bloodstains would, sooner or later, make it back to him. The night was pleasant for the time being. He decided to stay around awhile longer hoping Whitehead would get his fill and leave.

"He said what?" Whitehead roared, interrupting the entertainment. He slammed the mug down on the counter again, this time breaking it. An instant later he was back out in the middle of the room to confront Noah. He was incensed, the blood boiling in his face. Eddie Button overcame the urge to clean up the mess and remained perched on his stool behind the bar.

As Whitehead stood fuming in the middle of the saloon, Dunlavy mumbled something else to him. Noah was unable to make out what was said, but it appeared to only add to Whitehead's anger. Whatever was being discussed seemed to amuse Mississippi.

"Noah," Whitehead bellowed. He was shaking with anger.

"What," Noah asked, looking over his shoulder at Whitehead. "Now what's wrong?" He could have almost guessed this was coming. Dunlavy just couldn't help himself when it came to stirring up trouble.

"What you've been saying about me isn't one bit funny," Whitehead objected in a loud voice that was an octave higher than normal.

"Which part wasn't funny, Niles?" Noah responded. He turned toward Whitehead keeping his left elbow resting on the counter while scolding Dunlavy for an instant with his eyes. Dunlavy owned the patent on the confused look of innocence he wore on his face. "The part about the fencepost, or the part about the Kansas river?"

Taking a hurried step back to the bar, Whitehead grabbed Dunlavy's glass and drank the whiskey. The move left Dunlavy staring into the empty glass with disbelief. Whitehead returned to the middle of the room to face Noah again. "Someday you're going to push me too hard."

"Then what?" Noah challenged, and at once wished he hadn't. As it was, he was having a difficult time believing that Dunlavy was really stupid enough to get Whitehead this riled up. "Settle down, Niles, you're all liquored up now, and you ain't thinking straight. You ought to go unroll your blanket and sleep for awhile."

"What I ought to do is call you outside," Whitehead threatened.

"It's dark out there," Noah mused.

Whitehead looked out into the darkness a moment before storming out the door in a huff. Relieved, Noah watched Mississippi gulp down the last of his beer in a hurry to join Whitehead. Before Mississippi had a chance to set the empty mug down, Whitehead came storming back through the door. Noah turned his back to Whitehead in an effort to ignore him. He knew if things did not cool down in a hurry there was a good possibility for trouble. It had been a long time since he had seen Whitehead so worked up. He was not afraid of Whitehead, but he was afraid Whitehead might be drunk beyond reason.

"You should be glad it's dark out," Whitehead continued. "Anyway, it wouldn't be fair to Burt if I called you out. I can imagine how much he is looking forward to killing you. I'd better save you for him."

"Niles, you're fuller than a constipated pig," Noah remarked, in a voice that was calm and serious. The teasing was over. He looked back around at Whitehead. The mood of the night was suddenly dampened. "I'm telling you, you best be quiet and go on to sleep."

Noah turned back to rest his forearms on the bar with the hopes that Whitehead would simply leave. Instead, Whitehead took a step back into the doorway and drew his pistol. There was a scramble of chairs, and men moving to the far end of the counter to take advantage of what little cover it offered.

"Now, I don't want this in here," Eddie Button hollered. He abandoned his stool to get further away from Noah.

"Niles, you better think of what you're doing here," Dunlavy appealed, realizing things had gotten out of hand.

"Shut up, Lester," Whitehead ordered, knowing Dunlavy hated being called by his first name.

Slowly, and cautiously, Noah turned around to face Whitehead. The bar patrons, along with Dunlavy were all huddled behind Mississippi at the end of the counter. Noah looked at Mississippi and pictured where he was just in case he decided to jump in if it came down to a fight. Mississippi's gun hand was on the bar in plain sight.

Noah tried to gather his wits about him through the haze of alcohol. He knew the hammer thong on his holster was laid back out of the way. That was the sort of thing he was always aware of.

"I really don't want this in here," Eddie reiterated in a shrill voice. "Now, I'm going to close up early tonight. You fellows take this out of here with you, and settle it tomorrow."

Noah and Whitehead stood frozen in time, staring blankly into each other's eyes. Whitehead was poised with his pistol drawn and hanging at his side. Noah rested his thumb gently against his holster. The others in the saloon became inanimate objects. There was a strange silence that Noah had experienced before in these situations; it was the quick, dull drumming of his heartbeat echoing in his ears. He wondered for a split second if tonight was Whitehead's turn to go under, or his. Noah heard himself say, "Your hand's shaking, Niles."

As Whitehead started to bring up his gun, Noah could hear the hammer being cocked. In one smooth, lightning fast move, Noah drew and fired. The impact of the slug drove Whitehead out the door, into the darkness. Whitehead got off a shot on his way out, shattering the whiskey bottle at Noah's elbow. Noah then whirled his gun around to cover Mississippi. When Mississippi realized Noah already had the drop on him, his hand was only halfway to his gun. He quickly slapped it back up on the bar.

From outside came a sharp groan, then silence. The saloon was full of bitter, stinging sulfur smoke. Everyone exchanged glances, but no one let out a peep, or made a move. Finally, Eddie reached up and took the lantern down from where it hung. He had a dreadful look on his face as he came out from behind the bar. All at once everyone in the saloon wanted to go out to see what damage had been done to Whitehead. Eddie glanced back at Noah anxiously and it was obvious that the old barkeep did not actually want to see what he was sure to find.

"You go on out ahead of me," Noah instructed as Mississippi came around the bar. At that point, Mississippi was not about to argue with Noah and fell in behind Eddie – he was licking his mustache as if it was coated with honey. Dunlavy gave Noah a fretful gaze as he paraded by with the others on his way outside. Noah stuffed his pistol back in its holster as he shot Dunlavy a sour glance and told him, "Now look what you caused."

"Me?" Dunlavy responded innocently. "I didn't..." His words tailed off.

The men in the saloon went outside and huddled around Whitehead, who was lying further away from the door than Noah expected. While all their faces were brightly lit by the lantern, the limp form stretched out in the dirt was hard to see in the darkness. Whitehead's arms were sprawled out like he was on a cross and a bright red pool of blood ran from his chest. His eyes were closed and Noah watched to see if he would open them again.

"He's dead," Mississippi blurted out. He went to his horse and rode away, keeping a watchful eye on Noah the whole time.

"Do you think he's dead?" Eddie asked Noah.

"I think he's dead, Noah," Dunlavy offered.

"I suppose someone ought to let Frank Canfield know about this," Eddie suggested. He looked at the others to find another man nodding his head in agreement. Realizing Noah did not know who Frank Canfield was, Eddie added, "He's the law around here. The justice of the peace in Springwater."

"I suppose so," Noah agreed. He continued to watch for any signs of life. There were none. Niles Whitehead was dead.

CHAPTER THIRTEEN

The morning sky was filled with bright pillowy puffs of white clouds coming out of the southwest. Noah awoke early, as did a few others eager to see what the outcome of the shooting would be. It was unusual to have men gathering at the saloon so early in the day. Some had witnessed the bloody violence, including Dunlavy who ended up spending the night sleeping on the spare cot in Noah's cabin. Noah wanted Dunlavy as a witness.

Word of the shooting brought in a few men who had missed the action and they listened eagerly to firsthand accounts from Dunlavy and Eddie. Whitehead's body had been wrapped in an old blanket and laid out on the floor of the empty cabin. Noah walked away from the group of onlookers and went out to the corral to catch Pecos. The eyes of the men followed Noah in earnest, watching every move he made, and they mumbled continuously. A gust of wind chattered through the silvery leaves of cottonwoods and kicked up tan swirls of dust.

Pecos moved to the far side of the corral as Noah climbed through the rails. He started slowly toward the horse, but paused to watch as a wagon rattled to a halt beside the men who were gathered in front of the cabin where Whitehead's corpse was stored. Dunlavy had started out to join Noah, but his inquisitive nature overpowered him and he turned back to see who had arrived.

The man at the reins was thin and frail, with pallid skin and a pointed face. He couldn't have been more solemn if he had a noose around his neck. He wore a bright new straw skimmer. On the seat next to him sat a man who was a head taller and twice as broad. Noah knew the big man must be Frank Canfield. A nickel-plated badge stood out on the breast of his black suit coat, and he held onto a long, double-barreled shotgun. Still, he had a pleasant face and eyes that looked around with determination. The group of men greeted him with smiles.

Eddie did most of the talking, and when he pointed into the cabin at Whitehead's body, the men climbed down from the wagon. Canfield left the shotgun leaning up against the seat and followed the undertaker into the cabin. Eddie and a couple others crowded inside and the rest of the men milled around the doorway straining to see what was going on. Dunlavy was at the back of the pack and after a few minutes he turned to Noah and shrugged his shoulders. Canfield surged back outside through the onlookers followed by Eddie. Eddie motioned toward Noah and Canfield came over by himself.

"Noah, I'm Frank Canfield," he announced, and extended a calloused hand that felt like a bear trap when Noah shook it. "I came out with Harry Troost...he's our undertaker. We're taking Mister Whitehead's body back to Springwater." Noah was content to listen and nodded to Canfield that he understood. Canfield wrinkled his brow as he studied Noah. He then asked flatly, "Are you a wanted man anywhere? The reason I ask is that I'm going to have to make a report about all this to the territorial marshal in Boise."

"I had a little scrape in Wyoming last winter, but I settled the matter with the law before I left the area," Noah stated.

"Where abouts?" Canfield questioned.

"Around Medicine Bow," Noah replied.

Frank Canfield was a man that did not let his position turn him into a judgmental, self-righteous fool. He was direct and to the point in carrying out his duties, and courteous at the same time. Canfield had no trouble looking Noah in the eye while he was talking to him, and his voice was steady when he asked, "Did you kill Mister Whitehead?"

"Or be killed myself," Noah nodded. He leaned to look past Canfield and they both watched as the body was carried out of the cabin. The scrawny man with the straw skimmer oversaw the operation as though the men were moving a piano. Dunlavy saw Noah and Canfield looking his way and strolled over as the men finished loading Whitehead's corpse onto the undertaker's wagon.

"Mister Canfield, my name is Dunlavy," Dunlavy said casually. He stuck out his hand and Canfield clasped it. "I was a witness last night when Niles Whitehead got himself killed." He wiggled his fingers a couple times when Canfield let go of him.

"Pleased to meet you, Mister Dunlavy," Canfield responded with a smile.

"Are there any questions you want to ask me about it?" Dunlavy pursued.

"I don't think that will be necessary," Canfield told him, then looked to Noah. "I believe we can settle this matter right away. Noah, would you follow me into Springwater with the body? I need to make a written statement at my office."

Noah was not surprised by the request. He had already started to catch Pecos when Canfield and Troost showed up. "I can do that," Noah agreed. "You can go ahead and start out if you want, I'll saddle my horse and catch up to you."

It only took Canfield a second to decide to trust Noah's word. "That's fine," he nodded a farewell and walked off.

"Are you going in with him?" Dunlavy quizzed discreetly.

"Why not?" Noah asked. "I don't think he plans on putting me in jail. If they even have one. He seems like a fair man."

"Think you can trust him?" Dunlavy was by nature suspicious of everyone and everything. "You know how some of these folks in these farming towns feel about outsiders."

"He seems decent enough," Noah said, trying not to let Dunlavy's trepidation rub off. "I'm not going to fret over it."

"I don't reckon there's any need for it," Dunlavy began. "I heard the saloon-keeper and the older fellow both tell that lawman that if you hadn't shot Whitehead, he was getting ready to shoot you. They sounded pretty convincing. But, who knows, could be they were only saying that for my benefit because they know we're friends."

"Don't you have anything better to do than hang around here?" Noah griped. It was this part of Dunlavy that irritated Noah the worst – Dunlavy was always trying to make someone worry about things. Noah took a short piece of rope and looped it around Pecos's neck. He led the horse out of the corral toward the cabin where he kept his saddle.

"If I recall," Dunlavy reminded Noah, "it was your idea for me to stay here and put in a good word for you. And I can't figure out why just now. That lawman don't even want to hear what I have to say. They send telegraphs everywhere these days. What if they find out about that mess in Medicine Bow?"

"Dunlavy," Noah asked, annoyed, "are you wanted by the law anywhere?"

"Not for anything important," Dunlavy replied.

"Well, I'm not either," Noah insisted. "But even if the law ain't after you I can think of a couple of other men who would like to get you in their sights." It was Noah's turn to direct a few worrisome thoughts Dunlavy's way.

"What do you mean?" Dunlavy questioned, looking around anxiously. "Who are you talking about?"

When the undertaker's wagon pulled out, the gang of spectators who had gathered that morning followed it as far as the saloon. Dunlavy goaded Noah awhile longer to tell him who was out to get him.

"Think back and figure it out on your own," Noah told him, and Dunlavy soon gave up and joined the others in the saloon.

CHAPTER FOURTEEN

Noah caught up to the undertaker's wagon halfway to Springwater. Canfield looked around at him once with a tinge of relief. Pecos slowed to an easy walk, then grew nervous and started acting up. The horse could smell the cargo they carried in the wagon. Noah reined the gelding to the side where Canfield sat, upwind from Whitehead.

Flashes of lightning appeared in the black line of clouds on the southern horizon, too far away for the sound of thunder to reach them. "Good storm going on down there," Canfield spoke up. "I don't think it will blow this far north. Never can tell, though. One thing about this part of the country, you can usually see the weather heading your way. I think we can at least count on some wind."

Not long after Canfield spoke of the wind, a gust blew through herding a cluster of tumbleweed across the road ahead of them. A cloud of dust swept past them, causing the men to turn their faces from its bite. Troost's straw skimmer took off and he snatched it out of midair. The bony little man moved nearly as fast as a lizard's tongue picking off a fly.

"Got it," Troost called out, looking around at Noah and smiling broadly. He put the flat-topped hat woven of wheat straw back on his head, pulling it down tight. "Have to be careful with these kind of hats. You can break them."

"That's why I wear a Stetson," Noah stated.

As Troost continued smiling and looking over at Noah, he steered the front wheel of the wagon into a chuckhole. The bump nearly threw Troost and Canfield out of the wagon box, and tossed Whitehead's body out from under the blanket. The sight of Niles Whitehead dead in the sunlight took Noah by surprise. Whitehead had a ghastly look of anguish on his ashen face, his eyes sunken. The undertaker stopped the wagon to pull the blanket back over the cadaver.

Noah tried to recall how long he had known Niles Whitehead. He could remember trailing cows with him from west Texas to the railhead when it was still in Kansas. It suddenly seemed so long ago – far too long to know a man only to end up killing him. He had known Burt Perry for six or seven years. It seemed longer. Noah noticed Canfield studying him so he moved in front of the wagon to lead.

As the undertaker's wagon entered Springwater the people in the street turned to watch. The women went indoors as the men came outside. Curious shopkeepers followed their customers onto the board sidewalks. Troost pulled in behind Vanlew's Mercantile, close to the building for the shade it offered. One by one, the men wandered around to the back of the mercantile. Faint murmurs rose from the crowd as it gathered around the body.

The town office was a desk in the Masonic Temple, a shed-roofed addition attached to the side of the mercantile. Noah hitched Pecos to a rail along the street and waited for Canfield, who promptly came around to the front lugging the double-barreled shotgun.

"I understand that you were acquainted with Mister Whitehead," Canfield said as Noah followed him into the office. Before going to the desk, he hung the shotgun on a set of elk antlers mounted on the wall. "Eddie Button spoke as if you men might have been friends." He sat at the desk and opened a journal to make an entry.

"I knew him," Noah stated. He watched as Canfield dipped a pen in the inkwell and scratched out the date at the top of a fresh page. "I can't say we were friends. I worked with him here and there over the years."

"What kind of work was that?" Canfield focused on Noah's pistol a moment before looking up at him.

"On cattle ranches, mostly," Noah offered. There was a wide window seat near the desk. Noah sat back to rest on it. "I didn't know for sure that I would run into him up here."

"Were you drovers together?" Canfield pursued tactfully.

"He was kind of an amateur wrangler." Noah was so used to picking on Whitehead, he did it even after the man was dead.

"And you?" Canfield asked.

"Mister Canfield," Noah responded, "I think we both know what kind of work I do. I faced up to what I am years ago, and I have no shame over it."

"What I'd like to know is what happened between you and Mister Whitehead last night?" Canfield proceeded.

"Niles Whitehead and me have been having sort of a running feud for years," Noah explained. "Mostly ribbin' each other. Last night it got out of hand. I had no intentions of shooting him. It just turned out to be. I think he ended up drinking too much and forgot himself."

"But he did threaten you," Canfield said. He continued to probe for a definite reason for the killing.

"Men like Niles Whitehead are always threatening," Noah contended. He stood up from the window sill and leaned forward to rest his palms on the desk. "They are stupid, and they are reckless. If you want to hear from me that I killed him in self-defense, I'm telling you that's the way it was. Now, what else do you need to know?" he asked as he stood up straight.

"What he was doing around the Springwater Valley," Canfield said straightforward. He looked Noah in the eye and waited for his answer.

It was no mystery to Noah what Niles Whitehead was doing hereabouts, and he bet the justice of the peace had a good idea, too. For that reason, Noah did not feel obliged to explain it to him. "It doesn't matter now, does it? He'd have been better off being somewhere else."

Canfield stared at the page of the record book as he mulled over Noah's blunt observation. Noah watched as Canfield wrote out Whitehead's name and that he was killed by a gunshot. "That's a dandy saddle you have on that gelding," Canfield spoke as he dipped the pen and continued to scratch out words. "The tooling and silver work is excellent. It was done in Mexico, wasn't it?"

"I got it in New Mexico," Noah replied. "It was built by a Mexican saddle maker who opened a shop there."

"I'd like to take a closer look at it," Canfield said. After blowing the ink dry, he stood up from the desk and held the palms of his hands out to Noah. "That's what I use these for. I own the harness shop next door to the livery. I like making saddles, but I don't sell many. I've even tried my hand at tooling on them. I don't do too bad at it either. But mostly I make harness and I repair harness for a living."

"You're welcome to look at it all you want," Noah offered. He started for the door, glad this little inquiry was at an end.

"Noah," Canfield called to him. When Noah stopped, Canfield made sure he was looking him square in the eye. "I'm not a gunfighter. That's not what I do to earn a living. One time I did have to bring in a horse thief on the end of that scattergun I carry. There was a couple of tense moments while that was going on, too. But the territorial law takes care of the serious problems around these parts, while the Army keeps a tether on the Indians. We have a fairly peaceful valley here and I hope it stays that way. I try to stick to handing out marriage certificates."

"I can understand that," Noah responded. Rustlers were usually taken care of by the ranchers who hired men more capable of rubbing them out than the local law. And when it came to range wars, Noah knew few lawmen that wanted to get involved – though they would when there was trouble with Indians.

"Harry Troost is the haberdasher here in town," Canfield continued his train of thought. "He sells clothes and those fancy ladies hats a couple doors down the street. The only reason he became undertaker is because he cares enough about people who live in this valley to see that they have on a decent set of clothes when they're buried. He just kind of naturally fell into the job. Mister Whitehead will be buried wrapped in that blanket unless someone comes up with money for a coffin. Do you know if he has a family that can be notified? Otherwise, he'll be put in the potter's field."

"I might be able to find out about that and let you know," Noah said. Whitehead once spoke of family in Arkansas. Dunlavy might know something like that, he was always asking those types of questions.

"If I could get you to sign your name or make your mark for the record," Canfield said, turning the book around for Noah. "I need your full name and where you're from, please."

Noah looked at the pen laying on the page and tried to decide what he should do. He was reluctant to disclose the fact that his last name was Conklin. He was certain that Canfield knew Rose. Noah did not want her bothered with questions about him. There was a sudden commotion out front in the street and a man yelling for Canfield in an excited voice.

"Now what?" Canfield shook his head with wonder and went out the door. A wagon rumbled to a halt in front of the Masonic Temple. Noah could hear the men who had wandered out back to take a look at Whitehead come clamoring down along the side of the building.

After a moment of further deliberation, Noah signed the record book and joined the others, eager himself to find out what all the ruckus was about.

Percy McRull jumped into the back of the wagon as the crowd gathered around him. "You have to see what has happened, Mister Canfield," McRull harangued. Waving his arms around frantically, McRull motioned toward the sheep he had hauled in. There were three dead ones and a forth that was shot through a hind leg. The wounded lamb lay still, but was panting furiously.

"I want to know what you are going to do about this?" McRull demanded of Canfield.

"How did this happen?" Canfield wanted to know. The throng of men, now joined by a couple of wives, debated amongst themselves.

As far as Noah observed, the assemblage showed a respectable amount of concern over the dead and wounded sheep, but their anger lacked passion. Each and every one detested the cruelty of the act and they wore troubled looks on their faces. Noah suspected that if the truth be known, some of those present were not sympathetic to the woolly critters. They did defend the right to raise sheep though, because most of them were farmers, and farmers were normally interested in people's rights. And they were most interested in preserving their right to string barbed wire fences.

"This is the work of Jared Sowers," McRull blasted. An outcry of agreement poured from the group of onlookers. McRull knelt down beside a saddle blanket covering the dog.

"Jared Sowers?" Canfield questioned. "Are you certain it was Mister Sowers?"

"Aye, it was done by men hired by the blackguard. There was two of the cowards. That's not the worst of it," McRull cried out, pulling the blanket off the dead sheltie. "They killed my dog."

Sheep were sheep, but a dog was a different story. The men became outraged at the sight of the shot dog. The people of Springwater turned into a lynch mob, and shouts rang out demanding Canfield to take some kind of action. Noah had seen anger from citizens before and figured theirs would be short lived. He knew the quickest way to rid the average man of anger was to suggest that he take up the fight personally. When it came right down to it, the fighting should always be left to someone else.

"We'll get to the bottom of this," Canfield assured the mob. "What did these men look like?"

About halfway through the description given by McRull of the older and taller man who had raided his camp, Noah realized Canfield was staring at him. Canfield seemed surprised that the description fit Whitehead. "Where's Harry Troost," Canfield called out. "We need him out here."

"He's over at the store selling my wife a hat," a sodbuster yelled from the middle of the crowd.

"Will someone tell him to meet me over behind the mercantile," Canfield pleaded. "Percy, come see if you can recognize the dead man we've got out back here."

As the sodbuster lit out for the haberdashery to fetch Troost, Canfield guided McRull and the rest of the horde for another look at Whitehead's body – this time the women marched along. It was something Noah had already seen once too often that day, so he unhitched Pecos from the rail and led the tall gelding across the street toward Troost's clothing store.

"Mister Troost," Noah called to the undertaker as he came out of the haberdashery. He beckoned the little man over to him. "I was wondering what it might cost to have Whitehead put in a coffin, and maybe put a clean shirt on him."

"Ten dollars would get him a decent burial," Troost announced, and a smile came to his face when Noah started digging in his shirt pocket. "But his grave will still be dug in the potter's field."

"That's fine," Noah agreed, handing Troost a greenback. "Listen, you don't happen to have any fancy Chinese silk scarves for a woman do you?"

"I'm sorry, I don't," Troost apologized. He gave Noah a most woeful look and rubbed his chin. Then an idea struck Troost that perked him right up. "Say, I have some very elegant hats just in from New York City. Very popular."

True to his profession, Troost wanted to shirk his duties as undertaker, and take time to show Noah the hats. Noah begged off, insisting it was a silk scarf he was interested in. As the little man went on his way, Noah mounted Pecos and rode north out of Springwater.

CHAPTER FIFTEEN

Sitting on the ground by the fire pit, Perry used a whetstone to sharpen his skinning knife. He paused to watch Little One saunter off toward the river.

"I make good food, Perry," Alice uttered, gaining his attention. She had fatback and bread frying in the skillet. "Make you strong." He was already stronger than the mule he rode.

Responding with a grunt, Perry continued to work the blade up and down the stone. Alice gave him an alluring smile whenever he glanced at her. She'd been smiling at him since he first woke up. He felt the urge to get out of camp for awhile and decided that soon after breakfast he would ride out to look over the countryside. Little One came back up from the river with a buffalo bladder of water and hung it in the shade of the lean-to.

They ate together hunkered down around the skillet. Perry watched Little One as she ate a piece of fried bread she had rolled in sugar. He wondered how he could spend some time with her after they finished eating. He would most likely have to put it off awhile being Alice gave him the sheep's eye every time he blinked at her.

It was getting more difficult to please Alice these days when he found Little One so pleasing.

Almost the moment they had finished eating, Alice tossed the roll of carpet down at his side and stood swaying over him. Perry swore she could teach a dog to beg with that yearning look she had in her eyes.

"Go fetch me my jug," Perry ordered as he licked his fingers. He looked around for Little One and realized she had taken off again. He had been left alone with Alice who rolled out the carpet with a toe of her moccasin before going after the rum. It appeared that they had connived against him. Perry scoured his brain for an idea that would release him from his obligations.

"Not much, you got," Alice mentioned as she handed him the jug. She plopped down on the carpet next to him and hiked her buckskin skirt above her knees.

"This is the last of it," Perry announced. He knew Alice was fully aware of how much rum was in the camp. He pulled the cork and inspected the contents. There was enough to last him the rest of the day, or perhaps enough left to get Alice out of the way. "I'll have to go out today for supplies."

"Not go now, Perry," Alice appealed. Lifting the skirt up to expose herself with one hand, she reached out for Perry's crotch with the other.

"Not right now," Perry grumbled and came up with some quick sign language that meant no. "Later. I'm not going anywhere for awhile." He held out the jug for Alice and as she reached to take it, he asked, "Where did Little One take off to?"

"She go down river," Alice said. She was suspicious of Perry offering the last of the rum to her. "She look for fish."

"You go ahead and have a drink," Perry proposed getting up from the ground. He picked up the whetstone. "I want to put my sharpening stone away before it's lost. You drink up and I'll be right back." Perry hoped Alice's fondness for rum would make her forget about her fondness for him.

It made sense to him about Little One off fishing. She was an expert at catching fish, too. When it came to killing snakes or catching fish, Little One was hard to beat. He wished she would have waited awhile to go fishing though. It might have been easier to take care of Alice if Little One was around to help.

His plan seemed to be working for the moment. Alice was sipping as fast as she could swallow the fiery liquid. As long as she seemed content to leaving him alone, Perry took his time reorganizing his personal belongings. But before long she was over on top of him.

"Not now, I said," Perry hollered, pitching her off. "Go back over there and sit down on the carpet. Can't you see I'm in the middle of things here. When I'm done I'll come and drink some rum with you."

Grumbling under her breath in Caddoan, her native tongue, Alice complied with his demand. She sat down cross-legged on the rug and resumed drinking. Alice had the jug tipped up so often, it seemed she was trying to balance it on her nose. Perry finally came to the conclusion that he had better just do the deed and get it over with so he could take his ride.

"Hell and goddamn," Perry boomed, finding the jug nearly empty. "You goddamn hog. I said you could have a drink, not drink it all." This was all the excuse he needed to start a fight with Alice. "Now I have to goddamn go get something for me to drink." He gave the squaw a stout backhand that set her to whimpering and cowering. After a minute, Perry whopped her again and sent her off to catch his mule.

Once Perry was up out of the ravine, he rode along the bluff overlooking the Snake. His eyes scanned the bank of the river for Little One. He became anxious to find her and frustrated that he couldn't. If he could find Little One he would hump her. She was nowhere in sight. He suspected her of hiding from him, and the thought infuriated him.

Reining the mule away from the river, Perry set out to see if Sowers had purchased his rum yet. He struck the main route to the east rim of the Springwater Valley, then followed a game trail that wound thread-like along the crest of the burnt grass hills. Dark, foreboding clouds swept across the southern plain. Perry aimed the big mule into the breaks to elude the wind and below in the distance the valley lay pale green and gold.

Paying a call on Jared Sowers meant taking a chance on running into Noah Conklin. Perry felt a knot in his gut for an instant when the thought occurred to him. He wondered what it was about Noah that gave him the uneasy feeling. Noah was deadly with a pistol – he was quick and sure. But then, Perry told himself, so was he. Noah Conklin was too smart to get into it with him. It's best, he thought, when men like us leave each other alone. He'd take care of Noah when the time was right.

The mule was trotting at a steady gait across a meadow of range grass when movement in the distance caught Perry's attention. A rock outcrop studded with scrub pine jutted out at the upper end of the prairie. Holding tight in the cover against the wind gusts was a man watching over a small flock of sheep. Perry reined up and studied the country that surrounded him. The place was forlorn. He rode over to talk to the sheepherder.

The herder climbed down from the rocks as Perry approached. The olive-skinned man in his mid-twenties was short and elfin with round cheeks and exceptionally large ears. He was armed with a single barrel scattergun that he used for warding off predators.

"Morning," Perry greeted as he pulled up on the mule. "Which direction is the valley called Springwater?"

"Yes, there," the herder spoke with a foreign accent and pointed to the west with the muzzle of the gun. The sight of Perry made him uneasy. "Right there."

"That's what I thought," Perry nodded, looking back at it for a moment. He then began shaking his head slightly. "I swear, gets to be so goddamn much country out here at times. I thought maybe I got turned around somehow. I'm brand new to these parts. Haven't seen any buffalo around have you?" He gave the young man a curious grin as he patted the buffalo rifle in its scabbard.

"No," the herder replied. The thought of buffalo eased the man's mind and he smiled. "No buffalo. Sheep. I see sheep."

"I'm afraid you're right," Perry observed, disgruntled. "The buffalo are long gone. I bet there'll never be as many sheep as there once was buffalo." He spoke of the beasts with a strange reverence in his voice. "Never be a time like that again. A man killed all morning and skinned 'till dark. Always up to your elbows in blood."

The young herder listened politely and tried to imagine for a moment what it must have been like. "All the time, I see sheep," the herder stated when Perry stopped talking. "I never see a wild buffalo except in circus."

"Probably a good thing, too, with that little peashooter you're hauling around," Perry bantered. He placed a hand on the stock of his rifle. "Now this old fifty-four here is the tool for that job. This here one would knock a big bull down at two hundred yards. Send a young calf ass-end-over-teakettle."

Perry moved his hand from the stock of the rifle to the butt of his pistol. He hauled it out and shot the herder in the forehead. The young man never had time to suspect. The mule lurched slightly. "And this little Colt here is good for blowing out the back of a man's skull." Perry always got real talkative while he was preparing his mind to kill a person. He savored the anticipation.

Without leaving the saddle, Perry dropped the loop of his lariat over one of the herder's boots and dragged his body into a clump of juniper on the rocky hillside. Tying the mule out of sight, he dug in his saddlebags and found a portion of jerked elk wrapped in a bandanna. He grabbed the buffalo gun and returned to the herder's body. Perry sat down next to the man he had just executed and began to snack on the smoked meat. For a solid hour he sat idle, nibbling and staring out across the country. He eyes searched for any unnatural movement. Besides the sheep, the only thing he saw was two hawks circling the skies and a coyote drifting down the game trail.

When he had devoured the last piece of jerky, Perry pulled out his knife. He shooed away the yellow jackets drawn to the blood and cut the man's ears off. Again he noticed how enormous they seemed. He wrapped the severed parts in the bandanna and tucked them inside his shirt. After Perry stripped the dead man of his clothing, he sliced open his guts to attract predators. He knew the coyotes would take care of the body and have a howling good time doing it – and scatter the bones to boot.

Taking the bundle of clothes and scattergun with him, Perry rode out of the high meadow driving the flock of sheep ahead of him. He abandoned the nervous sheep a mile or so away in a grassy draw where there was a marsh spring and hoped they would hold tight for a day or two. By that time the herder's body would be hard to find. A little further along, he hid the clothes and gun in a pile of rocks.

A stiff breeze caused Perry to pull his hat on tight as he dropped down from the hills behind Sowers' ranch. He hitched the mule by the watering trough and took a chew from a plug of tobacco. Before long he saw the black man, Jules, trotting out the back of the house to one of the barns. Sowers soon came out and marched across the barnyard to where Perry was staring off in the distance. A storm was blowing in from the west. Faint sounds of thunder rolled over the land.

"I hope there's some rain with it," Sowers remarked. "When we get lightning storms this time of the year there is always the risk of prairie fires. We had lightning around here so bad one year I put lightning rods on the roofs. My wife was terrified of the lightning."

"Did you get my rum yet?" Perry asked as he looked at the lightning rod on the house. "I always thought for a long time they was to attract the lightning. They look like they would."

"No, it directs the lightning bolt into the ground," Sowers explained. "I have a man out right now with a wagon getting supplies. I suspect he's on his way back this moment, trying to beat the weather. Your rum should be here soon. Would you like to come in the house and wait? I'd like to talk to you."

"I don't like being inside," Perry declined and leaned back against the trough. "What do you want to talk about? Have you seen Noah Conklin?"

"No, I haven't," Sowers responded. "Have you?"

Perry started to grin before he realized Sowers was serious. "I reckon not or you would have knowed about it," Perry concluded.

"That's what I wanted to talk to you about," Sowers continued. "I thought maybe you had an idea what Mister Conklin is up to."

"What about him?" Perry asked.

"You haven't heard," Sowers declared, when he realized word of the shooting hadn't reached Perry. "Niles Whitehead was killed last night. I'm taking a few men to town to pay our respects later this afternoon."

The only surprise Perry showed was a slight rise of his eyebrows. "Goddamn. Noah finally drove Niles to it," Perry stated. "Never thought Niles was that stupid."

"He drew his gun on Mister Conklin," Sowers said.

"Niles must have been drunk," Perry pondered aloud, dropping his heavy brow to a squint. Somewhere in the depths of his mind he appeared to be trying to solve a problem.

"That's what I heard. They were all drinking at a saloon," Sowers acknowledged. "Two of my men saw it and they both say Niles drew first."

"It was Noah's doing," Perry suggested. He began to watch the road leading to the ranch for the wagon bringing his rum. The approaching thunder boomed, rolling up the valley, growing closer.

"Mister Conklin warned Niles, the way they tell it," Sowers maintained. "Tried to talk him out of it."

"It was Noah caused it," Perry argued. He gave Sowers a troubled look. "Noah's got this...pestering way about him. That's it, he can just sort of pester a man to death. When he doesn't like you he keeps coming after you and coming after you and I don't think he even knows he's doing it."

"Well, he killed one of my men," Sowers considered, "and he hasn't hired on himself. I hope he doesn't get in the way of things."

"I guarantee you, the son of a bitch won't get in my goddamn way," Perry growled. Noah's presence in the valley annoyed him, and he figured things would be better when Noah was no longer around. "If he gets in the way, I'll take care of him." He added, "No extra charge to you, or anyone else."

"Maybe it won't come to that," Sowers said. "I hope this doesn't end up becoming a big fight. If that happens, the territorial law could get involved and ruin everything. This is none of their business. I don't mind buying out squatters when they decide to move on west. You do understand I'm not against scaring them into selling, either. But I hope things stay on that level. We don't need unnecessary bloodshed."

"You do understand that it's the sight of blood that scares the fastest." Using his eyes and a slight gesture of his head, Perry beckoned Sowers to step away with their backs to the house. "You just need to be careful who's blood it is. I did run into the ghost of a sheepherder on my way over here."

"I'm not sure I know what you're talking about," Sowers replied. Whatever Perry was trying to tell him gave Sowers the same uneasy feeling of the impending storm – dark and menacing.

"Here," he offered, reaching in his shirt. Perry pulled out the bandanna and handed it to Sowers. "Look at how big those are."

"What have you got here?" Sowers questioned. Reluctantly, he reached out and took the odd package and stood there as if he had a handful of warm crap. As he began to unwrap the contents, one of the severed ears fell to the ground. Sowers quickly dropped the rest. All he saw was evil when he gazed up at Perry.

"That's what a man's ears look like when they been lopped off," Perry said. One thing was for certain to him, if there was any dirty work to be done, it wouldn't be Sowers doing it. "Look at the size," Perry continued out of pure meanness. "There ought to be a bounty on sheepherders, don't you think?"

"Mister Perry, please do something with those," Sowers ordered with as much authority as he could muster. He was shocked by the sight and was doing his best to conceal it. The wrinkled objects were barely recognizable as once belonging to a man. The wind started to blow the bandanna away and Perry stomped his foot on it. "I'm going in from the weather. You're welcome to wait for the wagon in the house, or on the porch," he said, watching Perry wrap up the grotesque souvenirs. He only invited Perry in to get away from him. A man as savage as Perry most likely meant it when he said he didn't like being indoors. Sowers imagined Perry lived in a tepee.

"Go ahead," Perry said, "I'll wait out here." He tucked the bandanna containing the ears back inside his shirt. He would spring them on the women when he got back to camp. Alice always got upset over that kind of joke. It would make her leave him alone for awhile.

"When can I expect to see you again?" Sowers inquired.

"I'll be around," Perry assured him.

"Very well," Sowers said and started to walk away.

"Mister Sowers," Perry called out. "I take care of goddamn business when I work for a man."

"If you feel it's absolutely necessary," Sowers replied. There was a moment when he wanted to ask Perry not to kill anyone on his way over next time. But he didn't know how to go about it and went inside his house wondering what the hell he'd gotten himself into.

While Perry waited for his rum to arrive, he noticed Sowers looking at him from behind the fancy curtains that hung in the windows. The ranch hand showed up with the wagon before long and the old buffalo hunter breathed a sigh of relief when the small cask of rum was handed to him. As the thunder closed in on him, Perry rode out with the wind.

CHAPTER SIXTEEN

Word of the killing of Niles Whitehead was sure to wend its way across the valley, and Noah knew it would become exaggerated and twisted by time and imagination. Niles was dead, gone now and forever more, but the way Noah saw it, only part of the blame could be laid at his feet. Looking back on it all, he wondered how it might have been avoided. He couldn't remember a time when men weren't killing each other. And though he wasn't exactly sure why, Noah felt it was important to explain the shooting to Rose, firsthand.

He nudged Pecos to an easy trot as he made his way along the crest of the rolling hills that sheltered the Springwater Valley from the west. As he topped each rise the creek with the road running beside could be seen in the distance below. At one point Noah recognized Tater driving his wagon toward Springwater. He studied the scattering of farms and wondered which one of them the boy called home.

Nestled at the base of the hills was a scanty set of buildings that almost resembled a farm. A small gray dog ran for what must have been a quarter of a mile across a field to bark at Tater's wagon before turning back home. Tater didn't slow a whisker and disappeared amongst the trees that lined Springwater Creek.

Noah continued northward along the hills. On the opposite side of the valley a large ranch came into view. It had whitewashed barns and fences. He suspected the place belonged to Jared Sowers. Gazing across at the ranch Noah already knew something about Sowers – the man had worked hard at one time in his life. It made him wonder what Sowers wanted, given all he had. He studied the valley a minute, surveying landmarks and saving the location of the ranch in his memory.

Circling past Rose's farm, Noah felt that same knot in his stomach as he rode down out of the hills behind the springhouse. From his viewpoint he could plainly see Mixy's house and barn a short distance downstream from Rose's. The old man's place was small, neat, and simple, with a barnyard full of geese and sheep.

Thunder boomed to the south over the Snake River country and echoed up the valley. Noah looked around for Rose, but she was nowhere to be seen. Smoke coming from the chimney of her house was swept away by a stiff breeze. As he rode down off the hill past the springhouse to the rear of the barn, he could see the dairy cows huddled along the cottonwoods a short distance downstream.

Noah loosened the cinch, but kept the saddle on Pecos and shut him in a stall inside the barn. He tossed the horse an armful of grass hay from the cows' manger and went outside.

He could smell the plums again as he strolled across the barnyard toward the kitchen door. When he neared the house he heard Rose in the front yard. She was humming a song. He found the sound of her voice soothing, and he walked quietly to where he could see her. She was standing at the butter churn with her back to him. He remembered hearing the tune before, but did not know the name. Noah leaned against the corner of the house to watch her. Rose swayed gently with the melody as she worked the handle up and down, and Noah caught himself staring at her waist and wiggling hips – and felt sure his pulse had quickened. He was afraid if Rose caught him she would think he was snooping on her.

"Rose," Noah called out softly. His voice startled her and she spun around to face him. "I didn't mean to spook you."

"Well, you did," Rose scolded. There was a moment of panic about her, then she seemed to calm down. "Noah, what in heaven's name are you doing sneaking around here?"

"I'm not sneaking around," Noah said, defensively. "I just wanted it to be sort of a private matter when I come see you. I don't need to be causing you any kind of trouble. You never know how people are going to react to certain things."

"What things? Are you in some kind of trouble?" Rose asked. The thought had crossed her mind since their last meeting. Maybe he was on the run.

"No, I'm not in any kind of trouble," Noah declared and a little smile broke out on him. It never ceased to amaze him how everyone suspected that he must be in 'some kind of trouble.' But, at the same time, he also had to wonder why a man who had so few brushes with the law was forced to defend himself so much with a gun – perhaps he was in trouble. All it meant to Noah was, the world had to be full of men worse than himself.

"Are you sure?" Rose questioned. Her concern was genuine.

"If I was in trouble, I don't think I would be up here in this country," Noah appealed, trying to reason with her. "I would most likely be lost somewhere down in Old Mexico."

"Alright," Rose said, shaking her head at him. "Anyway, I hope you aren't. But I still don't like you sneaking around out here."

"Next time I'll ride right through the front gate if that will make you happier," Noah proposed. "I don't have to sneak around. I was only thinking of you."

"Well, I thought we decided it would be best if you just rode back away from this place," Rose reminded him. She didn't want him finding out about Tater and asking her a bunch of questions.

"You decided that," Noah maintained, "I didn't. Last time I was here I didn't get to talk to you very much and I just couldn't put it off any longer. I still need to explain a couple things to you."

"Explain what? Are you going to tell me more about why you weren't happy here living a plain life?" Rose questioned. She had thought about the reason he had given for leaving her all alone in a primitive land, and she couldn't make much sense of it.

"No, I'm not even going to try," Noah replied. "I don't think I could ever explain that to you. I don't think I truly understand the reason why myself."

Rose turned back to the churn and started moving the wood handle up and down with a constant rhythm. "Noah, I really don't want you just showing up like this," she told him as he moved around to face her. "Do you have any plans? You're not going to stay around here, I hope?"

"Either way," Noah pursued, "what difference would it matter to you?"

"None, I suppose," Rose stated. She began to labor at the churn as the cream started turning to butter. "I guess it's just simple curiosity that makes me ask. The same reason that makes me wonder what you've been up to all these years."

A strong gust of wind blew Rose's skirt and petticoat up behind her. She reached back with one hand to smooth them down, and Noah took hold of the churn and kept the rhythm steady. He gripped the handle above Rose's hand, and she stared at him as they began working the churn together.

A loud thunderclap resounded over the valley. Noah looked behind him and could see the dark clouds sweeping toward them. Along the leading edge of the storm were rain squalls and angry flashes of lightning. It was the kind of weather that gave Noah an anxious feeling, and he could see by the look in Rose's eyes it did the same for her.

"This butter is starting to feel done," Noah remarked as he pumped the handle up and down forcefully. "Good thing, too. I'd say that storm is going to make it up here."

"I need to get this in the springhouse for now," Rose said with apprehension. She stopped working the handle and bent over to pick up the churn.

"Here, let me get that for you," Noah offered. He grabbed hold of the side opposite from Rose.

"I can get it fine," she said, and for a brief moment they engaged in a slight tug-of-war.

"I'm sure you can," he insisted, and held on firm to the churn. "But not while I'm right here."

Nature's tempest was at their heels and the lightning crackled through the air above them. Noah hurried toward the springhouse carrying the churn with Rose beside him. She swung open the door to the springhouse and he sat the churn inside. An instant later it was raining so hard they could hear the cold drops slamming into the ground.

"Let's make a run for it," Noah hollered and pulled the door shut. The barn was closer than the house and they made a dash for it. The clouds opened up and dumped a torrent of rain and the wind drove it sideways against them. Noah grabbed Rose's hand and pulled her along. By the time they made it through the barn door they were nearly soaked to the bone and they ended up resting against the manger, huddled together in the dim light. Water dripped from the brim of Noah's hat down his back, and when he looked at Rose she kind of reminded him of a wet cat. Her curls hung limp upon her freckled cheeks.

Thunder shook the barn and the old timbers creaked under the onslaught of the wind and rain. Pecos stood quietly in the stall, weathering out the storm. Rose shivered and Noah put his arms around her. He watched her as she gazed out into the pouring rain. Then she looked up at him and he saw a fear in her eyes that went beyond the force of the wind and thunder. She seemed frightened and frail as he held her, and she was so close he could smell the rain in her hair. Right then all he wanted to do was kiss her. She gently pulled away and he let her go.

"I just didn't want you to catch a chill," Noah sighed. She stared at him with her arms folded across her chest. "I've got a dry shirt in my bags you could put on."

"Please don't bother," she told him.

"It's no trouble," he assured her and started toward Pecos.

"Honest, Noah," Rose called him back, "I'm fine. I've been drenched much worse than this. I actually kind of like the lightning and thunder." She sat on the edge of the manger.

"I do, too, it's exciting," Noah admitted. He stood in front of Rose trying to think of a way to get his arms around her once more. "They have storms like this come crashing through Wyoming now and again. And winter blizzards that will freeze a cow solid and then blow it away." He smiled at her with a gleam in his eyes.

"Exactly what was it you came up here for?" Rose asked. She hoped it wasn't for what seemed to be on his mind right then. It was his eyes that gave him away.

"I came out here to see you," Noah said. He took off his hat and shook the water from it.

"I thought there was something you just had to tell me," Rose reminded him. She pulled a hanky from the cuff of her sleeve and dabbed the moisture from her face.

"Well, yes there was," he muttered, flustered. All of a sudden, telling Rose about killing Whitehead was more difficult than he had envisioned. If he remembered correctly, she had always been real queasy about things that were hurt or dead. And Noah was the kind of man that hated feeling nervous about anything, so to keep from fidgeting he stuck his hands in his pockets. "There was a shooting last night across the valley."

Her brow wrinkled with concern.

"It was nobody from around here," he said to ease her troubled curiosity. "It happened at a saloon above the river crossing."

"At Eddie Button's?" She quizzed.

"I can't imagine you've ever been to Eddie Button's saloon," Noah said with a dubious glance.

"No I haven't, but I know of it," she said.

"Anyway," Noah went on with his tale, "this man's name was Niles Whitehead. I knew him. We worked together some over the years." The vision of Niles' pale corpse laying dead in the wagon abruptly resurfaced in his memory. "And he's dead now."

"He was your friend?" she asked. If Rose had a fault, it was that she had too much compassion.

"No, I wouldn't consider him a friend," Noah informed her. He couldn't understand her getting all watery-eyed over the death of a scoundrel she never knew. "Rose, you shouldn't waste a minute grieving over the likes of him. Niles Whitehead was a no good rascal that would have only ended up hurting someone right here in this valley. Perhaps it'd been one of your friends."

"Were you there when it happened?" she wondered.

"The man was about to shoot me in the back and I shot him first," Noah admitted flat and quick. She simply stared at him with disbelief. "It was me or him."

"And the Indian who used to ride that horse," she pursued, gazing at Pecos. Rose believed she was starting to get the picture. "Did you kill him, too?"

"That man was an outlaw and a murderer," Noah argued. "Why hell, the stinking bastard butchered men and women in front of their children. He was a ruthless savage. It was a lucky day when he died, and let me tell you he wasn't all that easy to put down."

"Noah," Rose said with a shiver, "you're starting to frighten me." She looked around him to see out through the crack of the door.

"It is a frightening thing, Rose, when men fight and die," he pondered aloud. Noah had spoken the truth to her and dreaded having to do so.

"I don't know you anymore," she said, pushing open the door and shaking her head. "Please wait here."

The brunt of the storm had passed over them and a light drizzle was all that was left in its wake. The sky to the south was noticeably brighter. He watched as Rose dodged puddles on her way to the house. He couldn't be sure, but he thought she had taken the news rather well. He wondered if she truly understood the brutality of such things as men fighting and dying – and at the same time hoped that the day never came when she did.

He had known her since boyhood when his family moved to Kansas to live on the farm next to her folk's. She was ten years old then and they milked cows together. Now, he was discovering that he didn't really know Rose anymore either. Too much time had gone by. In her own way she had changed as much as he had.

A feeling as gloomy as the day was beginning to settle in on him when Rose came dashing back across the yard. She had wrapped herself in a wool shawl. The fact she was still talking to him was more than he felt he deserved right then and just watching her lifted his spirits.

"I don't understand about you and guns," Rose said coming through the door. "I mean, why was it you who shot that man last night. Why did he want to shoot you?"

"I don't know the exact answer to that," Noah stated.

"And the Indian?" Rose pursued. "Were you working with the law when you shot him?"

"No, I wasn't working with the law anymore," Noah submitted. "At the time and place I was the only thing that even resembled the law for a hundred miles in any direction. I have ridden with lawmen. But what good are most of them? On the other hand, most territorial marshals are pretty capable...and some Texas Rangers. Frank Canfield is a decent and honest man, but he's no gunfighter."

"I guess that's the part I don't understand, Noah," Rose said. "Why does it end up being you who is doing the fighting and the shooting?"

"Because I know how to use guns," Noah offered. "That's what I do, and so far I've done it good enough to live through it, and make a living at the same time. And, believe me, there were days when it was no easy chore just staying alive. Most of what takes place seems senseless as hell, but I like to believe there is some sort of purpose to it all."

"There's going to be trouble around here, isn't there?" she asked, pulling the shawl tighter around her shoulders.

"Now, tell me why you think that?" Noah asked.

"Just because," Rose concluded, "it appears to me that trouble has been following you around. Or, could it be, you follow it?"

"Maybe you're on to something," Noah agreed. "I've had more than a lion's share. But I promise you this; if there is trouble around here, it won't involve me anymore than it already has."

"And you don't know who Jared Sowers is?" Rose inquired. "Is he the kind of rancher you work for?"

"I've heard of him," Noah confessed. "I've never met him, but I know he's hiring men. You don't have to worry about me going to work for him."

"We all know he's up to something," Rose said, "all the folks around the valley, and we're all trying to figure out what it is." Almost everyone in the valley suspected that Sowers was up to no good, trying to buy up deeds to all the land that surrounded him. She wondered if Noah had come back for a reason he wasn't saying.

"Some people call it progress," Noah surmised, stepping outside from the barn. The rain had ceased and at the low end of the valley the sun broke in golden shafts through the mist that rose up from the earth. "There is so damn much country out here. Far too much for the taking, yet there are always going to be those who want more than their share."

"I don't," Rose said bluntly.

"I don't either," Noah agreed.

"Well, I suppose if there is trouble, something will come along to take care of it," Rose said, resolving the situation in her mind that simply.

"It does seem to work that way," Noah concurred. "Everything just kind of balances out in the end."

They talked awhile longer, mostly about the weather, and as Noah went for his horse he figured it was about time to pay a visit to Jared Sowers.

Riding away from Rose, Noah looked back at her as though it might be for the last time. Right then he wanted to stay where he was and be a thousand miles away all at the same time. Though the sky was clearing, clouds of trouble swept into his thoughts. Perhaps he had made a mistake by coming back to the Snake River country. Passing by the locust grove, he wished he could sit in the rope swing until he figured it all out.

CHAPTER SEVENTEEN

Springwater Creek was swollen by the heavy rain that had fallen earlier. Noah crossed at the fords through water up to his stirrups and when he reached the lower end of the valley he noticed a well-traveled road that ran off to the east. He had a feeling that it led to Sowers's ranch and stopped at the fork to stare up the road a few minutes before continuing south.

A new grave was being prepared in the potter's field next to the cemetery where the good citizens were buried. The hole was being dug in the middle of knee-deep weeds and a scattering of simple wooden markers and crosses. He knew the grave was for Niles Whitehead. A potbellied man rested on his shovel to watch him ride past.

As Noah looked back, he suddenly realized he had no idea where he was going, or what he was going to do. He fought the urge to gallop his thoroughbred when he struck the main route along the river. He had always thought that men with something to hide seemed to be in the biggest hurry. He felt as though he was running, but couldn't understand what he was running from. He held Pecos to a pace so as not to draw more attention than usual.

Arriving at the ferry crossing, Noah watched the salvage operation that was underway. A handful of bystanders stationed themselves along the river bank to gaze at the barge tethered in the middle of the river. A pair of men in the water hanging onto the side of the barge kept ducking their heads under. They seemed to be discussing the situation beneath the surface with other men standing on the deck. If they were making any progress on getting the wagon load of barbed wire to shore, none was obvious.

As Noah reined Pecos around in the direction of Eddie's Saloon, he saw the road leading on up the Snake to where Perry had made a camp. In an instant, Noah changed his mind and was on his way upriver. As soon as he was out of sight of the ferry crossing and new hotel, he spurred Pecos into a gallop.

Noah did not slow down until he came upon the rough trail that dropped into the blind ravine where Tater had his shooting range. The sun was warm following the storm, and the air was still and humid. Wiggling his toes, Noah deemed his socks were overdue for a washing, as was another stiff pair in his saddlebags.

Heading down to the river, he kept his ears open for the sound of gunfire. There was none to be heard. The gully and river bank were deserted and he was glad to have the place to himself. He peeled the saddle off Pecos and turned the horse loose to browse on the scattered patches of grass. Tossing the saddlebags over his shoulder, he went to the water. Around the eddy was a sand beach strewn with wood that had drifted in and piled up during spring floods.

Standing at the edge of the Snake, Noah watched the water flow past on its perpetual journey to the Columbia and on to the Pacific. His mind was busy kicking around thoughts of Rose. He found it hard to believe that the feelings for her were still alive in him. Whenever he was around her, a knot would form in his stomach and he got sort of jittery and weak-kneed. God, he felt as though he was fifteen years old again. Yet, there was also a strange calmness that came over him when they were together.

During the storm, when Rose was wet and frightened and he had held her in his arms, Noah had found himself swept back to another time. A time when he did things without thinking so much about them. When everything always seemed simpler – when a man never knew better. Noah felt as though he was on an endless journey to an unknown destination. Somewhere in life he'd gotten off the main trail and was wandering aimlessly on a series of side paths. It had been a long time since he found himself in such a quandary.

Close by was an area of sand blown clean and smooth by the wind. Lying at his feet was a forked stick with the bark and ends gnawed away by beaver. Noah picked up the stick and stuck it in the middle of the sandy area. For the next few minutes he scanned the walls of the small box canyon and the ridges above him – and he listened acutely. Except for Pecos the place was deserted. Tater had found a good spot to be alone.

Noah reached in the bottom of his saddlebags and found the doeskin bundle. It was a medicine bag that had been given to him by an Indian shaman named Bacanaro. Bacanaro was a medicine man who used his great powers to heal the people who lived along the Yaqui River.

The feel of the pouch always brought back memories of the past – memories both good and bad. Noah had tailed the Apache down into Old Mexico and ended up getting himself gut-shot before it was all over. The leathery old Indian with long silver hair had come out of nowhere to save his life. Bacanaro had carried Noah to the river when he was loco with fever and mixed up plant concoctions that took away the infection, giving him a chance to mend.

There were other things he learned during his stay with the Yaqui's – one was how to rid himself of confusion, like the type he now suffered from. The Indians describe the experience as seeking a vision.

Opening the pouch, Noah studied the contents as he spread the skin out on the sand. He saw the brightly polished stones of quartz and fire agate, and a small piece of bone – and a couple dozen peyote buttons from the mescal. With the tip of his knife he scraped away all the fuzz that he could from the center of one of the buttons. He then blew the button off and began chewing it. By the time he had eaten six of the peyote buttons, Noah wondered how the Indians discovered the magic powers of mescal in the first place, as bad as the stuff tasted. It was like having a mouthful of coal oil.

Before long, Noah had stripped naked and was on his hands and knees vomiting. When his stomach cramps went away he took the forked stick and drew a six-foot circle in the sand enclosing himself within. The unbroken line in the sand was to protect him from evil spirits. Facing east, he sat cross-legged in the center of the circle.

Time passed that he could not measure. Around him the sky was a kaleidoscope of brilliant colors. The sand had turned from white, to yellow, and finally to a burnt-red hue. The river looked as though it was the backs of a thousand turquoise buffaloes with manes of white foam. The swift current of the channel pulled the water in the eddy around like a vast, but gentle whirlpool.

His back became hot and Noah stood up, turning to face the sun. His eyes were closed to the world and his thoughts were a brilliant red and yellow, like fires that were burning out of control in his mind. The surge of the river echoed up the ravine with a constant roar.

At first he was walking slowly along the inside of the ring drawn in the sand. In his hand Noah rattled the sacred pieces of polished stones and bone. He began walking faster and taking bigger steps. Eight steps were cut to four to complete the circle. It seemed he was moving so fast, miniature dust devils began to dance in the sand around him. Looking up into the sky, he spun in the circle until he was too dizzy to remain standing.

Noah lay sprawled in the sand outside the line that had been obliterated by his footprints. The sanctuary of the circle was broken. Lying in the sand next to him were the sacred pieces where they had fallen from his hand. The pieces had landed in a perfect order, as if Noah had carefully laid them out in a line. The small chunk of quartz lay an inch away from one end of the bone, while the agate lay an equal distance from the opposite end.

Symbolically Noah was the piece of bone, and he was exactly between the two stones. Exactly what the position of the pieces might mean, he didn't know. In the past he had followed the quartz with its obvious clarity. Even now the quartz pointed toward the southwest – the general direction of California and work he felt he could do with a clear conscience. But the mystical colors of the

fire agate loomed in the depths of the stone. The darker
stone pulled equally at the bone. Noah picked up the
pieces and rattled them in his hand.

There was a sudden stillness about and the sound
of the river faded away. Behind him was the shuffle of
moccasined feet along the sand. Noah knew there was
no one at his back, but he couldn't help making sure.
When he looked around, the sight of his clothes strewn
out on the pile of driftwood gave him a start. Though he
was in the warm sun, gooseflesh covered him all over.

Rapidly scanning the horizon of the ravine where
it touched the sky, Noah couldn't shake the feeling of
being watched. But he knew Pecos would let him know
if anyone rode into the narrow canyon. The horse grazed
leisurely where the trail came down from above. As he
watched the gray gelding, he thought of the Apache who
once owned him. The Indian had been fearless and crazy
– and brutal. Noah had won the battle, but came out of
it shot through the stomach. He remembered feeling as
though he was suspended above hell for awhile during
that ordeal.

With his dirty socks and a worn chunk of lye soap
that was so hard it was nearly petrified, Noah walked
into the cold waters of the Snake. He scrubbed both pairs
of socks, then himself until he felt he'd removed the first
layer of skin. Beyond the chill, the water was cleansing
and seemed to wash the clouds of trouble that plagued
him away with the dirt. The only thing he really needed
to decide was whether or not to ride on, and where to if
he did. First he would meet with Jared Sowers to find
out what the man wanted. Then would be the time to
figure out what he should do.

After his bath, Noah wrung all the water he could out of the socks and strung them out on the pile of driftwood to bake dry in the sun. He stood facing the river, letting his mind drift along with the current while he burrowed his feet down into the hot sand. The waters flowed on and the roar of the rapids became a form of silence. He could feel the energy of the river's current crashing in waves against his naked body.

From behind him came the gentle clicking of a deer hoof rattle. And when Noah strained to hear, the hollow sound of chanting echoed from the ground surrounding him. He walked over to his clothes and put on his pants. Then he strapped his pistol around his waist. He returned to bury his feet in the sand again, only this time he stood with his back to the river. It seemed to Noah as if time was standing perfectly still. There was no sound except for the chanting and the clicking of the rattle. Beneath his feet he could feel a slight vibration in the earth.

Long before the spirit of Bacanaro appeared, Noah had recognized the song of the Yaqui shaman. The apparition simply rose up out of the sand a few yards in front of Noah and began to dance around in a circle.

"Oh-aay-aay-yea," the spirit of Bacanaro sang out. Over and over the sorrowful voice lamented, almost as if it were a warning. "Hey-oh-oh-aay."

The vision faded for a moment, leaving only the faint clicking sounds of the brittle deer hooves. Then like a sparkle on the water Bacanaro reappeared. He just stood there shaking the rattle and staring at Noah. The illusion was so vivid, Noah wondered if it weren't Bacanaro in the flesh. Perhaps the silver haired shaman had finally learned to fly.

Noah started to smile when the old Indian suddenly threw the deer hoof rattle right at his head. He quickly ducked, but felt the force of the wind from it as it passed by his ear. The wind was followed by a thunderous roar that rolled down the canyon. When Noah looked up again, the ghost of Bacanaro had vanished; replaced by the ghost of the dead Apache running toward him out of the canyon at a frightening speed. The Apache was snorting like a stampeding bull.

Noah dropped down on one knee as he drew his gun. Pulling back the hammer, he held the pistol straight out in front of him with both hands to take a steady aim. He looked down the barrel and lined it up on the middle of the forehead just above the eyes. At the instant he was going to pull the trigger, the wild Apache turned out to be Pecos bolting toward him.

Quickly, almost without thinking, Noah dove behind a nearby pile of driftwood. The heavy slug from a buffalo rifle splintered a chunk of wood above his head. It took the report of the rifle a second to catch up with the lead.

Noah realized the wind that had blown past his ear was a bullet meant for him and the boom of that first shot had spooked his horse. There was a fragment of time he couldn't account for. During that time he had been living on instinct alone – the instinct to survive.

With his pistol out in front of him, he stuck his head out of the driftwood pile and scanned the ridge above for any movement. He wished he had the Winchester that was sticking out of his saddle scabbard. It was too far and there was too much open ground for him to cross to get to it. Besides that, a .30 caliber was no match for Perry's big bore rifle from the distance the shots had been fired.

"Burt!" Noah bellowed out. "Perry!" His voice was caught by the steep walls and echoed back at him from the head of the canyon. "You no good chickenshit coward." Though he was certain in his mind who had taken the shots at him, he wasn't a bit surprised when there was no reply. Noah was trapped in the woodpile, but it didn't bother him all that much because he knew Perry wouldn't be able to sneak up on him without being exposed.

Huddling back down in the pile, Noah moved a chunk of wood out of the way to create a crack to look out through. He felt better about being able to keep an eye on his surroundings without having his head popped up like a prairie dog on a mound of dirt. Taking a deep breath, he settled back and tried to recall the series of events that had just occurred. Foremost on his mind was the fact that Perry had nearly been successful at killing him, and perhaps was waiting to try again. Noah still couldn't detect any movement except Pecos wandering back toward the canyon grasses.

A slight shiver ran down Noah's spine when he remembered what the blast of wind from Perry's first shot felt like as it whistled by his head. The force had stung his ear and he reached up and checked his fingers for blood. There was none, but it was as close as death ever came to him from ambush. Perry's accuracy with his buffalo rife was lethal. He knew Perry loved and counted on the element of surprise and if he hadn't ducked the shaman's rattle the bushwhacker's bullet would have found its mark.

Somehow it seemed the old Indian had saved him again. It was a mystifying experience and all Noah had to explain it was the peyote. Bacanaro had been a strong believer in the powers of the peyote and must have found a way to come to Noah through it.

There was a time years ago when Noah and Perry had hunted men together. The strategy Perry had always adhered to was to strike quick and hard, then run. That way a man might live to fight another day; a day that hopefully had the odds better in his favor. After a little while, Noah stood up from behind the driftwood and let his eyes search the ridges above him. On one hand, he was certain Perry was long gone, hightailing it for his own camp. On the other hand, Noah didn't waste any time putting on the rest of his clothes and saddling Pecos.

To Noah, reaching the rim of the small box canyon felt like being freed from a trap. Open land and the main road lay in sight ahead of him and there was no sign of Perry or anyone else. Now at least he would be able to conduct a running battle instead of being a sitting target. Buffalo hunters were not famous for hitting moving objects, except maybe Bill Cody. The poor bison of the plains just stood there watching other members of the herd drop around them until it was their turn to be rubbed out.

Noah suddenly realized the socks inside his boots were soaking wet. The discovery brought a wry smile to his face. In his haste, he hadn't noticed them being wet when he put them on. It was an annoyance he would have to live with for the time being. He rode Pecos along the upper rim until he could see down into the canyon. It wasn't long before he found the place from where Perry had attempted to kill him.

Studying the tracks left by the mule where it had been tied off, Noah concluded that Perry had watched him for quite a spell before pulling the trigger. Perry had made no attempt to cover the mule's tracks knowing full well Noah could recognize them in the dark.

Getting out of the saddle, Noah walked into a patch of sagebrush where there was a clear view of the river below. This position had given Perry a clear shot at him. The event had Noah's mind racing. He wondered if Perry was drunk, or whether he had merely decided to get the bad blood between them flowing faster. Or just to get it over with once and for all. He was about to climb back on Pecos when something shiny caught his eye. A shell casing was sitting on a nearby rock. Noah picked it up and dropped it in his jacket pocket without really looking at it. He knew it was a .54 caliber Sharps and had been purposely left for him to find.

Noah followed the mule's tracks down the river road until it was obvious Perry had headed back to his camp. It was the safest place he could go. His squaw would stand and fight with him if trouble came to their camp. Noah had never known an Indian woman who was afraid to pick up a gun or knife or war club and fight back to back with their men when times got tough.

From now on, if Noah couldn't stay out of Perry's way he would have to kill him. It wasn't much of a choice. Neither would be easy. He would have to deal with Perry later. Noah figured the time was right for a meeting with Jared Sowers.

CHAPTER EIGHTEEN

An old, weathered-out ranch came into view as Noah rode along a low bluff. There was a wisp of smoke rising from the chimney. He remembered the place from years before. It had once been owned by a horse trader and his wife and operated as a way station for travelers. The passage of time and the elements were beginning to take a heavy toll on the structures. The barn was leaning noticeably to one side and it seemed a couple of pole braces were all that kept it from toppling over. The roofline of the cabin resembled the spine of a swaybacked horse and patches of daylight could be seen beaming through the roof of the front porch. Lodgepole rails used for corral fences were all horse-chewed and sagged miserably.

The yard surrounding the cabin was filled with chickens and pigs, scratching and rooting around for a morsel of food. A retired milk cow, so old and skinny that hats could have been hung on her hip bones, roamed about freely. Laying in a shady spot on the porch, a hound dog raised its head as Noah rode in, but didn't bother to get up and bark.

An elderly man came out of the barn and shuffled toward the front of the cabin. The old-timer was all horse-crippled and bent, his arms hanging nearly to his knees. He had to twist his body sideways and hold up the front brim of his hat to look up at Noah.

"Afternoon," Noah said, staying in the saddle. He was sure it was the same horse trader from years ago.

"Yes sir," the horse trader said, squinting up at Noah. "What might I be able to do for you?"

"I'm hoping you can give me some directions," Noah told him. "There is a big ranch north of here a couple three miles or so. Do you know which place I mean?"

"This ranch of mine ain't worth a damn no more," the horse trader declared, motioning behind him at the shabby buildings with his free arm. "Everything's all burnt up around here. When I had the creek running down into here things was okay then. Pastures have all dried up and they is blowing away more every year. It's all falling down now. Ain't worth trying to fix up. Might as well set fire to it after I'm dead."

"Are you familiar with the place I'm talking about?" Noah asked. "It's about halfway up the valley."

"That ranch belongs to Jared Sowers," the horse trader answered. With the back of his hand, he folded the brim of his hat so it stayed up and was out of his way. The old man peered at Noah through one eye, then the other. "Did I ever sell you a horse? Would you recall that?" he asked, tapping his cheekbone with a nervous finger.

"No, I've never bought a horse from you," Noah assured him. "I would remember something like that."

The horse trader's wife came out of the cabin and crossed the yard to stand beside her husband. The dog woke up and followed her out. The hound came close to touching noses with Pecos before lying down at the woman's feet.

Plump and rosy faced, the horse trader's wife had an enormous bosom that hung down to her waist under a tent like dress. She had tiny feet and stood a full head above her husband, who appeared frail next to her. She scrutinized Noah in silence.

"It was Jared Sowers that stole our water," the horse trader grumbled. The wife gave her husband a troubled glance. "Well, it's true ain't it?" he responded to her. "We used to be able to raise horses here. We got fertile ground and no water. Now we try to get enough out of a piss ant well to live on. It weren't right. He stole the water and the law lets him keep it." The horse trader gazed around, shaking his head bitterly.

Noah took a moment to look around the dilapidated ranch, then asked, "What's the best way to get there from here?"

"Head off that way," the old man motioned out toward the back of the ranch. "When you run into a dry creek bed, follow it up the draw until you come to where Sowers dug the creek and built a dam so it would run the other way. Then you follow that new creek into the next set of meadows. First wagon road you come to will take you on up there."

The horse trader's wife murmured under her breath into her husband's ear as she continued to stare at Noah. "No, he says we never sold him a horse," he told his wife, then looked back up at Noah. "There's something familiar about you, mister."

"I appreciate the information," Noah nodded and tipped a finger to the elderly couple standing together in front of their dingy cabin. He picked up his reins from the saddle horn and started to leave.

"As poor as this old ramshackle ranch is," the horse trader spoke up, "it's all we got, or could ever get again. We can barely weed out a living, but for us it's a lot better than nothing."

Noah stared down upon the old horse trader and his rotund wife. He could see the fear of the unknown etched into their faces. "What's your name, sir?"

"My name's Armstead," the horse trader answered. "This is my wife."

"Mister Armstead, madam," Noah nodded, bidding them goodbye. "I'm sorry you lost your water." He touched his spurs to Pecos to ride away. The lazy hound stood up automatically when the horse's feet started moving.

The dry creek bed was but a short distance behind the ranch. The ride along it was easy. A sparse grass scrubland closed in gradually and ran up into a narrow canyon. Within a mile or so from the Armstead's broken down ranch, Noah came to an earthen dam. The dam had made it possible to divert the creek out of the canyon by raising the level of the water held in a large reservoir. Noah rode across the dam to where a new channel had been dug along a hillside for a few hundred feet. The creek that ran out of the distant wooded hills now flowed into another part of the valley. It just didn't seem right.

In Noah's opinion, Sowers had gone to a lot of trouble for the paltry amount of water that drained out onto a lush green patch of prairie. There was little more than a trickle remaining when he came to the road that would take him to Sowers's ranch.

Noah found the wagon road to be a gradual but constant climb and the Springwater Valley began to fall away behind him. There was a scattering of cattle grazing the land surrounding him. Sticking to the road, he was soon riding between rows of whitewashed fences. The bright lodgepole rails seemed to go on forever before the twin white barns came into view.

Coming up behind him on the road were a half dozen riders. They seemed to be approaching him with a sense of urgency. He reined up to wait for them.

The man out in front sat erect and confident on the back of a powerful white horse. He wore his long black suit coat open over a tightly buttoned vest, a stiff white shirt, and a white silk scarf that was wrapped around his neck and tucked down in the vest. His pant legs were tucked into a shiny pair of boots that came up nearly to his knees, and the boots sported the fanciest spurs most men ever laid eyes on. They had wide silver studded spur straps, silver heel chains, and silver jinglebobs that rang out persistently. He carried a small nickel plated .32 caliber pistol in a holster inside his jacket, and a large bore derringer in his boot top.

Cattle barons for the most part did have a pompous style about them, and the stately man on the big white gelding was no exception. Noah could only assume the man commanding the hodgepodge group of cowboys was none other than Jared Sowers.

Most of the men with Sowers appeared to be real working cowpunchers. But there were a couple of bad apples in the barrel, too. Mississippi was among them, as was another man that Noah was disappointed to see. The man's name was Wally Pomeroy. Wally was a short, stocky fellow with muscular arms and thick shoulders under his stubby neck, and he kept his sandy hair cropped off short. He was simple minded, hardly ever smiled, and had a hard time looking someone in the eye when he talked to them. Most idiots appear to be happy because they don't know any better – not Wally.

There were at least two things about the little bulldog of a man Noah didn't like: He was very efficient with his fists, having been a prize fighter; and pretty good with a pistol. Noah figured Wally Pomeroy was another of those men born without much conscience. Other than that, Noah and Wally treated each other in a civil manner.

"Afternoon," Sowers said, riding up. The other cowboys held up a few yards off.

"Howdy," Noah replied, meeting Sowers with his eyes. He then looked at Wally and nodded a greeting. He even gazed at Mississippi a moment to acknowledge his presence.

"I'm Jared Sowers." Sowers reined his horse in closer and extended his hand to Noah. Pecos felt threatened by the big gelding and laid his ears back quickly, nipping at the intruder.

"Whoa," Sowers exclaimed, as his horse sidestepped out of harm's way. "That's a spirited animal you've got there."

"My name's Noah Conklin." Noah pulled his horse's head back around and never did have a chance to shake Sowers's hand.

"That's what I understand from the men." Sowers aimed the big white horse toward home. "Ride on in with me," Sowers said, spurring his horse on. The request almost sounded like an order.

"I'm glad you decided to come on up here, Mister Conklin," Sowers spoke up as Noah rode alongside him.

"I just took a few hands to pay our last respects to Niles Whitehead. I have to admit I expected to see you at the burial. They buried him at Springwater in the potters' field."

"I know," Noah stated. "I was by there earlier this afternoon. There was no reason for me to stay around."

"I felt obliged, being the man was working for me," Sowers justified the reason for the trip to town. The other men had reluctantly tagged along when their boss suggested it was the only proper thing to do. The truth of the matter was, Sowers had used it as an excuse to go with the hope of running into Noah. He waited for Noah to look at him, before adding, "Now I'm a man short."

When they reached the front of the house, Sowers and Noah split off from the others who rode on to the horse corrals. Jules came out of the house to take charge of the horses.

"Jules will take care of your horse, Mister Conklin," Sowers instructed, and Jules started over to take the reins from Noah.

"He's fine," Noah politely refused, swinging down out of the saddle. "I see the water trough. I'll do it myself." As Jules led the gelding away, Noah watched the horse's movement.

"That's all quarter horse there," Sowers stated, noticing Noah's interest. "He can outrun that horse of yours for the first quarter mile," Sowers boasted, then quickly challenged, "Perhaps someday we can race them."

"Perhaps someday we will," Noah agreed.

"When he's watered," Sowers offered, "why don't you join me on the porch. Would you drink some peach wine?"

"That sounds good," Noah told him, heading for the trough with Pecos. He hitched the horse so it could leisurely get at the water and loosened the cinch before going to the house.

Sowers had not made it back outside yet, so Noah took the time to walk around all four sides of the house. Out back, the barns stood like sentinels guarding a spacious paddock. A massive whiteface seed bull had the whole space to himself. He stood, looking out between the fence rails toward the heifers on the open range.

Noah wandered back around and sat in a wicker chair beside the front door. From the chair, he was able to look out over much of the Springwater Valley. The screened door sprung open and Sowers came out carrying a decanter of wine and a couple of long-stemmed crystal glasses. He had traded in the black suit coat for the embroidered silk smoking jacket. Reddish shocks of unruly hair stuck out on his hatless head.

"I don't usually drink," Sowers informed him, pouring the wine and handing a glass to Noah. "I don't believe in it, but this is a special occasion." Sowers drank half the wine in his glass in one gulp. He then added, "It steals a man's dignity."

"Some men thinks it gives them dignity," Noah responded.

"Like Niles Whitehead?" Sowers queried.

"Some men it gives false courage." Noah sipped the sweet wine.

"What does it give you?" Sowers asked, refilling his own glass.

"I'm still trying to figure that out," Noah reasoned. He was admiring the handiwork on the Chinese silk jacket. "Is that dragon made out of real gold thread?"

"Yes, it is," Sowers answered. "But the jacket itself is very comfortable."

"Do they sell those kind of things around here?" Noah asked.

"Not right here," Sowers replied, "but there are a couple of merchants in Boise that sell fine clothing. All the haberdasher in Springwater sells is work clothes and itchy wool suits...and all kinds of ladies things."

"It's a real nice coat," Noah concluded, "but I honestly have to say that I've known an Indian or two who would've loved to run into you out on the plains wearing it."

"Mister Whitehead was a reckless man, wasn't he?" Sowers understood what Noah was getting at and smiled as he pursued his original train of thought.

"At times," Noah agreed.

"Like I said before," Sowers restated, "I'm a man short now and I heard you're responsible for that."

"I was only defending myself. You lost Niles Whitehead the minute he pulled his gun," Noah suggested, "no matter what the outcome would have been."

"How do you figure that?" Sowers asked.

"Because at the very least," Noah explained, "if he'd shot me in the back he would've had to leave the country. You still can't just go around shooting people."

"While we're on this subject, there is something you should see," Sowers insisted. He made sure both glasses were filled and motioned with his head for Noah to follow. "Come on, I want to show you something. In a way this is something you're also responsible for."

"I have no idea what you're talking about." Noah said as he walked with Sowers down the back stoop toward the holding pen.

"That bull is from down around Medicine Bow, Wyoming," Sowers announced, coming up on the fence where the bull stood on the other side watching them through the wooden rails. "He came from a bloodline of top producers in his breed. I bought him from a man named Decatur Bross when he was forced to cut back his herd."

The candor Sowers used when he spoke the name of Decatur Bross caught Noah off guard. Bross was the last man Noah had worked for. Sowers seemed to be waiting for some kind of a response from him.

"Look at the neck on that son of a bitch," Noah said with amazement. The bulls neck was so thick he could barely bend it to look around.

"He's a prize alright," Sowers agreed proudly. "Beef stock like him is sometimes hard to come by even if you can afford it. I was very pleased to be able to buy him." He moved around a little to face Noah. "I heard you used to work for Mister Bross and that you ended up shooting him. Is that true?"

"It's true," Noah stated flatly. Noah and Bross had gotten into a violent argument over the hanging of two starving Indians. In a fit of anger Bross had come after Noah with a gun.

"I heard the man ended up being a cripple in a wheelchair," Sowers remarked. "That's why he sold me that bull. What a horrible way for a man to end up. You should have just killed him."

"I tried to, he just didn't die," Noah said. "But, I s'pose you must have also heard that matter has all been settled."

Behind Sowers, Wally Pomeroy came out of the barn near the holding pen. He walked over to the fence and rested his forearms across the top rail while putting a boot up on the bottom one. The bull swiveled around on his hind legs to face Pomeroy. Noah determined Pomeroy was too far away to hear what he was discussing with Sowers.

"I heard it hasn't been settled completely," Sowers remarked. "What about Mister Perry?"

"You seem to know quite a lot," Noah replied. He noticed Pomeroy was looking his way every so often. "Anyway, whatever is between me and Burt Perry is a personal matter."

"Someone told me it was all over some Indians," Sowers pursued. "I guess I'm just curious to hear your side of the story."

"Mister Sowers," Noah said, smiling and nodding his head, "you need to keep hanging around Lester Dunlavy if you want to find out more about what happened. Or you can even talk to Wally Pomeroy over there. He was in Medicine Bow when it all took place. But personally I think it was a goddamn shame, and I really don't care to discuss it with you."

"I understand it was Burt Perry that hung those Indians because they were rustling calves," Sowers contended, looking over at Pomeroy who seemed to be ignoring them. "Maybe Mister Perry was working on his own? He doesn't seem the type of man you could give orders to."

"He takes orders fine if you order him to do something that he gets pleasure out of," Noah reasoned. "I'd have a bit more of that sweet wine if you offered." The two of them started back for the house. Sowers's glass was empty and he looked like his mind was laboring over some riddle.

"Maybe it's the lack of dance halls in this part of the territory," Sowers commented as he poured the peach wine. "It hasn't been easy to get good men to come all this way to work. But I hope to hire whatever it takes to get the job done. What about it, Mister Conklin, are you ready to hire on?"

"I'm not sure I know exactly what the job is," Noah said, hoping he was about to find out what he came for – a damn good reason to ride south and get on with his life. He could go on down to Bakersfield and find out how ornery a Mexican vaquero could be when he chose to rustle a white man's cows.

"Look at that valley, Mister Conklin," Sowers said. He leaned out over the porch railing and pointed with his wine glass. "A valley with grass and water like that could support a couple thousand beeves easy."

The high meadow where Sowers had built his ranch sloped off into the spacious valley of browns and greens, and the golds of ripening grain. The rich earth was studded with the occasional house and barn of a settler. Beyond the distant bluffs to the southwest, the river snaked its way like a silver ribbon across a land that disappeared into the afternoon haze.

Noah recalled the first time he ever laid eyes on the Snake River country. He had always felt there was something special about its jagged beauty. It had been the main reason he staked a land claim at the head of the valley many years ago. "Too bad you weren't here first," Noah concluded.

"Yes, too bad," Sowers agreed, then added, "but I'm here now and the valley still lays at my feet."

"And the people down there?" Noah posed the question as he gazed over the scattering of farms. He was thinking of Rose and wondered what would become of her. "What happens to them?"

"Look at all this country. You've ridden it. It's endless," Sowers contemplated. "This kind of land was put here by God to raise cattle on."

"Crops seem to do okay, too," Noah told him.

"You don't sound like a cattleman, Mister Conklin," Sowers said, giving Noah a puzzled glare. He swallowed the wine in his glass before pouring the last of it from the decanter. For a man who claimed he didn't believe in drinking, Sowers had no problem swilling down peach wine.

"I've been around cows so long I'm not sure anymore," Noah told him. "I can look one in the face now and know it ain't worth dying over."

"They're starting to raise sheep around here," Sowers declared. There were two things that seemed to irritate cattlemen more than anything else; sheep and farmers' fences. "And you can't hardly ride across that valley anymore without seeing barbed wire."

The thought didn't anger Noah like it did other men he knew. "Times are changing everywhere," he said calmly. He could tell Sowers was disappointed with him. Noah drank the last of his wine and sat the glass down on the porch rail. "There is still plenty of land out there to graze cattle on without having to run off settlers."

"I don't want to run off any of those settlers," Sowers explained. He looked at Noah with skepticism. "I more or less just want to help them along their way. Most of them was headed for Oregon to begin with when they squatted here in this valley. Some of them was too broke to continue on and I want to buy them out so they can afford to go on to Oregon. Fulfill their old dreams."

"Will it matter if they want to sell or not?" Noah asked.

"Well, hell," Sowers said, letting out a big breath of air. He appeared somewhat exasperated. After a moment of silent thought, he told Noah, "I would like to hire a man of your ability, but I'm not sure we could ever see eye to eye. This doesn't interest you very much, does it, Mister Conklin?"

"No, I reckon it don't," Noah stated. "Good day, Mister Sowers, and thank you for the wine." Noah went down the steps toward Pecos.

"Mister Conklin," Sowers spoke up, following after him, "I'm not out to get into a bunch of trouble, or kill anyone. Are you afraid because Burt Perry is working for me? There must be more to this than I think."

"Is that what you think?" Noah rebuffed as he approached his horse and began tightening the cinch. "You think I'm leaving because I'm afraid of Burt?"

"I was just wondering if that was part of the reason," Sowers said.

"I'm not afraid of Burt Perry," Noah said. He unhitched Pecos and swung up into the saddle. Looking down on Sowers sternly, he offered some advice, "But you should be. He is a savage and I don't know any man who can control him."

"Including you?" Sowers wondered aloud.

"I can only try to kill him if it ever comes down to it," Noah replied. Tipping a finger to his hat, Noah nodded a farewell to Sowers. Wally Pomeroy was still leaning on the fence and Noah looked his way before clicking the horse into a walk.

"Mister Conklin," Sowers called out, "you can't stop what is going to happen." The peach wine was having a warm, confident effect on him. "I'm going to end up with a big share of this valley with or without your help."

Reining Pecos around, Noah rode back over to Sowers. He looked around at the fine ranch as he commented, "You have it real nice here. Appears to me you have worked hard and made something out of your life." He looked down and caught Sowers's eye. "I'll never understand why a man who has all this can't be satisfied."

"It's part of man's nature to always want what he can't have," Sowers said with a slight grin. "The railroad is nipping at our heels and the market for beef is always strong. Especially for good beef. The rangy old longhorn is on his way out. I plan on putting that bull out back to work. He's going to increase my herd and I'm going to need more range."

Two stubborn men stared at each other a moment, and Noah finally concluded, "I believe that greed is the evil that dwells within a man's soul."

"Are you a student of philosophy, Mister Conklin?" Sowers asked.

"No, I'm simply an observer of life," Noah said, reining Pecos around toward the road.

As Sowers pondered the thought about greed and evil, he wondered what it was about Noah that intimidated him. Perhaps it was because he knew Noah wasn't intimidated by the power his money could wield.

"Before you go," Sowers said, halting Noah for a moment longer, "there is something I've been meaning to ask you. At the head of the valley is a widow woman by the name of Conklin. She wouldn't be a relative of yours, would she?"

Noah looked off in the direction Sowers spoke of and thought for moment before answering. "I don't have any blood kin within a thousand miles of here," he stated honestly, and urged Pecos into a trot.

CHAPTER NINETEEN

As Noah rode off he mulled over the reason why Sowers had referred to Rose as a widow. She had admitted to him they were still legally married. If she had remarried and lost her husband she would have a different last name, but even Sowers called her Conklin. It didn't make any sense unless she was telling everybody he was dead. As the years went by maybe she figured he was.

It began to dawn on Noah that she hadn't said much about what she'd been up to, but was always asking lots of questions about what he'd been doing. Every so often he got a feeling there was something she wasn't telling him. Now he would never find out. He tried to put it all out of his mind by telling himself it was none of his business anymore.

Right now it was hard to think of anything except getting back to Eddie Button's saloon. Emptiness gnawed at the pit of his stomach and his feet ached from wearing wet socks. Noah slumped down in the saddle and from time to time pushed Pecos into a fast lope across the open land. By the position of the sun in the sky he knew supper was being served.

Long before he passed the saloon on the way to his cabin Noah could smell food cooking. He stripped the saddle off Pecos and turned the tired horse loose in a small holding pen behind the cabin.

Leaving his saddle and bags lying on the ground, he hobbled over to the cabin stoop and tugged at his boots. They felt as though they were glued to his feet. He found the socks wadded up at the end of the toes. They looked like a couple of rags that had been used to wash the dirt from the inside of his boots and were dirtier now than before he scrubbed them in the river.

He took the time to wash up before trudging over to the saloon. A lone mule stood idle at the front rail while two customers stood at the bar drinking beer and talking with Eddie. The three of them seemed to be expecting Noah for they were looking his way when he walked in. The fact he was carrying his boots and socks and came in barefoot took them by surprise, and they all ended up staring down at his feet.

"Got my socks wet today," Noah announced to them, wryly. "I was wondering if I could hang them near the stove to dry for awhile."

"There's pegs in the rafters," Eddie told Noah as he watched the two farmers gulp down their beers. "Come on back behind the bar."

"We'll see you another time, Eddie," said one of the farmers. The pair of them sat down empty mugs and made their way toward the door.

"Aren't you hungry?" Eddie asked. "I thought maybe you came to have a bite of supper. I've got some good beans cooked up here. Lots of meat in the pot."

"We killed a goose this afternoon," the farmer said. And the two of them were out the door.

"I think maybe I'll just have a beer," Noah requested as he hung his wet socks in the rafters to dry. There was a mug of beer waiting when he came back around to the front of the bar. As he took a drink he looked around the empty saloon. Usually it was busy that time of day and without thinking, he remarked, "Kind of dead around here this evening, isn't it?"

Eddie gave Noah a strange look, but didn't respond to the comment. Outside, the mule trotted past the door carrying both of the farmers on its back.

"What'd you put in the beans today?" Noah finally asked after a long silence.

"Pig liver," Eddie said in sort of a take it or leave it tone of voice. He went over to get Noah a plate. "Are you ready to eat?"

As starved as Noah was, he had to think about beans cooked with liver for a minute. If he hadn't ridden all over the country that day and ended up barefooted, he might have been tempted to try out the dining room at the new hotel. Eddie stood staring at him, waiting for an answer. "I wonder what they are serving down at the hotel?" Noah thought aloud. "I never have tried their food."

"I don't know what he cooked today," Eddie said, still waiting for his answer. "Don't you like liver?"

"I like liver okay if it's cooked done," Noah explained. "I don't think I've ever had it boiled with beans before." He couldn't help making a face.

"It isn't that bad," Eddie insisted. "You ought to at least taste them. Hell, nobody's showing up to eat."

"Alright, give me a little taste," Noah gave in. "Not too many. I'll see what they're like."

As usual, the heap of beans that Eddie served up was dripping from the rim of the plate. Noah studied the mixture a moment before scooping up a spoonful. The beans with strips of pork liver turned out to look and smell better than they sounded. And they actually tasted better than they looked, but as Noah ate them he wondered if Eddie ever cooked steak and potatoes.

A buckboard drove up to the saloon and two men talked and laughed as they came inside. One of the men wore a blue tattered army cap from the war. Noah glanced up from his supper and they stopped laughing when they saw him. Eddie stood behind the bar waiting to serve them.

"You're not serving beans again today are you, Eddie?" the man with the army cap asked.

"Beans with nice tender strips of liver," Eddie said. He attempted to make the fare sound as appetizing as possible after the reaction he'd gotten from Noah.

The men glanced at each other and the man with the cap mumbled something under his breath. Then he spoke out, "I think we might try the hotel. I'm just about beaned out." Without waiting for any response from Eddie they retreated back outside.

"What's going on, Eddie?" It was obvious to Noah the men had a change of heart about eating at the saloon when they spied him.

"Can't say," Eddie shook his head. He went to the stove and gazed into the caldron as he stirred. It was impossible for the fuzzy-haired barkeep to hide his concern over the kettle of beans nobody seemed to want.

"Has Mister Dunlavy been in today?" Noah asked.

"He was here earlier." Moving over to the door, Eddie looked out like he was trying to conjure up hungry men.

"He didn't eat either. I guess everyone's still upset over last night."

"You think that's it?" Noah had a hard time believing that was the reason nobody wanted to eat. He chose to blame it on the liver. The word had got out to most everyone besides him. But perhaps Eddie was correct in his thinking – Noah had seen farmers act in strange ways before.

"Don't get upset with me for saying so," Eddie spoke from the doorway, "but there's a rumor that this place is getting to have a reputation as being a haven for disreputable characters." He hoped he wasn't being too vague and glanced over to see how Noah was taking the news. "I'm sure that's why business is so bad, why they're staying away."

"That's nonsense," Noah stopped eating to wash down the last of his beer. "I'm sure that somewhere over the years there has been a shooting here before last night."

"Oh," Eddie suddenly perked up, "that boy Tater was in this afternoon looking for you." He went back to his stool behind the bar. "He sat in here during the storm and wanted to hear all about the gunfight. I must of told him the story half a dozen times. I explained to him it wasn't your fault, that Mister Whitehead shouldn't have ever taken you on." He pointed to a bright spot on the log wall. "He even dug Mister Whitehead's lead slug out of the wall over there."

"I really don't think you have to worry so much about customers," Noah surmised. "You have whiskey. I've never seen a place yet that sold whiskey that someone don't eventually show up to buy it."

"That storm like to blowed the roof off this place," Eddie said, looking up at the ceiling. There was a section of rafters covered with canvas instead of shingles. "Tater climbed up there in the rain to nail that tarp over the hole." The barkeep became more solemn than ever. "It would be a crying shame if anything was to happen to that boy. It would most likely kill his ma. He shouldn't be messing with guns at his age." Eddie talked about Tater like an old schoolmarm.

"You're flat right about that," Noah agreed, wondering why it felt as though he was the one being scolded. Perhaps it was because he had felt some of the same concerns about the boy that Eddie did. "I must not have been as starving as I thought," he said, pushing the plate to the back of the bar. His hunger pains had eased and the beans lost their flavor in a hurry. "They aren't bad, I'm just full."

As Eddie took the plate away, Noah moved to a table by the window with a deck of cards and spread them out for a game of solitaire. He played the game by rules familiar to very few other solitaire players. He flipped through the deck, viewing only every third card. This method allowed him to move a few cards around on the table, but as the game progressed Noah started to realize he might be stumped. To keep the game alive, he had to create a move here and there, taking the bottom card and putting it on top of the deck to alter the order they came up in when he flipped them over. Of course, it was common rules to go through the deck as many times as necessary. But as the game further disintegrated, so did his honesty. By the end, he was lifting up the piles of face down cards on the table like he was playing three-card monte, looking for the ones he needed. With this technique he won a lot more games than the average player.

As the evening wore on, Noah got tired of winning at solitaire and started to think that maybe Eddie was right about the men staying away because of the shooting. The place was so deserted he was beginning to get an eerie feeling and was about to strike up a conversation with Eddie just to hear voices.

A horse and rider finally showed up and Noah got a worried look from Eddie. "Would you like for me to hide behind the bar 'till he buys a drink?" Noah asked, sarcastically.   Eddie didn't answer as he shifted his hopeful attention toward the door.

It was the old fellow with gray hair who played the harmonica. Spotting Noah at the card table, the man stopped just inside the door. "Come on in and have a drink," Noah offered before the old-timer had a chance to leave. "In fact, the first one's on me."

Within the hour, Noah had persuaded four reluctant customers to stand at the bar. Then Eddie took charge, insisting the men eat a helping of liver and beans. Noah sat off by himself flipping through the cards and sipping beer. Periodically one of the men at the bar would glance over at him. At first the conversation between the men was a series of short murmurs, but soon the amber spirits began to relax their nerves – and loosen their tongues.

"What do you gents do for women around these parts?" Noah blurted out of the blue. Startled, all the men looked at him at once with mute faces.

Then the harmonica player asked candidly, "A white woman, or Indian?"

"There gets to be times when it doesn't matter, does it?" Noah considered.

"Maybe he means one to keep," another man offered.

"No, just temporary," Noah said with an assuring glance.

"Hell," another boomed, "what difference does it make? One is as hard to come by as the other."

The men were chuckling it over, when the harmonica player confessed, "I go to Idaho City. It's quite a ways, but worth it. I think it's better than Boise for harlots. There's women in Idaho City all the way from New Orleans and Kansas City."

The men were all amused at the older man's frankness on such a delicate matter, including Noah.

"Kansas City?" one of the men questioned the harmonica player. "Why would a whore want to leave Kansas City to come all the way out here. The last time I was in Kansas City there was plenty of business there."

"I was too busy to ask her any stupid questions," the harmonica player gave a devil's smile. "That's where she said she'd come from. I remember her. She was a big woman. She was about as big as I can stand them."

"I like the big ones," the skinniest man among them divulged in a Tennessee accent. "They're the best in the winter for keeping the bed warm. My wife was a big, good woman," he lamented. The skinny man let out a woeful sigh as some tender memory of her came back to him.

"Idaho City is the best place to get a temporary white woman," Eddie informed them all. He spoke with the conviction of an expert on the subject. Noah's mug was empty and Eddie came out from behind the bar to refill it. "Most of the men around here that are seeking a woman to take care of them are constantly writing letters to the States. Every once in a while they'll snare one out here.

I'd probably have to recommend bringing your own when you come out...just to be on the safe side."

"Even then, they can't stand the life out here and move back on ya," the skinny man said. His wife spent one winter in the Snake River country before moving back to Tennessee.

"The Yanks at Boise are kept happy by the Indian squaws that are always hanging around the fort," Eddie continued. "There's generally a big camp of them around nearby, waiting for their 'hand outs'. Young little girls, too. Some of them is, anyway." Eddie put another beer in front of Noah and stayed at the table. "Now if I hadn't already got my fill of women, I'd go to Idaho City myself. But, you can't mind waiting in line with gold miners."

The man at the bar who'd been the most quiet the whole evening suddenly asked, "You don't work for Mister Sowers, do you?" The other men looked at each other with concern and the saloon became so still a moth could be heard beating its wings against the glass chimney of an oil lamp.

"No, I don't," Noah said firmly. He understood their anguish over the matter. "I just met the man today, and I have to honestly say I didn't think much of him."

"What do you think all of us that lives here should do?" the man from Tennessee asked.

"Stick together as much as you can," Noah advised them. "And never stop caring about what happens to the man next to you."

"That's not always easy as it sounds," the quiet man stated. "Sometimes it's hard enough just to get by on your own."

"Still, it's the best hope you got," Noah concluded.

"I know what I'd like to do," Eddie interjected as he went back behind the bar where he belonged. "If someone would give me enough for this place to start over, I'd be out of here tomorrow."

"Where to?" Noah questioned.

Eddie took a moment for serious consideration and a grin spread across his face from an idea. "Why, I believe I'd go to Idaho City and open a burlesque house," he declared.

The idea brought a cry of mixed emotions from his customers. Those men who counted on him for an occasional meal deemed him crazy for even thinking about it. While the man from Tennessee, who had a vision of the fat whore from Kansas City in his mind, volunteered to go along. The idea really didn't sound all that bad to Noah. At least the burlesque houses brought women to the rough frontier.

CHAPTER TWENTY

The men at the bar bickered over and drank to some of the women they had known in their lives. They hushed to listen as a horse trotted up to the saloon. Within moments Dunlavy strode in and at once Noah could tell he had just finished a meal. Whenever he stuffed himself, Dunlavy walked in sort of a stiff uncomfortable manner – and he patted his belly constantly.

"I'd like a glass of whiskey," Dunlavy called out to Eddie. When he spotted Noah, he was suddenly perplexed over something. He joined Noah at the table, and as he sat down he asked, "What are you doing here?"

"Where am I supposed to be?" Noah challenged.

"I don't know," Dunlavy said. "I didn't think you were around. I didn't see your horse anywhere."

"He's behind my cabin," Noah said, remembering. "I have to brush him and turn him out yet. Where did you come from?"

"I ate down at the hotel tonight," Dunlavy told him as he took the whiskey from Eddie. "The sound of liver with beans didn't ring my dinner bell."

"What did they have?" Noah knew better than to ask, but did anyway.

"Roast pork with taters and gravy," Dunlavy answered with a slight grunt. He bulged out his stomach and patted it, and sucked at his teeth. "They let you have a second helping, too." He tossed down the shot of whiskey.

"Keep me company while I take care of Pecos," Noah requested, grabbing his boots as he got up from the table. Roast pork was a favorite of his, especially with potatoes and gravy. And when he went behind the bar to fetch his dry socks, he felt like shooting a hole in Eddie's bean pot. The saloon patrons watched quietly as Noah strode out the door barefooted.

"What do you have your boots off for?" Dunlavy inquired, once they were outside.

"I got my socks wet," Noah replied.

"Anyway, I was hoping I would see you today," Dunlavy said. He was still making the vulgar noises with his mouth, searching for bits of food lodged between his teeth. "I wanted to tell you about Niles's funeral."

It was amazing to Noah that Dunlavy didn't have a string of questions to ask about his wet feet. "Did I ever tell you how annoying it is when you suck on your teeth?" he grumbled.

"Did I do something wrong?" Dunlavy wondered what was gnawing at Noah to put him in such a poor mood. "How did it all go at the jail this morning with old Canfield? Did he want to lock you up? You think maybe you ought to leave the country?"

"All he wanted was for me to make a formal statement," Noah explained to the ever wary Dunlavy. "Nothing out of the ordinary. As far as the law goes, it's all settled."

They paused a moment as a solitary horse cantered across the meadow toward the saloon. Frank Canfield rode a big bay mare and cradled the long-barreled scattergun in the crook of his elbow.

"And maybe it isn't," Dunlavy commented. "He was at the funeral this afternoon, talking with Sowers."

Canfield bypassed the saloon and rode directly over to them as they stood at the front of Noah's cabin.

"Mister Conklin," Canfield greeted, "I'm glad I found you here."

When Canfield addressed him by his last name, Noah knew the lawman had to have read it from the journal he'd signed. He was also certain that by now Frank Canfield had sent a telegraph to the territorial marshal to see if there were any warrants out for him – and most likely wired the authorities in Medicine Bow. He searched his mind a moment to recall anything else in his past dealings with the law that might still be following him around. He determined that there shouldn't be any problems other than that mess with Decatur Bross. And that shouldn't be a problem any longer.

"Is there some kind of problem, Mister Canfield?" Dunlavy asked.

"I don't think so," Canfield said, looking over toward the saloon. "It seems pretty quiet around here this evening. I wanted to ride out and take a look at that tooled saddle if it's no bother."

When he found out it was only a social call, Dunlavy relaxed slightly and volunteered to take care of Pecos.

Noah wished he hadn't left the saddle lying on the ground and hastily picked it up and slung it over the hitching rail at the corner of the cabin. "Go ahead and study it while I get my boots on," Noah suggested to

Canfield. He sat on the door stoop, putting on his socks as Dunlavy led Pecos toward the corral. Dunlavy made sure to get in a dubious glance to Noah behind Canfield's back.

"I can't recall the Mexican's name who did that tooling," Noah said, stomping his boots on as he joined Canfield. "But it was the same man who made the saddle. He has a shop along the Rio Grande in a little town called Socorro. I know his name, too. I've been trying to remember it ever since this morning."

"I've always thought the Mexicans pattern some of their designs after those of the Spaniards," Canfield commented, running his fingers over the work that had been done along the rim of the cantle. It was a series of sunbursts that took, as far as he could figure, no less than five different striking tools to create. "This type of design here takes a lot of patience. Those people seem to live at a different pace than us. Gives them time to do this kind of work. And the silver work sure dresses it all up."

"Have you been in the deserts?" Noah inquired.

"I lived in Santa Fe for awhile. I rode guard for the Atchison, Topeka and the Santa Fe for a couple of years," Canfield explained. "I thought that country was okay, but I like this type of country better. I guess that's why I got picked to do this job around here." He paused before adding, "Not much goes into aiming a shotgun."

"I imagine the hardest part is knowing when you need to, and when you don't," Noah concluded.

"Still," Canfield maintained, "I would just as soon never have to, at any time." He moved around the saddle to face Noah more directly. "I hear you're at the top of the pecking order most anywhere you go." Canfield stopped paying attention to the tooled leather and looked to Noah for a response.

"Where did you hear something like that?" Noah asked.

"I saw Jared Sowers at the graveyard this afternoon," Canfield told him. "I heard some of his men talking about Mister Whitehead, and about you. Mister Sowers told me he was hoping to offer you a job at his ranch. Some of the men seemed to have a great deal of respect for you."

"A couple of those men are plenty skilled in survival themselves," Noah stated. "When things get to be real tough, it's good to have them along."

"Do you think there's going to be trouble around here?" Canfield asked.

"Why are you asking me?" Noah countered.

"I guess," Canfield responded after a moment, "because I think you are a lot more familiar with what is really going on around Springwater right now than I am. I expect there could be more trouble. Some of the citizens think so. But to be honest with you, Mister Conklin, I really don't know what to expect." Canfield's gaze fell back to the ornate saddle. "How's all this work? What should I be on the lookout for? Was last night the start of it?"

The forthright manner of Canfield's approach caught Noah off guard. He looked at the shotgun resting in Canfield's arm and thought of how close a man had to be for the scattergun to be of much use. Then his mind shifted to Burt Perry and what a back-shooting coward he was. Noah suddenly felt obliged to offer a few words of advice to Canfield – a man who seemed to be more virtuous than bright.

"There's a better than average chance for a little trouble around here," Noah acknowledged, letting out a helpless sigh. "Mostly the farmers will feel the pressure of Sowers' growing cattle herd. And a few of them will most likely sell out when someone comes along and makes them a fair offer."

"You mean someone like Jared Sowers?" Canfield didn't want to leave himself with any doubt.

"Most likely," Noah said.

"And do you really think it will be a fair amount?" Canfield wondered aloud.

"I imagine it will be," Noah replied. "Sowers is rich; he can afford to buy what he wants. I don't think he can afford not to. He has too much to lose by taking chances. He has worked too hard to throw it all away by being stupid." As far as Noah had it figured, though, Sowers had already made the biggest blunder of them all – hiring Burt Perry. "Only time will tell how clever he really is. I don't think things will get too out of hand, but if they do, you'd best send for the troops." He quickly added, "And don't wait a day." Noah watched Dunlavy as he came out of the corral after brushing out Pecos.

"What do you mean, 'get out of hand'?" Canfield questioned.

"The day one of the local settlers gets hurt, or killed," Noah stated. "You send for the troops."

"Or a sheepherder," Canfield added.

"Or a sheepherder," Noah agreed. "In fact it might not be a bad idea to write a letter to the governor and explain the situation around here to him. He might send somebody to look into it."

"Do you really think it might get that serious?" Canfield became concerned. "Write to the governor?"

Noah grinned and nodded at Dunlavy who was making his way toward the saloon. "What the hell do you think all these fellows are showing up for? Their main job is to make the citizens nervous. They're a rough bunch of cowboys, wouldn't you say?"

"I'm going to get me a fresh pint," Dunlavy called out to Noah as he strolled by. "Do you want me to pick one up for you?"

After a short delay, Noah responded, "I reckon you might as well."

Thoughts of trouble weighed heavy on Canfield's brow. Noah had given a man, who he supposed was much better at repairing harness than settling range wars, a great deal to think about.

"Will you go to work for Sowers, too?" Canfield asked, running his hand over the Mexican saddle one more time.

Noah could tell the man dreamed of having the time to do some fancy leather tooling. "No, I won't," he announced, and waited until Canfield removed his hand before carrying the saddle into his cabin. "If it's okay with you, I'm riding out of here tomorrow."

"You're a free man as far as I'm concerned," Canfield assured Noah. "Is your friend going with you?" He hiked a thumb toward Dunlavy who was disappearing into the saloon.

"Why would you think that Lester Dunlavy is a friend of mine?" Noah asked.

"Isn't he?" Canfield persisted.

"We just work together now and again," Noah maintained.

"Like with Mister Whitehead," Canfield suggested. When Noah failed to respond, he continued, "Well, I suppose I could drink a beer before I ride back to town. I'll buy you one if you like...for letting me study your saddle."

"I better turn you down," Noah concluded. "I need to think about getting my outfit together."

It appeared Canfield had something more he wanted to say, but didn't and walked away leading his horse. He no sooner went into the saloon when Dunlavy came shuffling out. As Noah stopped to think about it, Dunlavy probably was the closest thing to a friend he had – not counting Pecos. It certainly was a sad commentary on the lonely life he'd led.

"He's got jinglebobs the size of watermelons. You gotta give him that," Dunlavy remarked, hurrying up to Noah with a pint of whiskey in each hand.

"Who, Canfield? He's okay," Noah reasoned. "I doubt he even thinks about it that way. I'll bet it's more of a feeling of obligation." Closing his cabin door, he took one of the bottles of whiskey from Dunlavy. "Come on and go for a walk with me."

Noah and Dunlavy followed the trail Tater had blazed through the wooded grove, and soon found themselves on a basalt ledge overlooking the Snake River. From their rocky perch the pair looked down on the hotel and ferry crossing. A westbound wagon was being pulled across on the barge and was near the spot in the river where the freight wagon was submerged. On the far shore, another wagon was already waiting its turn to make the crossing.

The bow lantern was lit in anticipation of dusk. It glowed brightly off the river's surface, while the sun became a giant orange ball of fire as it sagged into the dusty-rose haze of the western plain. Noah watched the nighthawks diving out of the sky. The wind sang through their wings as they swooped and soared off toward the heavens again.

"I still think Canfield is too meddlesome for his own good," Dunlavy fretted. "He was asking Sowers a lot of questions about Niles, and you."

"What questions?" Noah hesitated in asking. He almost knew better than to participate in this type of conversation with an alarmist such as Dunlavy.

"Like how long had Niles worked for him and if you weren't working for him, too," Dunlavy proceeded. "And things about Niles having a part in those sheep getting shot."

"And you see something strange about that? Any imbecile could've solved that one." At times Noah had to marvel at Dunlavy's suspicious nature. "Well, if Canfield turns out to be the one who saves your hide, I'm sure you'll forgive him for being so nosy."

"How could he do that?" Dunlavy took a swig of whiskey, then remarked, "Can you see him trying to put Burt in jail?"

The thought brought a smile to both their faces.

"To hell with Burt Perry," Noah exclaimed. "All that son of a bitch ever really does is ride around looking ugly. Hideous, like some old mangy mongrel."

"Ain't that a fact," Dunlavy agreed without thinking. Realizing his error, he quickly covered his foolish words. "You would never tell him I said that, would you?"

"I won't have to," Noah reasoned. "It will be flapping your own mouth that gets you killed."

"Burt might be the smart one here," Dunlavy contemplated, taking out his tobacco pouch to roll a smoke. "Hell, he never hangs around the ranch. Says he's 'taking care of goddamn business' on his own. He draws a wage and most of the time I bet he ain't doing any more than staying in camp all day humping his women."

"Women?" Noah was puzzled.

"He's humping with Little One, too," Dunlavy said.

"She's a little girl," Noah groaned with disbelief.

"When's the last time you saw her?" Dunlavy inquired with a sly grin. "She's showing womanhood pretty darn good." He finished rolling a cigarette, adding, "She's a cute little buttercup, too."

"Goddamn. It just ain't right," Noah scowled, taking the tobacco fixings from Dunlavy. "She's not old enough to be dealt such a rotten hand."

"Maybe not," Dunlavy admitted, putting a match to the cigarette.

"Definitely not and you know it," Noah argued. He was aggravated by the news. "Didn't you say anything about it to him?"

"Not me," Dunlavy uttered with astonishment at the mere notion. "That's strictly a private matter. If Alice don't slit his throat, why should I care?"

"That son of a bitch must be rabid," Noah declared, shaking his head with disgust. "He took a shot at me today." And for as much good as it would do, he added, "You don't need to tell anyone about it, either."

"I won't" Dunlavy pledged solemnly. He couldn't hide his concern over the gravity of the matter. "What are you going to do about it?"

"I'm not sure," Noah stated. "What would you do?"

"That's an easy one," Dunlavy responded at once, "I'd be on my way out of this country. Then I'd probably go by a different name just to be on the safe side."

"At the least, I need to stay out of sight for awhile," Noah announced, tossing the tobacco fixings to Dunlavy. "I have to figure out how to handle this one on my own."

Dunlavy sat quiet. He appeared to be working on a solution to the dilemma. If indeed he was, Noah didn't want to hear it.

"See that old road below us," Noah proceeded to change the subject. "That's the original trail to Oregon. This crossing wasn't even here. The old one was a good days travel upstream. Look at it. It's barely used enough now to keep from growing over in weeds."

"How do you know all that?" Dunlavy wondered aloud.

"I was out here when this country was first opening up," Noah announced. "Nearly twenty years ago. There was a lot of wagons coming along this trail then. Mostly emigrants. Now it's just one constant flow moving west through here. Mostly teamsters."

"What were you doing out here?" Dunlavy asked.

"Following the excitement," Noah explained, reflecting back. "I was sharing in the adventure of opening up a new land. A whole new way of life. Helping to build a brand new empire out here in this country."

"Was it really all that exciting?" Dunlavy questioned, looking at Noah like he was crazy.

"I'm still doing it, ain't I?" Noah concluded.

He stared down on the wild river and into the endless plain – and he envisioned the spirit of Bacanaro sailing over it all through the air with the nighthawks.

CHAPTER TWENTY-ONE

That night Noah woke up twice.

The first time, thoughts of Burt Perry roused him from his sleep. Noah tried to justify Burt's lunacy on the demons that are common to rum. He was all too aware that Perry drank more rum than was good for him and got meaner than usual when he did. With the events of the day running through his mind, it took a long time of lying in the still darkness for him to doze off again.

In the twilight of the morning, it was a noise that woke him with a jolt. He lay motionless on the cot with his pistol pointed at the door. A sudden fear came over him, sharpening his senses. He listened to the silence, but all he could hear was his own breathing...and when he held his breath he felt the beating of his heart. Noah began to wonder if he'd been dreaming and it had only been his imagination that woke him up. Perhaps Eddie had been out pissing, and he had heard him go back inside. Pecos may have snorted. What ever it was appeared to have gone away. The faint line of light coming in under the door was a welcome sight after a restless night.

Just as Noah began to relax, there was a scraping sound against the back wall of the cabin followed by a soft thud of something hitting the ground. The noise brought him to his feet and quickly out the door as though he'd found a skunk in his bed. And he was prepared for battle. Clear of the cabin, he danced around with his pistol out in front of him...his eyes scouring for any movement. Cautious and silent, Noah moved down the side of the cabin toward the back. He listened for the slightest sound. Everything was still.

Suddenly, out the corner of his eye was movement. Noah jerked the hammer back on his pistol and dropped into a crouch as he drew a bead on the strange object. It turned out to be nothing but a fat old porcupine lumbering off toward the tree line. The dark shadow of the prickly critter as it moved through the gray surroundings brought to Noah's attention that there was a heavy fog laying on the meadow and in the trees. The saloon was but a dim silhouette suspended in the mist with no visible horizon, and Pecos was a ghostly figure drifting slowly and silently across the corral. Noah let out a deep sigh of relief as he let off the hammer.

Standing outside in the first light of day he began to realize things that he'd been oblivious to until then due to his panic. The ground was so heavy with dew that it was gray, and his tracks were dark spots that seemed to follow him. The air was cold and clammy and attacked his bones with a shiver, and his feet were numb from the dampness. Dressed only in his union suit, he found the back flap hanging wide open, unbuttoned from tossing and turning throughout the night. It was a drafty predicament to be in and he looked around carefully to reassure himself that he was alone.

By the time he was dressed the fog was beginning to wane, and the morning sun broke across the land casting a reddish glow into the rising mist. Eddie was splitting kindling at the wood pile behind the saloon. Smoke already puffing from the chimney was a cheerful sight to Noah. He was having a hard time shaking the chill he'd caught during his early morning adventure.

Noah discovered the front door of the saloon closed tight and was about to go around to the back when he heard Eddie taking off the bolt. Eddie swung open the door and looked out as if greeting the new day for the first time. He was surprised to find Noah waiting there.

"You're out early this morning," Eddie commented. He went back and tossed more wood in the stove.

"I'm moving out of here today," Noah said, following Eddie in close to the stove. The wood inside was crackling and popping. "Is that fire putting off any heat yet?"

"A little," Eddie observed, laying his hand on the stove and drawing it back sharply. Closing the damper, he moved the bean pot off to the side away from the heat. "Do you want breakfast?"

"I don't think so," Noah considered, fixing his gaze on the kettle of leftover beans and liver. He had decided the night before to try out the food at the hotel first chance he got.

"That's too bad," Eddie remarked, putting an iron skillet over the hot spot on the stove. "I have some good lean salt pork and eggs, and a pan of biscuits ready to bake."

"Well," Noah quickly reconsidered. "Okay."

"You didn't think I was going to heat up them beans again, did you?" The thought even brought a look of disgust to Eddie. "Tell you the truth, I get tired of beans every once in a while." He sliced strips of fat pork and dropped it into the skillet to sizzle.

"I don't like eating them everyday," Noah admitted. "I like a good steak, preferably elk or moose."

"I like that, too," Eddie nodded. "Have you ever had beans stewed up with porcupine? That's really tasty."

"There was a big one prowling around my cabin this morning," Noah said. Though he'd heard of people eating porcupine, he never had – that he knew of. He could never quite figure out how to go about cleaning one. "I should have shot him for you."

"I wish you would have," Eddie stated. "I saw him out there wandering around in the fog but didn't want to shoot while you were sleeping. That brute was chewing on the wall next to my bed half the night. I sure would have cooked him up."

The coffee boiled and Eddie poured a cup for Noah, automatically adding a shot of whiskey.

"Tell me more about Idaho City," Noah sipped the strong coffee.

"About the whores, or what?" Eddie asked.

"That, and just what the place is like," Noah said.

"Like anywhere else around this country," Eddie offered. "Hot and dusty in the summer, freezing cold and ass deep in snow during the winter, and up to your axles in mud during the springtime...or whenever else it rains hard for that matter. Are you going there?"

"Maybe, someday," Noah replied.

"It's not all that bad for whores; except the weekends are too busy," Eddie continued. "Most of them is older and worn out some, but they do know how to please a man. I'd like to visit there again, myself."

"I thought you had your fill of them," Noah reminded him.

"I'd go just to do a little gambling," Eddie reasoned. Most gold miners were horrible card players. "They're still playing with gold dust around there."

"Sounds like a pretty lively place," Noah said, envisioning the old mining camps that he'd visited in Colorado. They were like a festering boil on the earth.

"Too much so for me," Eddie related, cracking eggs and dropping them in the hot fat. "Street brawls all the time, fist fighting and slicing each other up with knives. The doctor there is as busy as a seamstress sewing men up." He stopped cooking and gave Noah a solemn stare. "I just can't stand trouble anymore."

"I know what you mean," Noah responded. "Worst part is, I always seem to end up right smack dab in the middle of it."

After what Noah considered the best meal he'd eaten in days, he settled up with Eddie, packed his gear on Pecos and rode out. He had every intention of riding away from trouble, but instead found himself headed in the direction of Perry's camp. It was a situation that he knew he must respond to one way or another. Shots had been fired at him. It called for retaliation – the mangy buffalo hunter had one coming.

All along the way Noah tried to figure out what he was going to do once he got there. He crossed the trail that led down into the coulees where Perry was camped with Alice and Little One. A half mile further upriver he came to a narrow, brush covered ravine that ran down toward the water. It offered the seclusion he hoped for. He stripped Pecos and stashed his saddle and gear in a thicket of wild plum. And after hobbling the horse, he took off on foot toting his carbine.

Cautiously, Noah came out onto the bank of the river. His eyes scanned downstream, halfway expecting to see someone at the waters edge. It was all clear. He stayed close to the brush for cover as he moved slowly toward Perry's camp. If it wasn't for the women, Noah thought, he would walk right on in the back door, give Perry half of a chance before riddling him with holes – and then dump his worthless carcass in the river. Before long he found himself fantasizing about having to use Perry's own mule to drag the big man to the water. Maybe he should do it anyway – he could probably get Alice and Little One to help launch Perry on his journey to the sea.

Rounding a slight bend, Noah saw the smoke of a nearby fire drifting out over the river. He was getting close to their camp. Before him was an open stretch of land he would have to cross to reach it. Backtracking a few yards, he crept around in a patch of sage brush until he found a rock to sit on. A feeling of anxiety twisted in the pit of his stomach. It wouldn't have been so bad if he had a plan of attack, but he didn't. And by the time he decided to go in for a closer look, he had repeatedly checked the rifle and pistol to make sure they were loaded – and pissed twice. He was about to sneak across the clearing when he heard a clatter in the rocks behind him.

"Noah," a voice called out softly.

A surge of fear ran through him as he drew his pistol and spun around only to find Little One standing behind him. She was petrified as she stared down the barrel of two guns. Noah had the rifle aimed at her too, even though he was gripping it by the stock. He'd been startled by her casual manner and it ended up making him angry.

"Goddamn it, Little One," he scolded, "don't ever prowl up on a person like that." Noah let out a sharp breath and jammed his pistol back in its holster. He'd come within a whisker of shooting the young girl. Taking Little One by the arm, Noah marched her toward the bushes. "What are you doing out here? Where's Perry?"

"Sleeping," Little One answered, going along peacefully. She had no fear of Noah. He was a man she had always known and he had always been nice to her. When she was very young she could remember him giving her a little doll made of corn husks.

"How long have you been watching me?" Noah asked, skulking down once they hit cover.

"I saw you coming down the river," Little One said with a sly glance.

"Where's your ma?" Noah quizzed.

"Minding the fire and cooking," she explained. "Perry got awful drunk last night, and awful mean. We had to hide from him for awhile until he went to sleep. I don't think you should go see him. I think he would like to hurt you. He's always awful mad the next morning after he gets drunk on rum."

Little One didn't fully understand how dangerous the situation between Perry and him had become. Noah felt as jumpy as a frog in a frying pan while Little One seemed calm as the day was long. She gave Noah a bashful smile then looked down where she was drawing circles on the ground with the toe of her moccasin.

"I don't need to see him right now, anyway," Noah conceded. Perhaps there was another way to deal with Perry. Having been found lurking about by Little One changed everything – it was an event he hadn't counted on. "Walk back up the river with me a ways. I want to tell you a couple things you should know about Perry. Just between you and me."

"A secret?" Little One's eyes lit up.

"Sort of," Noah implied, hoping to raise her curiosity so she would follow him to a place where there was less chance of being discovered.

The morning sun was cutting a high arc through the clear sky. The air seemed thin to Noah – like mountaintop air that leaves a person woozy. He kept asking himself why he couldn't walk away from this mess. A job that made sense waited for him in Bakersfield. Wiping out Mexican rustlers was an activity he could wade right into instead of tiptoeing around here like a burlesque dancer. If he rode away there was chance he would never have to deal with Perry again. Burt Perry was hovering on the brink of insanity and he was trying to lure Noah into it, too.

He studied Little One out the corner of his eye as she walked beside him. It was obvious even in her loose fitting buckskin dress that she was growing mountains where there were only plains a short time ago. The sight made Noah wonder if what Dunlavy had said about Perry having his way with Little One was indeed happening. It was the type of thing Dunlavy might fantasize, making himself believe it was going on whether it was or not. If it was true, though, how could he make her understand that it was wrong. None of this whole rotten business was actually any of his concern. For once, why couldn't he just let it go?

"Little One, have you and Alice ever thought of going back to your people?" Noah asked. They stopped amongst a rubble of boulders at the mouth of a shallow wash. "Why don't you get away from Perry? Quit running and hiding and being hurt all the time."

"Alice told me that this is better than living on a reservation," Little One stated. "She told me there is no food to eat on the reservation. Anyway, Alice can't go. Perry says he bought and paid for her. And he says I'm part of the deal, too. I heard him tell Alice once that if she ran away he would kill her with a knife."

"Well, you can't own anybody in this country anymore," Noah informed her. "It's against the law now."

"Perry doesn't know the law," Little One remarked.

"He should at least know right from wrong," Noah said. The subject matter he was about to delve into was making him fidgety. With his free hand he picked up a couple of river pebbles and began shaking them in his fist, rattling them like a pair of dice. "There is certain things that he shouldn't do with you. Do you know what I mean? Very...uh, private things."

"You mean when he makes me be naked?" Little One offered without hesitation.

It had to be either simple innocence or ignorance that gave Little One a total lack of guilt about the subject. Noah wasn't sure which, but either way it left him speechless. He lacked practice in discussing such delicate matters. His mind went blank.

Untying a leather lace, Little One slipped off her dress before Noah had time to blink. With the buckskin garment laying down around her ankles, the young Indian girl was proud and naked as a newborn in front of him.

"Will you breed with me?" Little One asked, shamelessly.

"Good lord almighty," Noah mumbled under his breath. Frozen in time, his eyes wandered over her. Before him stood the mind of a little girl in the shape of a woman, pelt and all – and with breasts that were too big for the rest of her. The pebbles in his hand were starting to turn to dust.

"Do you want me to take your pants off?" Little One asked, reaching for his crotch. She had watched her mother use this tactic on Perry with occasional success.

"Whoa there!" Noah cried out, quickly dropping the pebbles and grabbing her wrist. "Listen here, it's a real nice offer but it ain't right. I'm too old for you."

"But you're nice," Little One said. She couldn't understand his reluctance. "It would be okay with you, Noah. I want to."

"That's just it," Noah argued. "It ain't okay. Little One, you are too young for this kind of business and that's all I'm going to say about it. Now put your dress back on." He gave her a sour look and turned his back to let her know he meant business.

After a moment Noah glanced around to find her dressed, but looking like she was about ready to bawl with her lower lip pouting out. "I'm sorry if I hurt your feelings," he explained, "but I didn't come down here for that kind of trouble. How would you like to do me a big favor?" He could tell she was still trying to figure out why he got upset with her. "I'll give you a silver dollar if you can keep a secret for me."

"Okay, what?" Little One's face lit up at the mention of money.

"This is real important, so you can't forget," Noah insisted. "I don't want you to tell Perry that you ever saw me out here this morning, and you can't tell your ma neither." As much as Noah would have liked to give the no good scoundrel something to worry about, he didn't want them to move their camp. At least Perry was easy to find in case Noah changed his mind about shooting him.

"Why not?" Little One was puzzled.

"Just because," Noah told her as he dug around in his pocket. "You got to promise me to keep our secret." He held out the silver coin for her. "And if anyone asks you where you got a dollar, tell them you found it along the river bank."

Little One quickly nodded and took the money and wandered off toward her camp, playing along the edge of the river as she went. Noah watched her for a few minutes before walking back up the draw to saddle Pecos.

With the vision of Little One's nakedness lingering fresh in his memory, Noah rode west. She had sparked a craving in him that wasn't going away – and it sounded like what he needed to satisfy it was in Idaho City, or perhaps the Army post at Boise.

CHAPTER TWENTY-TWO

The house was hot from canning all day. Rose placed a few fresh picked plums in her apron skirts and walked across the yard. It was milking time and she heard Tater cussing the cows in the barn. She knew he was getting to a point where he despised the twice daily burden of dairy cows. At one time the milk herd was up to nine, but now it was down to six – the number Rose had to reach before Tater quit bellyaching to her about the chore. He still complained to the cows, though.

Following the path through the locust grove, Rose passed by the idle swing and wandered down the creek toward Mixy's. She found him out in the pasture stringing barbed wire on a row of posts he had set in the ground. The donkey was pulling the cart and poked along beside Mixy without any coaxing. It was a scene the local residents were accustomed to – Mixy rambling around the Springwater Valley with his donkey cart full of work tools. This day his geese and sheep were tagging along, too. They shied away as Rose approached.

"Afternoon, Mizz Rose," Mixy called out.

"I picked you some plums, Mixy," Rose said, gently unloading the fruit onto the cart.

"Well, bless you," Mixy said with a broad smile. He carefully selected a plum and rubbed it on his shirt before taking a bite. "Mighty sweet, Mizz Rose, and mighty juicy. Won't you have one, too?"

"Goodness no, I been canning today," Rose explained. "I been eating plums all morning."

As Mixy ate the plum he looked back at the fence he was building and a worrisome expression came over him. "Do you think I'm doin' the right thing here?" It was as though he was asking permission and offering an excuse at the same time. "In the spring I'm gonna have a passel of lambs to look after. I just..." his voice tailed off for a moment, then he stated, "Mizz Rose, you know I like the open space much as anybody. I'm really not sure about fencin' this off."

"Why Mixy, you almost sound like a cattleman," Rose suggested.

"There's a big difference 'tween a cattleman and me," Mixy assured her. "I don't like to fence it because I don't feel like the prairies can belong to anyone. A cattleman don't like fences because he likes to think that it's all his."

"I suppose you heard there was a man killed down at Eddie Button's saloon," Rose mentioned, contemplating Mixy's fencing issue.

"Yes, Mizzy, I did," Mixy replied. "But did you hear why all that took place the way it did?"

"What's your version?" Rose wondered aloud. She'd heard Noah's story – and one from Tater that sounded like it was out of one of those dime novels.

"That man Master Noah killed worked for Master Sowers." Mixy sounded as if he believed there was some sort of honor in Noah's bloody action. "He'd been sent out earlier that night by Master Sowers hisself to run sheep off of open land so they could put cows on it. That Master Whitehead fellow ended up killin' some of them sheep and a dog, and I believe Master Noah shot him dead for it."

"I have to admit," Rose declared, "that's different from what I'd heard. Where did you come up with all that?"

"There's rumors goin' around this valley," Mixy said. He took one last bite and slipped the remains of the plum into the mouth of the donkey. The animal had been keeping a close eye on the treat and rattled the pit vigorously between its teeth. "I visit with Jules ever so often on down the creek. He told me that Master Sowers is gatherin' up a nest of rattlers." Mixy shook his head with concern. "Jules told me that there's this one man name of Burt Perry that is mean to the bone and he's after Master Noah for somethin'. It sounds bad, Mizzy."

"I don't know what Noah came back for." Rose was upset with the thought of Noah coming back into her life the way he did – with such turbulence. She was suddenly gazing on a sight that disturbed her even more. "Good lord, is that Jared Sowers? What in heavens name does he want now?"

Loping across the prairie was a white horse carrying a man dressed in black from hat to boots. Jared Sowers rode alone. There was no doubt in Rose's mind where he was headed. Mixy put on his pigskin gloves to return to his task of stretching wire.

"Must be a Saturday dance pretty soon." Mixy responded with a slight chuckle. "Mizz Rose, there sure has been some men ridin' across that prairie lately to call on you," He couldn't help but find her dilemma amusing. Over the years Rose had been sought out by all the lonely men for miles around. At the same time he felt sorrow in the fact that she had closed her heart to romance when Noah had ridden out of her life so long ago. "Yes Mizzy, there sure enough has."

"I can't understand it either." Rose gave him an exasperated look. "I haven't been setting out any bait for them. I suppose I'd better get up there and find out what he wants." She started toward home, adding, "Tater truly doesn't like that man, and I can't say as I blame him."

Rose had to hurry along the creek to intercept Sowers. She didn't want him running into Tater. Sowers saw her coming and changed his course to join her at the locust grove. Rose stopped to sit in the swing as he jumped his horse over the creek.

"Afternoon, Rose," Sowers smiled nervously as he tipped his hat. "Heavenly days, if you don't look pretty as a postcard sitting there in that swing. I should hire a photographer to make a picture of you."

"Why would you want to go to all that trouble?" Rose asked, admitting to herself that she was flattered by the idea.

"Because any man in his right mind would enjoy seeing such a splendid sight," Sowers explained. He swung down from the saddle and hitched his horse to a tree. "I don't imagine you can figure out why I came calling, can you?"

"Well, I know there's a dance coming up," Rose answered. "But, Jared, you know I won't..."

"Now, Rose," Sowers quickly interrupted, "before you turn me down again, I wish you would just listen to me for a minute." He shucked off a pair of goatskin gloves and began fidgeting with them. "I need a chance to explain something to you that I've been considering for some time now."

"You can speak your piece," Rose insisted, "but I can't think of anything you could tell me to change my mind. I can get to the dance on my own."

"I can't understand why you won't let me take you," Sowers complained. "After you hear what I have to say, maybe you'll take some time to reconsider." As he watched a cow come bellowing out of the barn toward the pasture, he began the speech he'd rehearsed in his mind on the ride over. "Rose, besides being a rancher, I have to be a businessman to run the size of operation I have. Seems I've always had better luck in my business dealings when I come directly and honestly to the point. Just spell things out the way they are. I came up here to talk to you about a proposition." Sowers struggled a moment to remember exactly how he was going to make his plea. He stuck the gloves in his jacket pocket and sat down on the bench near the swing.

"I'm listening," Rose urged him on.

"My wife has been back in the States for nearly two years," Sowers said, looking off to the east. "She's never coming back out here. Arabella never really cared for this rough country. I can understand a little about a woman's special needs, but I think she just wasn't suited for this kind of life. I don't imagine that there will ever be enough conveniences for a woman of Arabella's bloodlines. Anyway, I petitioned the courts and have been granted a divorce."

"I'm sorry to hear that," Rose said. She heard it had been his wife who sought the divorce and Sowers had fought it for awhile, but finally lost.

"I have old Jules to do the cooking and taking care of the house," Sowers explained, "but it's not the same as having the woman's touch around. Kind of the same as you having your darkie living out here to help you with the things that need tending to by a man."

"Jared, get to the point," Rose cut in sharply.

"Exactly," Sowers blurted out, suddenly full of optimism. "Rose, I think you've struggled on your own long enough. I want you to consider coming up to my ranch and letting me take care of you. I could give you all the things a woman like you deserves to have."

"Your proposition sounds more like a proposal than anything," Rose said, feeling somewhat stunned. As far as she was concerned the concept was absolutely ridiculous. She stood up slowly from the swing shaking her head with wonder.

"I guess I should feel honored by such a generous offer, but it's something I would never really even consider."

Sowers sprang up from the bench and folded his arms across his chest stubbornly. "Can you tell me why not?"

"I guess one reason would have to be that I don't care for you that way," Rose scoffed. "Truth of the matter is, I don't even know you all that well."

"I can understand you'd feel that way," Sowers reasoned. He was so wound up from being able to finally express his feelings to Rose that he was about to burst. "There would be plenty of time for all that to happen in kind of a natural way."

"What would I do with this place?" Rose was asking herself the question more than she was him. "I suppose you'll buy me out so you can run cattle in here."

"No. I've given that some thought, too," Sowers responded quickly. "I figure your boy is about the age where he will be taking a wife. You could turn this place over to him so he could keep your dairy business going."

Rose anticipated with mixed emotions the day when Tater would get married and go off on his own. She knew she would watch with pride the son she'd borne and raised take charge of his own future. Yet there was also the fear that Tater would go off to discover the world around him, leaving her for long periods of time – perhaps forever. The thought always left her hollow.

"Well?" Sowers quizzed anxiously.

"Jared, I told you there's nothing to consider," Rose restated. She looked across the meadow where she made a quick count of the milk cows. She knew Tater shooed each one out separately as he finished milking them. There were three head grazing together across the green meadow and a fourth hurrying out of the barn to join the others. "I'm afraid that right now you'll have to excuse me. Tater is about finished with his chores and I need to start supper. You haven't picked a very good time to show up here."

"Rose?" Sowers called, reaching out for her arm as she passed by on her way to the house.

She made a quick move to avoid his grasp.

"I said, you're going to have to excuse me," Rose insisted, stopping briefly. "I don't have time to listen to any more of this gibberish." She gave him a worried look before walking away.

"But you haven't heard the whole deal yet," Sowers called out loudly after Rose while he unhitched his horse. She was nearly to the house when he finally caught up to her. "How would you like to go on a genuine honeymoon? How would you like to go to Chicago and buy some new dresses and hats and shoes. Maybe some new dishes? Huh, how does that sound to you?"

"How about New York?" Rose added sarcastically. She could feel her composure wearing thin.

"Why not London, or Paris?" Sowers offered with a big smile. "That's a great idea. A steamship ride to Europe." He already knew such a plan was impossible, with all he had going on, but it sounded good for the moment – and it sweetened the matrimony pot. Just seeing Rose standing there all fired up with her hands on her hips made Sowers feel like their wedding night couldn't come soon enough.

"Is that what you're hiring all those men for, Jared?" Rose asked. "So you can go off to Europe on an extended honeymoon?"

"I've hired some extra cowboys because I plan on doubling my herd over the next couple of years," Sowers explained. "The railhead to the East is getting closer every day and I'll have the stock ready to go when they get here. The beef market is booming, Rose. I'm going to be a very rich and powerful man someday."

"It sounds to me that you are going to be too busy to go off on any long journeys," Rose stated. She tried to bite her lip, but the words found their way out. "Unless that's your plan, to be gone while your cowboys take over the valley."

By the sullen expression that came over Sowers, Rose could tell she'd struck a nerve. He turned his back to her to help conceal his anger. Rose took the opportunity to count the cows again. Tater was down to the last one.

"Now, listen to me, Rose." Sowers turned back to face her with piercing eyes. "I have made you a decent offer and you really should considerate it. Any reasonable woman in your position would jump at the chance."

"What position do you think I'm in?" Rose had worked hard for years to get where she was. She felt fine about her life and her lifestyle. She figured it was the likes of Jared Sowers who created unnecessary misery for others, taking all he wanted without regard to anyone except himself.

"You can't be happy living out on this frontier without a man to keep you satisfied," Sowers grumbled.

"If it weren't for men such as you, Mister Sowers, or those you have working for you, I don't think I'd have a worry in the world," Rose contended, bitterly.

With sudden force Sowers grabbed Rose by the forearm and dragged her close to him. "This is a rough and savage land. And the only law that counts is that of the strongest men." She struggled but was unable to break his grip. "You need a man to protect you more than you think."

Rose felt her emotions burst into anger. "Take your hands off of me!" she blasted, jerking from his grasp. "And get out of here before I take my broom to you." It was the same threat Rose made to the rogue roosters that got too aggressive around her.

"Mom?" Tater called from the doorway of the barn. He stood with clenched fists and appeared to be ready to tear into Sowers. "Is anything wrong?"

"I'll take care of this," Rose spoke to him sharply. "You finish what you're doing and get the milk up to the springhouse."

"But, Mom," Tater cried out in protest.

"Don't argue with me," she yelled. Rose was aware of her temper because she could feel it swelling inside her. "And get washed up for supper."

Sowers put on his gloves and climbed into the saddle. "Rose, you need to remember that Tater is going to have a wife and family of his own before you know it. And your darkie is getting old. You're going to need someone to look after you. I have more to offer than any other man around here, and you know that's the gospel truth."

A loud ruckus from the barn caught their attention for a few seconds. It sounded like a tin bucket was being used for a war drum and the last cow fled out into the pasture bellowing with fright. Tater had a temper of his own and finished up the tantrum he was throwing by uttering an inaudible oath toward the poor beast.

"Jared," Rose responded, having to bite her tongue to keep from giving him a lashing with it. "I'm asking you to ride out of here and leave us all alone. Just please leave us be and we'll get by somehow."

Sowers looked at her and shook his head with bewilderment as a stubborn smile came over his ruddy face. "See you at the dance, Rose," Sowers said, aiming his horse toward the open prairie. He tipped a finger to the brim of his hat and at the same time dug the fancy spurs into the flanks of his mount. The prize quarter horse raced off kicking up clods of dirt and farting as it did.

Clutching a dairy can in each hand, Tater came out of the barn in a huff. He sat the cans down and hurried to the corner of the barn to watch Sowers fade away into the afternoon plain. With all the authority he could muster Tater started toward his mother.

Rose took a deep breath and tried to regain her composure. The more she let things bother her the worse they affected Tater. Usually after Sowers came calling Tater wore a scowl for the rest of the day. She studied the look on his face as he marched across the yard. His blue-grey eyes were steady and void of emotion. This time his face was somber. He had the demeanor of a man who had just shot his favorite horse and faced a twenty mile hike to get back home.

"The very next time Jared Sowers shows up on our land, if you don't run him off with the shotgun, I will," Tater informed her in a calm, but determined voice. Before she was able to respond, he turned his back to her.

As Tater strode to the barn it was as if she was watching Noah when he was that age. There was no use arguing with him. Conklin men came into this world instilled with ideals; they found it impossible to let go of right, no matter how much wrong they had to pack along with it.

CHAPTER TWENTY-THREE

The following evening, after clearing the supper table, Rose picked up the shotgun and started outside. She tried to do this with a nonchalance that wouldn't draw Tater's attention.

"What's that for?" he asked before she could get through the door. Tater was in the process of moving a chair from the table to a window so he could capture the pale evening light on the pages of a new dime novel.

"I thought I saw a coyote up on the hill this afternoon" Rose said, hoping not to arouse his suspicions. "It might have even been a wolf."

"A wolf?" Tater stopped what he was doing. The image of an evil-eyed critter suffering from hydrophobia materialized in his mind's eye. "Wolves travel in packs. Maybe you ought to let me go hunting for them. I once read where a pack of slobbering wolves attacked a man when he was by himself."

"You just read your book," she instructed him. "I'm going to check the cows and chickens and sit by the creek in peace while it's still light. If I get attacked by a pack of slobbering wolves you'll most likely hear the shooting."

Tater flashed a smile and gave into the adventure of the book, leaving the wolf hunting to her.

The chickens were clucking and scratching around the barnyard while the cows were lying around an old crab apple tree in the lower meadow. An invasion of noisy black birds created a fracas in the sky as they swirled from one treetop to another. Downstream, Mixy's gaggle of geese sent out a clamor of their own. The air was unusually still and scented with the faint odor of burnt grass.

Striking the path that led to the swing, Rose scanned the hills that ran above the ranch to the west. The sun had disappeared below the horizon and the sky was scattered with high wisps of orange and purple clouds. Earlier that afternoon she'd noticed a strange rider headed north into the scrub juniper and pine dotting the foothills. The rider was too far away for her to recognize. Later, her eye had caught some sort of movement on the hill above the springhouse. She hoped it wasn't Noah hanging around to snoop on her.

Though the evening air was warm, an uncontrollable shiver gripped her for a moment. She came to a sudden halt, perceiving that something was terribly wrong. A thick column of brownish-grey smoke rose to a soft billowy cloud. The instant she realized the smoke was coming from Mixy's barn the entire roof ignited. Tumultuous flames licked red and yellow at the dense smoke. The fire was silent and all she could hear was Mixy's geese sounding the alarm.

Panic shot through her and she turned back to the house. She hoped Tater had seen the fire and was on his way to help out. When she didn't see him she screamed out his name. Almost without thinking she yanked back a hammer on the shotgun and pulled the trigger. The jerk and roar of the gun startled her, and it occurred to her that Tater would think she was being attacked by a pack of rabid wolves.

"Mixy's on fire," Rose shouted to Tater the moment he came out the door. "Bring a bucket and hurry."

Before Tater had time to respond another shot rang out down the creek. It was the sound of Mixy's single shot .22 Remington. The crack of the small caliber rifle was followed by the thunderous roar of a buffalo gun from somewhere out on the prairie.

"Mom! What's going on down there?" Tater still stood in the doorway trying to figure out what all the ruckus was about.

"I don't know!" Rose called out. She tried to make out any movement across the meadow where the booming report of the big bore rifle had come from. "But bring the deer rifle and a bucket, and hurry. And be careful," she warned him as she took off down the creek toward Mixy's.

As Rose came out of the clumps of willow that lined the banks of the creek another sharp crack rang out from Mixy's rifle. Pulling back the hammer on the second barrel of the shotgun she slowed to a walk and proceeded with caution. She knew the instant she saw the barn it would be impossible to extinguish the fire – it was being consumed by a torrent of flames. And now she was close enough to hear the roar of the heat and the crackling of the burning wood. Her heart pounded with fear while her mind raced to try to figure out what was taking place. Mixy was nowhere to be seen.

From the far side of the burning barn, the geese came running and flapping their wings with Mixy trotting behind them. He had his rifle out in front of him at the ready while he kept looking over his shoulder. The light from the flames created an eerie scene.

"Did you see him, too?" Mixy cried out when he saw Rose. His eyes were wide with frenzy.

"Who, Mixy?" Rose surveyed the fire anxiously. The heat was intense and drove them back. "Who was it?"

"The big man on the mule," Mixy answered. "I heard you shoot and he came ridin' across there yonder." He pointed to an open stretch of pasture between the creek willows and the burning barn. "I think it was him, Mizzy, the man Jules was tellin' about."

"Don't you worry, Mixy," Rose said, moving further away from the heat of the blaze. "We'll help you build a new barn."

"Yes, Mizz Rose," Mixy agreed as he solemnly watched the fire. "By the time I seen the fire it was already too late to do no good."

The settling dusk made the flames seem ever brighter. The land beyond the barn was lost in darkness. Rose couldn't help but think of the strange man Mixy had seen and wonder if he was watching the fire. Perhaps he was watching them. She felt a tinge of relief when she saw the familiar profile of Tater coming from the shadows along the creek.

"What was all the shooting about?" Tater asked, stepping into the light of the fire. He had a bucket in one hand and a rifle in the other. And the young man had broken his own rule – he had his gun belt strapped on over his bibbed overalls.

"Where did you get that gun?" Rose interjected before Mixy had time to speak.

"I bought it with my own money," Tater responded firmly, knowing full well she meant the pistol. "And I know how to use it, too."

The anger that began to surge in her turned to fear. Rose looked to Mixy for help, but he was mesmerized by the flames – engulfed by his own troubles. Seconds later the wooden framework gave out and the barn collapsed into a fiery heap. A column of sparks that looked like a million fireflies being set free at once created a greater spectacle than an Independence Day celebration.

"Should I go fetch Mister Canfield?" Tater asked.

"No," Mixy stared at Rose with concern as he spoke, "might be better if we didn't say nothin'."

CHAPTER TWENTY-FOUR

Plagued once again with a sense of unknown urgency, and despite the fact it was pouring down rain, Noah traveled the road to Idaho City. He was wet and cold and miserable – and he couldn't stop thinking about Rose. The distance he had put between them didn't seem to ease his mind. Besides, he felt he should be headed in the opposite direction; South, towards California.

He passed wagon after wagon loaded with supplies destined for the mining town. A few of the heavier wagons had fallen victim to the deluge and were bogged down in water filled ruts. Stranded teamsters had built roaring fires in an attempt to stay dry, and the crackling warmth taunted Noah as he rode along. A few days earlier he was roasting in the sun on the banks of the Snake River, and now he could see his breath as he huddled into his oilskin slicker.

The dismal cloak crept over the mountains and drifted through the dark green woods like a gathering of gray ghosts. Heavy clouds whisked by in blotches and whenever the sun broke through steam would rise from wherever it struck. A mule skinner along the way had told him the sudden change was more or less typical of the weather that comes in off the Pacific Ocean.

Ahead was a stretch of road that had taken on the appearance of a plowed field – row upon row of muddy ruts. A lone wagon stood in the middle of the quagmire, buried to its axles. There was no sign of the men or horses who had abandoned it. Noah studied the whole mess as he rode around it and wondered why any man in his right mind would choose to be a teamster. It was a thought he had every time he traveled the highways during nasty weather.

A few miles further along he came up behind a heavy wagon that was being dragged along the road by brute force. It was a sight seldom seen outside of wheat country; a fourteen-horse hitch. Noah had to stop and count them. Then he had to count the men. Nine. Nine men and fourteen horses all hooked to, and fretting over, one big wagon. There was a man on foot at each wheel helping turn the spokes by hand as others pushed on the rear of the wagon. The driver was out in front pulling on the bridle of the lead horse while another man walked along with the horses, swatting them on their rumps with a switch.

Noah assumed the cargo securely wrapped with tarps had to be mining equipment. It was the only thing he could think of that could be important enough to warrant that amount of effort. The men with the wagon were so intent upon their struggle they paid little attention to him as he went around them.

It began raining harder, but Noah knew it would hardly discourage such a determined lot. He grew disgusted with the thought of the men laboring so hard. Nothing could be worth that much trouble in this

miserable weather. Over the years it had become quite
clear to him: the wealthy sometimes feel that while time
is valuable, the sweat of man is cheap.

Rain fell in a constant drizzle throughout the
afternoon. Pecos hung his head wearily as he trudged
along. Noah had started looking for a place to seek
refuge when he saw a sign nailed to a tree along the road
ahead. The lettering read; 'HOT BATHS - 1/4 mile'. An
arrow pointed down a narrow lane through the woods.
He studied the sign for a minute before heading off in the
direction of the arrow. It occurred to him that someone
must be pulling a cruel hoax.

However, at the end of the road was a two story hotel
built from logs. The grand looking structure wore a
few coats of whitewash, almost giving it the look of a
hospital. At the rear of the hotel a bright plume of steam
rose into the gray sky. A Chinese coolie with an umbrella
came out to meet him as he rode up. Noah felt as though
he had stumbled onto paradise. After arranging for a
stall and a good ration of grain for Pecos, he took a room
in the hotel.

Exhausted, he shucked off his wet clothing and
tumbled into a cozy feather bed. He only intended to
take a short nap before having supper, but when he
opened his eyes again he knew he'd slept through the
night. It was daybreak and his room was filled with the
aroma of fresh baked sourdough. The smell of the bread
made his stomach rumble with hunger.

When Noah finished breakfast in the hotel dining
room, the Chinaman came out of the kitchen at once
to take his plate. "You have special hot bath now?" the
Chinaman asked in a sharp, high voice.

"That does sound good," Noah agreed without hesitation.

"I be back right away," the Chinaman said as he cleared the table. "Then, you follow."

The bath house at the rear of the hotel was a row of half-walled cubicles. In each semi-private room was a copper tub filled with hot water from a mineral spring. A faint odor of rotten eggs saturated the air while a steady stream of steamy water flowed into the tubs from a rusted pipe. A turkish towel had been placed on a chair beside the tub along with a sliver of soap, a few matches and a long, thin black cheroot.

"This is alright," Noah said with a half smile. He handed his clothes out to the Chinaman, who promised to launder and iron them within one hour for two bits.

The water turned out to be hotter than he was accustomed to. It took a couple minutes of oohing and aahing before he could submerge his entire body. After settling back in the tub, he struck a match on the bottom of the chair and put fire to the skinny cigar. He inhaled the mellow smoke deeply and thought for a moment of where he was at that very time the day before. His butt was stuck to a wet saddle and his muscles were aching from the damp cold. He closed his eyes peacefully as he exhaled a deep, smoke filled sigh.

"Feels pretty damn good, don't it?" The lazy voice of a man came from the next cubicle. There was a slight splashing of water. "I got to sit up on the chair for awhile. I'm half boiled."

"It's kind of hot," Noah responded.

"I could hear that you was taking your time getting in." The voice sounded a bit amused.

It only took about five minutes in the tub to render Noah helpless. He puffed away on the cigar, convinced that he had forgotten how to move his arms or legs. He couldn't feel the water either. It wasn't hot anymore, it was perfect. He heard the fellow next door get back in the tub.

"Did you have a chance to see the hurdy-gurdy dancers yet?" The unseen man asked. "Ain't they something."

"No, I haven't," Noah answered. "Where are they at?"

"They're at the theater that's built out of brick. I can't remember the name of the place," the man paused to think for a moment. "It's right along the main street."

"In Idaho City?" Noah asked.

"Where else?" the man was abrupt. "Soon as this rain stops they are headed for Warren and then they are traveling clean up to Pritchard Creek before winter. I hear that's almost in Canada. They would already be gone if it weren't for this weather."

Noah had no idea where the places were that the unseen bather spoke of. He could only presume they were other mining districts. At times miners could be speaking perfect English, but nobody else was able to understand a word of it. In the past, listening to miners, Noah had heard of things such as pegmatites and detritals but had never been interested enough in taking the time to find out what they were. Gold and silver miners. They also caused Noah to wonder why a man would choose that line of work. Especially the ones that tunneled into the ground. It had to be the gamble – a chance at striking it rich.

"Are you a miner?" Noah put down the cheroot and picked up the soap.

"I'm trying to be. This rain has washed me out of my placer," the man explained. "I welcome it. Right now Mother Nature's doing the heavy work for me. I think most of the color on my claim is from an alluvial deposit or perhaps a residual and the hydraulics of the flood will help free it."

Whatever that means, Noah thought to himself as he shook his head. "How far is Idaho City from here?"

There was a moment of silence before the man responded. "Are you serious?"

"I haven't been there yet," Noah explained. "I just came up from the south and ran across this place."

The sound of splashing came from the next cubicle as the miner got out of the water. "Well, you'll find a trail out by the stables that takes off through the woods in a northeast direction," the man explained.

"Idaho City is only about a ten minute hike on foot from here."

"I didn't realize I was that close," Noah said, washing his face with soap. He ducked his head under the water to rinse off.

"You better hurry," the miner said as Noah surfaced.

"What?" Noah asked as he saw the miner looking over the top of the short wall. The tall sandy-haired man with broad shoulders was putting on a shirt.

"If you plan on seeing the hurdy-gurdy girls you better hurry," the miner advised him. "This might be the last day they'll be here. I think it really is worth seeing. Four women dancing with their legs naked. Four superb looking women." The miner raised his eyebrows with delight. "Not like most of the whores around here."

"Sounds like a good excuse to head to town this afternoon," Noah said.

"Hope there is still some whiskey to be had," the miner said as if talking to himself. "I'm sick of beer." The man finished buttoning his shirt and focused on Noah. "I guess we really shouldn't gripe too much. Even though whiskey is hard to come by right now, there is plenty of beer and naked legged dancing girls." He concluded with a grin, "I reckon a man just can't have it all, all the time now, can he?"

"I 'spose not," Noah agreed.

A little while after the miner left the bathhouse, the Chinaman returned with Noah's freshly laundered clothes. "Do you know anything about a scarf for women made out of Chinese silk?" Noah climbed out of the tub to towel off. "Something real nice," Noah explained. "It is a present for a woman that I would like to send through the mail."

"I see what I can do," the Chinaman said with an adamant nod. He appeared at once to understand what Noah had in mind.

CHAPTER TWENTY-FIVE

The afternoon sky was brighter and less threatening with patches of blue and yellow sun breaking through. The path the miner spoke of was simple to find and Noah gave Pecos an armload of grass hay on his way past the stables. The miner's point-blank description of the hurdy-gurdy dancers had aroused his curiosity. 'Four superb looking women'. His craving for a woman had rekindled and he was looking forward to seeing them perform.

The trail was flat and easy to walk, and Noah soon came out of the woods on the edge of town. Surrounded by a pine forest, Idaho City was several rows of buildings situated along muddy furrows that were once streets. It was the biggest town he had seen since Cheyenne. Main streets and side streets, and there were even a few two story buildings.

It appeared to him that all the miners in the country had been flooded out of their claims and were spending their idle time promenading from one saloon to another. It was impossible for wagons to make it down the streets and plank footbridges had been laid across the water filled ruts. The men moving along them reminded Noah of a string of ants scurrying along twigs.

Saloons and gambling halls made up half the businesses in town where miners passed the hours swilling beer and squandering gold. Every saloon with a table and a deck of cards had its own resident gambler. It gave the drunken fortune hunters an opportunity to make wagers against real card players.

And though there was rarely a killing, it was not all that uncommon to hear gunfire echoing down the streets anytime during the day or night. That sort of racket was frowned upon heavily by the law. While it took a pack of lawyers to settle the feuds over placer claims, gambling disputes were often resolved on the spot by the shedding of a little blood.

Sticking to the high ground and stepping on every worn out tuft of grass he could find, Noah reached the system of boardwalks. He was about to enter the first beer hall he came to when the faint sound of men singing floated down the street. He could tell the singers were Irishmen. Whenever there were enough Irishmen in one place to make a group, they would always get together and start crooning ballads from the old country. It was some of Noah's favorite music to be around. He crossed the street on a set of planks where the traffic was moving in the direction of the tavern where the music came from.

A pathetic pair of men wearing striped Sunday suits with stiff collars and bowler derbies stood in front of the saloon. The suits looked brand-new except for a coating of mud that was nearly up to their knees. The men were drinking dark foamy ale from mugs. They talked at one another in slurs as they wavered around, each hanging onto the other's shoulder to keep from toppling over.

The rusty color of the ale sparked Noah's curiosity more than his pallet. Most of the dark variety tasted like it was brewed in an iron kettle, but now and then he came across some worth drinking. The search for the good kind was an adventure in itself. Noah was greeted by the familiar aroma of stale beer and tobacco smoke as he went inside. Hopefully someone standing at the bar would be able to tell him more about the hurdy-gurdy girls.

The saloon was crowded and unusually quiet. Most of the patrons watched with watery eyes as the trio of round-mouthed singers harmonized their voices. Another man accompanied them on a violin played so slow it whined. They sang a song about some fishermen who had drowned because of a storm at sea and about the wives crying for them on the shore.

A sudden outburst of anger disrupted the song.

In an instant a quiet game of poker had erupted into an uproar of hostile accusations and protests. There was a loud thump as a chair was knocked over at one of the card tables along the wall and a scuffle of men jumped to their feet, pushing and shoving.

When Noah got a closer look at the fracas he couldn't believe his eyes. Eddie Button was being forced up against the wall by a bearded giant twice his size. The big man's face was twisted ugly with rage as he drew a bowie knife from his belt and put it to Eddie's throat. He was preparing to give Eddie a bloody smile a couple inches under his chin.

Instinctively, Noah stepped into the crowd. He grabbed a heavy mug half-filled with ale from a nearby table and slammed it against the back of the bearded man's skull. The mug exploded in Noah's hand sending a shower of foam and broken glass on everyone involved.

The man let go of Eddie and turned around to face his assailant. He glared at Noah, seemingly unfazed by the blow. The big man held the knife out in front and was about to go on the attack when the heavy mug to the back of his skull finally registered. Noah took a step back as the man's eyes fluttered shut. In the blink of an eye the man's knees buckled under him and he fell to the floor in a heap. A second later three or four other men surrounding Noah drew their knives and flashed them at him. Noah dropped the mug handle and slipped his pistol from its holster. Eddie quickly moved in beside Noah, too scared to show any sign of relief.

"He ain't about to shoot in here," a man wearing a beaver top hat grumbled with a heavy Irish accent. He waved his knife in Noah's face as he took a step forward.

Noah thumbed back the hammer, and much to the man's surprise, blew the hat off his head. The thunderous roar of the pistol brought the whole lot to a standstill. With a look of uncertainty, the knife wielding Irishman reached up to feel his bare head as if he couldn't believe his hat was missing.

"What the hell are you doing here?" Noah asked as he grabbed Eddie by the arm and started for the front door.

"God, am I glad to see you," Eddie exclaimed. "I thought I was a goner. I wasn't cheating. I must have dropped it by accident."

"We're not out of here yet," Noah said, waving the gun at anyone who was in the way of the door. While there was a scramble of men getting out of their way, there was also a surge of angry men following close behind.

"He wouldn't listen," Eddie said. "None of them would. Hell, I was winning big, fair and square. Why would I risk getting cut up for cheating?"

Noah backed out the front door of the saloon dragging Eddie with him. They ran between the two drunks in the new suits who had come over to look in. Noah and Eddie departed the saloon with such haste they went off the wooden sidewalk and found themselves out in the middle of the street with the mud sucking at their boots. The angry men from the saloon had followed them out yelling and swearing angrily as they waved their knives about. There was a whole string of them hovering over the edge of the sidewalk. Noah kept a sharp eye for any sign of a gun. A couple of the miners who wore pistols wisely kept them holstered.

"You can't do that to me own brother and get by with it," the hatless Irishman snarled at Noah shaking his knife in the air. "I just won't let you off unscathed." He hopped off the wooden sidewalk into the muddy street. Eddie tried to retreat, but his foot was stuck in the mud and he went down on one knee.

Backing up, Noah's foot slipped into a murky brown rut that was so deep it only took a second for the cold water to fill his boot. Stepping in the mud-hole angered him as much as the pack of drunk men that were pursuing him like wolves. He aimed at the ground and fired another shot, this time as a warning. The slug splattered mud all over the angry Irishman.

"You better stop this," Noah sternly advised the vengeance seeking man. "If that's your brother that I bonked you ought to go take care of him. All we want to do is be on our way."

"I have some money laying in there," Eddie said. "Thirty-two dollars on the table and four more in the pot. He was going to cut my throat over it." He reached up to feel his neck and discovered his fingers were moist with blood when he checked them. "Oh God, I'm bleeding. I think he's killed me. Can you see where I'm sliced?" Eddie sounded like he was about to faint as he held his chin up for Noah to examine him.

"You're cut," Noah informed him. There was a small laceration on Eddie's Adam's apple with a trickle of blood dripping from it. "It doesn't look too bad."

"He cut my throat." Eddie's eyes stared wildly as he yelled frantically at the men who were after him. "My throat's been cut."

"Eddie, there's a little scratch on your neck." Noah tried to calm him. "You're gonna make it okay."

The vengeance seeking brother of the unconscious gambler who had jumped into the street after them, quickly tucked his knife away and climbed back onto the sidewalk. The majority of the others had already started wandering back inside the saloon.

"You there, in the street," came a deep, firm voice from behind Noah. "You toss that gun out in front of you. Any other ones you might have on you, too."

When Noah turned to see who was talking he saw three men wearing badges. All of them had a shotgun trained on him. Two other deputies with shotguns were tramping down the sidewalks toward him.

"Thank God," Eddie murmured.

Holding the pistol by the barrel with his left hand, Noah offered it to whoever had given the order. "Can I hand it to you?" Noah requested. "I'd just as soon not throw it in this mud. I'm not looking for more trouble.

There's been some kind of simple misunderstanding here."

Five lawmen with shotguns surrounded Noah and Eddie and closed in around them, having to wade out into the street. Noah turned his pistol over to the first man who reached for it while another man took his knife.

"I'm going to have to arrest you two until we can get this sorted out," said the man with the deep voice. He was the oldest with graying hair sticking out from around his hat and his badge read Sheriff instead of Deputy.

"I wasn't cheating," Eddie said to anyone who would listen as a deputy began to shackle his wrists behind his back. "Look," he offered holding his chin up, "they cut my throat. I need a doctor. I didn't do anything to deserve this."

"He's barely nicked," the deputy stated in a callous tone as he assessed the damage to Eddie's neck.

It wasn't the first time Noah had his hands shackled behind his back, but it gave him a feeling he knew he could never get used to – a sense of helplessness. He had to place his fate under the control of men he didn't know. But more importantly he was under the control of men who didn't know him. In the territories justice took on many forms. The Sheriff of Idaho City had an army of well trained, heavily armed deputies to ensure peace and tranquility among the citizens.

"Escort them to the office," the sheriff ordered his deputies.

A deputy on each side of Eddie grabbed him by the arms and started to walk him away. Eddie's boot was still mired down in the dark brown muck. The deputies tugged hard to help free him from the mud. This resulted in Eddie taking a couple of quick, long strides. His foot came out of his boot on the first step and out of his sock on the second.

"Wait a darn minute," Eddie protested loudly. He looked back to where his boot was sticking out of the mud. "I lost my boot, and my sock."

One of the deputies went back to retrieve the lost articles. Everyone found the situation humorous except for Eddie who wore a mournful expression.

It took a minute for everyone to make it up out of the boot-sucking mud. With the sheriff in the lead they made their way single file along the maze of wooden sidewalks and slick narrow planks down an alley between two buildings toward the jail.

"How did all this get started?" Noah looked back at Eddie who was walking directly behind him.

"Someone found a card on the floor under my chair," Eddie said. "It must of fallen off the table, but I was accused of trying to smuggle it out of the deck. It just happened to be the ace of hearts."

Before they had gone a block, a series of shots intermingled with the whoops and hollers of excited men came rumbling down the alleyways.

"Claude, get them to the office and sit them down," the sheriff barked the order to the deputy bringing up the rear. A moment later the sheriff was scampering off along the planks with the other three deputies.

"Busy day, Claude?" Noah looked past Eddie to the lone deputy.

"Average," the deputy responded and motioned with the barrel of the shotgun for them to move along. "Let's keep going."

They crossed another street near a two-story brick building that was the opera house. A nervous huddle of men stood at the front door hoping to get inside.

"Big crowd tonight to watch the hurdy-gurdy dancers," Eddie observed. "I was wanting to see them again, myself."

"I think this is their last night in town," Deputy Claude said. "Ain't they something?"

The crowd in front of the opera house suddenly let out a roar of approval. Noah tried in vain to imagine what it was over. Women's naked legs often had that affect on a group of lonesome men – cheering and howling. If he could get this mess he was in now settled quickly, he would go see for himself what all the men around were raving about.

CHAPTER TWENTY-SIX

The jail was located at the far edge of town and was built like an old Army forts. It was a low roofed log structure enclosed within a compound guarded by picket walls. The sheriff's office was well lit and warm. A fire burned in a big pot belly stove in the middle of the main room. The faint odor of wood smoke gave the jail a somewhat cheery atmosphere, except for the iron bar door on the back wall leading to the cellblock. A mute faced guard with a short barreled shotgun across his lap sat in a chair near the fire. He gave Noah and Eddie a thorough once over as they entered.

"Knife fighting and shooting off guns," Deputy Claude stated to the guard as he came in. The guard shook his head like he was saying, 'shame on you'. "Have a seat along the wall over there," the deputy ordered, motioning to a bench beside the cellblock door. "You can smoke if you want."

"What about these shackles?" Noah turned his back to the deputy and held his wrists out. Deputy Claude produced a key and removed the wrist shackles from Noah, then Eddie. Noah took a seat on the bench wishing he had some tobacco fixings right then.

"Am I still bleeding?" Eddie asked, stretching his neck for Noah to examine the wound. The stretching caused the cut to break open and a fresh trickle of blood started down his Adam's apple.

"You'll be okay if you stop craning your neck around," Noah insisted.

"Hey!" A prisoner bellowed from his obscure cell back in the dim-lit part of the jail. The caged man then let out a banshee scream that echoed from every corner of the building. Neither the guard nor the deputy paid any attention to the outburst. The guard stayed as still as a statue. Deputy Claude laid Noah's pistol and knife on the corner of a desk where he sat down to read a newspaper.

"I come up here to get away from danger and almost end up getting my throat slit," Eddie said, disheartened. He wiped what mud he could off his foot and shook out his sock. "That friend of yours, Dunlavy, came close to getting himself killed."

"Dunlavy?" Noah felt truly concerned. "What happened to him?"

"He nearly got me done in, too. He was having a drink at my bar when this Mexican walks in and throws a dagger at him," Eddie explained. "Whistled past his ear and stuck in the wall close to where I was standing. I was stirring the beans and minding my own beeswax and this pearl handled toadsticker missed me by a hair. Dunlavy got hot over it and scolded the Mexican, but he just laughed it off like it was nothing more than a harmless prank."

"That's all it was," Noah informed Eddie. "That was Pico. Fernando Pico, a Texas born Spaniard. He always does that sort of thing to get Dunlavy's goat."

Eddie gazed at Noah skeptically as he pulled on his muddy boot.

"I guarantee you that if Pico wanted to stick his knife in Dunlavy, he could have," Noah stated. "You came all the way up here because of that?"

Letting out a sigh, Eddie relaxed back against the wall. "Other things happening, too. Just too many peculiar things. Some sheepherder turned up missing, and Frank Canfield has been out looking for him. He asked me if I'd seen or heard anything."

The news made Noah instantly suspicious of Perry. He wondered if Sowers would give such an order. Sowers was crazy if he did.

"A couple days later someone burned down an old man's barn over in the valley," Eddie said. "I was getting so I felt spooked all the time wondering what was coming next." The scrawny, fuzzy-haired old man leaned closer to confide in Noah, and in a lowered tone added, "I just can't stand trouble anymore, and Jared Sowers is a real son of a bitch."

Noah had left the Springwater Valley to try to keep from thinking about everything Eddie was talking about. Right then all he wanted to do was go have some whiskey and see the dancing girls, but he knew he wasn't even supposed to leave the room he was in. The realization of being in trouble came on like a headache. Here he was once again having to explain his actions to another man wearing a nickel plated star.

The stomping of feet at the front of the jail announced the arrival of the sheriff and his men.

They came through the door chortling at one another.

"What was all the shooting over?" Deputy Claude asked. He seemed confused that the sheriff didn't have at least one prisoner with him. Discharging a firearm in Idaho City was generally an automatic trip to the hoosegow.

"Celebration," one of the deputies explained. "The whiskey wagon was pulling into town. Too bad you missed it. There were sixteen horses hitched to it."

Noah knew at once it had to be the tarp covered wagon he'd passed along the road. Finding out the wagon was loaded down with whiskey rather than mining equipment gave him an odd sense of relief. He silently exonerated those poor drowned souls for working so hard in the drenching rain.

"You two can get up from there now," the sheriff said, taking over the desk from Deputy Claude. Noah and Eddie got up from the bench and stood in front of the sheriff. The four deputies gathered around the potbelly stove to carry on quietly among themselves.

The sheriff dipped a pen in a bottle of ink before looking up at Eddie. "What's your name?"

"My name's Eddie Button." Eddie announced. Poor vision made him squint as he watched the sheriff put his name in the journal.

"What are you doing in Idaho City, Mister Button?" The sheriff dug two twenty dollar gold pieces from a pocket and slapped them on the desk.

"I come up here to play some cards," Eddie stated.

"That's your money from the poker table," the sheriff said as he shifted his attention to Noah. "Where are you from?"

"I'm on my way to California," Noah deliberately avoided the question as he watched Eddie scoop up the gold coins. "I was planning on waiting out the weather here is all."

"What's your name?" the sheriff asked, dipping the pen again.

"Noah Conklin." Noah started to relax. He figured the sheriff must have gotten to the bottom of the squabble between Eddie and the Irishmen.

"You two can get out of here," the sheriff informed them as he shook the remaining ink from the pen onto an ink-blackened splatter on the floor beside the desk. When Noah reached for his gun, the sheriff added firmly, "Mister Conklin, I hope you have a safe journey to California. As for you, Mister Button, try to find a friendlier game to sit in on. Don't either of you get in trouble again while you're here in Idaho City."

The group of deputies broke into a chorus of laughter as Noah headed for the door with Eddie at his heels.

"I'm glad you boys have time to skin the cat over there while you're soaking up the stove," the sheriff's sarcastic tone terminated the deputies elation. "My advice to you would be to get out there and keep some order around here. There's a wagon full of whiskey just showed up in a town full of restless miners. Let's keep a tight rein."

The sheriff didn't have to say any more. The deputies surged to the door and followed Noah and Eddie outside where they scurried away. Once Noah was beyond the picket wall he stopped to reload his pistol.

"Are you a relative of theirs?" Eddie's brow wrinkled as he mulled something around.

"Of who's?" Noah slowly spun the cylinder making sure he'd replaced all the spent cartridges.

"The Conklins living in the Springwater Valley," Eddie said. "That reminds me, she came to the saloon looking for you a couple days after you took off. I got the feeling it was important, too."

What woman would come to the saloon looking for him? Rose? It had to have been something urgent. "Who came looking for me?" Noah was troubled by Eddie's words. "A woman came to the saloon looking for me? Did she say what she wanted?"

"The widow, Rose," Eddie replied. "You do know her don't you? She talked like she knew you. She didn't really ever say, but I think it was something about Tater. That he had been going around wearing his gun belt. I could almost see it coming. I knew she wasn't going to go for it one bit."

"Eddie, what does Rose Conklin have to do with Tater?" Noah asked, hollow voiced.

"Rose Conklin is Tater's mother," Eddie declared. "Didn't you know that?"

Noah felt as though he'd been kicked by a mule. Confused. The news flat knocked the wind out of him and he couldn't seem to catch a breath. Eddie's words kept ringing over and over in his ears and he found a nearby step to sit on. He tried to picture Tater in his mind's eye, but the image was vague.

"Is there something wrong?" Eddie leaned over him. "Are you sick or something?"

"How old is Tater?" Noah wondered aloud. He could feel his mind churning and searching for answers. Why hadn't Rose told him she had a son?

"I think he's fifteen or better," Eddie replied, feeling for blood on his neck. "I know for a fact he's over fifteen. I won't serve whiskey or beer to boys under fifteen. I think a fourteen year old boy is too young to be drinking whiskey already."

It was like the pieces of an extraordinary puzzle suddenly began falling into place. A voice as cold and clear as an icicle slipped into Noah's deepest thoughts telling him it was his son, too. It was impossible for him to shake that feeling. He had carried some sort of a strange feeling around about the boy from the day he had met him.

"Want to go see the hurdy-gurdys?" Eddie offered, checking his fingertips. The bleeding had stopped.

"No," Noah replied, giving Eddie a blank stare. The only woman he wanted to see was Rose. It had become apparent to him that she had some explaining to do.

FAMILY REUNION

CHAPTER ONE

Turning over in his bedroll, Noah cracked open his tired eyes to gaze at Pecos. The horse was lying down, and it was a sight he seldom saw that time of day. The tall thoroughbred was usually browsing around the ground at first light for the tender shoots of sweet grass while they were still covered with dew.

"You must be tired as me," Noah said as he wiped the sleep from his eyes. The sound of his voice brought the horse quickly to its feet. Pecos greeted the day with a full body shake that left a tan cloud of dust, back-lighted by the early morning sun, hanging in the air.

A few yards away was the constant peaceful gurgling of Springwater Creek cascading over and around the boulders of the streambed. In a nearby willow thicket a chorus of songbirds mingled together creating a joyous melody to celebrate the new day. The beauty and tranquillity of the morning was suddenly splintered by the troubling thoughts that had plagued his mind for the last couple of days.

Noah began to dwell on Rose again, who was now only a couple of easy miles upstream. He had never learned to live with torment. And if ever there was a time in his life when he felt as tormented as he did right then, it had to be when he deserted Rose all those years ago.

What had caused him to do the things that were now coming back to haunt his conscience? What was it he could have told himself at the time to have justified his actions? Right then he couldn't remember the reasons, at least none that seemed good enough. He came face to face with the truth. While he tried to convince himself that the things he did was to help others, the fact was that in the process he had hurt some of them along the way. Nothing on earth Rose ever did to him made her deserve what he had done to her. And all she asked from him in the end was to be left alone – now he couldn't even do that.

Rolling out of his blanket, Noah pulled his boots on and took a razor, mirror and a bar of soap, and sat on a rock beside the creek. He cupped his hands and drank the cold water, savoring the clear sweet taste. He combed out and re-braided his hair, and as he prepared to shave, he stared into the mirror and noticed the lines weathered into his face by years of changing seasons. It was as though he discovered them for the first time. He found himself looking into the eyes of a man he wasn't sure he knew anymore. Noah felt like he had lost his sense of direction, or perhaps his sense of purpose – if he ever had one.

Could it actually be that the boy called Tater was his own son? If that was the case he should have at least had the right to have known. He should have at least been given the opportunity to make the right decision. To be responsible. Rose could have gotten the word to him if she had really wanted. She could have gotten word to his family; there had always been a way. A feeling of anxiety surged through him when he thought of confronting her about the truth.

Less than an hour later, Noah sat in the saddle, watching from the road that led to Mixy's little piece of ground. Through the trees he could see a barn raising and picnic were in progress. Under blue skies a crew of men with hammers and saws worked on the building like a swarm of yellow jackets on a rotten apple. Most of the framing for the barn had been completed and the structure was a dull yellow skeleton of new sawn wood waiting for its skin. Heavy wagons loaded down with stacks of boards were parked nearby. In the barnyard a circle of women hovered over gingham tablecloths as they set up a potluck dinner.

Noah touched his spurs to Pecos while he looked for Rose among the gathering of neighbors. He spied Mixy Alexander up on the roof nailing shake slats to the rafters. The old Negro stopped hammering when he saw Noah riding in. Mixy called out to the huddle of women, pointing toward Noah as he did. A moment later Rose emerged from the jury of skirts who took time out from the fried chicken, potato salads and deviled eggs to give Noah a disparaging eye.

"We are having the church services out here today," Rose said walking up to him, wiping her hands on her apron. "I heard you had left the country again."

"Is it Sunday?" Noah stepped down out of the saddle. "I guess I haven't been keeping good track of the days lately." From his position up in the rafters Mixy gave a slight wave and Noah tipped a finger to his hat. "I was over in Idaho City a couple days ago and came across Eddie Button."

"I heard his place was all boarded up," Rose said, as she began hiking up the path that led to her house.

"Who did you hear that from, Tater?" Noah asked as he started to followed her. "Isn't that your boy's name?"

Instead of giving him any sort of an answer, Rose stepped up the pace causing him to have to drag Pecos along by the reins to keep up with her. "That's what people around here call him," she turned back long enough to snap at him before lighting out quicker than ever.

"I rode a long way to talk to you," he insisted, swinging back up in the saddle. At the clip she was going, riding was the easiest way for him to keep up. "Rose, you should have let me know about the boy."

Looking down at her as he rode, Noah followed Rose to the house. She hadn't uttered another word, though she had turned to glare at him a couple times. As she started inside, he got off his horse. "I'm not going to leave until you talk to me," he informed her.

She changed her mind about going in the house and took off across the yard, past the chicken coop, and up the slope toward the springhouse. He tied Pecos to one of the clothesline posts and hurried after her.

When Rose finally stopped, she had climbed the hill above the springhouse to a spot where she could look out over the valley. Her eyes studied him warily as he caught up to her, then she focused her attention on the valley road winding off in the distance below. "You think you have it all figured out, don't you?"

"No, I don't," Noah replied, a bit winded from the hill. "In fact there isn't much that makes sense to me anymore. I'm kind of counting on you for a few answers."

"I don't owe you anything," she spat.

"Excuse me, Rose, but I take exception to that," Noah contended. "I think that perhaps you owe me some sort of an explanation here."

Brushing her auburn curls away from her eyes, she gave him a stubborn glance. "Why's that? You didn't give me one. I asked you why you left me out here on my own and all I hear is some cock-and-bull story about needing more out of life. I guess this kind of life wasn't enough of a challenge for you. Well it damn sure was challenge enough for me when I found myself all alone. For Christ's sake, what in the hell do you want from me?"

"When did you take up cussing?" He was always surprised to hear a proper woman use foul language.

Letting out a deep breath, Rose said, "Oh hell, Noah, I know all the words." She seemed concerned as her eyes scanned the valley road and across the vast prairie. "But I don't guess I should be speaking them on Sunday. Why in heaven's name did you have to come back here?"

"Because I need to know something," he said with a tongue so dry that it felt like the words came out in pieces, and right then he couldn't look her in the eye. "I need to know if that boy is my son."

His words hung in the tense air for a long moment as Rose seemed to be searching the ground around her feet for the answer. She couldn't face him either, or maybe she just couldn't face the truth. She finally mustered up the courage to look him in the eye, and replied, "No, he isn't. Now, is that what you've ridden all this way to hear?"

Not knowing what to say, Noah stood staring at her until it caused her to look away. Shaking his head with wonder, he took off his hat and wiped his brow with his shirtsleeve. "No, that's not what I came all this way for to hear."

A gentle breeze drifted in and it carried with it the distant pounding of hammers. Noah surveyed the progress on the new barn and put his hat back on. "Alright, Rose, I guess we'll just have to see," he said determined, and started back down the hill.

"Where are you going?" Rose called out anxiously.

"I'm going down and find out what Mixy knows about all this," Noah threatened, turning around to find Rose wringing her hands in her apron. "I came back here to find out about that boy, and I don't think you're going to tell me anything. So I'll see what Mixy has to say. I don't believe that old man ever did learn how to tell a lie." Noah acted like he was starting to leave again. "Now are you going to tell me, or do you want me to have to go find out from Mixy? Or maybe some of those other folks down there might know something."

"Wait," Rose said calmly, "I'll tell you what you want to know." She'd been afraid that he might show up again asking such questions and had already decided what was best to tell him. "But it's not what you think. I'll go ahead and tell you even if I don't feel like it's any of your darn business. And after I do tell you, you have to promise to stay away from us."

"Okay," Noah agreed, wondering if maybe he should have crossed his fingers. "I swear I won't bother you anymore. Now go ahead and tell me."

Skeptical as she was, Rose began, "Well, not long after you up and left me, a man showed up here..."

"What man?" Noah interrupted.

"Nobody you knew. A drifter," she said, stepping past him to maintain her vigil on the valley road. "He needed a place to stay and I needed the help. Anyway, he was such a decent man, and a good provider, and handsome, too. Before I..."

"This drifter, what was his name?" Noah stopped her.

"His name?" She gave him a blank stare.

"What was this handsome drifter's name?" Noah quizzed her. Cynicism was one of his fortes.

"His name was William," she answered quickly.

"William what?" Noah persisted.

"What possible difference could that make?" Her eyes were searching the ground again. "It was Brown. His name was William Brown."

"Okay, so this drifter named William Brown shows up here after I was gone." Noah was trying his best to picture the scene Rose was trying to paint. "Alright, go ahead."

"Anyway, at the time he was like an answer to a prayer," Rose continued. "He took away my loneliness and before I knew it I found myself in love with him. It was not..."

"Wait a second here," Noah butted in again. "How long was it after I left before he showed up?"

"Two months, maybe," Rose responded.

"Two months?" Noah was suddenly amazed by her story. "So you're telling me that within a few short weeks after I was gone, there was some handsome drifter living up here with you."

"It might have been longer than that, Noah, it was a long time ago," Rose declared. She hadn't planned on him asking so many questions. "Are you going to let me tell you about Tater's father, or are you going to keep interrupting me? This is going to take all day if you won't keep quiet for a minute."

"I'm sorry," Noah stated. "That just doesn't seem very long to me, Rose. Two months. Does that seem like a long time to you? But I'll try to keep my mouth shut. Go ahead with your story."

"Where was I?" Rose was getting flustered.

"You were in love with a drifter," Noah reminded her.

"It just happened," Rose went on with her tale, "it wasn't anything I was looking for. We were going to get married, but we didn't have time. The poor man died without ever getting to see his son." Her face was etched with sadness. "During that first winter he came down with the fever and died. That was Tater's father."

Far in the distance, a pair of wagons had made their way across the plain on a dusty old trail that meandered out of the foothills into the head of the valley. The wagons reached the main road and faded into the shadows of the trees that lined the banks of Springwater Creek. Rose had failed to notice them because she was too busy trying to read his reaction to her story.

Rose's yarn about William Brown was spinning through Noah's mind and some of the pieces just didn't fit. The day Tater and him had gone target shooting at the river the boy had mentioned something about his father's death. While his brain was busy trying to remember exactly what it was that Tater had told him, his tongue was busy wagging in the wrong direction. "I reckon back then preachers where pretty scarce out here on the prairie," he commented, hoping she would detect the sarcasm in his voice – and she did.

"What do you mean by that?" Rose asked.

"Well, it seems you couldn't find the time to get married to this fellow," Noah concluded, "but you certainly found the time to have his baby."

Rose threw a wicked right cross that landed squarely on Noah's cheek. The blinding flash of light rocked him backward, and it took him a moment to fully realize what had happened. Rose was hopping mad and came at him again with clenched fists. Noah quickly moved out of her range, complaining loudly, "What the hell was that for?"

"How dare you speak to me in such a manner," Rose snapped. There was fire in her green eyes that burned clean through him.

"If a man hit me like that..." Noah warned.

"Who gave you the right to show up here on my land and pass judgment on me, and mine?" Rose trembled with anger and her jaw was clenched tight. "I'd say you owe me an apology."

"Yeah, well I'd call it about even," he argued, rubbing the tender spot on his cheek with his fingers. He didn't come back to fight with her, and he certainly didn't expect to hear about her romance with another man so soon after him. It was his stupid pride that made him say things to provoke her. Maybe it was time for him to ride off for good.

There Rose stood, flushed with anger, sunlit curls danced on her forehead, her green eyes were ablaze, and her hands knotted in fists ready to clobber him. She looked upon him with scorn, and right at that moment she was the most beautiful sight he'd ever seen, and the fires of his heart were rekindled. And, he also recalled what it was Tater had told him that day at the river.

"So," he spoke as calm as he could, "what you're saying is that this William Brown fellow died of the fever while you were with child."

"Carrying Tater," she nodded. "That's right."

"And this drifter was your boy's real father?" Noah wanted to make sure he had the story straight.

"That's what I've been trying to explain to you," she assured him.

"Is he buried here on the place somewhere? Perhaps down by your rope swing." He craned his neck looking all around. "He's not buried out behind the barn is he?"

"No, he's not," Rose responded stubbornly. "I don't have to tell you where he's buried."

"Yes, you do," Noah stated flatly and leaned in close to her. "I want to see his grave with my own eyes. You want to know why? Because Tater told me that his daddy drowned in the river down there. Now if his daddy died of the fever, why did you tell Tater that he drowned in the river? So you see, I honestly don't know what the hell to believe anymore. In fact I hardly know what the hell I'm doing anymore at all. But I do know this; if the man you was in love with died while you had his baby growing inside you, you'd sure as hell know where he's buried. Rose, if you can show me a grave with William Brown's name on it I promise you I'll ride out of here and never look back."

Stone silent, she just stood looking down at his feet, arms folded across her breast, her hands grasping her own shoulders. Noah added, "Somebody's going to tell me the honest-to-God truth before I leave here."

This time he started down the hill without looking back even though she was calling out. He really didn't want to cause her any more trouble, or hurt her more than he already had, but he felt she had left him no choice. He was walking fast and could hear her coming after him, and he braced himself for another blow from her fists.

As he reached the springhouse, Rose grabbed his arm to stop him. "Noah, wait," she pleaded.

"I didn't mean for it to be this way," he told her. "I need to know what the truth is, that's all."

The anguish of the past rose to the surface once more, but the pain and the anger were dulled by time, and now she only felt numb. With the back of her hand, she wiped away a tear before it had a chance to run down her cheek. Suddenly exhausted, she sat down among the green tufts of grass that grew around the springhouse and gazed up at him with eyes that were soft and pleading – like those of the dying.

The sorrow in Rose's eyes as she fought back her tears put a lump in Noah's throat too large to swallow. He wished he could cradle her in his arms, where she would lay her head close to his heart and sob gently while she told him the truth about Tater. There was a long minute of silence before he could find his voice. "Tater is my son, isn't he?"

"Do you have any idea how bad you hurt me?" There was little emotion left in Rose – she was wrung out. "I turned around one day and found myself out here all alone, and expecting. There were times when I thought I was going to die from the hurt, and there were other times that I wished I could've. If it hadn't been for Mixy Alexander I really might have."

"You should have let me know, Rose," he reasoned. "I think I had the right to know about something like that. I should have at least been given the chance to do the right thing by you."

"The right thing by me?" Rose got up from the ground and swatted the dirt off her skirt. The tone of her voice let him know she had regained her strength. "You were my husband, Noah. The right thing was to be by my side, not drive me out here in a prairie schooner and dump me off like some stray hound you wanted to be rid of.

"I want a drink," she declared, moving over to the springhouse door. She reached into a dark corner and produced a large glass canning jar half filled with liquor. She took off the lid and drank down the contents as though it was nothing more than lemonade before offering it to him.

Before putting the jar to his lips, he took time to sniff the contents. It was a trick he'd learned over the years to keep from getting poisoned too bad – he had discovered right from the start that what some men called whiskey was little more than a distant cousin to whiskey found hanged from a limb of the turpentine family tree. This time, though, he was more interested in smelling it to find out what Rose liked to drink when she did. And he wasn't a bit surprised to find the jar contained a sweet smelling wine. The surprise came when he took a swallow. The vaporous concoction had a dry biting taste and lit such a fire in his furnace that he could feel his ears turning red. Fumes that formed in his throat drifted up to burn his nostrils and, it caused him to let out a snort.

"I make it out of rhubarb," Rose stated, taking the jar from him to down another swallow. She looked him square in the eye and told him, "If you take my son away from me, I would try to kill you if I could. You can't come back here after all this time and steal him away from me."

"I didn't come back here to steal him away. For Christ's sakes, I had no idea he even existed until a couple days ago." Her words puzzled him. "Why would you ever think that?"

"He reads all about that wild life prattle," Rose explained with a certain amount of disgust in her voice. She put the lid back on the jar and returned it to its hiding place. "Indian fighters and the such in those dime novels. He even goes down and reads to Mixy out of them. That boy can read about some poor soul living out there in the wilds wearing a set of buckskins that have turned black from blood and grease and a with pack of nits living in his hair, and Tater thinks it's romantic. Don't you understand? He sees you as one of them gun toting fools in those novels. I guess you know he has his own pistol, keeping it hid behind my back. And I heard about you giving him a shooting lesson. I don't want him to get all caught up in guns and fighting."

"There ain't nothing wrong with knowing about guns," Noah defended his actions. "You know enough about them to protect yourself if you needed to."

"I know how to use a gun good enough to fight for what I believe in if it comes to it," Rose's words almost sounded like a warning. "I can see too much of you in him at times. I can see that same wanderlust lurking in his eyes that lurks in yours. If he knew the truth about you, that you were his daddy, he'd most likely want to go off with you."

"So where is he?" Noah inquired as the sound of an old gospel song came wafting up through the trees on a wavering breeze. The benevolent neighbors that were gathered downstream for a good old fashioned barn raising were belting out Sunday hymns. "I didn't see him. Was he down there with the rest of them?"

"He's up in the foothills somewhere," Rose told him with a fitful glance, "and I'm not real sure when he'll be back. But I do hope you'll be gone by then." She looked around and realized that from the springhouse she wouldn't be able to see Tater coming until it was too late. "He's gone to help fetch a load of roof shakes for the new barn and I need to get back down and help with the potluck."

An old rusted railroad spike that stuck out of the mortar beneath the eaves of the springhouse caught Noah's attention. He could remember putting it there when he constructed the walls some seventeen years ago. He used to unbuckle his heavy tool belt and hang it on the spike when he took time out from his labors to sit inside where it was cool and damp – and he could sip the cold water. He had built a small wooden bench and placed it along the far wall where he used to lay back and dream in the wet darkness about going off and finding out what else there was in life besides scratching out a living from the earth.

Leaning into the darkness of the springhouse, he could see the old bench he had built to laze about on was still there – only now the legs were all but rotted off and it was jammed up against the wall with milk cans perched on it. Green velvety moss grew along where the wooden legs had settled into the damp earth. The sight of the decomposing bench was a stark reminder to him as to the amount of time that had passed. The endless days had turned into endless years. And as it turned out, all he really ever found was mostly insanity. What in the world would he find to say to his own son?

"Noah?" She interrupted his thoughts. "I do have to get back to the others. Lord knows they already have enough to gossip about."

"Yeah," he said, "I need to go take care of some things." The images of the two wagons out on the prairie rumbled across his memory. He started down the path toward Pecos, knowing that Tater could show up much sooner than Rose expected. "I haven't had much to eat since yesterday. Do you think I might get a few more plums or maybe a carrot before I leave?"

"The fruit is pretty much gone by now," she said.

Noah unhitched the reins of his horse and swung up into the saddle and rode in under the tree where he saw a couple of plums he could reach by standing up in the stirrups. Rose watched for a moment before going into the house.

When she came back out he was tucking the fruit inside his shirt. She brought a mason jar of canned plums, and a small paper bundle. "I wrapped up a couple pieces of chicken," she said, handing the food up to him. "And don't worry about returning the jar."

"Here, I have something for you, too," Noah said, pulling a wrapped package from his saddlebags as he stowed away the food. "When I seen this, it made me think of you." He held out the package, but she was hesitant to take it. "Go ahead," he insisted, "it won't bite you."

She slipped the string off and unwrapped the package to find a brightly colored chinese silk scarf. It was painted to look like the feathers of a peacock with his tail all fanned out shining for the peahen. The sun shone through the trees and fell on the scarf lighting it up like a church window. The colors were so brilliant they cast their glow upon her cheeks.

"It's for you," Noah assured her.

"I don't know if I can take this from you..." Rose's voice tailed off. She felt as though she were holding a rainbow in her hands.

"Sure you can," Noah insisted. "You once said a Chinese silk scarf would make your life better. I hope you're right, Rose, and that's how it really works."

CHAPTER TWO

Swiveling around in the saddle, Noah rode out slowly as he watched Rose making her way through the locust grove towards Mixy's. The songs from down the creek died out as did the gentle breeze. The air was dry and quiet, and the resounding silence seemed like it was that of time itself wearing away. She glanced back at him once, and he hoped he didn't look as lost as he felt inside. He could never remember feeling as alone as he did just then. He had no idea where he was going or what he was going to do. And it was almost frightening.

Pecos was given plenty of rein, but all the horse cared to do was trudge along, worn out by the hurried trip back from Idaho City. Noah had a hunch he could trust the instincts of the horse better than his own and let it pick the direction. He began eating the plums he had picked, content to maintain the pace the horse had chosen. They wandered into the head of the valley and made their way along the tree line of the foothills. The conversation he had hoped to have with Rose had somehow turned into a confrontation. He played it over in his mind again and again and thought of a dozen things he wished he'd said different and two dozen questions he wished he'd asked her. As far as he was still concerned, nothing ever got settled between them. He just couldn't understand why she had tried to hide the truth from him about having a son of his own, and why she didn't want the boy to know about him. The last thing in this world a man would ever hope to do was put his own child in harm's way. If he had any say in it at all, he would do whatever he could to make sure Tater stayed home where he belonged, and out of trouble as much as possible.

Noah thought back over the years to the miscellany of other women he'd run up against in a variety of different places and situations. Was it possible he had fathered other children, too? He quickly tried to put that idea out of his mind – after all none of the women ever went to the trouble to track him down to let him know. But then, neither did Rose. He wasn't able to really understand that either.

When he stopped daydreaming about all the 'what ifs' and 'what should have beens', he realized Pecos was all of a sudden following in the rut of an old road. Cut into the earth were the fresh tracks of a pair of heavy wagons. He studied the lay of the valley for a moment to get his bearings and determined they must have been made by the wagons Tater rode on to haul the cedar for the new barn roof.

Urging Pecos into an easy lope, he entered a scrub forest and within a quarter of a mile came to a grove of ancient cedars rimming the banks of a small marsh. Pairs of red-winged blackbirds called out from the patches of fuzzy topped cattails. The wagon tracks ended beside a freshly cut stump of a tree that was too big for one person to reach around. Reddish piles of sawdust left by the crosscut saws made an outline where the cedar had fallen. At the end of the sawdust piles lay the gray, weathered top of the century old tree with its tangle of gnarled limbs.

Draping the reins over the saddle horn, he slid down off Pecos. The horse moseyed over to the edge of the marsh for a drink while Noah trailed along digging in his saddlebags. He finally came up with a pint bottle and was disappointed to find less than an inch of whiskey left in the bottom. He pulled the cork and drank it down and pitched the empty bottle into the weeds.

Exhaustion began to seep into his bones, and he set about stripping the horse and stashing his gear on a carpet of needles beneath the boughs of a cedar that offered a natural shelter. After hobbling Pecos, he found the bundle Rose had given him, sat down on his saddle blanket and rested up against the trunk of the cedar. He unwrapped the paper to discover an assortment of necks and gizzards and backs, probably his least favorite of the parts a chicken had to offer. But hunger won out and he chewed the gizzards until his jaw ached and picked at the necks and backs until all that remained was a pile of delicate bones. He wadded them up in the paper and tossed them out into the bright sunlit day to draw away the ants and yellow jackets.

Peering out from under the branches, he settled back against the tree. The air was filled with the rich fragrance of the cedars and of the fertile soil of the marshlands. A few yards away were the brightly colored piles of sawdust on the dark ground. After studying the ladder like pattern for a moment he closed his eyes and wondered if there was any chance Tater might return for more cedar. He envisioned Tater shooting bottles at the river and knew that these were dangerous times for a young man who might think he knows all about the art of gun fighting from the dime novels. It's not like bringing down a white-tailed deer, Noah reasoned to himself – a hunted man can put up one hell of a battle. Life is hard to let go of for most.

Pulling his hat down over his eyes, he thought of the young hothead who called himself Mississippi. He figured Mississippi probably reads dime novels, too, if he can even read. His kind doesn't know any better than to go around inviting trouble into their lives, but he saw how fast death can come calling and he was startled by it. Then he began thinking about Niles Whitehead lying dead in a grave at the other end of the valley, and of how that misfit ended up in the Springwater cemetery. And Noah knew there was a strong likelihood that he was going to have to kill Burt Perry before it was all said and done. The thought of killing burdened him to sleep.

When he woke up it took him a minute to remember exactly where he was. The afternoon sun had slipped away leaving the long dark shadows of the trees across the tan grasses and cattails of the marsh. He knew he had slept longer than he should have and got right up and started gathering up his gear. As he saddled Pecos he felt the strange sense of urgency that had been pestering him a lot lately, except this time he knew where he was headed. He set out to try to make it down to the hotel at the ferry crossing by sundown and have a bite to eat and drink some whiskey, and to get a good night's sleep on a real feather mattress if possible.

Noah left the fading light of the forest behind and broke out onto the open range. He loped Pecos across the valley floor staying near the base of the foothills for as long as he could. His present course would take him close to Sowers' spread, so he rode up into the rolling hills and over the crest to pass unnoticed above the house and white washed barns. Scarlet colored wisps of clouds hung over the land and the sun was a bright crimson ball that seemed to be racing toward the horizon. He let his horse follow a game trail that wound down the backside of the hills into unfamiliar country, and he soon lost sight of the valley.

The landscape crumbled into a series of small meadows connected together by a maze of steep walled ravines. The meadows were confined on all sides by rock walls that were impassable on horseback. The game trail blended away into the meadows, but he was able to pick it up again when he rode through the narrow canyons. The bright light of the day began to dim, and he seemed to be drawn deeper into the sprawling labyrinth. Hopes of reaching the hotel by dark began to dwindle with every turn.

The horse spooked, jerking beneath him as he rode out of a steep walled canyon into a small isolated meadow. A meager flock of sheep bolted in front of them, bleating at the intrusion. Noah reined up and looked around the meadow and he let his eyes scan the rim of the rocky bluffs. There was no herder to be seen and the presence of the stray sheep seemed strangely out of place. He rode slowly toward the jittery flock for a closer look wondering all the while why they were out here on their own. Before he could reach the sheep, they scurried off into the narrow canyon he had just come from. Their cries of panic echoed off the stone walls that encompassed him. The lost flock of scraggly sheep gave Noah a bad case of the willies, and he could feel the hair on the back of his neck bristle up. He jammed his spurs into the flanks of Pecos and the horse grunted as it sped off at a gallop. The light was fading too fast and it became obvious to Noah that he would have to find his way in the dark if he was going to make it to the hotel in time for supper.

Racing through one ravine after another the country finally spread out into a wide prairie. He reined Pecos to a halt and could hear the animal panting and feel it tremble from fatigue. Ahead of him in the near distance were scrub pine and juniper studded outcroppings that reached into the meadow grasses like dark spiny fingers. He looked back to the western sky just in time to see a golden slice of sun sink below the horizon. He resigned himself to the sad fact that he wouldn't be able to make it to the warm comfort of the hotel and nudged the horse toward the stands of junipers to find a place to strike a camp.

He chose a boulder strewn point that gave him a good view of the prairie. If he was to spend the night in the open at least he could find a little shelter in the trees and build a modest fire to fight off the chill of darkness. He had just witnessed the sun forsaking the day, and already he pined for its return. It was getting to be too late in the summer to be in this part of the country. The days were growing noticeably shorter, and campfire or not, it seemed destined to be a long and lonely night. He knew he was out of whiskey at the moment, and he wasn't able to shake an anxious feeling that badgered him constantly.

He unloaded the gear from Pecos for the second time that day, and this time the horse seemed eager to give it up. He let Pecos have a good roll in the dirt before hobbling him out for the night. The horse was a pretty good watch dog and always stomped around and snorted a little when something tried sneaking up on him. Noah figured it was part of the horse's Apache training.

Walking into a tangle of junipers that had been ravaged by the seasonal winds, Noah began gathering kindling for the fire when out of the corner of his eye there was movement. Instinctively, he grabbed for his pistol and had it well out of its holster by the time he focused in on a grouse roosting in the branches of a nearby tree. He saw it was one of those big dumb grouse that will just sit there while a person unloads a gun trying to down it and only ruffle its feathers at all the racket. Noah dropped it with a single shot.

The first stars of the evening began to appear as he sat down beside a crackling juniper scented fire to roast the breast of the fat grouse on the end of a sharpened stick. He couldn't begin to count the number of meals he'd eaten off the end of a stick. Noah had lived much of his life this way, he ran himself and his poor horse ragged and always seemed to end up right back where he started, or stuck out in the middle of nowhere like he was now. Lately he felt like he was down to living a single day at a time, and right then from moment to moment – and with little joy.

By the time the grouse was cooked enough to eat, the fire had burned down to embers. The meat turned out to be tender and tasty, and somewhere in his saddlebags was a jar of plums for dessert. He dug around in the bags for the plums and came up with the doeskin bundle that held what was left of the peyote. The solitude of this night wasn't turning out to be too bad after all.

Noah ate a few of the peyote buttons, and after retching up the roast grouse began to gather wood until he had the makings of a small bonfire. Torrents of thick smoke billowed from the pile of wood while the fire began to build from the embers. A thick coil of gray smoke reached into the cobalt sky that glittered with stars. With a stick he drew a circle in the dirt and sat within it. He stared into the embers and his eyes followed the hypnotic smoke as it spiraled high above him.

The energy of the Yaqui saturated Noah's awareness as Bacanaro began to materialize. The leathery old spirit came flowing out of the smoke and danced around the fire like a whirlwind, exciting the flames. Noah pulled off his heavy boots and danced around with his mentor until he was woozy. His eyes were drawn to the column of smoke that was drifting toward the heavens like a prayer. Laying back on the ground, he smiled as he watched Bacanaro ride the smoke into the sky, where he would disappear among the stars only to reemerge from the fire to catch another ride. The Indian shaman had learned a wealth of magic since the last time Noah had seen him. Bacanaro had learned to play like a child again.

In his heart, Noah knew that the silver haired shaman no longer walked along the river – it was his spirit that lived on to guide those who sought his wisdom. The old

Indian had once told him that a man had to die before he could truly fly. Death was the only way to escape the physical world. Most men don't like to think about death; Bacanaro had thought about it constantly. While treating Noah's gunshot wound, the old Indian had kept asking him what it was like to be at death's door. Fortunately, Noah really didn't remember much after he felt the wind being knocked out of him by a bullet. But he would never forget the fever that burned like the fires of hell in his guts.

Bacanaro stopped dancing and flying and stood over Noah and looked down on him with glowing eyes that were the color of blue ice and it sent a chill through him. Then the Yaqui shaman stared into the smoke and with the cold light of his eyes projected a vision from the past that made Noah sit upright.

It was a vision of the very first time Noah had ever laid eyes on Burt Perry, and it had been indelibly etched into his memory. The big man had come riding in on his tall mule with Alice following a short distance behind him on a pony. Little One was a mere pip-squeak of a girl running along with them like a camp dog. And it didn't take long after he started working with Perry that Noah found out the stinking mongrel was nothing more than a merciless predator. He gazed back in time and realized he had come to hate Burt Perry more than any other human being that walked the good earth. It was a hatred so deep it consumed him.

The image began to fade as the heat of the fire drove away the smoke, and with a shuffling noise the bonfire caved in, sending a flurry of golden sparks skyward. Moments later the flames erupted with renewed energy. Bacanaro hovered above Noah and gazed down on him with troubled eyes and his lips moved but there was no voice. Then the old Indian pointed a long bony finger toward the fire. He looked to where Bacanaro was pointing and saw Burt Perry standing across the flames from him. Noah sprang to his feet and slid his pistol out of its holster and aimed it at the heart of the mangy brute. With his buffalo gun clutched to his chest, Perry remained motionless and he stared back at Noah with his own hatred.

A conspicuously odd object was laying on the ground at Perry's feet. At first it appeared to be a human body except Noah could nearly see through it. The torso seemed to be made of nothing more than a puff of smoke that was illuminated by the firelight. He was drawn to the strange entity and stepped around the fire for a closer look. He studied the body for a moment and got the feeling that there was something terribly wrong with what he was seeing. He thumbed back the hammer of the pistol and could hear his heart drumming in his ears.

Beyond the perimeter of light something moved and he felt the adrenaline surge through him. It was Rose coming in from the darkness. She wore a soiled and tattered wedding dress and was toting a double-barreled shotgun with her like she meant business. She went to the body and knelt down over it and looked at Noah searching his soul for an answer to it all – and he could feel her heart breaking. Noah's eyes frantically searched the fringes of the firelight for Tater, but the boy was nowhere to be found. And the wailing cries of the dead began drifting in from the prairie, their hollow sounds filling the night air.

Bacanaro floated past Noah with sorrow filled eyes... and with a shrill cry the old Yaqui was drawn into the fire and devoured by the flames. From somewhere in the deep recesses of Noah's mind the solemn voice of the silver haired shaman called out and told him, "It is the corpse of an angel." The words echoed through his head and he looked to Rose to see if she heard them, too. She hung her head and began to weep as Perry leered down at her like a rabid jackal, and a surge of terror struck Noah like a thunderbolt. He pulled the trigger.

The blast shocked the night air and the flash from the muzzle left bright spots of orange light in his eyes. In the fleeting moment it took the gunshot to reverberate across the prairie and escape into the darkness, the images before Noah were gone. Rose and Perry had vanished and the body of smoke was winging its way skyward, eventually dissipating into thin air. Noah crept back into the shadows of the rocks and sat huddled as he watched the fire burn down. The night encroached upon the dying firelight, and as it did a foreboding loneliness settled in on him.

CHAPTER THREE

As soon as the faint light of the new day began to gather, Noah unwrapped himself from his blanket. There was nothing left of the fire but a thread of smoke rising into the cold quiet morning. He was stiff from lying on the hard ground. Pecos stood nearby resting on three legs with his tired head hung down. It had turned into a long and eerie night for both of them with a prairie full of coyotes singing their seemingly endless serenade of lament. If Noah had gotten any sleep at all it wasn't much, and it certainly wasn't restful.

The peyote vision flashed back in his memory as he began to saddle his horse. He was troubled by the fact that he didn't understand what it all meant. When he slung the saddlebags over the animal's rump he thought about throwing away the last of the Peyote. Maybe he had just eaten one too many, or perhaps it was too old. The vision he sought had turned into an unpleasant journey. But one thing was clearer to him now than before; if he was ever going to be able to leave the Springwater Valley, he was going to have to kill Burt Perry first. His gut feeling told him there was no other way. So that's what he set out to do.

He rode down out of the junipers and across the prairie and watched as a lone coyote ambled away from him to vanish into the maze of canyons. He reined Pecos south toward the Snake and before long the river canyon came into view. Noah stayed atop the bluffs overlooking the river long enough to watch the sunrise. For a few minutes the river seemed to flow right out of the sun to become a winding strand of gold that stretched across the eastern plain. He welcomed the sun that day and tried to detect the slightest degree of warmth on his cheeks as the great sphere of golden fire broke free from the horizon. He found such beauty and solace in the sight that for the time being it erased the thoughts of killing from his mind.

He continued on and before long came across the old wagon trail that ran along the river. Noah headed downstream toward the ferry crossing. The road passed nearby the rear of the Rocky Bar Hotel and he arrived just in time to find Schwarting, the hotel cook, coming out of the basement root cellar. The large man stopped at the kitchen door and shook a cloud of flour dust out of his apron as he watched Noah ride past.

Noah reined up at the edge of the building where he was able to see the ferry crossing. The empty barge was tied up at the river's edge, but there was no sign of the ferryman or the team of oxen.

"Good morning," Noah called out when he noticed Schwarting was still watching him. "What time does the ferry start up?"

"It'll be a little while yet," Schwarting said. "It's still pretty early in the day. There's another man waiting in the dining room who wants to cross, too."

There was only one horse standing at the hitching rails in front of the hotel and it wasn't Dunlavy's lanky mare. Dunlavy was about the only person Noah could think of at the moment that he would like to run into. He needed information about the goings on at Sowers' ranch, and he knew he could count on Lester Dunlavy, meddler, to have it.

"You wouldn't happen to know a man named Dunlavy that might get a meal here from time to time, would you?" Noah asked, then added, "He's a pretty good eater."

"Rides a worn out bay, and always eats with his hat on," the cook offered.

"That's him." Noah rode over to talk with the cook. "When would be the best time to find him here?"

"That's hard to say. He has sort of peculiar eating habits," Schwarting told him. "He's been coming around fairly regular the last couple of weeks, though. Let's see," he continued, massaging his jowls for a moment as he thought, "he was showing up here in the middle of the day, but he has been coming in right around supper time recently. And he missed yesterday so I'd almost bet on seeing him today. Hardly ever misses two days in a row, anymore. I've never known him to eat breakfast here, though."

Schwarting was full of information and gave it out fast and free – and it crossed Noah's mind that Dunlavy and Schwarting would get along pretty well if they ever really got to talking. The cook could keep Dunlavy posted on the events around the hotel and ferry crossing, and Dunlavy could fill Schwarting in on what was going on in the rest of the whole world.

Before the conversation with Schwarting was concluded, Noah learned that the cook suspected the reason Dunlavy was such a good customer was that the hotel dining room always tried to feed a hungry traveler second helpings when it could. And by looking at Schwarting, Noah was sure the rotund cook believed in putting on the feed bag.

And he also found out that, after a couple of failed attempts, a young man working for a freight company had finally arrived and swam down to the bottom of the river with a hook on the end of a rope to recover the rolls of barbed wire and the wagon that had been lost in the ferry mishap. Noah still blamed that one on Perry.

Schwarting also suspected that 'Old Man Winter was just around the corner,' because the travelers had been telling him that they had seen areas where the trees and shrubs had been 'brushed with the yellows and reds of Jack Frost.' But best of all, for two-bits Noah was able to buy a cold pork chop and a couple of warm biscuits out the back door of the hotel without having to get down from his horse.

He rode down to the river and sat in the sun on a rock to eat his lavish breakfast while he waited for the ferryman to show up. The morning sun began to heat up the day as it climbed into the sky, and it was hard for him to believe that winter could be anywhere around.

It wasn't long until the ferryman came strolling down the road, and after he checked the dragline informed Noah they didn't have to wait for the team of oxen to cross the river. Noah walked Pecos onto the barge and the ferryman set them adrift across the Snake. They had barely left the shore when the man who had been waiting at the hotel came riding down to the crossing too late to make the trip. He seemed to be in a hurry and appeared upset that the ferry had left without him. The ferryman pointed up the road where his helper was coming with the team of oxen. The sight had a calming effect on the stranded traveler. It was a silent trip across the smooth surface of the water, taking only a few minutes for the slow tug of the river's current to carry them to the opposite shore.

When he was on dry land again, Noah swung up in the saddle and nudged Pecos into a steady trot upriver. The road headed out across the scrub plain away from the river canyons and he was soon out of sight of the ferry. He reined his horse off the road and picked his way along the river the best he could, always trying to keep the opposite shore in sight. He recognized the blind canyon where Tater had set up his shooting gallery of stove lids. The place was quiet and forlorn and he continued on his way. It was Burt Perry's campsite he was hoping to find.

After another mile or so, he spotted a puff of light gray smoke drifting out across the water. Noah knew at once it was more than likely from the rekindling of a morning campfire. He picketed Pecos and continued on foot lugging his saddle bags and Winchester along. Keeping his head down as best he could, he slowly and cautiously made his way through the brush before settling in amongst a clump of river willow directly across the river from the sheltered coulee where Perry had made his camp. High waters had laced the willow thicket with dried grasses and bulrushes and small branches creating a natural blind. It provided him good cover from view, but it wouldn't come close to stopping a slug from a buffalo gun.

Perry's campsite was still in the morning shade and the piles of driftwood and heavy brush with sparse open areas made the coulee a good hideout. Noah's eyes carefully explored for any movement other than the occasional puff of smoke that lifted out of the bushes and evaporated before it reached the top of the steep rock walls. There was none, not even hide nor hair of the big mule or the other ponies.

Noah had gotten up and moving so early that it felt to him like it must be at least noon, but he knew that wasn't the case. Maybe they just weren't up and about yet, he thought to himself. He took a small brass telescope from his saddlebags, extended it out and put it to his eye just in time to spot Alice coming out of the bushes. His view was good enough that he could see she had a Mexican saddle blanket draped around her shoulders like it was a shawl – and that she had a couple pieces of squaw bread in her hand. She crossed a small opening and handed the flat rounds of bread to Perry who was sitting with his back up against the smooth trunk of a tree left by the spring floods. He was wrapped in an elk hide robe and his hair and beard were all wild and unruly, and he kind of just blended in with the native habitat.

During the next hour Alice had made another trip across the clearing to feed Perry more fried bread, but other than that there was very little movement in the camp. Noah saw it as an opportunity to eat some of the canned plums Rose had given him, and as he sipped the juice he thought about her and knew she was only one of the reasons he was sitting on the bank of the Snake River just then trying to find out what Burt Perry was up to.

When Noah heard someone call out he put the lid back on the plums and resumed spying through the telescope. It was Perry who was hollering, and this time Alice came out into the clearing and they started yelling back and forth at each other. Noah couldn't make out what they were arguing about, but it was over quick and Perry got in the last word. Alice retreated back into the bushes.

Perry stretched his arms above his head like he was finally awake and wrestled himself up to where he was sitting on the weathered out tree. He leaned back and reached down behind the log and came up with a jug of liquor. He left the jug sitting in plain sight and wandered barefoot out into the sunshine at the river's edge. He stood there a moment and looked up and down the river to make sure he was all alone. Noah automatically hunkered down as he tried to keep the spyglass focused on Perry, who seemed to fill the entire lens. Cloaked in the elk hide and all grizzled, Perry resembled some sort of odd savage beast as much as he did a human.

Perry's gaze seemed to be fixed right on the willow thicket and through the telescope it felt to Noah like he was staring right into Perry's eyes, and Perry right back into his. Noah didn't flinch a muscle, confident that he was well hidden. A moment later, Perry bowed his head and threw open the robe. Noah was surprised to find himself watching Perry, who stood at the edge of the water in the morning sun, ghost-white naked and with a piss hard-on. It was by far the most intimate view of Burt Perry that Noah had ever witnessed, and he found himself grinning over it. As it turned out, it wasn't as impressive a display as one might imagine of such a large man, and he knew someday if the time was ever right he would have to tell Dunlavy all about it.

After pissing in the river, Perry walked back up to the clearing and threw off the elk hide and spread it out on the ground like a blanket. He sat down on the hide and laid back on his elbows.

"Now goddamn it," Perry bellowed out so loud the words crossed the river as clear as a bell.

Alice came out of the bushes and strode past Perry and sat down on the log next to the jug. A second later Little One appeared and walked over to Perry and slipped out of her dress before sitting down beside him. She played with him for a minute until he was hard again and then swung a leg over and straddled him like she was hopping on a pony and wiggled down on him.

The sight incensed Noah. He dropped the telescope and grabbed his Winchester and tried to draw a bead on Perry, but from that distance there was no kind of a shot. He told himself that he should have killed the mangy bastard when he was pissing in the river and he could have been on his way to Bakersfield right that minute. He laid down the rifle and raised the telescope to his eye again. Little One was still bouncing up and down on Perry while less than ten feet away, Alice just sat on the log swilling firewater and watching the whole thing as if it were an everyday occurrence – and Noah felt certain it must be. It was all over in a few minutes. Little One got up and grabbed her dress and headed for the river. Then Perry got up, stretched his arms out like he had just polished off Thanksgiving dinner, wrapped himself in the elk hide and went over and stood before Alice. The Indian woman handed over the jug and sulked off into the bushes as Perry sat down where he was earlier with his back up against the log.

When Little One reached the river, she hurried upstream until she was out of sight of the camp and hung her buckskin dress on a tree limb and waded out into the water for a swim. When she came out of the water she wandered naked along the river for awhile. The sun was bright and warm in the sky and there was a gentle breeze. The surface of the river was smooth and Noah couldn't help but watch her as she hunted for flat stones to skip across the water. Little One may have looked like a woman, but she still played like a child. Even though she was an Indian, and a pretty one at that, she was still just a little girl too young to be subjected to Perry's vile ways. Noah wondered how he would handle things if he had the opportunity with her again, if he would take advantage of the situation. It was a tempting sight, but there were some things and times that came along in life where a line had to be drawn. And he knew he would have to make an effort not to cross it. The mental dilemma caused him to put the spyglass away and stop snooping on Little One.

As the Indian girl wandered farther upstream away from the camp, Noah gathered up his things and crawled away from the willow thicket. Once he knew he was out of sight of Perry's camp he wasted no time in getting to Pecos and back across the ferry to the Rocky Bar Hotel. The dismal sense of urgency had returned and was after him like a swarm of hornets. He was bursting to talk to someone and hoped in vain that this was one of those days when Dunlavy was out before noon – and hungry.

When Noah didn't see any familiar horses hitched out in front of the hotel, he put the spurs to his tall gray thoroughbred. He rode up and away from the Snake, past the rocky outcrop where he had built the bonfire and back through the maze of narrow canyons. He circled above Sowers' ranch and crossed the head of the valley where he climbed into the foothills again to avoid being seen. And when the sun went down again, he was sitting on the crest of the hills that overlooked Rose's place.

Noah had to ask himself if he knew exactly what it was he was doing. It seemed that lately he had been running around in circles a lot, and the circle kept getting smaller, and ending up at Rose's. Maybe he was getting sick. His mouth was dry, his pulse was pounding in his ears, and his mind was spinning from one thought to another. And he wondered where the day had gone. Maybe the peyote buttons had somehow poisoned him for good. The only real thing he knew at that moment was he would do whatever it took to protect Rose and do whatever he could to keep Tater from getting himself into the kind of trouble he couldn't handle.

CHAPTER FOUR

As dusk fell and the landscape faded into nothing more than shadows, he came down out of the hills and crossed the road downstream from Mixy's. He made his way back up along the creek until he came to a large plum thicket that was so dense it seemed to trap whatever light was left. Leaving the horse to graze, Noah skirted around the thicket until Mixy's farm was in sight. The fresh sawn siding on Mixy's barn stood out across a small meadow. Noah hurried toward the bright new structure and as he reached the barnyard he ran into the geese, causing them to trumpet their warning.

Noah ducked into the darkness of the barn as the yellow glow of the oil lamp in Mixy's little cabin was quickly extinguished. The cabin door was open and he knew Mixy must be standing back in the darkness with a gun. It hadn't crossed his mind much before now to involve Mixy in all this, but he knew if he was to show up at Rose's front door again so soon he would only make things worse for her than they already were. There was nowhere else he could think of to go at that particular time, and he just had to talk to someone.

"Mixy," Noah called out just loud enough to be heard, "don't start shooting now."

"Who's out there?" The anxious voice came from inside the cabin.

"Mixy, it's Noah Conklin," he announced, and emerged from the barn where he could be seen. "I'd like to talk to you if it's alright."

"Why, Master Noah," Mixy came straight out the door, "I been hopin' you'd stop by sometime." He was unarmed.

"Well, it might be better if I didn't," Noah stated, shaking Mixy's hand. Even in the faint light of the evening Noah could see that the old negro was smiling. "I hope I didn't give you much of a start."

"I did have a little bit of trouble lately," Mixy acknowledged.

"That's what I understand" Noah said, turning to look at the new barn. "You can still smell the fire, can't you? Even over that green cut lumber. Mixy, you do own a gun, don't you?"

"All I got is a little twenty-two caliber rifle," Mixy explained, "I only use it to kill a pig now and again, and the prairie wolfs when they come too close. Master Noah, I'm plain scared that I won't be much help around here. I don't imagine I'm gonna be able to put up much of a struggle anymore."

"So, how'd your barn burn down?" Noah asked. Eddie Button had said something about somebody's barn burning down when he ran into him at Idaho City. "Wasn't lightning, was it?"

"The boy said it was that Burt Perry that set it," Mixy replied.

"What do you know about Burt Perry?" Noah was troubled by the mention of his name.

"Only what I hear from the boy," Mixy explained. "When I told him what the man looked like that burnt my barn down, he said it was that same man you had a fight with. And Jules, another man I know that takes care of Master Sowers, he told me about Burt Perry, too. He said he was no good. And that's all I knows."

"And you know for a fact that Burt Perry was the one who started your barn on fire?" Noah quizzed. Not that he didn't think Perry would do such a thing, he just wondered why Mixy seemed so sure it was him.

"I know what I seen. He was ridin' around out in that field," Mixy recalled, pointing off into the darkness, "a big man on a mule with a buffalo gun. He was all lit up by the fire and he was just watchin' it burn."

"Does Frank Canfield know what happened up here?" he asked. It disturbed him to think that Perry had come this close to Rose, and Tater.

"He most likely does," Mixy reasoned. "Can't hardly keep this kind of a secret. I guess you could see the fire half way down the valley. A few folks rode up here to look at it. But I didn't make no complaint."

"You could file one if you wanted to," Noah advised him. "It might get him to send for the marshal."

"Master Noah, I guess I still got too much of the past in me," Mixy explained, "I was taught that Negroes don't go to stirrin' up no trouble with the master. I been thinkin' tho, it might not be such a bad thing that this happened, 'cause it made the people that live around here in the valley get together so they could talk things over. They was talkin' about all sorts of things while they was sawin' and hammerin' away on my barn."

"Mixy," Noah was puzzled, "why do you think it is that someone wants to cause you any trouble? What have you done to make anyone want to burn you out of here?"

"That is what I've been havin' to ask myself," Mixy shook his head as he looked around. "It can't be for what I got, 'cept for maybe 'cause I keep a few sheep out back there, and I knows Master Sowers don't like sheep. I don't hold the title to no property. I'm just squattin' on a couple acres here where Mizz Rose said it was okay for me to do. Other than that I got a two room house and I'm gonna have a better barn than before." He stopped to ponder a moment, and added, "I figure in the end it must be 'cause of Mizz Rose."

"Why's that?" Noah asked.

"It's 'cause of the way Master Sowers comes sniffin' around Mizz Rose like some old hound dog that's sufferin' from confusion," Mixy stated. "It's kind of hard for me to explain, but I figure it must be 'cause she depends on me helpin' out some when need be. He must think if she didn't have no help up here, it might be too much for her all alone. But I swear, anymore the boy can do most anything needs to be done around here. Master Sowers told her that she should move up to his big house to live with him."

Rose had failed to mention to Noah that Sowers was courting her, but she did seem to know him fairly good. He felt like he had just been given another missing piece to a puzzle, but he had no idea where it fit. "So, how does Rose feel about that?" he quizzed Mixy.

"About Master Sowers?" Mixy chortled. "Shoot, Mizz Rose ain't got no use for that man, it's all she can do to keep a civil tongue in her head when he comes around to call on her. And Tater don't like him even worse. Why if you was to ask me, Master Noah, I'd have to say that Mizz Rose don't got no room in her heart for another man."

The subtle shadows of the evening were quickly disappearing into the darkness of night and Noah reminded himself he still had a horse wearing a saddle, waiting for him down along the creek. "Mixy, what do you think about me staying around here tonight?" he asked.

It took Mixy a moment to respond, then he said, "I would like that just fine."

"If you think it'd be better if I didn't, I'd understand," Noah added. "The last thing I want to do is cause trouble for Rose, or you."

"Master Noah," Mixy suggested, "it would probably be better all around if Mizz Rose didn't know you seen me or talked to me for awhile."

"I think you're probably right," Noah agreed. "And I have a horse that needs to hide out, too."

This time Mixy led the way through the plum thicket when it was almost too dark to see. They took Pecos on down the creek a short ways. Noah stripped the weary gelding and left him picketed in a grassy glade where Mixy assured him that the horse would be alright until morning. Then Noah followed the spry old colored man back through the night with the promise of a soft bed of grass hay in the corner of the barn.

Once back inside the barn, Mixy lit a lantern, keeping the wick low. He turned over a bucket to squat down on and seemed to be in no hurry to go back to his cabin. Noah leaned his Winchester up against the wall and spread out his bed roll in the pile of sweet smelling dried grass. When he was all settled in Mixy put out the light.

"Mixy, this is the best bed I've had in nearly a week," Noah declared, pulling off his boots. Only a small portion of the roof had cedar shakes nailed on and when Noah laid back he could see the night sky through the slats. "It's nice to have a roof over my head, even if I can see the stars through it."

"What's your plan, Master Noah?" Mixy asked softly. His voice seemed to just drift out of the darkness. "That is if you don't mind my askin'."

"I'm not sure I have one," Noah admitted. "What do you mean, a plan about what?"

"Well, I 'sposed you must have come back around here for a reason," Mixy said.

"There was. I heard about a well-heeled rancher having some kind of trouble and that he was hiring men," Noah told him. "I was looking for a job, but I didn't know for sure it was right here in this valley. I knew it had to be close, though. I swear ending up right back here and finding out all I have in the past few days has sort of taken me by storm."

"Did you find out what kind of trouble the rancher is havin'?" Mixy asked. Noah's eyes had adapted to the darkness well enough that he could see the old Negro was half grinning – like he knew exactly who and what Noah was talking about, but was pretending otherwise.

"Yeah, I did," Noah went along for a moment," his main problem is that he doesn't know when he's well off."

"They's a lot of men that have that same problem," Mixy interjected. "They'll never find no peace in this here life."

"You're right," Noah agreed, "I've met a few of them myself, you can be sure of that."

"That pile of hay you're layin' on was hauled in here by Lewis Morrey," Mixy said. "He has a little farm close to Master Sowers. Do you happen to know him?"

"I can't think of who you're talking about" he answered. Although Noah couldn't recall ever hearing the name, Morrey could have been one of the locals who hung around Eddie Button's saloon and eatery.

"Master Lewis is a decent man," Mixy continued, "and he's gettin' ready to move on to someplace called the Palouse. He's one of them kind that is always there with a lendin' hand when someone needs it. He's hopin' to wait till the springtime before he goes, but with the things that's been goin' on about, he's not sure what he's gonna do now. He said that Master Sowers made him a fair offer for his land and that he wants to go."

"Mixy, there's a real good chance that Jared Sowers will crowd some of the farmers out of this valley," Noah said. "I'm sure he's probably rich enough that he can afford to hire all the pea-brained idiots he cares to. And if he doesn't make too many mistakes there won't be much that can be done about it. But I think he's already made a mistake and only time will tell."

"Master Lewis told me that Master Sowers said to him that he wants to own as much of the valley as he can see from his front porch," Mixy appeared to be confused from thinking about it. "That is one reason I think it must have been over Master Sowers and Mizz Rose, I'm talkin' about burnin' down my barn, 'cause Master Sowers cain't see clear up to here. Master Noah, if it didn't turn out to be this here particular valley, would you have taken that job? I mean, if it wasn't for Mizz Rose bein' a part of it and all?"

"I wouldn't have taken it, anyway," Noah assured him. "I would have just rode off and left it to someone else."

"Who?" Mixy queried.

There was a moment of silence that was broken by the call of a barn owl sitting on a nearby branch – it seemed to be posing the same question. Who? Who indeed if not for him? It was the likes of Niles Whitehead or Wally Pomeroy or Burt Perry that took these kind of jobs. Men that Noah considered to not have good sense. He felt as though the effects of the peyote were still tormenting him. And he felt like he wanted a cigarette.

"Mixy do you have anything to smoke?" Noah began poking around in his saddle bags. "I think I can find some rolling papers."

Mixy had to go to his cabin for the tobacco and when he returned he handed Noah a soft leather pouch, saying, "That's a pretty good mixture." Noah had met men over the years who preferred to smoke tree bark, so he put the bag to his nose. It didn't have that unique aroma of good cut leaf tobacco, but smelled a bit strong, more like the native grown variety. "It all grows wild about," Mixy assured him, "it's pleasant tastin', you'll see."

Noah rolled a cigarette and Mixy struck a match and lit it for him, then put the flame to a brier pipe of his own. As the pungent leaves smoldered, a faint glow was cast on their faces. The smoking mixture turned out to be what Noah usually referred to as Indian tobacco, and they sat in silence blowing puffs of smoke into the darkness.

"I'm thinking of killing someone, Mixy," Noah said, the words just seemed to spill out of him.

"You mean besides the man at Eddie Button's?" Mixy asked.

"Christ almighty..." Noah let out a deep smoke-filled sigh. He tried to imagine what the ordinary person saw when they looked his way. He wasn't ashamed of the way he wore his gun, or proud of it either. Most of the time he was oblivious of the trouble it brought to him because he had always been able to deal with it. The faces of the dead flashed in his mind like gunshots in the dark. And the ashen corpse of Whitehead laying in the back of the undertakers wagon lingered fresh in his memory. "How I must seem to people around here," he muttered.

"Most around here says that you was left without no choice in the matter," Mixy said. "Someone told me they heard it was a miracle you is still here. That he was ready to shoot you in the back."

"What I'm thinking about is different," Noah stated. "Niles Whitehead and me were drinking whiskey at Eddie Button's and I was badgered into that fight, but this feels different. I feel like I'm having to plan this one and I'm not real sure how its gonna turn out. I have my reasons for wanting to do it, though. Damn good reasons, too."

"Well now, I guess you must be speakin' of Burt Perry." Mixy said. "Master Noah, I wouldn't want you to go to no trouble for me. This is gonna be a real good barn."

"I'm not thinking of shooting him for burning down your barn," Noah was amused by the thought and tossed his cigarette butt down by Mixy's feet. Mixy snuffed it out in the dirt. "He's become feebleminded. I mean it. I believe he's the only one that Mister Sowers has that is feebleminded enough to do something where somebody around here will end up hurt, or worse. Of course Jared Sowers will make sure he stays apart from it all. He will be in a room full of witnesses and swear he didn't know what was taking place. But with Perry out of the game, I don't think this would work for him anyway. Too many problems."

"You really think killin' this man will solve the problem?" Mixy asked.

"The worst part of it anyway." Noah surmised. He felt tired from riding all over the country and the Indian tobacco was making his thoughts heavy and he laid back in his bedroll. "I'll try to tell you the whole story of Perry sometime." He had wanted to try to talk about Tater and see what light Mixy could shed on that subject, but the smoke made him sleepy. It would have to wait until morning.

CHAPTER FIVE

The geese raised a ruckus as they hurried beside the barn to gather around Mixy as he came out of his cabin to greet the new day. Noah watched from his nest of hay as Mixy poured a line of grain along the ground from a can for the geese to squabble over. As Mixy started toward the barn, Noah sat up in his bedroll.

"It's early yet. Did they wake you up?" Mixy asked as he came in.

"That's alright," Noah assured him, "I need to get up and get out of your way here pretty quick, anyway."

"Now, take your time," Mixy stated, "and I'll be right back. I fixed a little bite to eat."

Noah pulled his boots on and worked at getting his bedroll together. A few minutes later Mixy returned with a pot of hot coffee and a skillet of fresh baked johnny cake that had a big lump of butter melting over it. Cups dangled from both his little fingers. The aroma made Noah realize how hungry he was and he stopped what he was doing to eat. The coffee turned out to be strong and the cornbread was sweet – just the way he liked – and he expressed his gratitude to Mixy in grunts of approval as he ate.

"Mixy, what can you tell me about Tater?" Noah helped himself to more coffee. "I'd really like to find out the truth."

"Yes sir," Mixy said, and walked over to look out the barn in the direction of Rose's. "You knew your pappy. I can still remember you talkin' 'bout him. You said he was a honest hardworkin' man, and you grew up livin' under his roof."

"Back in Missouri," Noah agreed.

"Can you ever remember me talkin' 'bout my pappy?" Mixy asked.

"I'm not sure," Noah said. "That was a long time ago."

"I never had the chance to know my pappy," the old man sighed, and his eyes seemed to wander back in time. "He got sold off to another plantation when I was still just a little child. I got sold off myself when I was a mite older and that's the last I ever seen of my real mama, too. I know I must have some brothers and sisters scattered about that is still alive, but I don't know where. We got all broke up. That was the worst part if you was a slave. Slave families didn't matter none to the masters."

Noah thought of his own father who had been dead for several years now. There were things between them that should have been resolved, but never were, and never could be now. His father never understood how he could abandon Rose the way he did, and never forgave him for doing so. Noah knew his own father had given up on him.

"The only thing I can really remember about my pappy is that I was cryin'," Mixy added. He walked back over and stared down at Noah. The old man had looked so far back in time that it made his eyes watery.

"I can still remember seein' my pappy cryin' and it made me cry, too. I don't remember what he looked like, but I can still see his tears runnin' down his cheeks. I would have liked to been able to known him."

"It seems to me, Mixy," Noah remarked, "that as long as I can remember, the world has always been somewhat out of kilter. Lots of things that ain't right. What I'd like to know for sure is if he's my son or not. If he is, I want the chance to get to know him. Can't talk to Rose about it."

"Most of the time, me and Mizz Rose sees eye to eye on most everythin' there is," Mixy stated, "but not about that boy. And if it means I have to pick up and move out of this place here, that's how strong I feel about the need for him to know what the truth is. The way I see it, there isn't nothin' that's more important than knowin' your own blood kin. You is that boy's pappy, Master Noah, and lightnin' can strike me down if I'm wrong."

"You're certain about this?" Noah picked up his gun belt and wandered over to look up toward Rose's place.

"I'm as sure as the sun came up this mornin'," Mixy tagged along. "And it would most likely be better for me if you didn't have to let her find out that I was the one that told you."

"I won't say anything," Noah vowed as he strapped on his gun. "I already figured it out on my own anyhow. I sure don't understand her way of thinking. I don't know what she expects me to do, knowing what I do now. I can't just ride off like it don't matter to me. I'm not really sure what I'm supposed to do." He looked back at Mixy and shook his head over his dilemma. "What the hell would any man do in this case?"

"If you wanted to you could leave your bedroll here," Mixy suggested. "Hide it in the hay and nobody will see it."

"Stay around here?" Noah wondered aloud as he considered the offer. "How would that work?" He couldn't imagine how Rose would react to his being so close. He wanted to try to iron things out with her, not upset her more. "I'm not sure that's a good idea."

Mixy gave Noah a mischievous glance, and lowered his voice to say, "We'd be fine long as Mizz Rose don't find out about it."

"Are you sure?" Noah was starting to warm to the idea. Having to lay low for awhile would provide him with a chance to catch up on some rest. A little rest might do him a world of good. It would give him a chance to sort things out. "I guess, if I was careful to stay out of sight."

"I'm goin' to be here all day splittin' shakes for the barn roof," Mixy informed him. "Sometime this mornin' Tater will be goin' to do his deliveries with the milk and eggs. I could hear him up there yellin' at the cows so I knows he's started on his milkin'. I'd watch over things 'round here if you want to go keep an eye on him."

While Mixy set about the morning chore of chasing his donkey and sheep out into the pasture, Noah used the time to change his shirt and shave. He peered into a large piece of broken mirror that hung on the side of the cabin and scraped the whiskers off his face with a razor, and he was suddenly fascinated by his luck. It was as if something had been leading him here the whole time. Staying at Mixy's was a perfect way to be able to make sure Jared Sowers left Rose out of his endeavors, and at the same time he could keep an eye on the boy and not have to get involved unless it involved him. It seemed like an ideal situation. This was working out better than he ever could have imagined.

The wind coming off the wings of a large bird sounded like a dog panting in the sky above him. Noah caught the dark entity out of the corner of his eye and he watched it sail over him and land on the branch of a locust tree that stood behind Mixy's cabin. It was an opalescent-black raven and it made him think of Bacanaro. The medicine man always had something to say about the crows and the ravens when they came around. He once told Noah that they were connected to the spirit world, and they carried the messages of the ancestors. His mind wandered back to the peyote vision when Bacanaro flew off with the gray smoke and vanished into the starlit night. The raven called out to him and took off again to ride the silent currents of the morning air. Noah's eyes followed the bird until it was only a black speck amongst the white wisps of clouds drifting across the pale sky.

When he lost sight of the raven, he noticed Mixy standing off a few yards looking at him. Noah could tell there was something bothering him by the furrow that cut across the old man's brow. If Mixy was worried about having him for a barn guest, he certainly understood that. Noah knew that his presence alone could bring more turmoil to this end of the valley. That was the biggest drawback to staying at Mixy's, and perhaps the former slave was becoming more aware of the real danger prowling about. Perhaps he could read it in Noah's eyes.

"You're not having second thoughts about me staying around here, are you?" Noah asked after washing the shaving soap off his face. "I'd understand if you are."

"No, Master Noah, that's not it at all," Mixy assured him.

"What is it then?" Noah asked.

"Well... It must not of been important," Mixy declared, "I forgot what it was I was goin' to tell you. I've been doin' that a lot lately." He shook his head and walked off.

Noah returned to the barn and prepared himself for the day. He would travel light, leaving everything behind but his gun belt and saddlebags. He left his Winchester leaning up against the wall along with a partial box of shells and buried the rest of his gear in the haystack. The only thing he planned on doing before coming straight back to lay low in Mixy's barn was trailing Tater for awhile to make sure that trouble left him alone.

"Master Noah," Mixy called out as he came through the back door of the barn, "you'd best stay out of sight for a little bit. I can hear the boy's wagon comin' along the road." The old man strode past him to peer out the front door toward the road that ran past his place. "And he's a mite early this mornin'. What's he up to?"

Noah moved into a dimly lit corner nearest to where Mixy was, and after a couple minutes he heard the wagon pass by. "Do you have any idea where he's headed? I mean right this minute."

"Into town," Mixy replied, walking outside. "He always goes to the mercantile first and then he might stop at the boardin' house if there's any extra milk or butter. You can come on, he's gone." When Noah emerged from the barn, Mixy continued, "Then he usually ends up at the hotel. Ever since Eddie Button left the area he's been gettin' back here earlier in the day. The only thing we have to worry about now is Mizz Rose showin' up here. She will mosey on down here sometimes after she has her tea," Mixy gave Noah a sheepish glance. "She checks up on me."

"I'm leaving my Winchester here for you with some extra cartridges," Noah told him. "You keep it where you think it will be the most handy. And don't forget, I'm going to come sneaking back here later. So please don't go shooting me with my own gun."

Looking at the rifle, the burden of concern returned to the old man. "No sir, I won't," Mixy swore somberly.

"Oh, quit worrying about things," Noah assured him, mustering up a crook of a smile. "We're only outnumbered here a half dozen to one. And we all know what you have to do when the odds are that poor."

"Retreat?" Mixy questioned.

"It might look like retreating to some tinhorn," Noah said, "but I like to look at it as giving them all something else to cope with. Me and you both know that there are times when everyday life itself is about all a person can manage. Now I gotta get out of here and try to dog that boy for awhile."

"Master Noah," Mixy spoke up as he followed Noah across the barnyard, "just because a man don't know exactly what it is he's lookin' for don't mean he can't find it anyway. Don't you believe that's true?"

Stopping to look back, Noah pondered for a moment and told him, "I guess that could be right." His answer seemed to satisfy the old black man so he took off down along the creek to catch Pecos.

CHAPTER SIX

The morning dew was heavy on the grass, and by the time Noah sat in the saddle the cuffs of his pants were soaking wet. When he reached the road he let his feet dangle out of the stirrups to dry his boots quicker. The horse acted like it was in the mood to cover the miles and Noah had to hold back some on the reins in fear of catching up to the wagon before he wanted.

The wagon wheels were rimmed with iron and it made an easy track to follow, embossing a pair of endless ribbons into the damp earth. As his eyes were drawn along, his mind explored the possibility of taking a shortcut across the valley and riding on ahead to the hotel where he could wait for Tater to show up. In the mean time there was always a chance he might run into Dunlavy. He felt that he should at least try to find out what Jared Sowers was up to these days. Sowers had men on the payroll that were capable of doing a lot more than burning down an old man's barn – and of trying to pester a neighbor out of his land. It seemed awfully quiet around the valley and even Perry appeared quite content just to laze around his camp.

He began to dwell on Perry. It was about this time yesterday that he was spying on Perry's river camp and he wondered if one of Little One's daily chores had become straddling that mangy son-of-a-bitch. Under his breath, he cursed Perry for humping with the Indian girl. That part of all this really didn't involve him anyway. Besides that, as far as he knew, there was no law against it. But he felt certain if and when things in the valley all blew up, it would be that crazy bastard who lit the fuse. Thoughts of fighting and killing didn't seem possible on a day that was starting out so pleasant and peaceful. If it hadn't been for Burt Perry, Noah would have been satisfied with just laying back at Mixy's. Unfortunately, that wouldn't make the problem go away for some of Rose's neighbors. Here he was again, looking for ways to redeem himself with her.

If he did end up doing everyone around these parts and the rest of the world the service of killing Burt Perry, he was sure it would just make her look down her nose on him even more – the way she looked at things. The surefire way in his mind right now to get her on his good side was to make certain that nothing happened to the boy.

There was a gnawing in the pit of his stomach, and it wasn't from hunger. Here he was within minutes of his own son. What was it that made it so hard just then for him to face the boy? For some reason he kept telling himself the best thing to do was stay back when he knew that the surest way of protecting Tater from harm was to keep him at his side. If there was one thing Noah had learned over the years, it was that in the blink of an eye or the beat of a heart things can happen that change a person's life forever, and he had almost found an excuse to ride off ahead. He contemplated catching up to the wagon.

With a call from above, the raven returned to invade his daydreams and he watched it come out of the sky and drift silently overhead to land in the nearby treetops. The pitch-black bird had drawn Noah's attention to a small clearing where the creek had meandered away from the road for awhile. When he looked ahead again, he realized the wagon tracks had vanished into thin air. But it was the image in his mind's eye that made his body jerk with surprise. He reined Pecos to such an abrupt halt that he was almost tossed out of the saddle. His boots were still dangling out of the stirrups and he had to grab onto the horn to keep from hitting the ground. His head snapped back around to the tree line where the raven sat mocking him as if it knew that Noah had been caught cold.

At the edge of the clearing, Tater sat atop his wagon and with a wave of his hand he picked up the reins and put the leather to the roan mare and started toward him. The voice in Noah's head told him that he was staring at his own flesh and blood, that the young man who drove his wagon back onto the road was his own son. If any profound change came over him, other than his heart was pounding away in his chest, right then he couldn't tell.

But he now realized what he was afraid of, and his mind was conjuring up a story like a storm while the distance between him and his son was withering away. He was afraid the boy would ask him questions that were too hard to answer, such as:

"Where did you come from?" Tater asked. He looked suspiciously at Noah's wet pant cuffs then back up the road toward home.

Sticking his feet in the stirrups, it took Noah a long moment to respond. "Back yonder a ways," he said, and before Tater had the chance to ask anything else, he asked, "Where are you going with those milk cans?"

"I'm doing my errands," Tater said. "I have to go to town and then on to the hotel. I kind of have a lot on my schedule today."

"Well shoot, I might just ride along with you for awhile," Noah offered. "You go on and I'll tail you."

"I guess you know that Eddie Button closed down the saloon for awhile," Tater remarked as he pulled out.

Noah stayed back far enough to avoid getting caught up in a conversation right away. Tater glanced back at him a couple times and then had to pay attention to driving the wagon because he was going about as fast as he could without spilling his load. The pace suited Pecos so Noah just went along for the ride.

He watched Tater as he drove along and Noah wasn't quite sure that he liked what he saw. The boy's demeanor had changed. Somehow he remembered Tater as being more or less a freckle faced farm boy. But, now he wasn't wearing his usual bibbed overalls. Instead he was wearing canvas work pants and a chambray shirt with a leather belt. Noah was disturbed by the change of clothes, for it made Tater look much older than he remembered. The youngster had lost that callowness – that divine innocence which somehow shelters most youngsters from great harm. He had taken on the appearance of a young man who is emerging from the shroud of innocence that protects him to face whatever destiny holds in store. It is a perilous age when young men become presumptuous enough to believe themselves to be virtually indestructible. He felt as though Tater had gone through some mystical time triggered metamorphosis, and it caused Noah to blow out a breath of remorse.

The wagon slowed to a crawl to ford the creek where there was no bridge. Tater waited on the other side for him to catch up and explained, "There's bridges to cross farther down, but it's pretty smooth going from here on."

"Don't worry about me," Noah assured him, "I can keep up. Don't you have to go to school anymore?"

"I already finished it," Tater said. "Grade eight is as far as you can go around here. I got my diploma at home. If I have to get anymore schooling, I'd have to do it through the mail...or go away for it."

Noah dropped back again and only caught up for a moment when they were passing the whitewashed building in the distance. "What's that place?" he quizzed.

"The grange hall," Tater answered. "That's where they start school after the harvest."

The sleepy little village overlooking the Snake River soon came into sight and Tater slowed down the pace. "There's Springwater," he said looking back at Noah.

"It might be better if I don't go into town with you," Noah suggested, and a look of relief washed over the boy's face. "If you weren't going to be too long I could wait on down the road for you."

They agreed on it and Tater stayed on the road to town while Noah cut a wide circle out across the scrubland surrounding the town. He saw the cemetery that seemed to just lie out in the middle of the prairie, and he thought of Niles Whitehead buried in the ground. By the time he came out onto the main road that ran along the river, it was only a short wait before Tater met up with him again. The boy had a peppermint stick hanging out of his mouth that reminded Noah of Dunlavy's toothpick after a big meal. Halting the wagon next to Pecos, the boy reached in his shirt pocket and offered Noah a piece of candy. Noah reached over to take the peppermint stick and he noticed a book stuck in the back pocket of the boy's pants.

"What kind of book do you have there?" Noah asked as he started Pecos down the road toward the hotel.

"It's nothing," Tater shrugged it off as he drove the wagon alongside Noah. "It's one of those dime novels I got at the mercantile. Mixy likes me to read the stories to him."

Rose had said something once about Tater liking to read the adventures spelled out in the dime novels. "It really ain't like they write about in them dime novels," Noah told him, sucking on the candy. "You know that don't you?" Noah had read one or two himself and realized right away that the writer definitely had seen things from a different angle than him. "It seems to me that most days life in a saddle can be as hard as trying to scratch one out on some poor dirt farm."

"Have you ever rode much on trains?" Tater quizzed. "I heard they're building a railroad from Chicago clear out to Seattle."

"Well, I see them laying more tracks everywhere I go anymore," Noah said. "In fact when I came up here from Medicine Bow I rode along part of the old Mormon trail to Ogden and took the Utah and Northern to Pocatello. I just stuck Pecos in a stock car and sat in a nice smooth seat for the next hundred and twenty or so miles."

"The Utah and Northern is part of the Union Pacific," Tater interjected.

"That's right," Noah continued, "and when I was on the train the word was that the Union Pacific is planning to build the Oregon branch that will run right along the Snake River here in the next few years."

When Tater heard this news his eyes grew wide with excitement. "You see," He remarked, "now that's what I'd like to do. Go to work on the railroads. I have enough schooling for that right now. I can read and write, and I'm not too bad at the numbers either. If I went to work for the railroad, I would get to see all those places you're talking about."

"What does your mother think about this idea?" Noah wondered.

"She thinks I should stay in the dairy business," Tater replied, disgruntled, and appeared to shake off the thought.

They came to a single lane bridge where it crossed a dry streambed. Noah held up to let the wagon go first and when Tater reached the other side he pulled off the road. He hopped down from the wagon and tied his horse to a clump of dead brush. "I know where there is a good drink of water."

As Noah got out of the saddle, he looked at the brackish brown puddles of water lying here and there. Stands of dried out cattails lined the sides of the wash.

A slight breeze rustled through the cattails and the sunlight was diffused by a passing cloud.

"Have you ever drank this water before?" Noah didn't see any water he wanted to swallow.

"All the time", Tater assured him. "Mixy would stop here every time to get a drink and look down on the river when I used to help him with the deliveries. This used to be a really nice creek." Tater gazed around, thinking back. "I can still remember how nice it used to run through here." The boy studied the log and plank bridge, adding, "They almost don't even need this bridge here anymore."

CHAPTER SEVEN

A lazy breeze touched Noah's face as he stood at the edge of the basalt bluffs. He stared out over the Snake River to the brown stretches of plains where the shafts of sunlight broke through the clouds illuminating the morning mist that rose up from the low valleys. A few yards behind him was a little spring where Tater had left him. Between the ancient flows of the volcanic rock, a steady gurgle of clean cold water gathered in pools along a layer of reddish-gray clay. On a ledge above the spring Pecos stood patiently waiting while tied to a sagebrush. And just beyond the horse, a freighter's wagon rumbled over the loose planks of the narrow bridge heading west on a stretch of the Oregon Trail.

Noah had agreed to wait there by the trickle of a spring while Tater finished up his errands at the hotel. For one reason or another, Noah and Tater both thought it was best that they not be seen traveling together – at least not in public places. It was Rose that they didn't want to find out, and each of them had their own reasons why. But as he started picking his way back up the dry creek bed toward his horse, Noah figured that no matter how hard they tried to conceal it, it was only a matter of time until the truth made it to the surface. Who knew what was best? He swung up into the saddle and took off to the Rocky Bar hotel with the hopes of seeing Lester Dunlavy.

From a lack of business, the ferrymen stood idle with the oxen at the river's edge. They watched him only long enough to determine that he was headed on up the road toward the hotel.

As Noah approached the hotel, he could see Tater's wagon parked out back by the kitchen door and felt fortunate that neither the boy or the cook were anywhere in sight. It was getting close to noon and there were a few horses tied to the rails, so he rode in for a closer inspection. Right away he identified a couple of familiar looking plow horses that used to wait outside of Eddie Button's saloon, but Dunlavy's lanky bay didn't turn up among them – and according to the cook he was still riding the same horse. Noah was about to leave when he heard someone calling out.

"Hey, mister," the voice yelled out again, drawing Noah's attention. The rotund cook in a soiled apron was standing at the back corner of the hotel with Tater at his side. Schwarting was waving for Noah to come over to him.

Noah rode over just close enough so they wouldn't have to holler at each other. There was a genuine look of surprise on Tater's face and the boy was trying to give Noah some sort of a hidden message through an odd stare.

"You just missed your friend," Schwarting announced. "He was sitting in there eating his breakfast less than an hour ago. I don't believe he's ever showed up here this early in the day before."

"Was he alone?" Noah tried his best to ignore Tater.

"He was with a Mexican," Schwarting replied. "I told him that you had been by and was asking about him."

It had to be Fernando Pico that Dunlavy was using for an accomplice these days. That was most likely a good thing, too. Noah figured Fernando to be a man that was blessed with the gift of common sense. "I don't suppose you saw them leaving?" Noah pursued.

"They rode off toward Springwater," Schwarting recalled.

"Thank you anyway," Noah told him, "I'm sure I'll catch up to him sooner or later."

Tipping a finger to the brim of his hat as a show of gratitude and farewell, Noah reined Pecos around and started toward Springwater. Something didn't make sense. If Dunlavy had gone to town like the cook said, Noah should have run into him somewhere along the trail. He twisted around in the saddle before he lost sight of the hotel and saw Tater standing alone at the corner of the building – still watching him.

When Noah came to the dry streambed, he stopped and waited in the saddle until he saw Tater's wagon coming in the distance, then he continued up the road. Pecos was encouraged to maintain an easy pace and Noah looked back often to make sure that the wagon was able to close the distance between them. Noah kept thinking that he should have gone ahead to the hotel when he'd had the chance early that morning. He would have found out what was going on with Jared Sowers.

"I have one more place I have to go," Tater yelled out as he finally caught up to Noah. "I know a shortcut back around the bend."

With Tater leading the way, they backtracked for a few minutes until the boy steered the wagon onto an old trail that wound its way out through the sagebrush. Once off the main road, Noah discovered that Tater wasn't the only one that knew about the shortcut – a pair of well shod horses had gone ahead of them. Noah poked the big gelding in the flanks and trotted out in front of the wagon to take the lead. The tracks looked to be fairly fresh and as he followed them, the little voice inside his skull was trying to convince him that they had been made by Lester Dunlavy and Fernando Pico.

"Who else knows about this cow path?" Noah asked, looking back at Tater.

"Lots of folks," Tater explained. "It's a shortcut to the ferry crossing if you live in the valley. You don't have to go clear into town first."

"Where is it exactly that you're going?" Noah asked.

"I have to see a man about something." Tater was a bit vague but insisted, "This really is the shortest way home for me. I know all the cutoffs."

"I guess I can go along a little ways farther," Noah suggested, and rode out ahead so that he could focus on the tracks of who ever it was out in front of them. After awhile the sage became more sparse and the old wagon road ran alongside the dry creek.

"It used to be real nice along here, too," Tater yelled after him, "when the water was still running." Swiveling around in the saddle, Noah gazed up and down where the creek used to flow like he was trying to imagine it. A little ways further, the trail strayed away from the dry streambed as it veered off into a brush-covered draw. The tumbleweeds finally gave way to the sun bleached grasslands and the old road was consumed by the prairie that stretched up into the low lying hills.

The morning had burned off nicely and Noah sensed that above all else it was a good day to be out riding. And the tracks they were still following, he finally reasoned, could have been left by most anyone – there were farms scattered all over the valley these days.

The low hills turned into a long and fairly steep grade, and by the time they reached the summit the mare was nearly winded from lugging Tater and the wagon. They pulled up to rest the horses as the vast expanse of the Springwater Valley unfurled before them.

From the crest of the hill, Noah was able to get his bearings for the first time since they left the main river trail. Just below them along the fringe of the foothills lay the old road leading into the valley. It was the original route that came past Eddie Button's saloon and ran in front of the old horse trader's place. It was the trail he remembered the most, from roughly two decades earlier. It was still well-worn.

"It might rain on us before the day's over," Tater commented.

"You think?" Noah glanced up at the bright sun that felt warm on his back.

"Well, it's raining over there," he said, pointing down the river gorge.

Beyond the village of Springwater sheets of rain were falling from a big dark-bottomed cloud. A gust of wind came up the canyon from the river bending the tall grasses in waves around them. It carried with it the smell of rain, and the wind seemed to whisper something as it passed by. There was a peacefulness about that seemed to slow down time – as if time itself was trying to cling to that precious moment for a little longer. And for a flicker of that moment, Noah felt like he was a part of all there ever was. Then the harsh cry of a raven pierced the drone of silence sending a chill down his spine.

"Mixy told me that you are my real dad," Tater said nonchalantly. "Is that true?" He turned his attention to the sky to watch a pair of ravens fly on toward the Snake.

The boy's words were erased by the wind, but they continued to echo through Noah's mind. There he was – a half worn out cowboy sitting on the top of a little hill with a marvelous grass valley sprawled before him and the Snake River gorge at his back – and on one side of him the sky was full of sunbeams and on the other side rain clouds were coming. And he was aware that Tater had turned his focus back to him and was waiting for some sort of an answer.

Noah was trapped in an awkward situation, and there was a long moment before he was finally able to face Tater. And as he gazed into the eyes of his own son, he witnessed the spirit of a young man come forward to take his rightful place. It was something in his son's eyes that was deep and searching. In a way, Noah felt as though he was looking at a reflection of himself. It was an experience that humbled Noah and he had to take a deep breath to keep his eyes from getting watery. "If it were true," he struggled with the words, "how would you feel about that?"

"I don't know how I'm supposed to feel," Tater responded with a shy grin. "Mixy told me not to think about the past too much and just be happy that I have the chance to spend some time around you." He kept hidden the secret thoughts that rumbled around in his dime novel mind. But if the truth was ever known, Tater was more than just a little pleased that his own dad had turned out to be a real gunfighter.

"I reckon it's so," Noah revealed. There was a feeling of serenity that came over him as the truth was set free by just speaking the words. Old Mixy had let the cat out of the bag, but he had done it in a way that made it seem alright that the cat was loose.

"What do you want me to call you?" Tater considered.

"What do you want to call me?" Noah asked.

"How about Noah?" Tater suggested.

"Well, I think that would be just fine," Noah smiled. "That's what my friends call me."

"Okay then," Tater agreed with a nod, "I will. But I need to keep going if I'm ever going to make it home for dinner." The mare was no longer panting and with a slight snap of the reins across her back they pressed on. Pecos took the lead again and within a few minutes they were traveling along the well-worn road.

Noah was busy persuading himself, now that the cards were all lying face up on the table he could dispense with the idle chatter. They had hardly said a word all day, and when they did talk it was about a creek that used to flow and whether or not the rain clouds would reach them or blow on by to the south. He did find out about Tater's ambition to go work on the railroad. Maybe he should talk to him more about that. The railroad could be a dangerous occupation at times. Then there was another thing that had been on his mind all day, too.

"What does your mother have to say about those clothes you're wearing now?" Noah asked. He wished Tater still looked like that harmless lad he'd first met, all freckled with beer foam dribbling from his peach fuzz moustache, still under that divine shelter.

"She don't like it much," Tater admitted, "but I'm getting too old to have my ear yanked anymore."

"I guess you can tell that she's mad at me right now for all this," Noah declared.

"She doesn't seem mad to me," Tater remarked.

"Well, all I know is," Noah contended, "that when I saw her a couple days ago she was wet hen mad at just the sight of me. You really don't think she's mad at me?"

"No," Tater reasoned, "I've seen her plenty mad before. Something important is bothering her. She likes to worry about things." Tater shook his head and added with a grimace, "Why, if she knew about all this, she would fret herself right into a fit – and I mean over me just plain talking to you." The mere thought of it obviously disturbed him. "You don't know her like I do, Noah."

The boy was right, Noah felt like he hardly knew Rose anymore. He knew his own son even less, and when he thought back about it there were only blank spaces where there should have been memories stored. And Noah vowed then and there while he rode alongside Tater to do whatever was necessary to remedy that fact. After all, what could Rose do about it even if she wanted?

Once again Tater abandoned a good road for two narrow strips of bare ground that wandered out through the prairie grasses. Noah was disappointed to discover that the same two horses they'd been trailing for the last hour had also chosen the very same cut off.

"Were you at Mixy's this morning?" Tater called out when Noah trotted around the wagon to take the lead.

"What would make you think that?" Noah quizzed him.

"Because that's where it looked like you were coming from when I first saw you today," Tater surmised.

"Besides that, you don't have a bedroll or your rain slicker – or your Winchester. Anyway if you didn't come from there, I think Mixy would sure like to talk to you."

"Mixy's a pretty good old fellow," Noah offered. "Isn't he?"

"Mixy's the greatest," Tater solemnly testified. "I can never remember a time when Mixy wasn't there helping us out."

Noah understood it was the sort of praise that could only be earned. A cloud moved in front of the sun and a shadowy curtain was drawn across the landscape.

"I don't know if you noticed or not," Tater continued on a different subject altogether, "but we have been following a couple riders ever since we turned off the river road. I'll bet they're some of Mister Sowers' hired hands."

"Now you don't know that," Noah stated. At the same time his own little voice was telling him again that the tracks had to belong to Dunlavy and Pico. "I'm going to ride out ahead some."

Noah followed the tracks to where they broke over a low windswept ridge. There the riders had left the trail and the hoofprints were lost in the prairie. He stopped to wait for Tater who was only a couple of minutes behind.

Thousands of acres of open range that made up the main floor of the Springwater Valley lay in front of him. His eyes explored the landscape for men on horseback. If it had been Dunlavy and Pico, they were long gone by now. The range was void of movement except for the wind against the grass. In the distant foothills he saw the two white-washed barns where Sowers kept his prize bulls. This was the worst part of the valley that Tater could possibly be headed for. When the wagon showed up, Tater was staring up the little ridge like he was looking for someone.

"Do you see something up there?" Noah automatically scanned the ridge.

"No, I haven't seen a soul," Tater replied. "I was just thinking about other things."

"So was I," Noah said. "For instance, who exactly is it you need to talk to bad enough to be clear over here in this part of the valley?"

"Mister Morrey. He's a friend of ours," Tater said, pointing. About a half mile away stood a locust grove. There was a farm scattered among the trees. "That's his farm over there."

"Uh-huh," Noah nodded. Lewis Morrey certainly was in the shadow of the Sowers empire. From his lofty perch, Jared Sowers had a great view looking down on Morrey's farm. "What do you have to see him about?"

"Mixy wants me to give him a message," Tater put the leather to the mares back and started on. "I'll only be a few minutes."

"We must be getting pretty dang close to being on Sowers' spread." Noah reasoned as he nudged Pecos to stay alongside the wagon.

"We're already on part of the land he claims," Tater mentioned, gawking off toward the ridge again.

The only peculiar thing Noah could see was a dark green patch of ground that stood out against the tans and yellows of late summer. "You never know who you might bump into around here," Noah warned.

"My mom says that no one has the right to tell another person where they can go or not," the boy informed him.

"Yeah," Noah scoffed and shook his head, "that works fine when there ain't a bunch of simpletons out running around all over the place."

"I guess you heard by now that it was Burt Perry that burned down Mixy's barn," Tater announced. "That buffalo hunter that you know. I've never seen him again since that day he came across on the ferry. But Mixy seen him watching the fire that night and we ain't supposed to tell anybody about it. They all think it got set on fire by some strange accident. Well, it didn't." It still rankled Tater when he thought back on it all. He snapped the reins and the mare suddenly broke into a trot, farting loudly as she did. Tater found some sort of humor in it and couldn't help but flash Noah a wide grin as he added, singing, "...goes the weasel."

"Not everybody," Noah told him, urging Pecos to keep up. "Mixy should have gone in town and signed a complaint with Frank Canfield."

"He thinks it would only stir up more trouble," Tater explained "And mom says he might be right."

"No, he ain't right," Noah contended, "it only lets them know they can get away with it. I'd say there's a good chance they'll be back someday."

They came to a string of barbed wire that Lewis Morrey had put up to keep the cows out of the crops. Inside the fence were well-tended rows of squash, corn and potatoes. The house and barn were just beyond the garden in the shade of the locust trees. It was a nice farm with evidence of hard work everywhere. Tater drove down the fence line that would take him around to the back of the barn.

"I hope they do come back," Tater threatened, "because the next time they won't be so lucky. We've

been watching for them – and waiting. Me and Mixy."
He gazed around like he was looking for trouble. "And
there's a couple of his gunmen right now hanging around
Mister Morrey's place," his voice wavering with alarm.

CHAPTER EIGHT

Lester Dunlavy and Fernando Pico were sitting on their horses out behind Morrey's barn – and even though they were too far off to speak with, they were almost within pistol range. Both of them were hunched over in their saddles, hands folded over the horn. And both of them were staring straight at Noah. It was the second time that day Noah had been caught by surprise and he was upset with himself. Dunlavy and Pico must have been on the other side of the barn, because he would have sworn that they weren't sitting there a minute ago. Noah cut in front of the mare and reined up forcing Tater to stop the wagon.

"You need to just stay put right here," Noah told Tater firmly. "I know these cowboys."

"I have my pistol here under my seat," Tater offered, earnestly, "do you want me to put it on?"

"No!" Noah was stern. "Now, they're just up to some monkey business. I'll go chase them off. Does Mister Morrey have any kids running around?"

"Two young ones," Tater stated. "The littlest is still going around without any pants on yet. Is there going to be a gunfight?"

"No, there isn't," Noah assured him, then insisted, "now I need for you to stay right here until I come back for you. Okay?"

"Alright," Tater reluctantly agreed with a nod of his head.

Noah approached slowly, and except for the two wayward cowboys and a few barnyard chickens taking dirt baths in the loose earth beneath the locust trees, he didn't see any signs of life. Dunlavy and Pico were passing a smoke back and forth. Noah knew right away what they were up to, they had been sent out here to intimidate Lewis Morrey. But neither one of them seemed too sure of why Noah had shown up. Dunlavy was trying to hide the fact that he was about as nervous as a skunk that had found its way into the chicken coop. Even though Noah had known both of these men for years, he was still wary. All of a sudden he felt like he was on a different side than them.

"I heard you was back around here," Dunlavy said with chagrin. Much of his attention was focused on Tater. "Isn't that the kid that used to hang around Eddie's Saloon?"

"Hola! Señor Pico," Noah deliberately ignored Dunlavy.

"Buenas tardes, Noah, mi amigo," Pico returned. It was apparent that the knife toting Spaniard was pleased to see Noah again and shook his hand.

"That's the kid, Noah," Dunlavy pursued. "He's always driving that wagon around."

"His name's Tater," Noah offered to appease Dunlavy's curiosity. "I'm using him for a little detective work I'm involved in."

"Detective work?" Dunlavy was puzzled.

"You know how boys are, Dunlavy," Noah explained, "sometimes they ain't nearly as dumb as you might think. They hear everybody around talking about things, and they don't know any better than to tell the truth. But you can't blame them for it because they're too young to know any better yet. As it turns out, the people living around here know they have a problem, and I think they're going to stick together pretty good, too."

"Are you working for the citizens these days, Noah?" Dunlavy asked bluntly.

"No, I'm working for me these days," Noah answered.

"Doing what?" Dunlavy inquired.

"More or less," Noah stated, "what I'm doing is trying to make sure Burt Perry doesn't cut any more ears off of innocent people. And I'll tell you the pay ain't very good either."

"I think you are too late," Pico commented. The Spaniard spoke good english.

"Oh," Noah looked to Dunlavy for the answer, "why is that?"

"There was a rumor going around," Dunlavy admitted, giving Pico a woeful look, "that Burt gave Mister Sowers a pair of ears that was still fresh. Supposedly, they had belonged to somebody that was rustling sheep."

"Rustling sheep?" Noah countered.

"The bunkhouse jokes these days is all about sheep rustlers being around Idaho," Dunlavy went on, "and how Burt is cleaning them up."

"If he did murder some sheepherder up in the hills," Pico interjected, "you could never really prove it anyway."

Noah thought back to the small flock of frightened sheep running wild in the canyons above Sowers' ranch.

They did seem out of place at the time. "You haven't seen Burt around lately, have you?"

"He hardly ever shows up around the ranch," Dunlavy said. "I don't know what he's up to. I really don't."

If Fernando Pico hadn't been there, Noah would have told Dunlavy exactly what the mangy scoundrel was up to, especially when it came to Little One – and about seeing Burt pissing in the river, too. "Is Wally Pomeroy still around?" Noah asked.

"Him and that Mississippi," Dunlavy said. "They been out actually herding cows around. Wally told Mister Sowers that if things didn't get rolling pretty quick he was quitting."

"You should not trust Wally," Pico spoke up, "I think he don't like you, Noah."

"Gracias, Fernando," Noah said, "I never really did trust him. I guess everybody can't like everybody else. For instance, Burt Perry don't like Dunlavy here at all." He focused on Dunlavy. "I wouldn't put it past him to just up and shoot you if you looked at him cross-eyed."

"Yeah, I'm not planning on looking at him cross-eyed anyway," Dunlavy rebuffed. He didn't find the thought as humorous as the other two, who were all smiles.

"Do you have any fixins'?" Noah asked Dunlavy as he started searching his shirt pockets for his rolling papers. He looked out at Tater who was still waiting patiently. It was obvious that somewhere along the way Rose had taught the boy to mind. Tater's full attention of course was centered on the gunmen's parley. And when Dunlavy handed over a pouch of tobacco, Noah quizzed, "Do you even know the man who lives here?"

"I've never met him," Dunlavy admitted. "I caught a glimpse of him when we rode up. He was out cutting hay."

When Noah looked to Pico for the answer, the Spaniard shook his head that he didn't know Morrey either. "You're about out of tobacco," Noah mentioned as he dug into the pouch.

"Help yourself," Dunlavy told him, "I need to get more anyway. I been trying to get into town."

"Tell me, Dunlavy," Noah reasoned, as he rolled a cigarette, "you're pretty good at distances and stuff. From up there where Jared Sowers is roosting, how many acres do you think he can see down here? Because I think he wants all he can see. Don't you?"

Burdened by thought, Dunlavy gazed up at Sowers' ranch and then out across the valley. "I imagine that there has to be over three thousand," he determined, "at least twenty-five hundred."

"And maybe eight, or ten farms, if that many," Noah stated. "How many acres do you think this little farm here takes up? I mean fenced in. Five?"

"Yeah, about that," Dunlavy said, looking around.

On the other side of the barn from the vegetable garden was another couple acres of meadow grass that Lewis Morrey had fenced off from the range cattle. There were patches where the tall grass had been hand cut with a scythe, and in one place the fresh cropped stalks lay where they fell to dry. There was plenty of good grass left that still needed to be cut and stacked. Noah imagined that the hay he had slept on in Mixy's barn must have come from that very field.

"For Christ's sake, Lester," Noah reasoned, licking the cigarette into shape, "what's five acres here and ten down the road. We're surrounded by a thousand square miles of open range." He stretched his arms open wide. "Tell me, why the hell is it that Jared Sowers thinks he can't live without this little speck of dirt right here?"

"I don't think we're breaking any laws for being around here," Dunlavy defended himself. "None that I'm familiar with anyhow." He transformed into a true picture of innocence, like he really didn't know any better. "Why are you taking this all so personal?"

"I don't know," Noah declared, "but I do know there is something wrong about it. Maybe it's because I grew up on a farm the same as you did." As a general rule, when Noah and Dunlavy were kids most anyone that was born west of the Mississippi River grew up on a farm. "And I do know that when you scratch a living from the earth, at least it's an honest life. I don't know, Dunlavy," he looked around at Morrey's place and lit the cigarette, "maybe you ought to stop pestering the folks that live here and let them get on with their harvest."

"We're not out here to hurt anybody," Dunlavy replied, the color draining from his cheeks. He seemed to take Noah's advice as a warning.

"I know that," Noah admitted, "but does this poor fellow living here know that?"

There was nothing but silence for a little while as they all looked around at the lifeless farm. They couldn't even see the chickens kicking up dust from where they were, however, they did hear some horses or cows kicking around inside the barn once in a while.

"This farmer could lose his ears, too, amigo," Pico cautioned Noah. "Lester might talk them off him if they ever meet each other."

"Alright, why don't you pick on me?" The color started to return to Dunlavy's face. It always agitated him when someone called him by his first name.

Noah understood it was what Pico intended, to in fact soothe the situation down. He spoke to the Spaniard as if Dunlavy wasn't even there, "Or he'd be teaching his children to make ugly faces."

This brought a chuckle from everyone but Dunlavy who just grimaced and shook his head – he knew when it was best to shut up. Lester Dunlavy couldn't hide the fact that he liked children, and in the past both Noah and Pico had witnessed him teaching kids to make the most grotesque expressions whenever he had the chance. In the end Dunlavy was laughing, too. Even he knew it was a good joke on him.

The laughter relieved the tension that Noah had felt ever since he'd been caught off guard by the shady pair of cowboys. They all ended up looking at each other like nothing made sense anymore. "Fernando," Noah questioned, "is this what you want to be doing?"

"Now don't start on him," Dunlavy butted in, "he's just out here trying to look busy until he can draw his wages, and then he's going to California. Fernando's off to fight with the bandidos."

"Bandidos?" Noah prodded Dunlavy. "You're going with him aren't you?"

"He's too frightened," Pico said.

"I am not," Dunlavy argued.

"Do you want to go with me, Noah?" Pico continued. "The end of the month is next week and when I get paid I'm leaving. At least down there I can understand when I hear them plotting to kill me."

"You hear that, Dunlavy?" Noah mused, "you shouldn't let Fernando out of your sight, and you'll probably be okay."

"He's going by sea from Astoria to San Francisco," Dunlavy informed him. "Right now, I don't know what I'm going to do. I'm thinking of trying to find some honest work for a change."

"He is afraid to go out on the sea," Pico explained to Noah.

"I'm not scared of it," Dunlavy reasoned. "I just don't care to be on water that much. I'd go that way, Noah, if you were to go, too. If I do end up going with Fernando, though, you shouldn't stay around here by yourself to take on Burt," he looked off toward Tater, "and most likely Wally, too. You won't have a friend left in these parts."

"Sailing on a ship and fighting with Mexican rustlers does sound exciting," Noah stated, "but I feel like I should stay around here awhile longer."

Lester Dunlavy's instincts were as keen as ever and he figured that there was more to the story than Noah was admitting. There was something more personal than the bad blood between Noah and Burt. But more than likely he would never know what it was unless Noah wanted him to. Dunlavy let out a deep sigh and said, "I think I might ride into town and get some tobacco. Where are you staying?"

"I'm staying in an old camp over on Springwater Creek not too far from the grange hall," Noah lied. He began to see the telltale signs that signaled Dunlavy was getting ready to leave. Dunlavy was looking around like he was trying to figure out which way he was going calculating the path of least resistance.

But there was one more thing that continued to baffle Noah. "I heard that Burt burned down some old man's barn at the head of the valley," he pursued while he still had the opportunity. "I wonder what that has to do with Jared Sowers' master plan for taking over the valley?"

"I guess that he's courting some woman that lives up around there," Dunlavy told him. "The widow Rose. Sounds like she's a real belle, too."

"How do you know that?" Noah questioned. To hear Dunlavy talking about Rose like that nearly made the hair bristle up on the back of his neck.

"That's how Señor Sowers tells it," Pico offered. "He speaks of her like she's some prize heifer."

"Have you ever been up at the head of the valley?" Dunlavy wondered.

"Yep, I have," Noah said. "Have you?"

"No," Dunlavy said. "What's up there?"

"Nothing," Noah assured him.

Dunlavy spent the next few minutes convincing a reluctant Pico into riding into Springwater for tobacco. And on a promise of seeing each other again sometime, Noah watched as the two men set off across the valley toward town. Dunlavy twisted around in the saddle and stared back like he had forgotten something. Tater waved at them from the wagon and after a moment both cowboys waved back. Then they seemed to set their sights on some unknown landmark.

CHAPTER NINE

Longing to rest his tailbone a spell, Noah slid down from the saddle and walked his horse back out to where Tater was waiting impatiently with the wagon. The rain clouds had blown in a bit closer and Noah searched for Dunlavy and Pico, but they had already dissolved into the distance. By the looks of it though, Dunlavy had ended up riding into rain – and he had talked Fernando Pico into going with him.

"What's it mean when somebody's up to monkey business?" Tater asked the moment he had the chance. It was a term he was unfamiliar with – and he had spent the entire time he was waiting trying to notice any unusual behavior by Noah's old cohorts. Tater had only seen a couple real monkeys in his whole life, and both times they were in a cage.

"It's when somebody is going out of their way just trying to stir up some trouble," Noah explained.

"Oh," Tater pondered, "I get it."

"I heard that your friend is home," Noah said, "but I didn't see anybody around."

"If you're talking about Mister Morrey, he just went in the house," Tater informed Noah. "He was out in the barn all along."

"You mean while I was over there with them two cowboys?" Noah looked back to where he'd met with Dunlavy and Pico. They had to have been within a few short feet of the barn. Morrey was probably some of the bumping around noises coming from the shadows within – and he must have listened in on every word. "What is it that you're suppose to tell him?"

"Mixy told me to tell Mister Morrey," Tater recalled, "that he should hold on for as long as he can. And to tell him that there are people in the valley that know what's going on and might try to help him. And I was to thank him again for the load of hay."

"Uh-huh," Noah considered, "that's good. You can tell him, too, that if he sees them same two fellows hanging around again that they shouldn't give him any trouble. He ought to just go on about his business."

"Why don't you tell him yourself?" Tater queried.

"I best wait out here," Noah reasoned, "he's had enough strange company for one day. And tell him that you don't know about any others, but for the ones that was just here. So let's hope he got a good look at them."

"What should I tell him about you?" Tater asked.

After a brief deliberation, Noah couldn't think of anything, so concluded, "I suppose it would probably be better to keep this under his hat for a little while if he can."

Noah took his canteen from the saddle and watched as Tater parked the wagon on the very spot where he had just met with Dunlavy and Pico. When Lewis Morrey came out of the house, the boy got down and went in the barn to talk with him.

Taking a swallow of water, Noah wondered what it meant now that Dunlavy and Pico were quitting and clearing out. With his gang beginning to dwindle, Sowers might start to panic. The job of harassing Morrey would most likely be turned over to Wally Pomeroy, and since Niles Whitehead was dead, that left only Mississippi to help out with such tasks – and Dunlavy had mentioned that even Wally was starting to get restless. Wally was a dimwit with a mean streak.

It was only a matter of minutes until Tater was on his way back out. And as he pulled up in the wagon, he asked, "Which way do you want to go?"

"I need to get back over by the grange," Noah suggested, swinging up in the saddle. "I'll follow you if you're headed that way."

"We can go back the way we came to the valley road," Tater considered, looking back toward Morrey's barn, "or there's a shorter way, but it means we'd have to go down Sowers' road for a little ways. Either way will take you past the grange."

Turning the wagon around, Tater led the way back past the small farm. Lewis Morrey, who had resumed cutting hay, stopped swinging the scythe a minute to watch them pass by. He was a tall, stout looking man who was leathered by the sun from working the fields. Noah didn't recognize him as any of the men he'd seen at Eddie's saloon.

Even though it was Tater who had suggested that they could take this route, he became apprehensive about running into Jared Sowers. And when they came to the road that led to Sowers' ranch, he stopped for a moment and looked up and down making sure it was deserted. A loud thunderclap startled them and in the distance rain fell from the dark clouds that churned along the river gorge. At least going this way might keep them from getting wet, but as far as Tater was concerned the sooner they were off this road the better. The boy snapped the reins across the mare's back and started down the road at a good clip.

"Is something bothering you?" Noah asked, trotting his horse behind the wagon as it rattled along the well worn ruts. The fast pace suited him just fine, because his stomach was starting to grumble from the lack of food.

"I don't come this way much anymore," Tater stated, looking back over his shoulder at Sowers' ranch in the hills above the valley. "I don't want to run into Mister Sowers. It would just give him an excuse to come see my mom. And if he saw me with you, I'm sure he would show up in a hurry to find out what's going on."

"Mixy says that your mom don't like him much," Noah commented. He gave himself away on purpose. The thought crossed his mind that Jared Sowers could be paying Rose a visit right that minute.

"She hates him, just like me," Tater said, twisting clear around in his seat to look at Noah. "So you have talked to Mixy."

"He thinks I ought to stay with him for a couple nights," Noah divulged.

"Hey, I think that's a real good idea," Tater urged. "He's there all alone. Do you think you're going to do it? We have an old army cot I could bring down for you."

"And you don't think your mom would mind too much," Noah remarked.

"Oh, she'll have a real conniption fit," the boy exclaimed with concern. The thought made him shake his head. She had been in a strange mood for quite some time now, but Tater had assumed it was because of all the trouble going on in the valley – and the fact that Jared Sowers was coming around to see her. "Why, when mom found out we were together at the river shooting guns that time," he recollected, "she was so upset with me that she didn't cook anything for me to eat for two days."

Tater drove on in silence trying to figure out a way that Noah could stay at Mixy's without his mother finding out. She usually went down to see Mixy during the day while he was off running errands. She seldom went down after supper unless it was something important. Even then he could run ahead and warn them that she was coming. Tater's heart was set on Noah staying at Mixy's place. He envisioned sitting around in the evenings watching Mixy smoking his pipe and listening to the stories that Noah would dispense about his adventures on the trail – and the tales he had to tell of gunfighting.

They left Sowers' road to follow another set of ruts out across the prairie. The whitewashed grange hall stood on a small knoll that rose up from the valley floor. It didn't appear as if anyone was around at that time of day – the string of hitching rails was empty. Twin privies sat fifty feet out back. The hitching rails and the outhouses had been whitewashed, too. Noah couldn't quite figure out why they thought they needed two privies except for the fact that there were no trees close by. There was a hand pump sitting over a well and a wooden trough to water the horses. A quarter mile beyond the grange to the west the willows and the cottonwoods and the aspen groves grew along Springwater Creek the length of the valley.

Tater reined up near the water trough to give the mare a chance to catch her breath. His desire to leave that part of the valley behind as soon as possible had caused the old horse to lather up around the harness.

Noah held up at the nearest outhouse to tend to a chore that he had put off that morning in order to keep up with Tater. As he slid down from the saddle, he noticed that the thoroughbred's flanks were dark with sweat. They had covered a lot of ground in the last twenty minutes.

When Noah came out of the privy, he saw Tater standing beside the wagon staring out at the low end of the valley where an immense dust devil spun silently across the prairie. Above the whirlwind, a crooked finger of blowing dirt pointed into the sky. He grabbed the reins and wandered over to stand next to his son who seemed to be mesmerized by the approaching turbulence.

The dust devil continued toward them until it bumped into the base of the knoll and then it just seemed to blow apart sending a strong gust of wind up the rise. They watched the grasses bend in waves as the gust raced toward them. Noah and Tater automatically turned their backs to the gritty wind that made the tufts of dried grass hiss around their boots as it blew past.

It was late enough in the day that the sun cast the shadows of dimension across the earth. Noah gazed upon a landscape that was far more splendid and dramatic than any artist's painting he had ever seen. And it was a living thing. The golds and faded greens of the valley floor and the hills were bathed in the sun's luminance, but above the hills the sky was so dark it absorbed the sunlight. A bolt of lightening flashed out of the angry clouds that hovered above the twin white barns belonging to Jared Sowers. Noah had about given up on hearing thunder when it rumbled throughout the heavens – and as rain swept across the hills a brilliant rainbow formed.

"That's beautiful, isn't it?" Tater commented softly as if not to disturb anything.

"Mother Nature's paint brush," he answered. The full arc of the rainbow framed Jared Sowers' ranch perfectly. It almost gave the impression that whoever lived there must lead a charmed life. Noah hoped that wasn't the case – and at the same time he was glad Bacanaro couldn't see this picture. The wise old Indian would probably view it as a bad omen and warn Noah to ride away while he still could.

Instead Noah said, "If you thought that there was a way to keep your mom from finding out, I wouldn't mind taking Mixy up on his offer. I could use the rest." He knew that if he made Tater an ally, then at least he wouldn't have to hide out from him, too. Noah hated having to sneak around behind somebody's back. He'd done it before with a woman, and he looked back on the overall experience as a poor one. He was certain, too, that if he did stay at Mixy's for any length of time, the chances that Rose wouldn't find out anyway were slim to none. He would leave her alone and out of it if that's what she wanted, but it was the best opportunity he had to get to know his son. And just then that seemed more important than trying to make amends with her.

"It would be a lot better if she didn't know, that's for sure," Tater agreed. "You might have to stay away during the day. When I'm there, I could run ahead and warn you if she was coming down. And Mixy's a good cook, too, if you don't already know it."

The thought of food got them moving again and shortly after leaving the grange hall they came to the main road that ran along Springwater Creek. Noah trailed back a couple hundred yards again just in case they met up with any of Tater's neighbors.

The rain clouds had moved on to the east and the wind died down. The air that followed the storm was fresh smelling, but to Noah it also felt cooler, especially in the shaded areas along the creek. After awhile, the boy pulled off the road again into the little clearing along the creek where they had met unexpectedly that morning.

By the time Noah caught up, Tater was climbing back up in the box of the wagon. He had changed his clothes and was now wearing his regular bibbed-overalls. He drove back out onto the road and looked at Noah and shook his head with resolve. "I just don't want her fretting over this, too," he told Noah. "She's been upset with me enough lately. I don't want her to stop cooking again."

CHAPTER TEN

They split up below Mixy's place and Noah left Pecos tethered in the glade. He spent a few minutes at the creek washing the trail dirt off his hands and face with high hopes of supper, and then took off up the foot path toward Mixy's cabin. Along the way he encountered a half dozen friendly sheep running loose with a small long-eared donkey. The odd mix of critters followed him until he entered the plum thicket.

Inside the thicket, the path wound around like a maze through the tangle of burgundy-colored branches. Ahead he could hear somebody pounding away on something, and when he emerged from the prickly trees he saw Mixy out behind the barn with a froe and wooden mallet splitting cedar shakes.

A sudden rush of anxiety made Noah stop right where he was. He'd been caught cold twice that day already, first by Tater and then by Dunlavy and Pico. When he thought of getting caught by Rose, it was absolute dread he felt. It made him wonder if staying at Mixy's was such a good idea after all. The geese weren't around to announce his arrival, so in order to get Mixy's attention Noah snapped his finger. On the third snap, Mixy finally became cognizant of the sound and turned around to find Noah standing at the edge of the plum thicket like he was waiting for the okay. The old man put down his work and went over to the corner of the barn and looked up toward Rose's a few seconds before waving him on in.

"Is the coast clear?" Noah asked, ducking into the shadows of the barn.

"For the time bein' anyway," Mixy considered, mopping his forehead. "Why, you must've been right behind that boy, he just went by here a short while ago."

"How was things around here today?" Noah asked. "Anybody come by?" What he really wanted to know was if Jared Sowers had been around. Noah wondered how often it was that Sowers came calling. And he especially wondered how the well-to-do rancher would react if he knew Noah was staying so close to Rose. He knew that Tater had it right – Sowers was the kind that would have to know what the circumstances were that two different people with the same last name ended up as next-door neighbors. He would most likely suspect it was more than pure happenstance.

"Not a soul," Mixy stated. "I got a little supper fixed if you're hungry. This would be a good time for us to eat. They'll be busy up yonder for awhile with the milkin' and havin' their own supper."

"I'm hungry," Noah admitted.

"Then I'll get washed up," Mixy said, "and bring it out to the barn." He began to roll up his sleeves as he started off toward the creek.

Noah used the time to take off his gun belt and spurs, and dig his bedroll and bags out of the haystack. He rummaged around in his saddlebags to see if he had anything to contribute to supper and all he came up with was three pilot biscuits that were starting to show a little wear. He should have stopped in Springwater earlier and picked up a couple things. He was out of tobacco and out of whiskey and was down to very little to eat. Like always, his trail diet was pitiful.

"Master Noah," Mixy warned, as he came through the barn with some urgency, "there's somebody comin' down the trail."

Noah took up a position in a dim lit corner where he could see out in the direction that Mixy had gone. He pressed further back into the corner when he saw Tater coming down along the creek toward Mixy's cabin. The old man was able to head the boy off and talked to him for a moment before shooing him back toward home. Mixy stayed put until he was satisfied the boy was gone and then went inside his cabin.

"What did he want?" Noah asked, coming out to the edge of the light as Mixy showed up with a chair in each hand. "Is Rose coming?"

"I don't think so," Mixy responded, somewhat puzzled by the thought. "I'm not quite sure what's goin' on. I couldn't make much sense of it." He put the chairs down so that one was inside the barn and the other was out just far enough so he could keep a lookout while they ate. "Said he was lookin' for the milk cows. Hold on..." Mixy hustled over to the cabin and after a minute came back with two plates of food.

"I hope you like sugar on your squash," Mixy said, handing Noah a plate of food.

Sitting down with the plate in his lap, Noah studied the fare. There was a piece of baked hubbard squash that took up the whole plate and in the cavity was a pile of sliced meat. Noah guessed it to be boiled tongue and as hungry as he was it seemed like an awful lot. And he tried to remember the last time he had the opportunity to eat tongue. He started on the baked squash first.

From up the creek, the woeful bellow of a mistreated milk cow severed the quiet evening. "I'm afraid that boy is too short on patience to be a dairy farmer," Mixy remarked, grinning and sticking another chunk of meat in his mouth.

Noah picked up a slice of the meat and sniffed it. It had a slightly pungent odor. "He'll probably end up working for the railroad anyway," he suggested.

Suddenly confounded, Mixy stopped chewing. "That boy seemed to think that you might be down here," he stated. "He acted like he was lookin' for the cows, but said he was goin' to stay up there just in case Mizz Rose was to come down this way. Why would he think you was here?"

"Oh hell," Noah replied, "he knows the whole kit-and-caboodle. I talked to him for awhile today and he knows that I'm his daddy and everything." He took a cautious bite of the meat.

"That's what I wanted to tell you this mornin' before you went off after him," Mixy admitted. "I've been tryin' to tell you how important I feel family is. I was goin' to tell you that he already knew the truth about you. I know it was none of my business to meddle, but..."

"Don't fret about it. I suppose it was best anyway," Noah proposed, chewing. "I don't seem to have the gumption for that sort of thing. I don't know if or when or how I would have ever got around to telling him myself, especially the way Rose feels about me coming back around here."

"But he don't know you're stayin' down here, does he?" Mixy questioned, wiping his mouth with the back of his hand as he assessed the problems that could create. "I 'spose so," Noah said, still chewing. He looked at Mixy who was lost in thought. The old black man's brow had a deep furrow of concern etched into it and he stared up toward Rose's place.

"You don't need to worry about Tater, he's in our camp. He's suppose to come and warn us if Rose heads down here," Noah tried to console him, finally swallowing the peculiar tasting meat. "What is this I'm eating?"

"Do you like it?" Mixy asked.

"It's different," Noah insisted. "It sort of reminds me of tongue."

"That's right. It's pickled sheep's tongue," Mixy said. "The man who told me how to do it said that it was a delicacy in some places."

"These are the kinds of things you need to grow up eating," Noah reasoned. "My own favorite pickled thing is a pickle." But by the time Noah had finished a second piece of pickled tongue he admitted to himself that it wasn't all that bad.

After supper when the day's light grew dim, Noah spotted Mixy out behind the barn standing idle at the edge of the prairie. A handful of twinkling stars were scattered across the deep blue above and a bright half-moon hung in the western sky – and there was a faint smell of wood smoke in the cool air. Near Mixy's feet was a grave marked by a simple wooden cross with the name 'SARLA' carved into it.

"Why do you think it is, Master Noah," Mixy spoke softly as Noah approached, "that there is so darn much sufferin' in life? I'm not talkin' about havin' to work hard to make a livin'. That's just work. I'm talkin' about all the sufferin'. You know what I'm talkin' about, I know you seen it."

"I know what you mean," Noah told him. "I've seen things that I don't think I'll ever be able to get out of my head. Killing and such. Things that come stealing into my dreams on the darkest damn nights. I know I've had my share of restless nights to be sure."

There was a long spell of silence.

"Do you think that God is mad at us?" Mixy pondered seriously.

"I wouldn't know about such things, Mixy," Noah reasoned. As far as he was concerned there was no real answer for a question like that – and he made it a point not to dwell upon those kind of questions anyway. Not questions about God – not even when he was eating peyote. "You would have to ask a preacher about that."

"In her whole life, Mizz Sarla here knew nothin' but sufferin'," Mixy said, "and she was the kindest and gentlest bein' I ever knew. And I swear all she got in return was a lifetime of burden and sufferin'."

Noah could tell Mixy was getting all sad and watery thinking about her. "Well it sounds to me," Noah offered, putting a hand on the old man's shoulder, "that she knew something else, too. It sounds to me, Mixy, like she knew about being loved. And there are some that will never know that in their whole life."

Nodding his head, Mixy looked in Noah's eyes. "Mizz Rose is one of the finest women I've ever known," he proposed, "and I wish that all this trouble would just up and go away and leave her alone."

It sounded to Noah like he was included in Mixy's wish for Rose and it took him by surprise. "I told you that anytime you think my staying here isn't a good idea I can find somewhere else."

"Oh please no, Master Noah," Mixy declared at once, "I wasn't meanin' you. Why, the way I see it, you is heaven sent."

"I don't know about that," Noah scoffed.

"Who else do you think would stand up for us?" Mixy asked. "I want you to know that I got some money saved up and I was goin' to tell you that I would pay you some for your help..."

"No, Mixy, I could never take your money," Noah interjected. "After all you have done for Rose and Tater..." His words faded out and looked up into the stars. "I just realized that I don't even know my own son's given name."

"It's Eli," Mixy answered.

That was Noah's grandfather's name. Eli Conklin had owned a river bottom farm in Missouri and never drank whiskey or beer. He remembered his grandfather as being a very charismatic, free-spirited man that somehow knew everybody for twenty square miles – and got along well with most all of them. Noah admired him. Rose adored him. When she was a young girl, he used to tease her and make her laugh until she rolled around on the ground. The melancholia set in. Rose had ended up naming his son after his grandfather.

"Mizz Rose says she still can't think of your grandpappy Eli without smilin'," Mixy added.

A few moments later, Noah determined, "God has every right to be mad at me."

"Maybe this is your punishment, Master Noah," Mixy cogitated. "God has sent you back up here to help out us more helpless folks." He was smiling.

"Maybe so," Noah admitted. He couldn't help but smile along with Mixy over the odd way things can sometimes end up.

"Still," Mixy offered, "if you can use a little money..."

"No," Noah responded firmly, "I don't need your money. I got a little saved up myself. Letting me stay in your barn is plenty enough. And besides that, this is really my fight more than anyone else's around here. And I think Jared Sowers is going to find out that he hasn't got what it takes. You'll see."

"All I know is that when Mizz Rose finds out what all I been up to, she is going to be hoppin' mad at me," Mixy said, thinking of the more immediate problems they faced. He stuck his little fingers in the corners of his mouth and let out a shrill whistle. A few minutes later the long eared donkey showed up with the sheep in tow. Mixy shut his critters up in a fenced pasture and the men went back to the barn for a smoke before turning in for the night.

Noah had barely crawled into his bedroll when Mixy showed up with an extra quilt for him. "It's a clear night," he explained. And as he was leaving, his voice came out of the darkness: "Master Noah, thank you for what you said to me about Mizz Sarla, that's a real nice thought."

Pulling the quilt over him, Noah cozied up on his soft grass pallet. He liked sleeping in barns once he got over his fear of mice he'd had as a little boy. It was his older cousins that had put that fear in him in the first place. In the summers when they were allowed to sleep in the barn, they wanted to be rid of the little kids. And the thought of mice running over you while you were sleeping did the trick for awhile. He looked for the stars through the roof slats, but they were gone – Mixy had nailed the shakes on that part of the roof.

It had been a full day and his mind grew weary. He could hear Mixy's sheep bawling at each other. It reminded him of the scraggly flock of sheep he'd seen running in the high breaks above Sowers's ranch. He lay in the dark listening, and after a little while all was still. Dunlavy and Pico seemed to think that Burt might have already murdered somebody since he showed up in these parts. What else could it have been that Burt had given Sowers? If he indeed had, what was the reason?

Images of the night Niles Whitehead died played back in his memory. There was no real reason for it either, other than stupidity. It could have easily blown on by if Noah had just let it go. In the dark chambers of his mind he knew the truth – and the truth was that he hadn't given Niles Whitehead a chance. Compared to Perry, Niles wasn't really all that bad and somehow Noah wished the lanky misfit was still hanging around.

Wally Pomeroy could be a problem. He could get real mean and liked to fistfight and would beat a man past the point that was necessary. The little bulldog of a man liked to hurt people. Wally would stick around as long as Perry did just to see what kind of crazy things Perry could come up with. But when it came to Mississippi, Noah had no idea what he was capable of. He should have asked Dunlavy when he had the chance.

The thought of Perry leaving the country stirred his mind. Noah Conklin had a sudden revelation: he didn't want to have to leave the Springwater Valley. And if Perry left the country Noah knew he would most likely go after him – at least for a while. For however long it took to shoot him. For some reason, Burt just didn't see the wrong in killing and Noah knew the best thing he could do was to see the scoundrel buried in the ground. He should just go get it over with before someone else had to die.

Once again, Noah caught himself trying to get to sleep with killing on his mind, and right then the thought of having to go away was unfathomable. Maybe he was just getting tired of wandering around. There was no doubt he was tired of the bloodletting though he was certain there would be more in store for him.

He found solace in the thought of Rose and Tater being close by and safe in their beds – at least for now. And as Noah drifted off to sleep he knew that this little part of the valley above the Snake River was where he would finally make his stand.

CHAPTER ELEVEN

The encampment on the Snake River that morning was like living in the clouds. Perry woke up shivering cold at first light and started to build the fire. The fog was settled in so heavy that everything was soaked including the kindling, and as a result the sputtering fire put out more smoke than heat. Usually he would kick Alice out of her bed to start the fire, but not that morning.

Leaning over to blow on the smoldering embers, Perry felt a sharp pang in his groin. He glanced down beneath his elk hide robe and discovered a large black and blue mark on the inside of his right thigh. Last night had turned out to be one hell of an ordeal, and shards of it were starting to come back to him. He had swilled a quart of whiskey single-handedly and wound up fighting with Alice over Little One. The Indian woman didn't want him humping with her young daughter anymore, and when he tried to anyway, she went after him with her war club. He examined the bruised area closer and came to the conclusion that she had caught him a pretty good one – and she wasn't too far off the mark either.

Then he remembered that he had punched Alice in the face and knocked her out. Perry could not summon much memory after the brawl except that he had awakened down by the river in the middle of the night naked and half froze on the hard cold ground.

The fire began to flare up so he threw on another piece of wood and when Alice heard him stirring around she poked her head out from under her blankets. The disheveled Indian looked like she had been kicked in the head by Perry's big mule. Both her eyes were blackened and her nose was red and swollen. She stayed beneath the covers and glared at him a moment before turning her back to him. Beside Alice, nestled safely under the blankets, was a lump where Little One was all curled up in a ball still sound asleep.

As Perry gazed at the motionless forms he thought it would probably be best if he was up and gone before Alice had a chance to look at herself in a mirror – but the damp chill of the night had settled in his joints and made it hard for him to get up and moving. He had been in a foul mood for the last few days anyway, and now he was even angry at the weather. Just yesterday a storm had blown through and let loose a thunderbolt that struck the rim of the coulee directly above his camp. Now the sudden drop in the temperature seemed to help make up his mind with a shiver that he would be gone from the Snake River canyon long before the snows came. He already planned on setting up a winter camp at a hot spring he knew of down along the Bear River among the herds of migrating elk.

The warmth of the fire began to drive the cold from Perry's bones, and as he heated up his buckskins he started to dwell on Noah Conklin. The news from Wally Pomeroy that Noah had skipped the country still puzzled him. Perry couldn't help but think back to when he took a shot at him along the river, but couldn't convince himself that was the cause of Noah's sudden departure. He knew his adversary had more backbone than that. Noah had been shot at on more than one occasion in the past, and it had never deterred him from what he had set out to do. And Burt Perry was certain that Noah Conklin felt like he had a personal vendetta to settle for the two Indians that were hanged last autumn in Wyoming.

What was it that caused Noah to just pick up and leave? Perry pulled on his pants and wondered why Sowers needed him anymore now that Noah was gone from the mix. That's what he needed to go find out. The steam from the warm buckskins rolled off his back as he wandered into the brush to catch the mule.

By the time he was saddled up and ready to leave, the fog was beginning to lift off the river and Alice and Little One were awake and sitting up in their bed. Perry was troubled by what he saw and rode over to them.

Little One must have told her mother how her face looked, because Alice was staring up at him like she was plotting his demise. They both had on their bright gingham cotton dresses that they only wore when they had a chance to go to church.

"That's what you get for coming after me," Perry stated. It was his way of apologizing. Then he warned her, "And if you're thinking of running away, you just go ahead. But if you ain't here when I come back, I'm going to track you down and put you under. Then it will just be me and Little One with you out of the way," he added, tapping the mule in the flanks and riding off.

The sight of Alice and Little One in their fancy white woman's garments was reason for concern. Those store bought dresses were like treasures to the Indian women and they had slept in them like they were nightshirts. To Perry it was a sign of bad medicine. He twisted around in the saddle and scoffed at Alice. There was no fear in those bloodshot eyes of hers that morning – just vengeance. He was going to have to keep a keen watch on her for awhile. Alice could be a real scrapper when she wanted.

The mule lunged as it climbed up the steep terrain above the river sending a sharp stab of pain through Perry's groin. He cursed his squaw under his breath. She had taken a vicious swipe at his manhood, and if she'd cracked him there he probably wouldn't be able to walk, let alone ride. And if she had knocked him on the head she would have surely split his skull. His head already felt terrible from drinking too much whiskey.

Reaching the high ridges that overlooked the river canyon, Perry stopped to rest in the warm sun. The dense fog had lifted high above the pale green water like a long cloud that ran the breadth of the land from east to west. Instinctively he scanned the surrounding country for anything that moved, and though the landscape was void of life there was something always pestering his mind. Somewhere out there was Noah Conklin – and he could be almost anywhere. Perry knew he would be looking back over his shoulder as long as Noah was alive. He grunted at the thought.

In the sky above him, a large flock of Canada geese broke formation in pandemonium, honking at each other to get out of the way. They rode through the air on bent wings down toward the waters of the Snake River. Winter was on its way. The best thing Perry could do was to move on and give Alice something else to think about – just tend to business for awhile. Life on the trail would help calm things down between them. He figured he would even leave Little One alone for a short spell.

When Perry trotted his mule into the back yard of Sower's ranch he found Wally Pomeroy sitting in a chair in the front of the bunkhouse sipping coffee and soaking up the morning sun. Old Jules was peering out a back window of the main house.

"Seems like you're out and about kind of early," Wally said as Perry reined up. He noticed that the big buffalo hunter grimaced with pain as he swung down out of the saddle, and asked, "What happened to you?"

"Me and that squaw bitch of mine got in a fight," Perry offered. Wally was the one man around that Perry could confide in. The simple man had grown up hard and mostly on his own the same as Perry. Wally Pomeroy had spent several years in prison for killing a man in a fist fight, and he wasn't a bit squeamish at the sight of blood. "What have you been up to lately?"

"Twiddling my thumbs mostly," Wally stated. He failed to mention to Perry that he had been herding cows around. "I really don't think Mister Sowers has much of a plan going around here."

"Well, he'd better get one," Perry said, "because I'm about to pull up stakes."

"Well, goddamn it," Wally said, disgustedly, tossing out a swirl of coffee grounds from the bottom of the cup, "this whole goddamn mess is falling apart. Dunlavy and Fernando took out of here at the crack of dawn this morning. They were talking about heading down to California. If you go and quit, that just leaves me."

"Them two is useless anyhow," Perry reasoned, "they got no stomach. Is there anymore of that coffee?"

Just then Mississippi stepped out of the bunkhouse and the sight of Perry prompted him to wipe the sleep from the corners of his eyes and smooth out his mustache. Mississippi had seen Perry around from time to time, but had never been introduced to him or ever talked to him. He had heard early on from Niles Whitehead that the huge grizzled man had a tendency not to be very friendly.

"I guess you always got him to back you up," Perry muttered.

"Hey, Mississippi," Wally called out, pitching the cup to the young sleepy eyed cowboy, "go bring my friend Burt here a cup of that coffee."

With one hand Mississippi snatched the cup out of midair and ducked back inside.

"He sure can talk a good one," Wally commented, half under his breath.

"Come on," Perry told Wally, "I'm gonna give the mule some water." Perry's groin was beginning to ache from standing around and he needed to try to walk off the soreness. The big man favored one leg as he led his mule toward the main house.

"Did Alice do that to you?" Wally asked as he fell in beside Perry.

"She whacked me with her war club," Perry reported candidly. "She almost got me in the balls, too."

"How come you was fighting with her?" Wally quizzed.

"She don't want me humpin' with Little One anymore. At all." Perry explained. Just thinking about the whole situation made him shake his head with wonder. "Like it makes some kind of difference...as if anybody really gives a good goddamn. Well, I blacked her eyes for her over it. Maybe she learned her lesson."

"Yeah, well still," Wally cautioned him, "you'd better watch yourself over that kind of thing." He had always taken a shine to Alice, but knew enough to side with Perry in such matters. "That Indian will slit your gizzard while you're snoring. I don't have to tell you how mean them squaws can get, especially when they drink a little snake venom."

"I got half a notion to take that fat sow back to her own people so they can cut off her nose," Perry scowled. He decided not to tell Pomeroy about Alice and Little One sleeping in their store bought dresses. Perry hadn't figured out yet what that was all about, but he was almost certain that sooner or later he would learn what their fancy pajamas was suppose to signify.

"You ought to just get rid of her," Wally remarked. It sounded like he knew what he was talking about. "I'm telling you she will try to do you harm over that kind of deal...it's a mothering thing."

"She does anything stupid," Perry declared, "and I'll get rid of her for good. The problem is I want to keep Little One. She ain't mean and lazy like her ma and she can hunt and fish like nothing you ever saw. I mean she's a lot of fun to have around. You know what I mean."

"I can imagine," Wally Pomeroy commented, putting his hands in his pockets. "It's too bad you can't do something with Alice, that way you would naturally be stuck with Little One all alone. Where the hell else would that young one have to go? She would have to stay with you to get by. How many goddamn white lawmen do you know out in the territories that give a hoot or a holler about what happens to some squaw Indian? Why, you proved that down in Medicine Bow. You can do what you want with them two."

When they arrived at the trough, Perry splashed the surface of the water with his hand to attract the mules attention. The animal sipped at the water while Perry pondered Pomeroy's words. Wally was right; Little One had never really lived around any normal people as far back as he could recall. The young Indian didn't even know her own tribe anymore. There was no one else to look after the uncivilized girl except for him and Alice.

The subject of Perry's family problems fell silent when Mississippi came around the house balancing a cup of coffee out in front of him as he walked. "Here comes Mister Sowers," Mississippi said, nodding toward the house.

Jared Sowers stood on the porch, watching the men who were gathering in his front yard. He was putting on a pair of riding gloves and was all spruced up like he had some kind of official business to take care of. He wore a dark brown Spanish style suit like a lot of the gentlemen ranchers of Texas seemed to prefer, and as he came down the porch stairs toward them, the rows of jinglebobs on his ornate spurs rang out on his heels.

"That's how I'm going to look someday when I own my own ranch" Mississippi stated, handing the cup to Perry.

"He looks like he's on his way to a Mexican pig roast," Perry suggested, chortling at his own wit and sipping from the cup. The coffee was warm and strong and Perry hoped it would help ease some of the pounding inside his skull.

"I've heard that Noah Conklin is back in the valley," Sowers announced as he approached them. "What do any of...

"Where'd you hear that?" Perry interrupted. The news did more to clear his head than the bitter coffee.

"From that worthless pair I ran off this morning," Sowers declared. "They had it in their minds that Mister Conklin is joining sides with the immigrants and they didn't want any part of this anymore. So I fired them both."

That made sense to Perry when he thought about it. Dunlavy and Fernando were always friendly toward Noah, so in order to avoid the possibility of a fight with him, they would have to get out of the way. "They might have got it right," Perry concluded. "He might be watching out for the squatters."

"How do the rest of you feel?" Sowers asked. "Is Noah Conklin a problem for anyone else?"

"He ain't a goddamn problem for me," Perry responded sharply, and Pomeroy and Mississippi quickly agreed with him. "Well good," Perry proposed with a scowl, "maybe now we can get down to some goddamn business around here before the snow flies."

"Do you have any suggestions, Mister Perry?" Sowers queried. "We haven't chased off one farmer yet, and I've lost three hired hands all because of Mister Conklin."

"We need to find out where Noah is staying," Perry stated. "That's the first thing we need to do."

"And that's precisely what I intend to do, Mister Perry," Sowers said. "I'm riding down to the hotel and into town to see if anyone has seen him around."

"I doubt you'll find him that way," Perry told him. "Noah won't be living out in plain sight. I'd say you're going to have to try to flush him out."

"And how do I do that?" Sowers was puzzled.

"I'm not real sure right now," Perry was pondering away. "I already burned down that old darkie's barn. And what good did that do?"

"None at all," Sowers lamented. As far as he was concerned, the only thing the razing of Mixy's barn accomplished was the canceling of the grange dance and a chance to see Rose socially.

"I guess maybe you should have burnt down his house, too," Mississippi suggested, grooming his mustache with his fingers.

Pomeroy glanced at the young man like he didn't know what he was talking about.

"Then he wouldn't still have a place to live," Mississippi explained to him.

"Well why don't you just go help yourself now," Perry jumped in. "Just what the hell would you know about burning down a goddamn house, huh?"

"I have a couple uncles that are experts at getting rid of the darkies back home in Mississippi," he bragged. "I been to a lynching."

"But you ain't never really done none of this by yourself?" Perry challenged.

"Mister Sowers," Mississippi insisted, "I'll do it if that's what you want done."

"If that's what you want to do," Sowers reasoned, "I guess I don't see any harm in it."

"Then I'll do it tonight," Mississippi said, licking his upper lip. He was thrilled at the chance to gain some respect from the seasoned hands. "All I need is some kerosene and a pillow case. I'll pull a night raid on him and burn him out. I'll bet you it's been a long time since that old darkie's seen a real night rider." And he strode away, talking to himself, "There's things in the barn I can use for a torch."

"I'm not going with him," Wally stated firmly. He felt there was something cockeyed about the whole idea.

"Sounds like he won't need your help anyhow," Sowers agreed and sent Wally off to saddle his horse. Wally Pomeroy was a pretty fair wrangler – he had never met a horse he couldn't match wits with. And though he wasn't quite as strong as a horse, Wally was quicker.

"What do you really think about Mississippi's plan?" Sowers knew that burning old Mixy out would most likely stir things up good. "I could still call it off if I needed to. How much trouble could it cause?"

"None for you if you blamed it on Lester Dunlavy," Perry suggested, digging in his saddlebags. "That little skunk will be long gone by the time they start looking for him." Gnawing on a twist of chewing tobacco, he added, "And besides that if they was to catch up to him, it would be his word against yours."

Sowers scrutinized Perry as the grizzled old hunter packed a wad of tobacco into his cheek with a grimy finger. He was amazed that such a crude man could come up with such an idea. Sowers thought it was a stroke of genius, he didn't realize it was just Perry's natural way of thinking. This plan was getting better by the minute. He'd been looking for an excuse to go see Rose and this might be just the thing. He could ride on over and show his concern and assure her that he had nothing to do with any of it. He'd even offer to help out if he had to.

"I've been meaning to get up to see the widow Rose," Sowers boasted. "Naturally I would have to go and see about something like that. She's probably been wondering about me by now anyway." He tried to make it sound like she was interested in him.

"It just might work," Perry submitted, spitting. "If Noah is working for the squatters, that just might flush him out. If it matters to him, he'll show himself."

Sowers saw Wally come around the house leading his horse. "Well I'll make sure Mississippi does the task then," he told Perry, "even if I have to send Wally along, too."

"He won't go with him," Perry said bluntly, "he already told you that."

"But he works for me," Sowers contended.

"That don't matter none. Besides, it'd be better if he didn't go along," Perry explained, "you might find Wally handy when it comes time to deal with Noah. He ain't got the sense to be scared of nothing."

"When the time comes, how are we going to deal with him?" Sowers asked.

"Its hard to say," Perry spit a stream of tobacco juice, "but I'm sure we'll know what to do...when the time comes." He flashed the rancher a big rotten tooth grin, and bragged loud enough for Wally to hear, "Don't you fret about it though, Mister Sowers, and I'll bring you a set of fresh ears."

That kind of open talk bothered Sowers and he didn't waste any time saddling up. "How will you know when I do find him?"

"I'll be starting to check with you every couple of days," Perry assured him. He took one last swallow of the cold coffee, flung the last of it out and tossed the cup to Wally. "And when you do find out where Noah is, make sure Wally here knows the way."

Perry and Wally and the mule stood together watching as Jared Sowers pranced his big white horse down between the rows of white fence leading into the valley.

"When we find Noah, me and you will go take care of goddamn business." Perry grimaced as he climbed up on the mule. "What do you think?"

"You come and get me," Wally called out as he quick stepped it toward the outhouse.

Sitting atop his mule, Perry took a minute to survey the Springwater Valley. The blue-gray smoke from the breakfast fires still hung in the cool morning air and he let his eyes roam along the stretch of trees that lined the banks of the creek. The entire valley could be scouted out in a days time – it was mostly open prairie that didn't offer many places to hide. And somewhere down in the peaceful looking valley was Noah. Perry knew he was going to have to figure out a way to get Noah to come to him. He watched as Sowers rode out onto the valley floor and he could sense that it was finally starting. He felt anxious to get back to the familiarity of his own camp, but at the same time he didn't feel up to having to deal with Alice.

Perry reined the mule around and started out at a slow walk. He rode across the back yard and Mississippi sauntered out of one of the barns holding a gunny sack.

Perry grunted, knowing that everyone would find out soon enough if the young hand was blowing wind.

"Master Perry," Jules yelled at him from the back steps. He was holding a quart bottle of rum in each hand. "Don't you want to take your ration?"

The demon spirits was the last thing on his mind right then, but Perry packed them in his saddlebags and nodded at Jules and rode back out the way he came.

By the time he reached the bluffs that overlooked the river, his skull was throbbing from the spent whiskey and a dull ache had settled in his groin. Perry undid his pants and opened them wide hoping the fresh air or the warm sunlight would make it feel better. Then he pulled one of the quart bottles out of his saddlebags and uncorked it. He reckoned that the way he felt, a couple swallows of the sweet rum couldn't make matters worse.

The skies above the Snake River were full of geese. Perry looked back to the north to see if that's where they were all coming from, but couldn't tell. Below the high white wisps of clouds there were vees of honking geese flying in all different directions. He drank a swallow of the rum and thought of Little One and how skilled she was at hunting and fishing. The Indian girl could catch a goose alive and fish seemed to come to her. What did they need Alice for, anybody can boil meat and make fry bread. Wally was right.

Lurking in the back of his mind was the fact that Little One was getting harder to catch and her squaw mom wouldn't serve her up any more. If Alice kept getting in the way he would crack her skull with a river boulder and make it seem like a mishap to fool Little One. He'd been tempted to do it before, but she had better not tempt him again, or else he'd have the girl all to himself. Perry cursed Alice under his breath, swearing that he wasn't going to give her a chance to seek vengeance on him.

The distant boom from a hunter's shotgun echoed along the bluffs. The sound drew Perry's attention to the miles of small coulees and dense thickets along the banks of the river. The Snake River canyon offered a myriad of secluded campsites. For that reason alone, Perry had a hunch that Noah must be camped out somewhere along the river, same as him. And as troubling as that thought was, he would have much rather faced Noah right then than Alice.

A cold breeze came down the canyon from the east. Perry took one last gulp of rum and put the bottle away. He examined his wound again and frowned at what he saw – his flesh had turned a few different shades of yellows and purples. And for the first time he noticed that the skin had broken open and there was a trickle of fresh blood. Letting out a deep breath, he did his pants up and urged the mule down the trail. Maybe he could get Little One to put a poultice on it – Alice couldn't object to that. As far as Burt Perry was concerned, she didn't have the right to take Little One away from him.

CHAPTER TWELVE

It was barely light out when Noah first woke up. He burrowed deeper into the warmth of the haystack and dozed off again. The next time he opened his eyes, bright sunlight was filtering through the cracks in the barn and Mixy was standing over him.

"Master Noah, that boy has took off in that wagon already," there was panic in Mixy's voice, "and Mizz Rose is gonna be down here before you know it." The look on his face suggested it was already too late.

Noah couldn't make himself wake up fast enough. He sat straight up in his bedroll and started pulling on his pants. If Rose was going to show up, he at least wanted to have some pants on.

"I don't know what's goin' on here," Mixy added and hurried off toward his cabin.

In the time it took Mixy to make a sprightly trip to his cabin and back, Noah was dressed and his bedroll was concealed in the pile of hay.

"Are you all ready?" Mixy was carrying a tin cup and a skillet. "I'll go with you a little ways." He handed the cup of coffee to Noah, but hung on to the skillet of fried salt pork.

Noah flung his saddlebags over his shoulder and followed Mixy out of the barn. The old man hustled along holding the skillet out behind him offering the pieces of meat, but Noah was unable to keep up without spilling the coffee – and it almost felt as though Mixy was luring him into the plum thicket with a few strips of salt pork in a frying pan. Noah looked back over his shoulder, grateful that Rose was nowhere to be seen.

When they were well secluded in the dense thicket, Mixy stopped so that Noah could catch up. "What would you need a shovel for to cut firewood?"

"What do you mean?" Noah started on the meat.

"And that's the other thing" Mixy considered, shaking the skillet at Noah. "He says he wants to go cut firewood by his self. Maybe he can fool his own mamma, but he ain't foolin' me. I'm tellin' you he's gonna go and get his self into trouble."

"What are you talking about?" Noah asked, chewing.

"I'm talkin' about Tater," Mixy explained, "he's suppose to be cuttin' firewood, but he took my shovel with him. Do you know what that boy is up to?"

Noah shook his head, wondering what difference it made if Tater took a shovel along or not.

"He's up in the pines," Mixy pointed with the skillet, "and I'm suppose to tell you that he's gonna wait for you there."

"Where?" Noah looked around. From inside the thorny maze he couldn't tell which way was which.

Mixy pondered for a moment rubbing his chin, and then his eyes lit up and he inquired, "Do you remember where we cut the logs for that old barn of yours?"

"I'm sure I can find it again," Noah assured him. He remembered it was at the head of the valley, not far from where Tater and the other men had just cut the cedar to make the roof shingles for Mixy's new barn.

"He says he'll mark the trail for you," Mixy relayed the last of Tater's message to Noah as he set the skillet on the ground beside the foot path. "Just leave those things here when you finish eatin' and I'll fetch them after awhile. I need to get back home before Mizz Rose comes huntin' for me." He was distraught.

"Mixy, you stop worrying now," Noah tried to ease the old man's mind. "I'll go meet up with Tater and see what I can find out for you."

Mixy started back and Noah called after him, "And I promise I won't let him get into any trouble."

Noah finished his stand up breakfast and went to the glade where he saddled Pecos. But instead of heading toward town as he had originally planned, he rode out to find Tater, following the wagon tracks and the route that had been marked for him.

Every now and then Tater had taken the time to stop and stack up a couple of rocks in the middle of the road. But the most obvious trail to follow was the sprinkling of shells from the half dozen or so hard-boiled eggs and the chewed cores from a couple of apples that the boy had disposed of along the way.

When Noah reached the head of the valley, he rode along the edge of the forest until he came across an arrow of rocks laid out on the ground that pointed the way into the woods. He reined up for a moment and gazed out over the quiet land. The sun was beginning to burn through the morning haze and he could see two big white specks that were Jared Sowers' barns up in the foothills to the east, and in the distance to the south a bank of gray clouds laid in the river canyon. Noah tried to locate the cluster of buildings that made up the little town of Springwater, but they were too far away. As he yawned, Noah reminded himself that less than an hour ago he was still snug in the haystack dreaming about things he could no longer remember.

He longed for a pouch of real tobacco and a pint of decent whiskey, and the only place around to get such items was beyond his sight. He hoped there would still be time before the sun went down again to make it to the other end of the valley. After all, it was early yet and it felt like it was going to be a nice day.

A few hundred feet back in the woods, Noah spotted the wagon parked in an area heavy with deadfall, and it was already half loaded with cordwood. The old mare had been unhitched from the wagon and was tied to the limb of a tree. Tater was busy cutting off the end of a log with a one-man buck saw – and there was a cigarette hanging from his mouth. When he saw Noah coming, he stopped sawing, took one last puff from the cigarette and ground the butt out in the dirt with his boot heel.

"I guess you found my markers okay," Tater said. He was flushed and sweaty from the hard labor.

"What's that undertaker's name?" Noah asked. He noticed a short-handled shovel leaning up against a fallen log as he stepped down from the saddle.

"Mister Troost," Tater replied. "What about him?"

"Mister Troost could have tracked you down if he'd just followed all them eggshells and apple cores," Noah reasoned. And as he tied Pecos to a branch, Noah began to think that perhaps Mixy was onto something. Why had Tater found it necessary to unhitch the old mare? It didn't appear as though it was going to take all that long to get a load of wood.

"How long have you been here, anyway?" Noah asked. He picked up a length of cordwood lying in the nearby weeds and put it in the wagon.

"I can get those," Tater insisted.

"Want me to saw for awhile then?" Noah offered.

The expression on Tater's face told Noah that the young student of the dime novels never suspected that a man who's livelihood was the gun would know anything about firewooding. Noah liked putting up firewood, it gave him the time to reflect on life for awhile.

"Back in Missouri, when I was a lot younger than you are," Noah started out, "I used to have to cut cordwood with a bowsaw. And I don't mean this soft juniper or pine, I'm talking about hickory and oak and hedge, wood that's hard as a rock. If you ever spend a winter down in Wyoming, make darn sure you lay in a real good supply, too. It's wintertime six months out of the year around the Yellowstone.

"I'd roll myself a cigarette if you had any extra tobacco until I can get to the mercantile," he added.

"What's Missouri like?" Tater took a pouch out from under the wagon seat and handed it to Noah. "Mom says that where she grew up in Kansas, it's too hot to sleep at night sometimes, and that the rivers are all muddy."

"That's about how I remember Missouri, too," Noah replied as he worked on the cigarette. A fragment of time from out of the past crept in and he recalled how much Rose used to like hearing the cicadas droning up in the elm trees on those humid summer nights.

"You see that big ol' buckskin over there?" Noah continued his original thought. He pointed at a dead tree that had weathered out of its bark and was now a silvery spire amidst the boughs of dark green. "Those are the kind the woodcutters look for if they are still good and solid. But you ought to have a two-man saw to cut that one down."

"Mixy's got one hanging on the wall in his cabin," Tater informed him, looking up at the top of the tree. "He keeps it sharp as a razor, too."

The mention of Mixy's name reminded Noah to ask, "What'd you bring that shovel for?"

The only explanation Tater could come up with was a blank stare. Noah tossed the tobacco pouch to the boy, waiting for an answer.

"Would you go look at something with me?" Tater implored. "It's kind of hard to explain. You'd almost have to see it in person to understand what's going on."

"Where?" Noah asked, striking a match on the iron rim of the wagon wheel.

"Just up in the hills a little ways," Tater said. "It wouldn't take very long."

Blowing out a cloud of smoke, Noah agreed to accompany his son on the secretive journey. After all, he'd told Mixy that he would try to find out what the boy was up to. Perhaps the old man's suspicions were justified. Besides that, Noah's own personal curiosity had been aroused.

Tater put the saw in the wagon and slipped a bridle on the old mare. He laid a small blanket across the horse's back and swung up on her without a saddle. Then he leaned down and grabbed the shovel.

"I know a short cut," the boy declared. There was a spark of excitement in his eyes, like he was on his way to raid the local watermelon patch. He rode off through the forest with the reins in one hand and the shovel in the other – and he had his gun belt strapped on over his bibbed overalls.

After a little while of winding through the trees dodging low hanging branches, they came to the marsh where the cedars grew. They rode past the ancient grove of cedars and around the clumps of cattails to a small clearing by a pool of open water. A pair of noisy mallards were spooked into the sky.

"There's been a herd of elk in here," Tater observed, pointing around the ground with the shovel. Elk droppings were scattered everywhere.

They left the clearing and followed the game trail single file up into the foothills. Free of the wagon, the old mare was quick and agile and Tater rode the bareback horse as good as an Indian scout. The boy knew his way around the forested hills like he was in his own backyard, and he set a steadfast pace.

They crossed over two windswept ridges and came to a small creek in the bottom of a ravine and they followed the water down out of the trees and across a narrow gully that lay between a pair of blunted hills. At the far end of the gully was a large pond. They reined up near the dam where the pond flowed into the new channel that ran along the hillside, and eventually onto Jared Sowers's rangeland.

"Mister Sowers has dammed it up here so he can steal this water," Tater submitted, agitated. "He filed for the water rights all legal and proper, but most people say it's just plain stealing. There's an old man and his wife that lives down where the creek used to run and he had to stop raising horses when he lost his water. Mister and Missus Armstead is their names, and I don't think that's right. What do you think?"

Gazing around, Noah thought of his brief encounter with the Armsteads – and that the old-timer had even complained to him about the water rights. "So, what do you intend to do," Noah inquired, "dig the dam back out with that shovel?"

The earthen dam was about four feet wide and nearly a hundred feet long. The pond itself didn't appear to be very deep, but still, the dam held back quite a large amount of water that came within a couple feet of the top.

"I would if I could," the boy vowed. "No, I'll show you what I've been planning to do."

They rode around to the other side of the pond and got down off their sweaty horses and walked out on the narrow dam until they were standing above the original streambed that was bone dry.

"Mister Sowers should at least have to share this creek with Mister Armstead," Tater proposed, stomping the blade of the shovel in the dam. "If I dug a little ditch right across here it would let some of the water run down the creek again. That way, Mister..." The boy noticed that Noah was grinning at him. "What?"

"The way Mixy was talking," Noah chuckled. "He just about had me believing that you took that shovel to bury a dead body or something."

"Why, what did he tell you?" Tater seemed perturbed.

"He said you were going to get into trouble if you weren't careful," Noah stated.

"Well, even Mixy says it's not right what has happened to Mister Armstead," Tater maintained. "So you don't think its a good idea, either?"

"Well..." Noah considered. "I'd have to think about it some." He started across the dam, surveying the project as he went.

"Can I ask you a kind of personal question?" Tater tailed along.

"I 'spose," Noah said.

"That day at the river when we were shooting and then went swimming," Tater mused. "I was wondering, how did you get that scar on your stomach?"

"I got shot by an Apache Indian." Noah realized it was most likely the answer his son anticipated.

"What'd you do to him?" Tater challenged.

"Not a thing," Noah said.

"So, he shot you and you didn't do anything back to him?" Tater was perplexed.

"I ended up killing him," Noah admitted somberly.

"Well, I don't blame you," the boy concluded, "I'd say he had it coming."

"But not for shooting me," Noah explained. "I killed him because he murdered some helpless settlers. That's why I went after him in the first place. It ain't like you think it is, boy. There ain't a bunch of fancy gunplay. It just happens. And I was damn lucky he didn't kill me, too."

"How come Indians are mean?" Tater pondered.

"Most of them aren't," Noah assured him as they arrived at the end of the dam where the water was flowing out. "At least the ones I've got to know weren't. Most of them are as nice as anybody else, and funny – they got their own strange way of looking at things."

Noah continued on along the berm of dirt that had been excavated from the new channel. "There's not all that much water running out of here," he observed. "I'm not sure you can let out any more without drying up this one."

"The way I see it," Tater reasoned, "some water's better than none at all."

"And all I'm saying is it might be trickier than you realize," Noah advised him.

They followed the scant creek around the hillside until the Springwater Valley came into view below them. The whitewashed grange stood out on the low promontory in the center of the valley. There were a half dozen patchwork homesteads strewn about the valley floor, including Lewis Morrey's small farm. Far to the south, silent flocks of geese flew in dark strings above the river as the bright gray fog bank drifted high in the sky to be melted away by the heat of the sun.

With the little stream of water gurgling at his feet, it was hard for Noah to imagine that anything other than peace could ever prevail in a place of such beauty.

"What do you think we should do?" Tater wondered.

"You sure you want to do this?" Noah questioned.

"I think it's only right," Tater affirmed. "Don't you?"

Just then Noah didn't want to have to think about right or wrong. He didn't care what Sowers had up his sleeve or that Dunlavy was planning to leave. And he even told himself that it didn't matter what Burt Perry was doing. But taking back some water could turn out to be the diversion Noah had been looking for – it might just give everyone something else to think about for awhile.

"Why not," Noah reasoned, starting back toward the dam. "It will probably be awhile before he even realizes that someone has been up here letting out some water."

"It runs across the main trail down by the hotel," Tater reminded him. "I bet that by tomorrow everybody in Springwater will most likely be talking about it."

"I doubt that," Noah surmised. "As dry as that creek bed is it might take days to soak in that far. The little bit there is to let out right now, it might not start going good again until the spring thaw."

Tater wasted no time getting started on digging a narrow ditch across the top of the dam. "This won't take very long," he remarked, looking around nervously.

"I bet your mom's still upset with me?" Noah quizzed as he looked on.

"I guess so," Tater replied, focused on the task at hand.

"Why, what does she say about me?" Noah delved.

"Nothing," the boy assured him. "I don't think she has any idea that you're still around. All she said was that she hopes you go away before you cause any more trouble."

Noah wished he hadn't asked about Rose – the truth was burdening. He let out a sigh of despair and stepped across the ditch. "I'll go keep an eye on the other stream."

"Noah, I can't talk to her about you," Tater said, pausing for a moment. "She doesn't know that I know about you...I mean that you are my dad. And besides that, she's really kind of mean to men. She especially doesn't like any of them that tries to hang around too much. I don't think it's your fault."

Noah walked away wondering who's fault it was, if not his. He figured Tater must still be naive about such matters between men and women. Matters of the heart. The boy obviously hadn't been through that labyrinth of life yet. He gazed back at his son who was busy tossing shovelfuls of dirt into the pond – intent on doing the right thing.

With Rose on his mind, Noah stopped at the mouth of the new channel and it took a minute for him to realize that the water had quit running. He turned around to yell at Tater and knew at once that something had gone wrong. The boy was trying to shovel dirt back into the ditch faster than he'd dug it out.

Noah hurried back to find a swift torrent of water pouring out of the pond and down the old streambed. The sides of the newly dug ditch were sloughing off and being swept away as muddy clouds. By now all Tater could do was stand and watch...there was no way to slow it down.

"I didn't think you were going to let out that much," Noah declared half teasing.

"I couldn't stop it," the boy exclaimed, white with fear. Moment by moment the gap widened and more water surged out.

While there was still time, Noah jumped across the ditch only to have the soil crumble beneath his feet. Tater quickly offered his hand and Noah was able to pull himself onto firm ground, but not before he got a boot wet. Simple logic compelled them both to retreat from the dam and they became lost in their own worlds of thought – mesmerized by the force of the water tearing at the dirt.

It only took a few minutes for the pond to breach a twenty foot hole in the dam and escape down the canyon like a Colorado flash flood. A flock of sage grouse were flushed out of the brush to higher ground. The water roared away picking up any loose debris that was in its path. Noah kept thinking of his conversation with

Mixy earlier that morning and could hardly keep from laughing.

"I don't think it's funny," Tater cautioned him. He looked like he was on his way to the gallows.

"You will someday when you look back on it," Noah enlightened him. "I just finished promising Mixy that I would make sure that you stayed out of trouble, but I guess it's a little late now. I didn't realize you were going to wreck the whole dam."

"It was an accident." Tater countered sharply. He wasn't the least bit amused. "When Mixy hears about this, he is going to know who did it." The boy took off toward his horse with urgent strides.

"Where are you going in such a hurry?" Noah quizzed, trying to keep from being left behind.

"Back to the wagon," Tater said. "Don't you think we ought to get out of here?"

"I think what we ought to do," Noah suggested, catching up to his son, "is ride down and make sure Mister and Misses Armstead didn't get washed away. And you probably ought to ditch that shovel for awhile."

This time Noah took the lead with Tater lagging a short distance behind. They rode in silence, inspecting the aftermath of the flood. The high water had left a myriad of pools and mud puddles behind that were still draining into the main stream that was now flowing.

"I bet you're right," Noah called out over his shoulder, "everybody will most likely be talking about this tomorrow." He continued to find the entire calamity quite entertaining.

Tater was trying his best to ignore the bantering. Noah had given him something else to dwell on besides the fact that he was going to have to face Mixy, who had been warning him a lot lately about stirring up more trouble: What if they found Mister and Misses Armstead drowned?

"I just wish that Lester Dunlavy could have been here to witness all of this. This is like something he'd do. Oh, and by the by," Noah slowed down so Tater could catch up to him, "I didn't come back here to cause your mom any trouble. And I never even knew that you existed."

"Why did you come back then?" Tater asked. He was miffed at Noah's lack of concern and rode on past, setting a vigilant gait.

The tone of the question caught Noah by surprise and he didn't have an immediate answer. He had used Burt Perry and Jared Sowers for an excuse, but he knew deep down it was the thought of seeing Rose again that was the real reason for his being there. The truth was, everything had turned out different than he had imagined – or hoped.

"I guess I thought I could help out," Noah finally considered, and called out after him. "Besides, there's a whole lot worse things that can happen in this world than a stupid dam breaking."

The canyon walls opened out onto the scrublands and the old worn out ranch came into sight. When they rode in, they discovered Mister Armstead stripped down to his underwear floundering around in the muddy creek. The hound lay in a near by puddle, its tail slapping the water as they reined up.

"Are you okay, Mister Armstead?" Tater queried. His imagination was such from worrying that when he first spotted Armstead in the creek, Tater would have sworn the old man was drowning. He kept looking around, hoping for any sign of Misses Armstead.

"Well, hello there laddie," Armstead greeted, craning up at them. His eyes were twinkling with joy. "Glory be, would you look at this. I wonder what would have caused this to happen?"

"It was an accident," Tater blurted out.

"That would be my guess, too," Noah quickly added, discreetly kicking his son's foot. "There must have been some sort of an accident."

"I'd say that the dam must've busted," the bent old man said, looking around like he had misplaced something. "You should've seen the way the water came down through here."

From the saddle, Noah and Tater saw Armstead's big wife coming up the road leading the rack of bones cow toward the barn that was more hazard than shelter.

"There's Misses Armstead," Tater announced with relief. The boy slapped his leg and the dog got up and shook off a spray of water to be patted on the head.

"Winifred lit out of here in all the commotion," Armstead stated.

Noah wondered for a moment if Armstead was talking about his wife or the cow. "I guess everything else is okay around here then?"

"At least for now," Armstead nodded. "You could hear it coming." He squinted up at Noah, still trying to remember where he knew him from. "I can't seem to remember your name, mister."

"I'm Noah Conklin," he told him.

Armstead stared right through Noah into the past and the pieces began falling into place in his mind, then his attention shifted to Tater. "Oh, then this is your boy," the old horse trader concluded.

Noah could have denied it, and most likely Tater would have understood why, but he didn't. He met his son's gaze and replied to the old man sitting in the creek, "Yes sir, he is."

CHAPTER THIRTEEN

The sun had wandered into the bright blue western skies by the time Noah arrived back at Mixy's. He wished he would have crossed paths with Dunlavy somewhere along the way, but he didn't. It had turned out to be a fairly exciting day and Noah was eager to tell someone about the events while they burned fresh in his memory. There was still enough daylight left for him to make it to the mercantile and back, but now he lacked the ambition.

Mixy was on the peak of the roof nailing fresh split cedar shakes along the ridge. He had already seen Tater pass by with the wagon load of firewood and was watching for Noah. He came down the ladder and followed Noah inside the barn – and soon found out what had happened.

"I told him to stay away from there," Mixy said, annoyed. He went over to where he could glare up the creek like he couldn't wait to see Tater again.

"Don't blame him too much," Noah reasoned, "it was, more or less, an accident. Besides, it just might keep some of them hired hands up on the hill busy for awhile." It would definitely make Dunlavy's decision to leave a lot easier. Building dams was hard labor. Noah was certain that the slacker would quit long before he became involved in any endeavor requiring that much effort.

"Still, trouble is trouble," Mixy argued. "There is already plenty enough to go around without stirrin' up more." What honestly bothered Mixy the most was the thought of Tater not minding him – and ending up in trouble with the law. "Me and Mizz Rose have preached our best sermons to steer that boy onto the right path."

"I 'spose it's as much my fault as it is his," Noah offered. "If there's a problem, I'll go and have a talk with Frank Canfield myself."

While Mixy contemplated the unknown consequences of the future, Noah fought the urge to interrogate him about Rose's visit. He was anxious to know whether or not his name was mentioned, but he remembered where his curiosity had gotten him earlier that day at the dam. He decided it was best to wait until Mixy brought it up.

That evening after dinner, Tater brought the shovel back down to Mixy's and leaned it up by the door of the cabin. The three of them gathered just inside the barn where they could keep an eye on the trail to Rose's. And Noah couldn't help but notice the scolding that his son was getting from Mixy's eyes.

"Well, it turned out to be a lot trickier than I thought it'd be," Tater announced with a frail smile. He had decided to adopt Noah's attitude and tried to make light of the whole incident.

With the images of the fiasco still clear in their minds, Noah and Tater were finally able to share the humor in it all. They were chuckling back and forth as they reminisced to Mixy about how fast the water escaped, and about how they found Mister Armstead sitting in the cold muddy water in his underwear, and that how the flash flood scared off their old cow – and they couldn't get the old Negro to crack a single smile.

"Ya'll just better hope that Mizz Rose don't find out what the pair of you have been up to," Mixy remarked, putting an end to the revelry. He shook his head at them, realizing that they were a lot more alike than he had ever imagined.

"The way I see it," Tater considered, "we're all squared up now. If Mister Sowers wants to burn down a man's barn, it cost him a washed out dam."

That angle hadn't even crossed Noah's mind, and he could tell that Mixy was mulling it over, too. The boy had come up with a good way to look at it.

"No real harm done then, I guess," Mixy said, rubbing his chin. He appeared satisfied by the thought of being avenged. "That is if they don't find out who done it."

"Outside of us three," Noah stated, "nobody really knows what happened."

"Then there will be nothin' more ever spoke of it," Mixy declared and spit on the ground at their feet.

"Nothing ever more," Tater affirmed, spitting on the ground, too. When Noah didn't respond, the boy quizzed him, "Well, are you going to pledge a oath of silence?"

Noah ended up swearing that he would never mention the subject again, and spit on the ground near their feet. He felt as though he'd just been initiated into some sort of secret society as he watched his son hurry off toward home.

When Tater reached the trees, he waved back at them and then he jumped up, like any boy would, and slapped at the low hanging tree branches.

The last dim shadows of the day ebbed away and the evening sky began to fill with bright twinkling stars. Noah walked out behind the barn to the edge of the prairie where he found himself in the middle of Mixy's menagerie. The small flock of sheep stood off a few yards bleating at him while the donkey came over and sniffed him up and down like a dog would.

With a whistle, Mixy summoned the critters and shut them in the barbed wire corral for the night. He then joined Noah out in the dusky light with an offering of smoke.

"It sure would be nice to have a fire," Noah wished aloud. There was a chill in the air since the sun went down. He used his last paper to roll a cigarette from the old man's special mixture.

"We could build one if you want," Mixy said.

"I don't 'spose I ought to be sitting around a fire this close to Rose," Noah submitted, "I wouldn't want to be casting any long shadows up her way."

"No," Mixy agreed, puffing on his pipe, distracted by the ghostly call of a hoot owl off in the distance. "We could have the first killin' frost come creepin' in on this kind of night."

The crisp air and the thought of winter made Noah want to change the subject. "Tater's a pretty good kid, ain't he?"

"Most of the time," Mixy said. "The both of you seem to get along just fine."

"Well," Noah said, letting out a deep sigh, "I do have to admit though, that Rose is right. He's too young to be getting involved in this kind of stuff."

"Yes, he is," Mixy concurred. "But I just wish that he minded better."

"He minds about the same way I did when I was his age. I was sneaking over to see Rose in the middle of the night trying to steal kisses from her through her bedroom window. Mixy, you want to know what the best part of this whole mess is?" Noah continued on before the old man had a chance to respond. "I liked Tater the first time I met him, before I even knew who he was. I've come to like him a lot. It's just too bad things aren't better between me and Rose, but I can't blame her for the way she feels."

"Give her time, Master Noah, and she'll come around," Mixy said.

"You think so?" Noah was dubious. "What does she have to say about me?"

"She don't like to talk about you much," Mixy replied, "But from what I've seen, womenfolks can be mighty forgivin'."

"I've known men who treated women terrible," Noah related. "Getting drunk all the time and whipping them, or always running off – and then somehow they can kind of ease their way back under the blankets with them just about anytime they want."

"They call them kind easy women," Mixy informed him. "And there ain't nothin' easy about Mizz Rose."

The hollow cry of the hoot owl drew their attention to the trees that lined the creek. A half moon had risen over the foothills to the east casting a faint blue glow across the land. Their eyes had become accustomed to the night and they looked in vain for the owl that was hidden somewhere in the deep shadows of the branches. Noah and Mixy started back toward the barn.

"I'm not sure that I would even know how to do it anymore, Mixy," Noah conceded.

"What's that, Master Noah?" Mixy asked.

"Live under the same roof with a woman," Noah divulged. "I've been thinking about it a lot for the last few weeks. I haven't spent more than a day or two here and there with any woman other than Rose. Seems like it used to just come natural back then."

There was a long pause, then Mixy insisted, "Why, I'm sure you could do it again if you had a mind to."

"I hope so," Noah said, "because lately there are times that the thought of growing old by myself scares me worse than the thought of death. I just wish there was a way to patch things up with her."

"Maybe you ought to go and talk to her again," Mixy suggested.

"And what would I say?" Noah was open to any advice the old Negro had to offer.

"Whatever you have to," Mixy stated.

"All we ever do is argue," Noah confided in him.

"All that means is there is still things that need to be settled." Mixy tried to encourage him.

"Nothing ever gets settled," Noah said. "I doubt she could ever find the time to forgive me."

"I'm tellin' you," Mixy declared, "lately Mizz Rose is havin' a hard time understandin' that some things just is because they is – and that's that."

"What do you mean?" Noah questioned.

"She's frettin' over just what's goin' on here," Mixy explained. "She's scared that you is still around the valley and that you'll be seein' Tater again."

"I 'spose I ought to go and try to talk to her some more," Noah relented. "When do you think would be the best time?"

"Whenever," Mixy told him, "but let me know when you is goin' to see her and I'll take the boy and go shoot some of them Canada geese that has been flyin' over. I don't believe Mizz Rose is ready to see you and him together yet. Do you like smoked goose?"

"Yes, I do," Noah assured him.

"That way, too," Mixy quipped, "her shotgun will be out of the house when you show up there."

CHAPTER FOURTEEN

When Noah turned in for the night, he closed the barn doors to try and trap whatever heat was left from the day. From his bedroll he stared into the pitch black. The idea of confronting Rose was discomfiting, even though Mixy seemed to think it would be alright. Noah wasn't sure he could ever make a woman happy anymore, even if he wanted to. Perhaps it was too late for him after all that he had witnessed in his life and been a part of. Maybe the best he could hope for now was that Rose didn't end up thinking any worse of him than she already did. He'd just have to wait and see how it went. See what fate had to offer.

Noah felt lost and he searched the darkness for the way. His eyes were heavy from the long day and his thoughts drifted away into slumber. Somewhere off in the distance he could hear the geese and the sheep. They were running toward him sounding the alarm and he was afraid that Rose was coming down the creek and she was going to find him. Noah tried to quiet the noisy lot, but it was too late – he could see Rose standing nearby cradling her shotgun in the crook of her arm.

The image jerked Noah awake and his instincts warned him at once that there was some kind of trouble lurking about. The geese and the sheep were still all riled up, and he could hear a horse tromping around close by. He listened intently as a solitary rider trotted alongside the barn. Noah quickly slipped his pants on and grabbed his gun belt. And as he made his way through the darkness he heard what sounded like a whiskey bottle being dropped on a rock.

"Hey," a voice yelled out and another bottle was shattered. "Are you in there?" The intruder was mumbling and chuckling to himself.

Noah didn't recognize the voice, and though the man's tone wasn't very friendly, he was certain it wasn't Burt Perry. He wondered for a second as he reached the door if maybe he was being too wary. Perhaps it was just one of the locals who had drunk himself belligerent and was paying Mixy a late night visit.

Cracking open the door, Noah saw someone sitting on a horse over near Mixy's cabin – and there was enough moon out to see that something was peculiar about the man's appearance. He was trying to figure out what it was when the rider struck a match and lit a torch that flared up in the darkness. Whoever it was that had come calling in the night had what looked like a flour sack over his head with holes cut in it to see out.

"You hear me, you old pickaninny," the hooded man called out. "You better stay put so I don't have to..."

"Hey!" Noah cried out, throwing open the door and stepping out of the barn. It was obviously not a neighborly call.

"God damn," the intruder uttered, jerking back on the reins as his horse was spooked by Noah. "I didn't know you'd be here."

"Do I know you?" Noah inquired. Now there was something about the voice that seemed familiar. The heavy smell of kerosene permeated the air.

"I'm not afraid of you," Mississippi announced, stripping off the hood so he could be plainly seen in the flickering torchlight. On the trip over, the young cowboy had sipped a half of a bottle of fruit brandy that Sowers had given him to ward off the evening chill.

"Mississippi?" Noah queried. "What the hell do you think you're doing?"

"This ain't no concern of yours" Mississippi stated, cocky and full of himself. "I came here to burn that old darkie out and that's what I'm doing."

"No, you're not," Noah cautioned him, his voice was stern and unwavering. He tightened his grip on the butt of his revolver. "You need to ride out of here right this second before you get yourself in trouble, boy."

Finding Noah at Mixy's farm had caught Mississippi completely off guard, but at the same time it seemed to be his big chance to earn some respect from Jared Sowers and Burt Perry and everybody else. The moment that he had played out in his mind so many times was upon him. In one swift motion Mississippi threw down the torch as a diversion while he slid off the rump of his horse to shield himself from Noah.

The move impressed Noah enough that he let the holster slip away from his pistol and fall to the ground. He was already in the process of pulling back the hammer when a bright flash of light came from behind the horse. He felt something smack his cheek and a thunderous report filled the darkness. The image of Mississippi was etched in his memory like a picture captured by lightning, and as Noah crouched down he fired into the image. He was momentarily blinded by the muzzle flash, but he heard the bullet knock the wind out of the young cowboy, followed by the sound of galloping hooves. The blasts of gunfire had frightened the horse off into the night. Mississippi gasped loudly for air, and then there was a span of pure silence. Noah stayed low to the ground and ready.

"I'm shot...I been shot...and I can't find my gun," Mississippi's voice came out of the stillness. It was soft and deliberate.

The torch had landed among the shards of broken bottles, and the flames fueled by the kerosene began to build on the corner of Mixy's cabin. The fire cast a dull yellow light, and Noah saw Mississippi was down on the ground. He stood up and moved toward him cautiously.

"Am I gonna die?" Mississippi asked.

Noah knew he was a silhouette in the firelight – a prime target for a bushwhacker. "Is there anybody with you?"

"No," Mississippi responded, "I came by myself. Will you help me find my gun and catch my horse so I can go home?"

"Can you get up?" Noah wondered.

Mississippi grunted a couple of times as he struggled to stand up. "No, I can't get up," he reported, and there was panic in his voice. "Am I dying?"

"I don't know," Noah answered. The light around them grew brighter as the fire began to creep up the wall of the log cabin. He picked up Mississippi's pistol and tucked it in the waistband of his pants. The front of the young cowboy's jacket was soaked dark with blood and Noah could see the reflection of the flames flickering in it.

"Mixy," Noah yelled out, "you better get out here."

The door to the cabin creaked opened, but Mixy seemed a bit reluctant to come out. Emerging slowly, he was much more concerned over the sight of Mississippi laying in the dirt than he was over the fact that the flames were climbing up the wall of his cabin.

"Master Noah, is you alright?" Mixy asked.

"I'm fine," Noah assured him.

It was getting more difficult for Mississippi to catch a breath and he let out a low groan.

"Oh, Master Noah," Mixy lamented.

"Mixy, you better go put that fire out before your house burns down," Noah instructed him. "Then bring your lantern out here so we can see how bad he's hurt."

"Oh, Master Noah," Mixy reiterated, hurrying off. He grabbed the shovel that had been left leaning against the front of the cabin and began throwing shovelfuls of dirt on the flames to smother them out.

Standing over Mississippi in the dark, Noah realized his cheek was smarting. He discovered a splinter of wood the size of a match stuck in him and he winced when he pulled it out. He wiped away the wet sticky blood with the back of his hand.

"Mississippi," Noah called out when he couldn't hear him breathing anymore.

"Do you think I could sleep here tonight?" Mississippi responded. "I'll find my horse in the morning." He sounded tired.

"I 'spose that would be okay," he agreed. Ever since Noah saw how much blood was pouring out of the young cowboy, he figured that Mississippi was most likely going to die – and just then there wasn't anything anybody could do about it. The dismal truth caused him to sigh.

"Mixy," he urged the old man to hurry.

When Mixy finally showed up with the lantern, he told Noah, "I couldn't hardly light the wick my hands are shakin' so."

"Well, just settle down," Noah reasoned. "None of this is your fault. Hold that light down here so I can see." He leaned over the young man who looked up at him almost peacefully, his eyes blinking slowly.

"Mamma," Mississippi suddenly uttered, like a lost little boy. He tried to raise up, looking past Noah with eyes that were glazed over in the golden light. Then he slumped back down and let out a deep breath.

The lantern handle squeaked as the light was jerked away. There was a shuffle of feet, and Mixy cried out, "No, Mizzy!"

Noah twisted around to find Rose glaring at him. She had come down the creek in her night clothes – a simple white housecoat that almost glowed in the dark – and she had her shotgun leveled at him. Mixy jumped in the way to prevent her from shooting. Everything had happened so fast that Noah forgot all about Rose and the possibility that she would come running.

A moment later, Tater bolted into the circle of light. He was wearing a striped nightshirt that looked like it had been sewn from old mattress ticking. He had his pistol with him, and his eyes were as big as saucers. The boy's jaw literally dropped open when he saw Mississippi sprawled on the ground next to a small pool of blood.

"It's Master Noah," Mixy told Rose, grabbing the barrel of the shotgun and aiming it away.

"What is this?" Rose was frantic. "What's going on here?"

"That man was tryin' to set my place on fire," Mixy quickly explained. "Master Noah had to stop him."

"What are you doing here?" she demanded of Noah.

He was tongue-tied. For an instant, with her long hair hanging loose Rose looked like she was sixteen years old again. And it suddenly dawned on Noah this was a lot like the vision he had of her around the bonfire that night when he ate the peyote. A chill ran through him that gave him gooseflesh.

"Mizz Rose, if it wasn't for Master Noah I don't know what..." Mixy intervened.

"Nobody asked him to show up here," Noah declared, pointing at Mississippi with his gun.

"So you shot him," Rose was incensed. When she bent down to get a better look, Mixy held the light closer for her.

"When he tried to shoot me," Noah argued.

"Is he dead?" Rose asked.

"I think he's probably dying," Noah admitted softly so Mississippi couldn't hear.

Tater was as still as a statue.

"Mississippi," Noah called out, like he was trying to wake him up. When there was no response, he stooped down to feel Mississippi's wrist.

"So you know him?" Rose queried.

"He's one of Jared Sowers' boys. I don't know what his real name is. He calls himself Mississippi." Noah looked up at her admitting somberly, "I can't feel no pulse."

Mississippi's eyes were still open and he appeared to be staring up at Rose.

Shaking her head, Rose condemned Noah with a single glance. "I don't want nothing to do with none of this," she stated bluntly. "Let's get home. This doesn't concern us."

Rose headed back up the path along the creek. Tater, who hadn't let out a peep the whole time he was there, followed her obediently.

"You go light the way for them," Noah insisted of Mixy. "And tell Tater that the first thing in the morning he needs to go get Frank Canfield."

"Yes sir," Mixy nodded, setting out at once.

The golden light of the lantern dimmed and blinked and then disappeared into the trees along the creek. So much for fate, thought Noah. Now look what had happened. He could not have imagined a more dreadful circumstance whereby Rose would find out he was staying at Mixy's.

"Mississippi," Noah blurted out loud enough to rouse most anyone. He would have been surprised to get any kind of response. It was all over and Noah was grateful that the young man didn't appear to have suffered very much. Of course he couldn't really tell what Mississippi had felt those last moments.

Noah still had the case of gooseflesh Rose had given him and he shivered in the dark silence. He went back to the barn to wait for Mixy, picking up his gun belt along the way. The events of the night began replaying over in his mind. It had all happened so fast. The young cowboy was quick with his gun, too much so for his own good. And if he had been a better shot, it might have been Noah lying dead in the dirt while Mixy's cabin was burning to the ground – most likely with the poor old man in it. After all, it was Mixy that Mississippi had meant to harm. Noah kept assuring himself that he only did what he had to.

When Mixy returned they covered Mississippi with an old piece of tarp and then they both agreed the best thing they could do was try to get some sleep.

Noah crawled back into his bedroll to face the night. Being in the company of death again made him think of Bacanaro who was always thinking about dying. The wise old shaman had once told him that to help out those in need was a noble way for a man to live a life. But just then Noah didn't feel very noble, and he was suddenly overwhelmed by grief. He felt like he wanted to cry, but had forgotten how – and he came as close as he ever did to praying for help.

He was unable to shut out the images of Mississippi bleeding on the ground in the glow of the lantern. The young man had seemed to know that he was facing the great unknown and had struggled briefly before crossing into it. Mississippi didn't die right away, he had time to feel fear. Not like Whitehead. Niles Whitehead was dead almost the moment he hit the ground. Same as the Apache. Noah's bullet had struck the Apache in the head and knocked him off his horse into the Yaqui River. The Indian was dead before he hit the water. It was much different with the Mexican...he died an agonizing death. It took the Mexican half a day to die and he was sweating and swearing the whole time. The images drifted in and out.

CHAPTER FIFTEEN

It turned into a restless night and it felt like the new day was already coming over the horizon before he fell asleep. And it seemed too early in the morning when Mixy came in the barn and told him that he could hear a wagon coming up the road. Tired as he was, Noah rolled out at once and got dressed. He left his own gun belt with his bedroll, but stuck Mississippi's pistol in the waistband of his pants before going outside.

Blue-gray puffs of smoke were coming out of the stovepipe as Mixy worked at firing up the cookstove. A few feet away from the cabin was the body of Mississippi lying in the yard with his boots sticking out from under the piece of tarp. The dead cowboy was not stretched out straight, ready for the coffin, but still sprawled out much like he had fallen. It was a grim scene to be greeted by in the bright morning light.

A moment later Tater came trotting down from the main road on the old bareback mare. He passed by Noah giving him a slight shake of the head, his face covered with doom and gloom. One would think it was him who had pulled the trigger. He rode over and tied his horse to a tree near where the path led to Rose's.

Then the wagon carrying Frank Canfield came rattling into the yard. The justice of the peace was packing his long-barreled scattergun and he had his badge on. Harry Troost was at the reins. The haberdasher who also served as the village undertaker had on winter gloves and a narrow-brimmed felt Stetson pulled down low to keep his ears warm. They were followed by another man who was on horseback, also armed with a pistol and a Henry rifle. The armed guard held up at the edge of the yard and kept an eye on Noah. The man looked uncomfortable, like he would much rather be doing something else.

When the wagon passed by Noah, Canfield greeted him with a raise of his eyebrows. Troost fought with the reins for a moment making the horse turn a sharp circle around the body before stopping the wagon beside it.

As Frank Canfield climbed down off the wagon, Rose came out of the trees and gave the mare a pat on the rump. Tater was starting to wander over toward the wagon and she called him back to her side. She stood there with her arms folded sternly across her chest and a scowl on her face. She wouldn't even look at Noah.

"Mixy," Canfield greeted as the old man stepped from his cabin. He laid his shotgun in the bed of the wagon before going over to examine the broken bottles and scorch marks up the side of the log wall. "Looks like you had some more trouble up here."

"Yes sir, Master Canfield," Mixy said, "they nearly burnt me out."

"Another one of Jared Sowers' hired hands," Noah stated as he joined them. He pulled the pistol from his waist band and handed it to Canfield butt first. "That belonged to him." Noah tilted his head toward the body.

"Do you know who he is?" Canfield asked.

"Not really," Noah explained, "just some young hothead calling himself Mississippi. But I never knew his real name. The first time I ever saw him was when I came to this valley. He was riding with Niles Whitehead."

"So," Canfield queried, "you were already here when he showed up?"

"I was sleeping in the barn," Noah admitted in a low tone while Rose and Tater moved in closer so they could hear what was going on. He knew Rose wouldn't miss this for the world. Somewhere along the way she would let it be known how she felt about this sort of thing – and most likely try to blame it all on him.

Obviously disgruntled, Rose focused her attention off in the distance as she listened in. Tater persisted in giving him a bleak stare, and the boy couldn't stop chewing on his lower lip. In spite of it all, Noah began to recount the events of the previous night. He told how the young cowboy had come riding in carrying a torch and wearing a hood over his head.

"Oh, goodness," Mixy suddenly exclaimed, "you have to see this." The old Negro hurried into his cabin and brought out the pillowcase with the eye holes cut out. "I found this layin' out here this mornin'."

"Well, what do you make of this?" Canfield was puzzled. "It's got a monogram embroidered on it. A.S. Who do you think that might be?"

"Arabella Sowers," Rose announced, grabbing the fancy pillowcase. Her brow wrinkled as she examined it.

"Let me see that," Harry Troost called out. Tying off the reins, he got down from the wagon to look. "I can remember sending back East for that exact set of linens. Arabella ordered them special."

Even the guard rode over and gazed down at the item briefly before returning to his spot. He didn't seem to understand what it all meant.

"Well," Canfield declared, "if that don't point the finger."

"It doesn't mean anything," Noah shrugged. "Don't prove nothing. Mississippi was staying up there. All Mister Sowers has to say is that he stole it."

"I think we all know better," Rose argued. As far as she was concerned, the pillow case was definite proof that Jared Sowers had sent Mississippi to burn out Mixy Alexander. It was perhaps the first time Rose felt true hatred toward another person. "It was Jared Sowers who put that poor dead boy over there up to no good." And she finally concluded, "This is all just senseless."

"Show me what happened here," Canfield addressed Noah, "I still have to go and try to find out what caused the bridge down by the new hotel to wash out." He turned and looked at the boots sticking out from under the tarp.

Exchanging glances with Tater, they both knew what caused it and the boy's cheeks flushed red with guilt. It was all that Noah could do to hold in his reaction to the news – to conceal his amusement. Noah figured that was why Tater had been making all the long faces and being unnaturally quiet. He must have heard about the bridge washing out when he went into town to get Frank Canfield. Mixy spit on the ground by their feet.

"I had just come out of the barn," Noah recalled. He went over to where he'd been standing when Mississippi shot at him. They all trailed along and when he showed Canfield were Mississippi's bullet struck, Noah realized just how close the young cowboy had come to killing him.

"That's where his bullet hit," Noah said, touching his cheek. The side of his face was tender and he could feel some dried blood matted in the stubble of his beard. He scratched at the blood and found himself staring into Rose's eyes. Her scowl had softened to more of a look of despair.

"Where's his horse?" Canfield wondered aloud, causing Rose to look away.

"It ran off when the shooting started," Noah replied, leading everyone over near the body where the horse's hooves had gouged into the earth. "You can see where it bolted. I 'spose it headed back to the barn, or else its still running around loose with its saddle."

Canfield stood quiet for a minute while he looked around and tried to visualize in his mind how it all must have happened. Then he reached down and pulled the tarp off so he could have a look at the body. The sight of the dead man was startling. His eyes were still wide open and they looked empty, dried out and dull. One of his arms was twisted under him from trying to get up, and a thick black pool of dried blood was on the ground at his side. Rose caught a quick breath and quickly turned away.

"Must have hit him in the liver," Harry Troost said as he bent over and tried to close Mississippi's eyes.

As Tater watched the proceedings, the color drained from his face until he was as pale as Mississippi. For a moment it appeared that he was going to faint. He was petrified by the reality and stared at the corpse with an intensity of having just discovered mortality. And when the undertaker started going through the dead cowboy's pockets, the boy went over and stood next to his mother.

"At least he can have a proper burial," Troost said, finding some money.

"If you'll give me a hand loading him, Mister Conklin," Canfield suggested. Noah took one side of Mississippi while the justice of the peace took the other and the undertaker grabbed the feet. And as they lifted the rigid corpse of the young man into the back of the wagon, Canfield was thinking aloud, "It seems like there has been a lot going on around lately. Percy McRull's dog and sheep got shot. And there's another sheep herder that is lost somewheres.

"Then, first there was that wagon that rolled off the ferry into the river, and now there's a bridge that washed out when it wasn't even raining. Not to mention Mixy's barn burning down." Canfield caught Noah's eye. "This is the second killing in almost as many weeks. I think it's time to dispatch a telegraph to the marshal's office in Boise. He could end up sending a deputy."

"Master Canfield," Mixy intervened, "if it weren't for Master Noah, that man might have kilt me."

"I know, Mixy," Canfield acknowledged. He retrieved his shotgun from the wagon bed and climbed up in the box. "Far as I'm concerned, this shooting was justified and that's what I'll write in my report. That young man came here looking for trouble – and he got more than he could handle."

"That's for sure," Harry Troost concurred as he covered up Mississippi.

Rose had been drawn in by the conversation and listened intently. Tater was starting to get a little color back in his cheeks, but was still at his mother's side. And

Mixy was glad to see that they were taking the old piece of tarp away – after what it had been used for.

"I'll need you to stop by the village office and sign the record the next time you come into Springwater," Canfield said, extending his hand to Noah.

"I'll come by today," Noah nodded, shaking Canfield's big hand.

"Whenever," Canfield said. "I want to thank you, Mister Conklin. Most of the folks around the valley here realize what you're doing."

Harry Troost climbed up on the wagon seat and pulled his hat down over his ears and put on his gloves. "By the way, Rose," he spoke up, as he took the reins, "I have a new shipment of wool piece goods in the store. Winter's coming, you know." And with a snap of the reins they drove off, Canfield bidding them farewell by tipping his hat. This time the heavily armed man on horseback lead the way. The clatter of the wagon soon faded, and the only sounds to be heard were those of the birds singing in the treetops.

"You see, Mizz Rose," Mixy insisted, when he noticed the surly look on her face, "it weren't Master Noah's fault."

Rose didn't respond right away, but stared at them with eyes that seemed to question everything she held true. She was befuddled by the fact that the local justice of the peace had ended up thanking Noah for killing another man, and even shook his hand for it. Perhaps it was best that he had been there to defend them, but on the other hand she had been betrayed – and to Rose that was a whole different matter. Besides, deep down she still had the feeling that it all had more to do with Noah than he was letting on. "I think that man came here after you."

"Nobody knew I was here," Noah insisted.

"What are we supposed to do," Tater jumped in, "just sit by while Mister Sowers is up to his monkey business?" The boy was feeling much better now that he hadn't been hauled off in shackles for destroying the bridge.

"You still have milking to do," Rose reminded him.

"I will in a minute," Tater told her. "You could go fix me some breakfast." He was desperate to find out what he should do concerning the bridge and needed a minute alone with Noah and Mixy.

"Listen, young man..." Rose snapped. She reached over to twist his ear like she always had when she was upset with him.

Tater slapped her hand away, defiantly, "I'm too old for that anymore."

"You better go on now boy and do as your mamma says." Mixy encouraged him not to make things any worse. "You can come down and talk later."

With a grimace, the boy did as he was told. He went over and jumped on the mare's back and laid flat along her neck to avoid the low hanging branches as the horse trotted off up the path along the creek.

"By the way," Rose inquired of Noah, "where's your horse?" She was sure it was hidden somewhere out of sight, all part of them sneaking around behind her back. The anger from a lifetime of frustration simmered in her. "The trouble all started when you showed up," she stated. "I ask you to please stay away from here. And Mixy, after all I have done for you..." She shook her head.

Noah and Mixy stood silent. There was nothing either one of them could summon up to defend themselves.

"They should have taken this with them," she glared. Somehow Rose had ended up holding the pillow case. She tossed it to Noah. "That has to prove something. It does to me."

"It proves something to me, too," Noah assured her.

"And me, too," Mixy added.

"I still don't know how I feel about all this," Rose concluded, "or if I'm ever going to like it. Meanwhile, the both of you can just stay the hell away from me." And with a swirl of her skirt, Rose strode off toward home.

"Mizzy..." Mixy called after her to no avail.

Noah could hear the disappointment in the old man's voice. Disgusted with himself, Noah took a deep breath and let it back out. "I swear, Mixy," he promised when Rose was out of sight, "I'll make this up to you somehow. Goddamn it! Should I go and try to talk to her now?"

"Oh, I don't think so," he advised Noah. Just the thought of it made Mixy quiver. "Not when she's upset like she is. We ought to let her cool out some."

"If she ever will," Noah said.

"You heard her," Mixy said, "she's startin' to accept what's happenin'." He looked at Noah with wonder. "You haven't spent much time around women have you? You got to learn what they mean when they say somethin'."

All Noah heard was that the two of them were supposed to stay away from Rose. And to him, she sounded like she meant what she said.

"Well, it's my fault she's mad at you," Noah admitted. "I should have never got you involved in all this in the first place."

"Mizz Rose will be okay," Mixy assured him. "You'll see. 'Cause I know what we is doin' here is the right thing." Somehow the old man had learned to be an enduring optimist despite a life filled with adversity.

"I hope so. In the meantime, why don't you hang on to this for me," Noah said, giving the pillow case to Mixy. "Keep it handy for when Jared Sowers shows up."

"Why, you don't think he'll show his face around here now, do you?" Mixy pondered.

"A man with money goes anywhere he wants," Noah reasoned. "It would be a sign of weakness if he didn't – and a sign of guilt. I don't think Mississippi would've come up here and tried what he did without the boss's permission. On the other hand there's really no way of knowing if he was sent, or not."

Noah filled the basin at the side of the cabin and washed the dried blood off his face. He wanted to go take care of his business in Springwater and get back in case Sowers did show up. While he shaved he watched Mixy out of the corner of his eye as the old man dug a small hole along the tree line. Mixy then used the shovel to scrape up the thick dark puddle of blood from the ground where Mississippi had died and solemnly buried it.

A short time later Noah hurried off through the plum thicket, and when he approached the grassy glade he found Mississippi's horse keeping Pecos company. The stray critter was an awful sight with scuff marks on its neck and back. The saddle was still on, but had been pushed over to the side. It appeared that the animal had stepped on a rein while it was running loose and had taken a bad tumble. Noah considered that the poor horse was lucky it hadn't broken its neck. It was too tired and sore to move and stood idle while Noah saddled Pecos. When he was finished with Pecos, Noah straightened the saddle on Mississippi's horse, tied the stirrups under its belly to keep them from flopping about, and took the lost animal along with him.

CHAPTER SIXTEEN

There was a dark cloud hanging over Noah's head that followed him all the way to Springwater. He couldn't get Rose out of his thoughts. Even though Mixy kept telling him that things were going along fine with her, Noah just couldn't see it. His hopes of ever being able to mend the fence with her again had faded. Maybe he should start thinking about moving on with Dunlavy and Pico. As usual he ended up thinking of Perry. It was about the time of morning the mangy cur would be starting his day in the Indian camp, and Noah felt sorry for Little One.

The first thing he did when he reached Springwater was to drop Mississippi's horse off at the livery barn, that way Frank Canfield could figure out what to do with it. The liveryman informed Noah that Canfield had already ridden out to investigate the bridge disaster. But Harry Troost, who had been watching for Noah from the haberdashery, showed up and let him in the town office to sign the record.

"Mister Canfield wanted me to ask you..." Troost stated, "if it was at all possible...he would like for you to stay around and meet with the deputy marshal. He will be here in two or three days."

"I'll plan on being around," Noah agreed. He was busy reading, for the second time, the statement that Canfield had recounted of the killing. Mississippi had been described as a drifter, a term that had been applied to Noah in Medicine Bow. But this time the justice of the peace had described Noah as a local citizen.

"He also wanted me to tell you," Troost continued, "that there is going to be a special meeting at the grange on Saturday. He thought it might be a good time for you to meet the folks living around Springwater."

"I'm not sure..." Noah hesitated. "I'll have to give that some thought."   He already knew that Rose wouldn't like that idea one bit.

He signed his name to the record and Harry Troost went back to selling ladies' feathered hats.

By the time Noah left Springwater, back toward Mixy's, his saddlebags were bulging with provisions from the mercantile – and the black cloud hanging over his head had evaporated. He'd acquired a quart of good whiskey, two pouches of real tobacco and a handful of cheroots. He also got some coffee, cornmeal and a side of smoked salmon that was so big its tail stuck out of the saddlebags.

At first Noah was disappointed that he didn't have an opportunity to talk to Canfield about the missing herder. Perhaps it was better if he waited to tell the deputy marshal the rumor he'd heard about the ears, and about the lost flock of sheep that he had seen running around in the foothills. It was the sort of burden the local justice of the peace really didn't need anyhow.

The grange hall soon came into view and Noah reined Pecos toward the comfort of a whitewashed privy. And as he approached the well-kept structures, he remembered a cattle rancher he had worked for a few years back who was vehemently opposed to the building of a grange in his part of the territory. According to the rancher: "Grange halls are worse than barbed wire – they're the beginning of the end to open range."

Noah came out of the privy and washed up in the horse trough. When he started to mount up again, he noticed a couple of flies buzzing around the chunk of smoked fish sticking out of the saddlebags. He pulled out his knife and cut enough off the tail so that he could close the flap. And with his back up against the grange, he sat on the ground to snack on the meat.

The sky above was clear and blue and the air was still – like it was waiting for a breeze to come along. Noah bathed in the warm rays of the sun as he watched the trees that lined the creek. From time to time he had caught a glimpse of a wagon coming down the road, and he soon realized it was Tater heading to town for the second time that day. This time he was hauling the dairy goods. For a little while the boy was out in the open and he was driving the old mare at a fast trot. Noah suspected Tater must be in a hurry to get his errands done as quick as possible so he could get back home. He knew the boy was probably worrying himself sick over the bridge mishap.

Silently in the distance, Tater passed by and proceeded on toward Springwater. Noah couldn't help but wonder what might have happened if he hadn't been at Mixy's when Mississippi came calling. What might have happened if Tater would have been down reading to Mixy? His own son would have probably challenged Mississippi, and he couldn't bear to think what the outcome would have been. Perhaps it was fate that was guiding him.

As Noah rode on, he twisted around in the saddle and looked back at the neatly whitewashed building. He was just now beginning to understand what the rancher had meant about the grange – it was a symbol of the community. It was a sign of unity. The Springwater Valley is where men and women had settled to build a life and raise their children. He stared out past the grange to the twin barns up in the foothills and he knew in his heart that families were a lot more important than cows.

Touching the spurs to Pecos, Noah couldn't wait to get back to Mixy's. When he had shown up at the old man's place a couple of days earlier, it was because he had nowhere else to go. Now he felt like there was no place he would rather be, and Mixy seemed so certain that it was the right thing.

When Noah reached the cabin he spotted Mixy standing at the edge of the prairie and rode out to join him. The old man was visiting Sarla's grave, and there was a bunch of fresh cut purple and yellow flowers lying at the base of the simple wooden cross.

"I can't think of a good reason to hide the horse anymore," Noah said as he reined up. "Can you?"

"No," Mixy smiled up at him, "I guess there ain't."

"Where'd you get the flowers?" Noah quizzed, knowing that the bouquet must have come from Rose's garden.

"I went up to see Mizz Rose," Mixy offered. "I just had to talk to her about things."

"So what did she have to say?" Noah asked, swinging down from the saddle.

"She didn't say much at all," Mixy reported, "but I know she was listenin'...and that's the most important thing. I ain't even sure what all I had to say, but I know I spoke my piece. And I know I must have said somethin' that made some sense to her, too."

"How do you know that?" Noah wondered.

"'Cause she cut those flowers for me to put on Mizz Sarla's grave, didn't she," Mixy answered.

"Well, I'm gonna try to stay clear of her for a couple of days," Noah considered. "If she wants to talk to me, I'm right here."

"Did you happen across Tater along the way?" Mixy inquired.

"I saw him," Noah declared, "but I didn't get a chance to talk to him. I was off the road for awhile. He sure looked like he was in a hurry, though. Did you see him making all those faces this morning?"

"He must've found out about the bridge when he first got to town," Mixy stated. "I swear that boy has never got by with nothin' his whole life. He can't never hide nothin.'"

"That's exactly what I thought, too," Noah chuckled. "Just wait till he finds out that the deputy marshal is coming for sure. We're gonna have to try to teach that kid not to look so gall-darned guilty."

Mixy failed to see the humor in the situation because of his concern for Noah. "You don't think they'll have a trial, do you?"

"I don't think so," Noah answered. Mixy's remark was worthy of Lester Dunlavy. It had the same effect, too – it gave him something to ponder over. He had

ended up at a hearing before a circuit judge in Medicine
Bow, but that was a whole different set of circumstances.
"At least I hope not. As a matter-of-fact, I'm kind of glad
they're sending a deputy out to see what's going on
around here.

"Anyway, I've never really had much of that sort
of trouble," Noah reflected. He was trying to reassure
himself as much as he was trying to console Mixy who
was staring out across the land with worried eyes. "I've
run into quite a few lawmen over the years...I even rode
with them...and usually when we get to talking it doesn't
take too long for them to figure out which side I'm on."

"And which side is that, Master Noah?" Mixy queried.

"Why, I'm on your side, Mixy," Noah assured him.

"That's good," the old man insisted, "'cause here
comes Master Sowers with his gang of men."

Noah followed Mixy's anxious gaze out across the
plain to find five riders coming toward them with the big
white gelding leading the way. The group of men held
up for a minute and the three honest cowhands were left
behind. Then Jared Sowers proceeded on with Wally
Pomeroy close by his side.

"I'd like you to take Pecos and shut him in the barn,
Mixy," Noah said calmly, handing over the reins, "and
bring back my Winchester and that pillow slip with the
eye-holes cut in it."

"Yes sir, Master Noah," Mixy acknowledged and set
out at once.

Noah wandered a few yards away from the grave, and
when Sowers and Wally were close enough so that they
couldn't help but notice, he undid the hammer thong on
his holster. His actions caused the pair to mutter back
and forth as they reined up at a respectable distance. The

three men who stayed behind had dismounted and were sitting on the ground holding the reins of their horses.

"Well," Sowers spoke up, "what I heard must be true."

"What'd you hear?" Noah asked, keeping a good eye on their hands. It was apparent that they had been in a hurry to get there, the horses were dark with sweat.

"That you've been staying around up here," Sowers sputtered. He was red in the face. "And is it true that you killed another one of my boys?"

Noah figured Sowers had shown up out of curiosity and to blow off a little steam, but he wasn't sure what the numbskull that he'd brought with him was thinking.

"Wally, you didn't ride up here looking for trouble did you?" Noah asked, resting the heel of his palm on the butt of the pistol.

"No," Wally answered quickly and clearly. He might not have been the smartest cowboy sitting on a horse, but he certainly knew better than to tangle with Noah in this type of situation – all alone so to speak. Secretly, he was hoping that his boss wouldn't end up picking a fight with Noah.

The speed and manner in which Wally had kowtowed to Noah bothered Sowers. He had expected his hired-gun to stand up to him somewhat. But it was the complete confidence and the total lack of fear that Noah exhibited that was so intimidating. "We only came up here to find out what happened for ourselves is all," Sowers stated.

"I'm just curious where you might have heard such things." Noah was surprised by how fast the news had traveled even by his nosy friend's standards. "My first guess would have to be Mister Dunlavy."

"I ran that laggard off yesterday morning," Sowers said. "Him and that Mexican, both. And you can be sure that they've hightailed it out of the country by now."

"Is that right, Wally?" Noah questioned.

"Far as I know," Wally nodded. "They were talking about going on down to Bakersfield."

"They weren't worth their salt, so I fired them," Sowers ranted. "But before they left, they wrecked my dam and caused the bridge down by the hotel to wash out."

"Huh?" Noah couldn't believe what he was hearing. He quizzed Wally with his eyes and the stocky cowboy merely shrugged his shoulders.

"That's right," Sowers continued, "and I paid them for the whole month, too. That's the thanks I get. I did put the law onto them, though. No, I ran into Frank Canfield when I went down to see about the bridge and he told me what was going on up here, and that you'd gunned down Mississippi."

The two men shifted their attention past Noah and at first he assumed that Mixy must be on his way back out, but then Sowers straightened up as tall as he could in the saddle and adjusted his Stetson while Wally worked at making sure his shirttail was tucked in. Their attempt to look more presentable caused Noah to glance around to discover Rose treading briskly out across the field to join them.

"What do you want now?" Rose inquired in a huff. Her cheeks were flushed and she was nearly out of breath from hurrying. A lock of her auburn hair had shaken loose from the neat bun on top of her head and hung down on her cheek.

"I came to find out what's going on up here," Sowers told her. "And I still haven't heard anyone admit to killing another one of my hired hands."

"Mister Sowers, if you don't want to lose any more of your boys," Noah warned, "then you better keep them home. They got no business coming up here. That goes for you, too, Wally," he added, perturbed by the way the simpleton was evaluating Rose.

"And you don't have any business around here anymore, either," Rose added, glaring at Sowers.

"One of my men was killed up here," Sowers said. "I'd say that makes it my business."

"The only reason that boy died is because you sent him up here to do your bidding," Rose argued. "You're as much to blame as anybody else."

"I didn't send him anywhere," Sowers insisted. "I don't know what you're talking about. He must have come up here on his own doing."

"Where's that pillow case?" She quizzed Noah.

"Mixy went to get it," Noah replied, looking back just in time to see the old man come out from behind the barn. He had the pillow case in one hand and the rifle in the other. Mixy kept his eyes aimed at the ground as he walked toward them.

"What is this?" Sowers questioned.

"You'll see," she told him. The sight of Mixy with the Winchester added to Rose's concern, but when she caught Noah's attention she could see that old spark of adventure in his eyes. Rose was somewhat reassured by his gaze – he appeared to be enjoying the confrontation with Sowers. She realized that Noah was in his element and it was Jared Sowers who was uneasy.

"Answer me this, Rose," Sowers implored. "What the hell's the connection here?" The prosperous rancher finally got around to his real reason for showing up the way he did. Mississippi was his excuse, but Rose was his true reason. And he didn't like what he saw, she had never looked at him the way she was looking at Noah. "What are you two, cousins or something like that?"

Rose continued to stare at Noah and in a voice that sounded as though she was reminding him, stated, "We were married once."

"Well," Sowers uttered, "I'll be go to hell."

Mixy had gotten back just in time to hear Rose's confession and he gave Noah sort of an odd look like he knew he had missed something important, but wasn't sure what it was. He held the Winchester out for Noah. "You just hang onto that for me," Noah told him.

"But you can give me that," Rose said, taking the pillow case from Mixy. "This is what that poor boy came up here wearing over his head," Rose said in a scathing tone as she held it up for Sowers to see.

"What?" Sowers disputed. "Why, that doesn't mean a darn thing. These are the old ones, so I used them in the bunkhouse. Isn't that right, Wally?"

"Huh?" Wally was busy gawking at Rose. He was still trying to figure out what she had said about being married to Noah.

"Oh, never mind," Sowers grumbled. Rose's admission of her true relationship to Noah continued to burn in his brain and the red-faced rancher could barely contain his anger. "So, this is the way it's going to be?"

"It's the way it is, Mister Sowers," Noah reasoned. "People are standing up for what's right – protecting what's theirs. There's more than enough open prairie to graze your cows on. You ought to be able to see that from up there on your perch. So what if there's a few little farms scattered around?...like Lewis Morrey...they really don't take up much land. They only fence off a few acres to try to make their livings. This ain't just a parcel of graze land anymore, this is a community of people. These folks have chose this valley to settle down and raise their kids. They're all neighbors. Why, most of these people would even accept the likes of you for a neighbor if you'd of given them half a chance. You need to think it over."

When Noah ran out of things to say, Rose seemed to add an exclamation point to his speech by tossing the pillow case to Sowers who instinctively caught it.

"I don't need to listen to anybody preaching to me," Sowers said, turning a shade darker and throwing the pillow case on the ground. He reined around sinking his fancy spurs in the flanks of the big white quarter horse, riding away at a gallop.

Even a half-wit like Wally Pomeroy knew better than to leave any evidence laying around if it could be helped. He swung down out of the saddle to pick up the pillow case that had been used as a hood.

"You can just leave that there, Wally," Noah said, taking his Winchester from Mixy.

Wally did as he was told and quickly climbed back up on his horse. Then the stocky cowboy tipped his hat as polite as he could be. "Ma'am," he bid farewell to Rose and rode off.

Noah watched for a minute as Sowers and Wally joined the other cowboys who had mounted up again. Together the riders all headed off across the plain kicking up dirt clods and dust as they went.

"Well," Rose broke the silence after a long minute, "I guess that's that." She tucked the loose bit of hair back into the tight bun. "I have bread in the oven," she remarked and started walking away.

"Rose," Noah called after her, "Frank Canfield sent for the deputy marshal and he wants me to stay around a couple days until I can talk to him."

She paused for a moment and looked back, nodding like she understood. "I guess that would be alright," she replied before continuing on her way.

"Do you think that's that, Master Noah?" Mixy wondered. He was looking out across the prairie like he was expecting Jared Sowers and his gang to come back.

"Not hardly," Noah reasoned. "Not with Burt Perry still out there." He started back toward the barn, catching the last glimpse of Rose as she disappeared among the trees along the creek. "I need to go take the saddle off my horse."

"I rarely do this," Mixy said, following behind Noah, "but I think while things is quiet, I'm gonna lay down and try to catch me a short nap."

CHAPTER SEVENTEEN

After Mixy went into his cabin, Noah opened up the doors on both ends of the barn, letting a fresh breeze coming across the valley sweep through. He stripped the saddle off Pecos and took a currycomb to the horse before picketing him in a patch of grass near the plum thicket.

All of Noah's gear was in one place for the first time since he began staying at Mixy's. He took the opportunity to wipe the trail dirt of the last few days off his saddle and reorganize the saddlebags. It also gave him an opportunity to taste the fancy-labeled whiskey – and he was quite pleased with the smooth burning taste. He rolled a cigarette and smoked it while he cleaned and oiled the Winchester. When Noah began to clean his pistol, he found the empty cartridge still in the cylinder. It was a grim reminder of the previous night.

Despite the recent turn of events, having killed Mississippi and then getting caught hiding out at Mixy's by Rose, Noah couldn't help but feel like things might be starting to go his way a little. At least the truth was finally out in the open. Firsthand truth about the kind of life he led – and the truth about Tater. But the thing that made him feel the best was having witnessed for himself the fact that Rose truly didn't like Jared Sowers, even if he was rich. As usual, Rose had been ill-tempered when she came scurrying down the creek, but this time she had directed her anger more at Sowers than at him. It brought a smile to Noah's face when he thought of the way she had lit into her pompous neighbor. His smile was short lived though, for he knew that a man like Sowers wasn't going to just go away quietly, not with a scoundrel like Burt Perry in his arsenal.

Rummaging to the bottom of his carpetbag, Noah pulled out a set of work clothes. The faded pair of dungarees and chambray shirt had lined the bottom of the bag for so long they had permanent creases worn in them. By donning the work clothes, Noah hoped it would show Mixy and Rose that he was more that willing to earn his keep as long as he was staying around. He could help lay in wood for the winter fires, or help with the harvest, or hunt. And when Noah came out of the barn wearing the set of old clothes, Pecos ceased grazing and looked up at him unsure at first who it was.

A few yards up the path toward Rose's place, Noah located a small tree-sheltered clearing at the edge of the creek. If he was living out on the trail it would make an ideal location for a camp – tucked back into the tree line with fresh running water close at hand. He was determined to sit around a fire for awhile and this was a perfect spot. He gathered rocks from along the banks of the creek to lay a circle for the fire and when he was done with that he began to scour the surrounding woods for deadfall and downed branches, anything that could be used to feed a campfire.

The bright golden sun had slipped lazily past its zenith into the pale afternoon sky as Noah widened his search for camp wood. He wondered what could be taking Tater so long in returning from town. And by the time he finally heard the boy's wagon go up the road he had piled up enough wood to last well into the night. He lugged a couple rounds of cordwood from Mixy's woodshed so that there would be a place for him and the old man to sit around the fire. He finished up his project by bringing his saddlebags and Winchester out to his spot.

The breeze had died away and the call of an unseen meadowlark came across the prairie. The colors of the distant hills had taken on the hues of autumn. From time to time large numbers of honking geese passed high overhead on their journey to the Snake River canyon.

Pulling up tufts of dried grass and adding strips of birch bark he had scavenged from the woods, Noah laid the base for his fire. He broke small twigs and carefully stacked them on the dry tinder, then struck a match and lit a fire. Dense smoke from the grass billowed up only a few seconds before flames shot up and the bark and twigs began to crackle. Noah sat down and rolled a cigarette and smoked while he tended his campfire. He took a sip of whiskey and kept the bottle down beside his cordwood stool. He sat facing the empty plain and was content to be there watching over things. He felt relieved that Tater was back.

After awhile, Mixy came out of his cabin and saw the wisps of smoke rising from the fire. He moseyed over and looked around at Noah's day camp. The old man was still trying to wake up and there was worry in his sleepy eyes.

"What's the matter?" Noah quizzed.

"Nothin'," Mixy responded, shaking his head as if he was trying to lose a thought. Sullenly, he gazed out over the prairie. "I shouldn't of took a nap. I ended up havin' a terrible nightmare."

"Can you remember it?" Noah wondered. "I have awful nightmares sometimes. I wake up in a sweat in the middle of the night, but by the morning I can hardly remember what they was about."

"I don't want to talk about it," Mixy stated. "If you tell what it is it might come true."

"Oh, that's just old superstition," Noah insisted, reaching down for the bottle of whiskey. He pulled the cork and offered Mixy a drink. "Here take a slug of this, it will make you forget your troubles."

Mixy didn't hesitate to take Noah up on his offer and after taking a drink, said, "I don't know, Master Noah, I just got a bad feelin' that I cain't seem to shake."

"Well, Mixy, sometimes you have to go with what your gut tells you. But I think things are going to turn out okay," Noah tried to console the old man, though he was having the same kind of feeling. There was some sort of foreboding hanging around him, too, but there always seemed to be. So much so recently, that he had almost grown used to the feeling.

"I'm sure you're right," the old man relented, and took another swallow of whiskey. "Thanks, Master Noah, that's some good southern mash." He studied the label a moment before handing back the bottle. "Says it's made over in Tennessee."

"I thought we ought to sit around a fire for awhile to kind of celebrate," Noah said.

"Celebrate what?" Mixy was perplexed. As far as he was concerned the events of the last couple of days gave no reason to celebrate.

"Well for one thing," Noah enlightened him, "we don't have to sneak around anymore. And for another thing, we ain't the only ones Rose is mad at anymore."

"I told you she would get things figured out," Mixy reminded him. The warmth of the whiskey began to relax the old black man and he sat down on the cordwood seat that Noah had provided for him.

"She really don't seem to like Jared Sowers very much at all," Noah said, hoping that Mixy would agree.

"And I told you that, too," Mixy stated. The sound of a bellowing cow could be heard off in the distance. "Did that boy ever get back home?"

"Yes he did," Noah replied, "but he sure took his sweet time about it. He must be up there doing his chores 'cause I heard another cow bawling a short while ago."

Looking up to see where the sun hung in the sky, Mixy concluded, "Seems a bit early for milkin'. This mess he's got hisself into has him all out of kilter."

The remark reminded Noah to tell Mixy about how Jared Sowers suspected Lester Dunlavy and Fernando Pico for breaching the dam. That led him to have to explain who Dunlavy was. Noah even ended up admitting to Mixy that over the years Lester Dunlavy was probably as close as he came to having a real friend.

"I don't think you should tell Tater about what Master Sowers thinks happened," Mixy was pondering. "That boy will think that lets him off the hook. And it might do him some good to worry about it awhile, so the next time he gets some wild idea maybe he will think twice about it." And when Noah didn't say anything, the old man quizzed, "Do you think that's mean?"

"Not nearly as mean as someone stealing an old man's water," Noah suggested. "But I 'spose it won't hurt to let him dangle a bit longer."

Just then Tater came rambling down the path carrying a blanket and pillow, and an old Army cot. When he saw Noah and Mixy sitting around the fire he came to an abrupt halt. "What are you doing out here?"

"Relaxing," Noah told him. "What's all that for?"

"Mom told me to bring it down," Tater explained. "What's going on, Mixy? She's acting real strange."

"Oh?" Mixy wondered. "How so?"

"She's being nice," the boy offered, suspiciously. "Where should I put this, in the cabin or in the barn?"

"In the cabin," Mixy said. He got up to lead the way.

"She's even cooking supper for me," Tater added. Then he gave Noah the once over. "Where'd you get those clothes?"

"I've always had them," Noah told him, following along.

While Mixy and Tater were setting up the cot, Noah gathered up his belongings and moved them from the barn into the cabin. Mixy's cabin was tidy and well-swept – almost too much so for a single man living alone, Noah thought. Along the side wall away from the door was a wood range, a counter, and a stack of shelves full of canned goods and an assortment of storage containers. A rope was strung across the back wall with an old quilt hung from it as a partition to afford some privacy for Mixy's bed. There was a small table and a couple of chairs against the front wall. The cot had been placed along the side wall just inside the door. A well-used two man bucksaw hung on the wall above the cot.

As Noah tossed his own bedroll down on the hard and narrow cot, and stowed his carpet bag beneath it, he wondered if he had been better off in the soft, sprawling grass hay out in the barn. But he knew that if Rose had sent down a bed of nails for him to sleep on, that's what he would have done. It was the least he could do to show his gratitude.

"It's not much, Master Noah," Mixy mentioned.

"It's nice, Mixy," Noah insisted, heading outside. "I'm sure I'll be real comfortable."

CHAPTER EIGHTEEN

Back at the fire, Noah threw on several pieces of wood before uncorking the whiskey bottle again. The shafts of smokey light breaking through the trees were slanted from the late afternoon sun. He took a drink as he looked out between the branches. Tater was just coming out of Mixy's woodshed with an axe and another round of cordwood. The sad grimace on the boy's face was enough to ruin the mood around the campfire.

For the first time since staying at Eddie Button's saloon – eating square meals and being able to bicker with Lester Dunlavy now and again – Noah was comfortable where he was. All he wanted to do was sit around the fire and drink some whiskey and smoke some tobacco...and tell some stories in hopes of finding something to laugh about. He was having a devil of a time feeling content while the boy was still tormented by the wrecked dam. He sensed that Mixy wasn't really enjoying the situation either. Tater's anguish hung over them all.

"Mixy," he stated, turning back to the fire, "I think I ought to tell that lad what's going on with the dam before he just ups and confesses to his mother."

Mixy agreed by nodding his head.

"We'll let him suffer, though, as long as we can stand it," Noah added.

An unruly plume of gray-brown smoke rose up from the fire forcing Noah to move out of its way. He offered the bottle to Mixy who took a swallow and gave it right back. Both men moved around the fire together as the smoke swirled toward them.

When Tater joined the men again he didn't look at either of them. He placed the cordwood seat down near the fire and began chopping on the pile of branches that Noah had hauled in. And hardly a single minute had passed before the boy stopped swinging the axe, leaving it stuck in a hard and twisted branch of black locust.

"Mixy," he blurted out, "I know I ain't supposed to bring this up anymore," his eyes shifted from Mixy to Noah, "but I went down to where the bridge used to be." He added quickly, "I just had to see it for myself."

"I figured that's what had took you so long." Mixy grumbled. He shook his head and spit. "You just cain't leave things alone now."

"It was completely gone," Tater informed Noah. "I mean there was only a couple of planks left and they were over the edge. The rest of the bridge had washed over the bluff clear down in the river. Wagons were having to drive across at the old ford. There was a lot of people down there looking at it – including Mister Canfield."

The smoke had chased all three of them around the fire while Tater was telling his story. Noah stopped to rummage in his saddlebags. Mixy appeared as though he was trying not to listen.

"Here, eat some of this," Noah offered. He set the side of smoked salmon out on one of the cordwood seats and broke off a chunk to chew on. "It's really good. It's Indian smoked."

Mixy didn't hesitate to try a piece of the fish.

"So did Mister Canfield have anybody under suspicion yet?" Noah asked.

"He didn't say anything about that," Tater replied. "Mostly all they talked about was the gunfight, and how you shot and killed that Mississippi last night. Mister Canfield was telling how it all happened...and he told everyone that it was a clear case of self-defense."

"So nothing was said about the bridge washing out?" Noah was perplexed. He dug in his saddle bags again and brought out a couple of cheroots and handed one to Mixy.

"One man said that he thought it was worth the bridge being wrecked so that the creek was running down through there again." Tater watched with interest as the men took a firebrand and started smoking the small black cigars.

"Did you happen to see Mister Sowers down there, too?" Noah took a few quick puffs that caused the end of the cheroot to glow a bright smoldering orange.

"No, why?" the boy asked. "Where did you get those little cigars?"

"I got them at the mercantile when I went to town this morning," Noah said. "Same as the salmon. Don't you want to eat any of this smoked fish?" The boy didn't seem the least bit interested in even tasting the salmon.

"I'm not very hungry," Tater said. "How many of those things did you get?"

"They're cheroots," Noah said, letting out a long breath of smoke. "I got a few. Why?"

"I'd like to try smoking one if you had any to spare," the boy said.

"You know your mamma doesn't like you smokin'," Mixy reminded Tater in a scolding tone. The words seemed to come out of the old man automatically.

"Oh, Mixy, she knows I have a smoke ever now and then," Tater argued. "She really don't mind that much."

"I guess it ain't up to me nohow," Mixy gave in.

"Why hell, Mixy, I bet you and me both took up smoking when we was littler than him," Noah said. "These are pretty strong tasting, though," he cautioned the boy. "I have some rolling tobacco if you'd rather have that."

"They can't be any stronger tasting than that kinnikinnick stuff that grows around here," Tater insisted.

"If I give you one of these..." Noah said, pulling another cheroot from his saddlebags. He handed it over to the boy on the condition, "If you don't like the way it tastes just let it go out and give it back to me. They're too good too waste," Noah added, exhaling a cloud of dingy-gray smoke.

"I will," Tater vowed. He put the cheroot up to his nose and began to sniff it.

"I 'spose you ought to know," Noah spoke up as Tater bent down to find a firebrand to light the cheroot, "that Mister Sowers paid us a visit today. Seems he's pretty sure that he knows who ruined his dam."

"Well..." Tater's cheeks flushed and he stood up straight, forgetting all about the cheroot. He struggled with the problem for a moment. "How do you think he found out?" Then the boy surmised aloud, "Maybe Mister Armstead..." His words faded away and he figured if that was the case it was because old man Armstead was too scared not to tell. "Mom doesn't know yet, does she?"

"No, she doesn't," Noah assured him, "and there ain't any reason why she ever should. Do you remember those two cowboys we saw at Mister Morrey's a couple days back?" he went on to explain. "Well, it seems Mister Sowers fired them off his ranch and he thinks that it was them who washed out his dam for spite."

Tater realized that there was still a problem, but wasn't sure exactly what. "What will happen if Mister Canfield goes after them?" he wondered.

"Nothing," Noah stated, "he could never really prove those two did it, anyway."

"How do you figure?" Tater pondered.

"Well, for one reason," Noah reminded the boy, "they really didn't do it."

"That's right," Mixy restated, "they surely didn't."

The fire crackled a bit and flames began reaching up through the wood driving away the smoke. Noah sat with his back to the footpath so he could keep an eye on the fire and prairie at the same time. "I wonder if anybody besides Jared Sowers really even gives a hoot," he continued. "On the other hand, how could they prove it was you? Nobody seen you except for me and I ain't telling. And I'd be willing to bet that Mister Armstead won't tattle either." He puffed on the cheroot and smiled. "There's a good chance nothing will ever come of it – unless of course Mixy tells on you."

"No, Master Noah, I'm just gonna tend to my own business," Mixy declared, then added, "Like a young man that I knows should do from now on.

"So, does that mean we got away with it?" Tater pondered. Noah and Mixy both looked at him at the same time, neither saying a word. "At least for the time being?" he pleaded.

"For the time being, anyway," Noah exonerated him.

A minute earlier Tater couldn't have mustered a smile if someone had taken a feather to his foot. And now he could barely contain himself. Somewhat elated, he lit the cheroot with the flaming end of a stick from the fire and choked on the first draw of smoke. Reddish blotches flushed his cheeks.

"I warned you they was strong," Noah recalled. He traded smiles with Mixy, further embarrassing the boy.

"No, it's good," Tater assured him, puffing on the cheroot. "I was just thinking about something else, but I don't know if you'll think it's funny, or not. Remember the other day when we were at that bridge and I told you they didn't even need it there anymore. Well, that was because the creek was dried up, but now that the water is running through there again the bridge is gone. Don't you think that's sort of odd?"

"I 'spose," Noah agreed.

"But there was something else, too," Tater resumed. "All last night, after the shoot-out, I couldn't stop thinking about something. Remember when you told me yesterday that there was a lot worse things that could happen besides a stupid dam breaking. Did you mean like having to kill that Mississippi fellow?"

"Worse than that," Noah surmised. "No, I meant something like your mother catching me staying down here in the middle of the night."

They all laughed aloud together. Even Mixy, who still felt troubled over the chain of recent events, saw the humor in that. Tater was grinning from ear to ear, puffing away, when he suddenly flicked the freshly lit cheroot out of his mouth and into the flames of the campfire. And before Noah had a chance to react, and lodge his complaint about the little cigar going to waste, the boy called out, "Hi, Mom."

"Mizz Rose," Mixy greeted her. The old man and the boy glanced at each other with concern.

Looking back over his shoulder, Noah spied Rose standing along the path peering into the little clearing. She was clutching her Bible to her chest and the sight brought him to his feet.

"We was just relaxing around the fire," Tater told her. "Where are you going?"

"I see that," Rose said, starting over to join them. As she approached Noah, she gave him and his work clothes a good once-over. "I was about to sit in my swing for awhile and I couldn't figure out why there was smoke coming out of here."

"It's mostly to keep the mosquitoes away," Noah told her.

"Your supper's waiting for you on the table," Rose informed Tater as she passed by him. "And I want you to go eat it before the flies get to it."

"I'm hungry, too," Tater announced, starting off at once. He was glad to have an excuse to get out of there before she said something about his smoking in front of Noah. "I'll be back later."

"And you know I don't like you smoking yet," Rose yelled after him as he fled. Then she addressed Noah, "I think you took up smoking when you were about twelve or thirteen." She moseyed on around the fire and looked down at the Winchester leaning by the saddle bags and at the bottle of bourbon that stood beside a cordwood seat. She ended up gazing out over the vast plain with her back to the men – and with a sigh, lamented, "I thought I should say a prayer for that boy who died here last night."

After a long moment of silence, Mixy finally spoke up, "While you're at it, Mizzy, you might say one for me, too." He seemed uneasy.

"I will, Mixy," Rose vowed, turning around to face them again, "I surely will."

"Well...then I guess I ought to go and see to my chores," the old Negro said. He gave Noah a peculiar squint and strode off without saying another word.

CHAPTER NINETEEN

Noah was left standing alone with Rose and he wasn't sure if the look Mixy had given him was one of encouragement – or uncertainty. And it was then that he recognized the Bible she was cradling in her arms – it was the old family Bible she had been given on their wedding day. She had a finger stuck between the pages and Noah wondered what ancient wisdom or lesson she was pointing to. The thing he found most disconcerting, though, was the fact that she wasn't scowling at him. It was the first time since he had come riding back into her life that Rose wasn't giving him a spiteful eye.

"Why don't you have a seat and talk to me for a minute or two, Rose," Noah invited. He sat back down and tapped the cheroot out on the heel of his boot and stuck it away in his shirt pocket.

After deliberating for a few seconds she sat down. Only a few feet and the fire separated them and they sat staring at one another through the heat waves of the flames. A simple dress hung from her curves and her hair was loose with a set of horn combs holding it back out of her face. To Noah, Rose looked like a desert mirage – the slight distortion of the heated air erased the lines of age and he saw her more as he remembered her in her youth. Her beauty reminded him of how long it had been since he'd felt the gentle touch of a woman. A primal desire began to seep into his soul. It was longer than he cared to remember since he'd felt the way he did at that moment. She must have noticed the wistful look in his eyes because a shy smile formed on her lips.

"What did you want to talk about?" she queried.

"I just wanted you to know that I didn't have any choice last night, but to do what I did," Noah said. "I tried to run him off, but he was bent on burning Mixy's cabin down to the ground."

"I'm still not convinced that he didn't come up here looking for you," Rose said.

"I doubt that he would've come up here at all if he'd known I was around," Noah boasted. "I didn't even know him that much. The most I knew about him is that he was in with an ornery bunch. The first time I ever laid eyes on him he was riding around with Niles Whitehead."

"The man who was killed at Eddie Button's?" Rose questioned.

"Mississippi was there at the saloon that night," he informed her. "He was mixed up in all that mess, too."

"Now what was the cause of all that?" she mocked him. "Were they trying to burn down the saloon?"

"No," he shook his head, amused by the thought. "I'd have to say it was mostly whiskey and stupidity that caused it. But there's a darn good chance that if Niles was still around he would have been here last night, too.

"As a matter of fact, those two had just come in from shooting up that sheepherder's camp. I'm sure you heard about that. I told you that you shouldn't grieve over their kind, Rose. They were setting out to hurt people. These sort of men are used to living in the middle of trouble, and if there isn't any they'll try to stir some up."

"Well, I don't know why they want to come up here and cause us trouble," Rose said, "if not for you."

"Sure you do," Noah declared. "I heard that Jared Sowers is sweet on you." Just thinking about it sent a pang of jealousy through him.

"Why," her cheeks flushed, "where did you hear such a thing as that?"

"In the wind," Noah told her.

"Well, it's an ill wind you're listening to," Rose assured him. "As a matter of fact, I got more than a good tickle this afternoon over the way he took off out of here. I've been trying to make that arrogant so-and-so feel unwelcome around here ever since his wife moved back to the East. But I must say, the way you stood up to him... well, most of the men around here are fearful of him... you can hear it in their voices..."

"They are afraid of his money," Noah interjected, "because of what it can buy. That's all."

"Then why aren't you?" she asked.

"I learned a long time ago, Rose, that all the gold in the hills can't save you from dying," Noah stated. "Plenty of rich men have got it in the neck, too. Only difference is they leave more stuff behind."

"But he was afraid of you," Rose said.

"And that's what made him so darn mad," Noah said, with a half-grin, "that you were there to see it."

Rose mulled it over for a few seconds, then implored of him, "Why don't you tell me a story, Noah?"

"What story?" Noah asked.

"A story...your story," she said. "I have heard the ones that Tater tells me about in those dime novels. Tell me your story. How did you get mixed up in all this sort of business? How did you start all this killing?"

"Men have been killing each other since the days of Cain and Abel," Noah insisted. "When we was kids Mister Kline shot and killed Mister McGee. Remember, Rose? And they were some of our neighbors. And then there was that time they hung those two Negro boys for what they did to some woman. Don't you remember any of that?"

"Yes, I remember," Rose said. "That was then and it was someone else...this is now and it's you. And I also remember talking about it at the time and that neither one of us could understand how one person could kill another person like that. Even you couldn't understand it at the time, and now it seems you've become part of it all. How in heavens name did that happen, Noah? I'm still having a hard time trying to understand is all. I know you weren't brought up that way."

"You sure you want to hear about it?" he pondered. He didn't want to say anything to spoil the mood she was in – it was more than amiable as far as he could judge.

"Yes," she nodded, "for some odd reason I do. I want to know about the men you've killed. That is if you can remember them."

"Of course I can remember them," he insisted. "It's not something you can forget that easy." Even so, Noah had to stop and think about it while he stared into the fire. "The first time was six years ago last July. I ended up having to kill this Mexican bandit..."

"See, that's what I mean," Rose interrupted him, "why did you end up having to kill him?"

"I guess the main reason would be the fact that he was trying to kill me," Noah told her. "He just came galloping out of a patch of greasewood down this dry wash shooting at me with a pistol. Them bullets were hitting so close in the rocks around me that it was making this old sorrel I was riding dance around something awful. For some reason instead of running I stood my ground and shot him with an old Henry rifle I had. And fortunately I was quick about it. And lucky to have stopped him at all, even though he was an awful big target."

"Did you ever find out why he would just come riding and shooting at you?" Rose queried.

"Well hell, I already knew that," Noah stated. "It was 'cause I was chasing after him. I thought I told you he was a bandit."

Starting to show signs of aggravation, Rose carefully laid the Bible down on top of his saddlebags, losing the place she had saved with her finger. Her eyes narrowed at him. "So why were you chasing after a Mexican bandit?"

"Okay, I see what you mean," Noah said. "Why it was me. Well it was me because I was working as a cowboy for this big cattle ranch in Texas. Seemed like it was about a million acres. Anyway, there was three or four of these Mexican bandits running around the countryside together robbing folks. On top of that they rustled and cooked and ate one of the calves from the ranch. So me and a few of the other cowboys was sent out by the boss to chase them back across the border. We all got split up and I was riding along following his tracks and the next thing I know he was coming after me shooting."

There was something off in the distance that caught Noah's eye. He got up and moved around the fire so he wasn't looking through the heat and the whiffs of smoke. He stared intently out across the prairie, more curious than concerned. Beneath a cobalt sky, the valley floor was bathed in the golden hues of summer by the late afternoon sun. A lone rider carrying a long rifle moved tediously across the rich landscape.

"It's nothing," Noah told Rose when she stood up to see what had distracted him. "Just one of the locals."

"How can you tell?" Rose wondered as she watched the speck moving across the distant plain. The horseman was too far away for her to discern whether it was a white man, or an Indian – and over time she had seen both kinds riding around out there.

"I've seen him down at the saloon before," Noah explained. "Probably just out hunting." He lost interest in the rider and went over to the dwindling side of smoked salmon. He broke off a chunk and handed it to Rose, assuring her, "Indian smoked, it's good."

Sitting back down, Noah relit the cheroot with the smoldering end of a branch and sucked in a couple deep breaths of smoke while Rose returned to her seat and nibbled on the fish. The middle had burned out of the fire and he began tossing the leftover ends onto the hot embers. He let his mind drift back to the past.

"It was that following spring," he began, "I got tired of Texas life and was headed out to California..."

"What ever became of that Mexican?" she stopped him.

"They buried him," Noah replied, looking up at her.

She narrowed her eyes at him again.

"Oh," he responded quickly, "a couple of young Texas Rangers rode out and made a report and that was that. They knew who he was, that he was a bandit and all, but there wasn't any reward out for him, or anything."

That seemed to satisfy her.

"Anyhow, I was making my way along the Santa Fe trail..." Noah's words faded away for a moment and his face grew somber thinking back on it, "...when I got caught up in something real bad.

"I came across this territorial marshal who was leading a posse of men. They had been in the saddle for over a week and were nearly beat to the bone. They were chasing after this Apache Indian who was murdering everything in sight. Those men seemed desperate to catch up to that Indian. So I joined up with them...and I don't think I could describe to you what I saw before that day was over."

As he spoke, he watched the fingers of smoke that began to rise from the camp fire. "We came to this place out in the middle of a cactus flat, the poorest dirt farm you would ever hope to see. It wasn't much more than a mud hut with some corn and squash planted around.

"That Apache had murdered and scalped this man and his wife in front of their two small children. Butchered them would probably be a better term. And then he just left them two helpless kids to perish in the dust. I'd seen a lot of things, Rose, but I had never witnessed that kind of brutality before...that kind of violence. Something inside me changed forever that day. I felt a rage building up in me. I don't care how bad a hand life deals you, it doesn't justify that kind of behavior."

The flames kicked up chasing away the smoke. Noah glanced over at Rose and she looked like she was about to cry. He hadn't meant to spoil her mood and certainly didn't want to make it any worse. He knew it was best if he didn't tell her that the woman had been violated before she was killed. Or about the old gray-haired couple they found the next day that had been shot in the

dirt like they were rabid dogs, or something. He had
better just skip to the end and tell her about killing the
Apache. But knowing her, even that wouldn't cheer her
up again.

"Take my word for it," Noah proceeded before the
tears had a chance to flow, "that son-of-a-bitch was pure
evil. Pardon my language. And when the marshal was
sure that the murdering bastard had made it back into
Old Mexico they had to give up the chase. But I didn't.
I left the posse behind and kept after him. Another man
from the posse volunteered to go along with me, too, but
he only lasted a couple days. I really didn't care, though,
he was just slowing me down.

"I mean how can you just let someone like that get
away with what he did? It took me nearly a week, but I
finally came across him. He was just sitting on his horse
in the middle of some muddy little river – on Pecos, that
horse I'm riding now. And he was as calm as the day is
long. I think that Indian knew he was going to die because
men like him choose the grave over being caught. I shot
him in the head with my pistol and he tumbled right off
into the water. There wasn't a man in that posse who
wouldn't have wanted to kill that Apache."

Noah got up and went around the fire to Rose and
lifted up his shirt, adding, "But he got me, too." Although
the old wound was quite visible he pointed it out to her.
"That Indian put a bullet right through my innards. He
almost used my belly button for a bull's-eye. Barely
missed my backbone."

She studied the scar on his stomach with genuine
concern for a few seconds then looked up at him with
a frown. "You're lucky to be alive," she scolded, like he
was a little boy who had done something stupid.

"I almost did die," he admitted. "If I hadn't been taken in by this old Indian medicine man, I wouldn't be here talking to you now. His name was Bacanaro. Some people called Bacanaro a witch doctor, but I know for a fact that he was a honest to goodness medicine man. I'm living proof. He brought me back from the gates of Hell. I'm telling you, Rose, that bullet burned like the devil."

The cheroot had gone out on its own so Noah put it back in his shirt pocket. He pulled the ax from where Tater had stuck it, but instead of chopping on the gnarly piece of locust, he laid it across the flames to burn it in half.

"Life sure can be full of strange events, can't it?" Noah talked while he fussed with the fire. "I mean...I was nearly killed by an Indian that I ended up killing – and I was found by another Indian who ended up saving my life. It just seems odd when I look back on it. I was laid out flat for a few weeks and it sure gave me a chance to talk to myself about how I was living my life. I spent an awful lot of the time while I was convalescing doing what you might call some soul work. I 'spose it's only natural for a person to do that when they're laying at death's door." He placed another thick branch across the fire and went back over and sat down. The story of his time with Bacanaro seemed to be cheering her up.

"I don't even know if old Bacanaro is still alive, or not, but he sure had a way of making me think about things that had never even entered my mind before," he said, lighting the cheroot again.

"Like what?" Rose quizzed.

"Like he was sure that he had almost figured out how to fly..." Noah told her, blowing out smoke, "without a balloon." He tapped his finger to his temple. "He said that the secrets of life are locked up in here, and all you have to do is find the right key to unlock them."

"Being able to fly..." Rose scoffed. "That's plain and simple nonsense. And you probably believed him. You don't think you might have been delirious with a fever?" She couldn't help but smile.

"If you would have known him," Noah contended, "you would have believed him, too. You would have got on good with old Bacanaro. He told me once that there was a powerful spirit watching out for me. Who knows, maybe he's right. All I know is, I never really feel afraid when it's going on, anymore. You know, when the bullets start flying. You got to admit, that's pretty strange."

"Or slow-witted," Rose quipped. "You should write your own dime novel. It would make quite an interesting story...about flying witch doctors, and all. But now that I think about it, you've always been a good storyteller."

"Well, I guess I must have kept in practice by sitting around camp fires with Texans," he stated. As far as he could figure, story telling was just part of the cowboy life. And for some cowboys like Lester Dunlavy, it was a way of life. "But everything I've been telling you is true.

"Then think about this one, Rose. Bacanaro told me that; 'in a lawless land it is men of conscience that maintain order'." He recited the old shaman's words as if they might be from a page in the Bible. "And I think that I'm finally starting to understand what he meant. It feels like I've been sort of working my way back up here ever since I left his place. I almost feel like I've been guided back up here, like some kind of spell has been cast over me."

"And what did you expect to find, Noah?" Rose asked.

"I had no idea," he admitted. "I didn't know what to expect...and I still don't."

They sat quiet for a minute staring at each other through the heat and smoke of the fire and listening to the gurgle of the nearby creek as it flowed along.

"Well, Rose, I guess that's my story you wanted to hear," he concluded. He didn't see any reason for bringing up the incident with Decatur Bross. Even though at the time, Noah wanted to kill Bross for turning Burt Perry loose on those helpless Indians. "That's all there's been... well, except for these two of Sowers' hired men since I've been back up here. And when I say hired men, I mean gunmen. I guess I'm just tired of those kind of men. Just sick and tired of them, and all the darn trouble."

"But it's not over yet, is it? What about the man with Jared today?" Rose quizzed.

"Wally Pomeroy," Noah scoffed, "he's a half wit. I look for him to be leaving the country soon enough."

"And what about the other man?" she pressed. "Or has he already left the country?"

"What other man?" Noah played dumb.

"The one who burned down Mixy's barn," Rose said. "Rumor has it that you and Mister Perry are at odds with one another. I hear it's something private between you and him."

"Where'd you hear all that?" he asked. It was almost as if Dunlavy had been around. The mere thought of discussing Burt Perry with Rose made him uneasy. He wasn't sure he wanted to even get started on that sore subject. He didn't want to say anything that would spoil her mood again.

"In the wind," she responded. "So?"

"Burt Perry," the words began to flow from Noah's mouth, "to put it simply is a heartless killer. Think of him as one of the sons of Satan. I honestly believe that the world would be a better place without him. He likes to kill. He's killed thousands of buffalo single-handed – and hired a crew of men to do the skinning. All Burt wanted to do was kill them critters one after the other. All day long, day after day. He takes pleasure in it."

"There are lots of men who made their living for awhile by killing buffalo," Rose stated. "That's what put you at odds with him?"

"Look, Rose," Noah told her, "there's other things, too. He lynched some poor Indians when there was really no call for it. There was a couple of starving Indians that had culled this old heifer out of the herd to feed their family. Burt caught them and hanged them as rustlers. One of the Indians was a harmless enough looking man and the other one was just a boy about Tater's age. He left them dangling side by side from a tree limb. Just left them strung up there to rot. That all just happened last fall over in Wyoming."

He stopped short of telling her how he found them with their ears lopped off, and the yellow jackets chewing on them. But maybe it was better that he told her about Burt Perry. That way if it ever did come down to him fighting with Burt, at least she might have a better understanding of the reason why. The look in her eyes showed more concern than sadness.

"The way I look at it," Noah reasoned, "Burt helped kill off all the buffalo and it didn't leave much for them people to eat. They was the kind of Indians that used to follow along with the buffalo herd. Then the mangy bastard turns around and hangs them for killing some stringy old heifer that was about to die of old age, anyway. And there's a darn good chance he has already killed someone around these parts, too," he added.

"Who?" Rose questioned. "I know everyone around here and I didn't hear anything about any other killings."

"That sheepherder who Frank Canfield said was missing up in the hills somewhere," Noah related. "I heard a rumor. I think that's the way he does it, the way he gets by with killing. He goes after those who won't be missed, or has lost contact with their kin. Those kind of people that nobody really seems to care about. Like sheepherders. And Indians.

"He has these two Indian women slaving for him that he treats worse than you would a dog." Noah couldn't think of a way to tell her what was happening to Little One. "I've run across a lot of people out there, Rose," he was somber, "that nobody in the whole world honestly cares about. At least it seems that way to me."

"So what are you going to do about it?" Rose asked. "About Mister Perry?"

"I've been trying to figure that out from the moment I found them two poor Indians hung up that way," he told her. "I know what I ought to do."

"Maybe you ought to talk to the deputy when he gets here," Rose suggested. "See what he thinks."

"I already planned on doing that, but I don't see what good it will do," Noah surmised. "I don't think the law is after him anywhere and there isn't any kind of real proof that he has done anything wrong. Nothing I can prove, anyway. And besides, if I could prove him guilty of anything, I still couldn't let anyone go after Burt without me. I don't think that deputy would have any idea of what he was riding into. I'm pretty sure I know old Burt too good. He's the worst kind of animal there is." He paused a moment, and told her, "Burt Perry is the worst kind of evil – he is ignorant."

"Well...I guess you might as well just go kill him yourself and get it over with. You most likely know what's best in these situations." The tone of her voice was calm and casual like that's what she expected he was going to do anyway. She stood and picked up her bible. "At least then you can decide what you're going to do next." When she came around the fire Noah got up and she stopped close to him and looked him in the eyes. "But whatever you end up having to do, when it comes to these sort of matters, you leave my son out of it. That's all I ask of you."

"I'd never let anything happen to him," he insisted.

"I know," she said, looking up the path. "Mixy tells me that you've been watching out for Tater, making sure he doesn't get into trouble. He's hard headed, Noah, just like you. But..." She took in a deep breath and let it back out. "I guess the Christian thing to do is to thank you for watching out for us." She reached out and took his hand in hers for a moment. "Tater and Mixy are all I have on this earth. So I thank you."

When he tried to take her hand in his, she slipped it away, saying, "I need to be getting on home before Tater comes back down here. I'm keeping him in tonight. We didn't get much sleep last night and I want him to get to bed early. He has firewood to cut tomorrow. I don't think you have any idea how upset he is over all this."

"I think he's seen for himself that killing is a grim business," Noah tried to explain it away, knowing she was still in the dark about the dam and the bridge. "I'm sure he'll be a lot better tomorrow. You know how boys are, they get over things in a hurry. I'd almost bet you by this time tomorrow he'll be his old happy-go-lucky self again."

"I don't know," Rose said, suddenly annoyed. "I can't help but think of that young man who died here last night. What on earth is his mother going to think?"

The look of despair on Noah's face was because he couldn't think of a way to keep Rose from leaving.

"I guess you ought to know," she said, "that I wrote a letter to your mother and told her you were back around here...and that you seemed to be well. I hope you don't mind."

"No, I guess that's fine," Noah said.

"The last letter I got from her she said she hadn't heard from you for so long that she didn't know if you were still alive," Rose lectured. "I didn't tell her what you've been up to." She seemed disgusted with him.

"Do you ever wear that fancy scarf?" Noah asked. He wanted desperately to change the subject.

"Not yet," she said. "I haven't had an occasion to."

"You don't need an occasion," Noah proposed with a sly smile. "I'd sure like to see it on you someday."

"I'm going home," she told him and started off.

"I'd come up for dinner anytime I was invited," he brazenly called after her.

She stopped and turned back like she had some sharp-tongued response. But then she just looked at him and there was something in her eyes that seemed to be pleased with him. There was a softness about her that he hadn't seen for so many years that he had almost forgotten what a sweet woman she could be.

"I'd be an easy man to keep around, Rose," he smiled at her.

"I'll pray for you too, Noah," Rose said, walking away shaking her head.

As soon as she was out of sight, Noah went over and uncorked the bottle and swallowed the sour mash until it burned his throat. He felt like he had just confessed and had been saved or something – or forgiven. It made him think of Fernando Pico who couldn't ride past a mission without going in and telling the friar everything he had been up to, and drop off a few Pesos to seal the deal. It was like the crafty Spaniard could start fresh in life every time he came across a mission.

The last look Rose had given him lingered in his memory and seemed to give him some sort of hope, if only just for a moment. But hope for what? He knew it was probably just his mind trying to will things to happen, but for the time being anyway he didn't feel all alone and empty. He wondered if maybe that was one of a woman's tasks while she was here on earth; to give men hope.

He wondered if she had found something in her Bible that let her be okay with the way things were. He told himself that maybe he ought to thumb through the Bible again someday.

Noah stayed out at the campfire until it was nothing but a glow of ash covered embers. Then he stumbled off to bed, thinking that the cot wouldn't be so bad, it was off the ground...and the half quart of corn whiskey would soften it right up.

CHAPTER TWENTY

The next morning began much too early for Noah. His head throbbed from imbibing too much around the fire and he was already in the saddle chasing after Tater. Mixy had roused him out of a sound sleep to let him know that the boy had already stopped by with the wagon and gone on ahead to cut firewood.

The new day sun shone bright and clear...yet there was a chill lying across the land. The brisk clean air buffeting Noah's face and rushing into his lungs was strangely refreshing. As he loped along on Pecos, he suspected that the label on the whiskey bottle was much too fancy for the contents. The amber poison had made his brain feel swollen and made it difficult to think.

A large flock of Canada geese circled around him low in the sky and they began to break formation, honking sporadically as if quarreling about where they were going to land. They finally settled on a place a good distance away from Noah out in the middle of the prairie grasses. He turned in the saddle to watch them and discovered that in addition to his aching head his body was stiff from sleeping on the hard cot. It was days like this that made him wish he'd taken up trapping or prospecting where he would be lost to the world, out in the middle of the wilderness, free of any and all responsibilities. He could even stay in his bedroll all day if he wanted.

When he reached the head of the valley he spotted the boy's wagon along the tree line. Tater must have been on the lookout because he had reined up the old roan mare to wait for him.

"I knew you'd be coming along," Tater called out as Noah rode up.

"And how did you know that?" Noah quizzed.

"I guess I was just hoping," Tater said. "Mom told me not to bother you unless you wanted to come along, but she packed some extra food for you...just in case. She really liked the way you chased off old man Sowers. She found it most amusing."

"She said that?" Noah questioned.

"No... But I could tell by the way she was talking about it," Tater explained. "I know she's glad you did it, that's all. I wish I could have seen it."

"Well, if he comes around again," Noah said, flatly, "maybe you still can." He could feel the sweat beading up on his forehead and he took his hat off and wiped his brow with his sleeve. Faint plumes of steam rose from atop his head and from out of his hat. He knew it was all the venom that he'd drank the night before seeping out of him.

"Are you okay?" Tater wondered.

"I'm fine," Noah assured him. He sat on Pecos and his gaze wandered off in the distance to the low end of the valley where a dense fog lay like white clouds along the river. "To be honest with you, though, I sure don't know if I feel like cutting firewood this morning. But I guess it's got to be done."

"What would you rather do?" Tater asked.

"I'd like to take a leisurely ride down to the river and stick my head under the water," Noah replied, pulling his hat on again. "Wash my socks and shirt...maybe take a nap in the warm sand."

"Well, I was kind of hoping that we could pay Mister Armstead a visit, anyway," Tater said. "Just to let him know that Mister Sowers thinks it was those other two men who wrecked his dam...and the bridge." He was still doing all he could to cover his tracks. "And maybe while we're down at the river we can do some more shooting."

"Are you s'pose to be gone all day long just to get a load of firewood?" Noah wondered if he might be better off leaving the boy behind this time, especially if he did end up down along the river. He wasn't really quite sure himself why he wanted to go down there, or who he figured he might run into, but he already knew that he was going. There was a jumble of thoughts running through his head that kept changing from dark to light, and back to dark again. And besides, just the thought of shooting guns made his head pulse. He told Tater, "You shouldn't be trying to add to your mom's worries these days."

"She knows I won't be back till late," the boy insisted. "I told her about the elk signs we saw the other day and I'm suppose to scout them out. She said that as long as you're around to help maybe we could kill and hang an elk this year."

"She said that?" Noah was leery.

"Yep," Tater affirmed. "And canned elk is the best. So do you think we can go talk to Mister Armstead?"

"I `spose," he relented. His mood abruptly shifted back to the bright side. It sounded as though Rose had been talking about him to the boy – and Noah was still trying to unravel a few things she had said the day before when she came along with her Bible. Her change of temperament had been so sudden that it made him suspicious that she might be up to something. Perhaps he should spend the day with Tater until he could make better sense of things. "But let's go deal with the firewood first."

"Follow me then." Tater popped the reins across the old mare's back. "It'll be a lot easier than you think."

The wagon yanked to a start and rattled off into the woods and Noah trailed along. After a few minutes they came to a dense stand of jack pines where a row of firewood had already been cut to length and ricked between trees ready to be hauled away. The boy parked the wagon next to the row and began unhitching the horse.

"I stack a load or two ahead in case I have things I want to do instead of cutting firewood," Tater explained. "I don't want to load it though, until I get back. Mom's been warning me about being careful not to break a spoke or a spindle by hauling too much. She keeps saying how this old wagon's about worn out. Mixy keeps fixing it."

"Aren't you afraid somebody will come in here and help themselves to this wood?" Noah rode around looking at the stack of wood Tater had cut. "There's a hell of a lot of work here."

"You mean somebody steal some of it?" he questioned. "Why would anybody do that?"

"To keep from freezing," Noah told him.

"Well...if they're freezing...they're welcome to it," Tater reasoned.

"Apparently you've never met some of the lazy sort I've known," Noah muttered. Other than that, he didn't have the will to argue about the unattended woodpile. But Tater was definitely Rose's son, it was logic straight from the way she looked at things.

"I brought my regular clothes, too," Tater said. He went behind the wagon and shucked off his bibbed overalls and began putting on a set of dungarees.

"Oh..." Noah replied, looking down at himself. He hadn't even thought of wearing his work clothes when he rolled out that morning. The idea of actually cutting firewood hadn't even crossed his mind. He tried to shake the numbness out of his skull and longed for the river.

After Tater finished changing his clothes, he strapped on his revolver, packed the food Rose had sent along into Noah's saddlebags, and swung up on the little mare. They set off to scout out the marsh where the big cedars grew with hopes of finding fresh signs of the elk herd – both agreeing that the quickest way to get there was by going back out onto the prairie instead of cutting through the woods. This time Noah led the way.

And by the time they came out onto the prairie again they had decided to put off looking for the elk until later that day when they came back for the wagon. It was Noah's idea to save them even more time. The new plan was to head straight for the river, stopping along the way only long enough to pay Mister Armstead a visit. This arrangement suited them both; because Tater figured that the sooner Mister Armstead knew what was going on, the better; and because Noah thought a nap at the river might help his headache to go away.

In the time it took them to journey to the other end of the Springwater Valley, the sun had pleasantly warmed the air and the cloud bank along the river had vanished into the blue sky. The boy had chattered the entire way about railroads. Noah might have ridden on a train before, but Tater knew most everything there was to know about the railroads back East. And all about how the Union Pacific was built...from reading books.

The railroad stories faded away when the Armstead ranch came into view. As they rode in closer Noah and Tater couldn't help but look at each other, and they both wore the same curious smile. Lately, the run-down horse ranch was where unusual sights seemed to be almost common place.

The withered old horse trader and his plump wife had brought out chairs from the house so that they could sit next to the newly restored creek. The flea-bitten hound lay at their feet thumping its tail on the ground. In fact the whole barnyard full of animals was out there with them. The emaciated dairy cow along with some pigs and chickens were all enjoying the trickling of the water.

"At least he got tired of sitting in the creek," Noah mumbled under his breath.

"Will you do the talking?" Tater urged. "You know more about what old man Sowers said than I do."

"Morning," Noah greeted as they reined up across the creek from Mr. and Mrs. Armstead. The hound got up and waded the creek for Tater to reach down and pat it on the nose, while their horses took the opportunity to get a drink. "Certainly looks peaceful enough around here."

"For the time being, anyway," Mr. Armstead agreed twisting in the chair to look up at them. "I guess you already heard that after the water came through here it took out the bridge down by the ferry."

"Yeah, I did hear that," Noah said. "Mister Sowers must've been around to see you by now."

"Yep, him and his bunch," he stated. "Five of them altogether. That was yesterday morning. Said they was on their way to see what was left of his dam. Mister Sowers told me it was a couple of men he'd run off his ranch that done it."

"That's what we heard too, ain't it, Noah?" Tater prompted. "That it was some of his own men."

"I `spose," Noah confirmed. He could feel Tater's eyes on him. "That's the rumor going around, anyway."

"Well...whoever it was that done it, laddie, I sure would like to thank them." Mr. Armstead nodded and winked at Tater. "I told Mister Sowers that I didn't see any strangers riding by at all. Told him we was busy chasing after the cow."

"I hope whoever did it gets away clean," Tater concluded. "Except for what happened to the bridge, I'm glad the creek's running by here again."

"Me too," Mr. Armstead agreed. "I'm thinking about raising horses again now that I got the water back." The old man's wife looked over at him like he was crazy. "I know a man less than a day away who's got some good horse stock, for cheap."

"I wonder if the saloon's still closed," Noah said, looking for an excuse to leave. A dull throb in his head told him it was time to continue on down to the river.

"Last I heard," Mr. Armstead said.

"The hotel is where the bachelors are drinking these days," Mrs. Armstead remarked. There was a slight degree of scorn in the tone of her voice.

CHAPTER TWENTY-ONE

They left the Armsteads sitting beside the creek and fifteen minutes later were gazing at Eddie Button's saloon in the near distance. The log buildings were a rusty-brown among the silvery cottonwoods. And there was someone slinking around out behind the saloon who made a quick dash into the privy.

"Did you see that?" Tater's voice reflected his surprise. He expected the place to be deserted.

"You just stay behind me," Noah told the boy, urging his horse into a brisk walk. Tater followed along a few yards behind on the little mare. As they rode around to the back of the saloon Pecos snorted and nickered like he could smell a strange horse. Then a big black mule stuck its head out of the barn into the sunlight, braying back at the intrusion. Noah slipped the hammer thong from his pistol as he reined up next to the outhouse.

"If you came to use the privy," the man's voice from inside informed them, "there's somebody in here already."

"Eddie," Tater called out. "When did you get back?" He rode up beside Noah.

"Who's out there?" Eddie said. They could hear him undoing the latch to come out.

"It's me...Tater." The boy slid down off the mare. "Noah's here, too?"

"Noah Conklin?" The scrawny white haired man came out of the privy and studied the pair of them a moment. He was still road-haggard from traveling and it looked like he hadn't shaved for a week.

"Well, Mister Button," Noah greeted. "I see you made it back all in one piece."

"Got here last night...after dark," Eddie stated.

"Oh hell, I wasn't doing any business in there. I just run in there when I seen somebody coming. I don't want anybody to know I'm back, yet, not until the beer wagon from Boise gets here. The word will get out soon enough."

"You mean you haven't got any beer?" Tater sounded disappointed.

"The only thing I got right now is a few bottles of rotgut whiskey." Eddie looked to see if Noah showed any interest in having a drink. "It'll probably be a couple days until I get stocked up again."

The news even disappointed Noah. He was thinking perhaps a beer would help settle his stomach. He stared at the mule that was still sticking its head out of the barn. "Who's critter is that?" he asked. It sure looked a lot like the one Burt Perry rode.

"Mine now," Eddie boasted. "Won it in a card game up in Idaho City."

"What in the world are you going to do with a mule?" Noah wondered aloud.

"That's a damn good mule I'll have you know," Eddie said. "You can put a saddle on her, or you can harness her. I'm thinking about buying a buggy to ride around in.

"You want a drink of whiskey?" he asked. It seemed to him that Noah was being a little reluctant. "Come on, it's on the house. I'm sure there's something around here to chew on, too. All I ask is that you put your horses out of sight in case someone comes riding by."

Tater led the horses off to tie them out behind the barn and Noah followed Eddie into the back room of the saloon where a trap door in the floor was laid open.

"I was about to go down in the cellar," Eddie explained as he lit a lantern. "I store everything down here when I go away." He put on a pair of cuffed gloves made of heavy leather like the kind the teamsters wore to handle a set of reins. "There's black widow spiders down there sometimes."

"Oh," Noah said, peering down into the dark hole.

"I wondered where you took off to so fast," Eddie said, descending cautiously into the cellar with the lantern lighting the way. "So are you and Tater related?"

"Yes we are, Eddie," Noah told him straight out. Everybody in the Springwater Valley was going to know sooner than later, anyway. "As it turns out, Tater's my own son."

"You're his real pa?" The news made Eddie forget about what he was looking for and even about the black widow spiders. He stared up out of the cellar at Noah. He was obviously confused and scratched at his whiskered jaw with a gloved hand as he pondered.

"Flesh and blood," Noah assured him.

"So you were married to the widow Rose?" Eddie questioned.

"Still am...I 'spose," Noah told him, and then mimicked her words. "But not in her eyes, or the eyes of

God." His comment seemed to baffle Eddie even more. Then he added, "And she ain't no widow either."

When Eddie finally remembered the spiders it only took him a few seconds to find what he needed from the cellar. He handed up a well-worn cracker tin, three glasses and a quart of whiskey that didn't even have a label on it.

"Well, it bothers me to see boys like him grow up in such a hurry out here on the frontier," Eddie said, coming up out of the cellar. "Toting a gun and all." He closed the trap door, blew out the lantern and took off the gloves.

"I know what you mean," Noah replied. He knew Eddie was talking about Tater, and that it was just out of concern for the youngster. "But, it seems like the world is all messed up these days."

About that time, having taken care of the horses, Tater came sauntering in the back door.

"Set that in on the bar," Eddie said, handing the cracker tin to Tater.

They all traipsed into the saloon and took their rightful places; Noah and Tater sitting on stools, and Eddie behind the bar. The front door was closed and the window shutters battened down so the place smelled like stale beer and cigars. The only light and fresh air filtered in from the back room where the silhouettes of flies buzzed around in the doorway.

Eddie poured the whiskey generously. He even sat a glass in front of Tater and poured him a shot. "I guess if you're old enough to wear a side arm in public you're old enough to start drinking hard liquor in public."

"Thank you," Tater said. The offer to drink whiskey in front of Noah and Eddie was public enough for him. He took a swallow of the amber liquid and made a horrible face. "It still tastes like medicine."

"It tastes like nectar from the gods to me," Noah suggested after taking a sip. He determined that the whiskey in the plain bottle tasted smoother than the hooch he had the night before – fancy label and all.

"So what's been going on around here? What have you been up to?" Eddie's questions were directed at Tater. He opened the cracker tin and it was full of jerked venison. "What happened to the bridge?"

While Tater jabbered away, they all three drank whiskey and gnawed on dried meat. Noah was content to just listen to the boy's account of the wrecked dam and bridge. The story hit on all the key ingredients of the disaster, except the truth about who was really at fault. Tater would glance over at Noah now and then, making sure he was keeping the story straight. In fact if Noah hadn't been an eyewitness to the truth, he would have thought that Dunlavy and Fernando Pico had caused the bridge to wash out. After all, Jared Sowers himself said it was so.

Not only could his son spin a good yarn, Noah thought, he was clever about it, too. Tater knew that Eddie would spread his rendition of the story throughout the valley as soon as the men started drinking and eating at the saloon again. It was also apparent to Noah that Tater and Eddie had been swapping lies and scattering gossip around for a long time. He was amused by it all and even thought his stomach was feeling much better. The whiskey had almost cured his headache and his mind was starting to wander all over the place.

The thing that snapped Noah out of his trance was the rotten odor of pickled eggs. At first he thought someone had opened up the smelling salts. Eddie had started spooning out the last of the hard-boiled eggs that were still swirling around in the murky, bitter stench of vinegar. Eddie got one on the spoon and held it out to Noah.

The egg was a pale shade of gray-green and the only reason Noah took it was because he was hungry. He hadn't had any breakfast that morning and his jaw was tired from chewing jerky. Besides, it wasn't all that bad washed down with whiskey...but one was all he wanted.

Tater must have eaten three or four of the nasty things before asking Noah, "Should we say anything about Mississippi?"

"You can go ahead and tell him," Noah said. "You know what all took place up there."

When his son told Eddie why and how Mississippi was killed at Mixy's cabin there was a sadness to the story. Eddie remembered who he was – the young cowboy with the droopy mustache. There wasn't much of anything Noah could have added to what Tater told Eddie about the incident.

"It was really kind of spooky, Eddie," Tater related. "I was wearing gooseflesh and I wasn't even cold. I had a feeling that there was goblins hanging around out in the shadows that night. You could really tell that he was dead... I saw him die."

There was a long moment of silence. Eddie poured another round of drinks and thought back to the night he saw Niles Whitehead dead in the lantern light.

"So how many of those kind of men do you think old Sowers has left?" Eddie asked Noah.

"Only two that I know of," Noah told him. "But, unfortunately they are the worst of the lot."

"Well...I passed one of his men on the road between here and Boise just yesterday," Eddie said. "That knife throwing Mexican I told you about."

"Fernando Pico?" Noah asked. "Wasn't Dunlavy with him?"

"Far as I could tell he was traveling by himself," Eddie pondered. "He talked to me for a minute. Said he was going sailing. I don't know what he meant by it."

"So you didn't see Lester Dunlavy anywhere along the way?" Noah was puzzled.

"I'm sure I would have remembered seeing him," Eddie stated, with a shrug of his shoulders. He found another egg floating around in the crock and gave it to Tater. "I guess your pa must have told you by now how he saved my hide over in Idaho city."

That whole episode had completely slipped Noah's mind. The only thing he remembered about that night was feeling a sense of urgency to get back to the Springwater Valley so he could talk to Rose. That was the night he found out Tater was most likely his son.

But, now it was Eddie's turn to tell Tater about his adventures and misadventures in Idaho City. His story was cut and dry, blunt and to the point. Eddie told the lad how a drunk gold miner had accused him of cheating at cards. And that Noah had to conk the man over the head with a mug of beer to save Eddie from having his throat cut. He even showed them the scar on his neck, that Tater pretended to be able to find.

The light must have been too dim for Noah to see any kind of mark, or maybe there were too many whiskers in the way. But, mostly it was because Noah didn't really care. He had something else on his mind and was not paying attention. Eddie and Tater's voices had become nothing more than a distant echo in the room. Noah was too busy trying to figure out where Dunlavy was if he hadn't gone to California with Fernando Pico.

"You should have stuck around Idaho City another day," Eddie was speaking to Noah. "I finally got to see the hurdy-gurdies. It was their last performance before going on up north. Three of them ladies were dancing up on the stage together...stark naked."

"Stark naked?" Noah quizzed. He heard that...and forgot all about Lester Dunlavy for the moment. He had heard these types of stories before – the figments of a man's imagination.

"The sheriff himself was guarding the stage," Eddie continued. "You'd think everyone would be whooping it up and hollering, but most of the time it was as quiet as a monk's funeral."

"Three of them at the same time?" Noah asked.

"Uh-huh," Eddie stated, then looked over at Tater. "You probably ain't never seen a stark naked woman yet in that kind of way. Have you?"

Even in the poor light they could see Tater turning a dark red like he was some kind of chameleon. The lad finished his whiskey in a single gulp, made a wretched face. He turned his glass upside down on the counter because he had read in a dime novel once that it meant a man was done drinking. And before anymore could be said about anything he excused himself to use the outhouse.

"I don't think he's been introduced to that yet," Eddie said, after he'd heard Tater go in the privy. "But, I'll tell you, after watching those bawdy women dancing around up there in front of everybody like they did...well, I went over and waited my turn in line at the Tainted Lady Hotel." Eddie winked at the end of his confession.

The privy door squeaked as it swung open, and when Tater came out in the daylight he didn't want to go back in the saloon again. He was eager to get on down to the river and do some shooting so he took it upon himself to go bring the horses around.

When Tater showed up at the back door with the horses Noah had a good idea what was going on. Besides, he was ready to leave, too. Noah had already spent more time than he'd planned, eating and drinking and getting caught up on all the news, and he'd drunk enough whiskey that he almost felt cured from last night's bout.

Noah left Eddie Button sitting alone in the saloon pouring himself another drink. The white-haired man sat on his little stool behind the bar and was still reminiscing to himself about the women he had seen on his trip to Idaho City, and other women that were still stuck in his head. Women rarely patronized his saloon and at times he longed just to hear the sweet voice of a female. Eddie Button had never been married. When he got his buggy, he told himself, he would go to town more often.

CHAPTER TWENTY-TWO

The quickest way to the river from the saloon was off through the trees and down Tater's little switchback wagon trail, but Noah wanted to go the long way that would take them past the Rocky Bar Hotel. He didn't give a reason why...and Tater didn't ask. Noah's curiosity had gotten the best of him. He couldn't get Dunlavy off his mind and thought perhaps the hotel cook might have seen him hanging around. Dunlavy was usually easy enough to track down if you knew where to look. The best place to start was always the local eateries.

As the Snake River came into view the ferry bell rang out from the opposite shore. Noah and Tater could see the flatboat as it started to drift away from the bank to pick up the fare waiting across the water. And when they reached the hotel they found Schwarting in his usual place outside the kitchen door, watching as a freight wagon was being driven onto the ferry.

"I don't know why they don't just build a bridge across here, too," the big man in a soiled apron commented as Noah and Tater rode up to him. "The wagons will never stop coming."

Over the years, Schwarting had watched men and women and whole families opening up the new territories in the West one prairie schooner at a time – and commerce following along building new towns with a constant stream of freight wagons.

When Noah asked about Dunlavy, the cook answered with a shake of his jowls. Schwarting couldn't remember exactly when he saw him last, but he knew it had been at least two or three days. Inside the hotel kitchen, someone started calling for Schwarting and he had to go back to work.

Still baffled over the disappearance of Dunlavy, Noah sat atop Pecos and stared out as the oxen began pulling the ferry back across the river.

"Are you hungry?" Tater asked, swatting at a wasp that was buzzing around him. "We could go down and sit by the water and eat."

"That sounds alright," Noah replied, lost in his own thoughts. But instead of leading the way as usual, he just sat there and continued to watch the goings on at the ferry crossing.

"Is there something wrong?" Tater wondered. It appeared to him as though Noah was especially interested in that particular freight wagon coming across on the flatboat.

"Huh?" Noah grunted.

"You act like something's bothering you," Tater said.

"Oh...it's nothing," Noah explained. "I was just thinking of old Lester Dunlavy. You know who he is. Well he's kind of a friend of mine and I was just trying to figure out if he's gone ahead to California, or not."

Then he touched a spur to Pecos and as the horse started off, he said, "Let's go down by the river while we eat."

"You ain't going to California, are you?" Tater called after him, trying to catch up to the long-legged thoroughbred.

"I wasn't planning on it," he stated. There was something in Tater's voice that made Noah look back at him. His son bore the most sorrowful expression so he slowed up for him. "I don't want to go anywhere, but around here." And when Tater rode up beside him, he clapped him on the arm, insisting, "I'm not going to go anywhere. You don't need to worry about that."

That momentary look of anguish on Tater's face troubled Noah deeply. He felt like his heart was sinking and it stirred a wave of emotion that washed over him like a great burden – and it instantly brought Bacanaro to mind. The old medicine man had a word for the way he felt right then, but he couldn't think of it. It wasn't a Spanish word either, it was in English.

They hitched the horses a couple hundred feet upstream from the ferry among the sagebrush that grew along the banks of the Snake. Noah took the saddlebags with the food and found a nice smooth boulder near the waters edge to sit on. Rose had packed fried egg sandwiches and pieces of apple cobbler for their lunch.

Tater took a sandwich and moseyed off along the shoreline, kicking little stones around with the toe of his boot as he ate his lunch. Sulking about like that, the boy appeared as though he was still dwelling on the possibility of Noah going away.

And as Noah watched his son, he knew if he ever did leave the Springwater Valley again it would never be for long. More time had passed than he cared to admit since anyone had shown that kind of concern over where he went, or for that matter what he did, let alone what might happen to him along the way. Somewhere between the saloon and the rock where he sat to have a bite to eat, Noah ended up with dark clouds stirring through his mind again. He still couldn't think of Bacanaro's word... but he knew he was still suffering from whatever it meant.

Having wolfed down his sandwich, Tater was already coming back for some apple cobbler. He still wore a long face.

"Noah," Tater asked, solemnly, "do you think they'll ever build a railroad along the Snake here? You know rivers are good places for a railroad to follow because of the grade they need."

"Well," Noah reasoned, "if that's the case, I'm sure they will then." His words seemed to brighten the boy's spirits. "In fact, you just heard the old cook there, what he said about all the freight coming this way. Why even Mister Sowers up there is planning on shipping beef out of here to the East. I 'spose they'll need a set of tracks around here somewhere so they can haul freight in and take cows back with them."

"Do you think I could ever get a job working for the railroad?" Tater questioned.

"I don't see why not," Noah assured him, "with as much as you already seem to know about trains."

Taking a piece of apple cobbler with him, Tater wandered off along the river bank again. This time instead of kicking rocks around he was finding flat ones to throw out across the water while he had his dessert. He suddenly had mixed emotions about old man Sowers

– secretly hoping for a booming cattle business in the Springwater Valley. And he was daydreaming about blowing a steam whistle.

As Noah finished his sandwich he watched a freckle faced kid playing along a river, eating apple cobbler with one hand and skipping stones with the other – and wearing a gun. Eddie Button was right, boys like Tater were too green to have a pistol strapped to their hip in such a fashion. He should still be trying to knock over tin cans with a slingshot.

Rose and Mixy were right, too, Tater was far too young to be mixed up in a mess like the one Sowers had stirred up. Noah tried to imagine how worried Rose must be when the boy was off running around the countryside alone. Now, the mere sight of Tater wearing a gun began to annoy Noah.

From somewhere up the river, the boom of a large bore gun rolled like thunder along the water and echoed off the basalt bluffs. A second shot followed moments later. The reports sounded to Noah like a buffalo gun and had instantly brought Burt Perry to mind.

The gunfire caught Tater's attention and he headed back toward Noah, and as he drew near, stated flatly, "Ten-gauge. Somebody shot a goose."

"That's probably it," Noah agreed, squinting up into the bright blue day. The skies above the Snake River had a few white wispy clouds floating around and the flocks of Canada geese appeared as crooked black lines moving across them in random order. Noah knew they were being pushed down from the north by the approaching winter.

A surge of urgency pulsed through Noah that got him up from his rock. He needed to try to think about other things besides winter being right around the bend – and Burt Perry just up the road a spell. He decided to save his piece of apple cobbler until later and started for the horses with Tater a step behind him.

"What would you do if you worked for the railroad?" Noah asked, throwing the saddle bags across Pecos's rump.

"I want to learn how to drive a locomotive," Tater answered, hopping up on the back of the old mare. He gazed up the well worn road toward Springwater. "Do you want to go have a look at the bridge?"

"Not especially," Noah answered, mounting up. "We'd better get a move on if we're going to make it back with a load of wood before your mom starts to worry."

With Noah leading the way they headed back past the hotel to the old road that went upriver toward Tater's ravine, but more importantly toward the coulee where Perry was camped.

No matter how hard he tried, Noah couldn't chase Burt Perry out of his thoughts. And he began to dwell on something Rose had said around the fire. She had said something about him having to take care of Perry before he could figure out what he was going to do next. Besides, as long as there was trouble lurking about the Springwater Valley how could he ask Tater not to wear a gun. Noah set a brisk pace.

"Where are we going?" Tater called out as they rode past the trail that led down into the little ravine where he had his shooting range set up.

"On," was all Noah offered and the boy didn't say anything.

As he came to the rim of the coulee where Perry was camped, Noah finally slowed Pecos to a lazy walk. He twisted around in the saddle and motioned for Tater to stay back a little. Noah surveyed the ground as he crossed the trail that led down into Perry's camp and there were no signs of fresh tracks to be found anywhere. He really couldn't tell how long it had been since anyone had been in or out, but it looked to him like the most recent tracks were days old. He sniffed the air for any scent of a campfire.

Noah continued on for a little ways and then reined up to wait for Tater. He felt troubled and stared back toward the coulee. Now he wasn't even sure if Burt Perry was still around. He thought that perhaps the dirty mongrel had moved his camp just to be on the safe side. Or, maybe he was down in there holed up with Alice and Little One and was simply too drunk and lazy to come out.

"Do you want to go back down in there?" Tater asked.

"Nope," Noah shook his head.

"What's down there?" Tater was curious. He still didn't know what they were doing, but he had an idea something was going on because of Noah's dark mood.

"That's where the old buffalo hunter made his camp," Noah told him.

"Is he down there now?" Tater asked, looking back with renewed interest.

"Don't know," Noah said.

"Well do you think those Indians are down there?" Tater wondered aloud.

"I just don't know," Noah replied.

"Maybe we could sneak up on them and see," Tater suggested.

"That's an idea alright," Noah said. He felt Pecos's head come up sharply and the horses ears were pointed in the direction of two men on the road ahead that were riding toward them. The men were leading an old bony packhorse and they weren't wasting any daylight getting where ever it was they were going. It only took a minute for them to pass by Noah and Tater and they all nodded a cordial greeting while studying each other curiously. The packhorse was all lathered up from its load and was dragging its feet kicking up puffs of tan dust, and it was wheezing as it trotted past.

"That poor ol' nag," Tater said under his breath. And when they were out of range, stated, "I'd have to guess that them fellows are headed for the gold fields." Living along the Oregon Trail, it had become a habit for Tater to imagine where travelers were headed – and the thought of finding gold stirred his imagination. "Have you ever panned for gold, Noah?"

"Nope, never have," Noah answered. "Been around it though..." He watched the pair as they rode away, dragging the packhorse along. And the men were gone almost as quickly as they had appeared. Perhaps Tater was right because they sure looked like they couldn't wait to strike it rich. "But, I'll be the first one to admit that I've never been greedy enough to work that hard. Believe me, Tater, dairy farming is an easy life compared to gold mining."

"Well...I think riding in a steam locomotive would be fun," Tater considered. "And that wouldn't seem like work at all. Don't you think?"

"It sounds to me like you've got it all figured out," Noah told him, urging Pecos into an easy walk. "Come on, let's keep going."

They continued on in silence and he glanced over at the pistol slapping against the boy's leg. Noah needed to find out where Burt Perry was, and there was only one way to know for sure if he was still camped down in the coulee. He'd have to walk in.

A few minutes later they came to the narrow brush covered ravine where Noah had hid Pecos the last time he was going to trek down the river to shoot Perry – the day he ran into Little One. Noah steered his horse off the road and when he was out of sight of any other travelers who might ride by he swung down from the saddle and looped the reins over a tree limb. Tater had followed. He slid off the mare and hitched her to some brush.

"I want you to stay here and mind the horses," Noah instructed. And even though he already knew his pistol was fully loaded, he pulled it out and clicked the cylinder slowly to make sure. He slipped the pistol back in its holster and looked up at Tater and he wished he would have waited until he was on his way down the river before he had checked his gun. The boys eyes were filled with uncertainty, almost fearful.

"What are you gonna do?" Tater questioned.

"I'm just going for a little hike down the river," he told him. "I'll be right back."

"Maybe we ought to just go and get that load of firewood," Tater suggested. "Even you said if we're gone too long that it will worry mom. Huh?"

"Listen, I need to go and see if Burt Perry is still around," Noah insisted, "and I want you to stay here and wait for me. It's important. Do you understand?"

"Yes sir." Tater was reluctant, but gave a nod.

"Okay then," Noah said, and started to leave.

"Noah..." Tater called out. And when Noah stopped and turned back to him, declared, "The other night...that was the first time I ever seen anybody get shot to death."

It was obvious by the expression on his son's face that the event weighed heavy in his thoughts.

"Oh...everything will be just fine," Noah told him. He tried to act as casual as he could. "Just stay here and try to keep out of sight and I'll be back before you know it. You could see if the horses want a drink."

CHAPTER TWENTY-THREE

Without any further discussion, Noah walked out to the edge of the Snake River where he could see down the shoreline toward Perry's camp. Noah had known all along exactly what it was that he had set out to do that morning, and he couldn't stop himself. Rose's words had only made sense to him. With Perry out of the way it would all be finished. Jared Sowers would be out of gunmen except for Wally. And Noah would give odds that Wally Pomeroy would clear out in a hurry thinking he might be next. The fact of the matter was there seemed to be no other solution to the problem, but to just go kill Burt Perry and get it over with, once and forever. Then he could try to figure out what he was going to do next... like Rose said.

As far as Noah could tell the river was deserted; so he started toward Perry's camp. He stayed close to the willows that grew along the flood plains and after only going about fifty feet came to a small clearing that he ducked into for a minute so that he could think. He didn't feel like he was prepared for what he was setting out to do. He wondered if he wasn't as crazy as the rest of them the way he was thinking – here he was sneaking down the river bank on his way to kill a man – almost as if he was obliged to do it. Noah's mind was racing with a myriad of thoughts. Why didn't he remember to bring the Winchester along? Why didn't he think to buy a bottle of that no-brand whiskey from Eddie Button? Why didn't he have enough sense to just leave Tater behind? He should have kept him away from all this bloody business.

Tater. That was the one flaw in Noah's plan that he was unable to overlook. What if something was to happen and he couldn't make it back to the horses? Sooner or later he knew that Tater was bound to come looking for him. Especially if he heard gunfire. It was in the boy's nature. The realization seemed to strengthen Noah's determination that he couldn't fail. With his son in the mix there was no margin for mistakes.

He looked at his hands and they were tough from the years and calloused from the reins. And even though he couldn't see it they had the blood of other men on them. When he thought about such things it made his life seem like some kind of mistake. He felt like he had taken so many bad turns over the years that he was right back where he started. Despite it all his hands were steady.

He also realized that he was about to commit murder and that, one way or another, he would probably have to answer for it. Noah sucked in a deep breath and compared the way he felt right then to taking a bath in freezing cold water, he couldn't think about it, he just had to do it. He blew out the breath and started on his way again and as he stepped out of the clearing he was startled by the sight of Little One coming out from behind a clump of bulrushes at the edge of the river. Noah's hand jumped to the butt of his pistol and Little One about jumped out of her skin.

"Noah," the young Indian girl cried out, startled.

"God almighty, Little One," he scolded. But before she had a chance to react to the tone of his voice, Noah forced a smile and waved her toward him. "Come on over here. I wish you'd quit sneaking up on me."

"I didn't mean to," she stated.

"What in thunder are you doing way out here?" he asked. "Where's Perry?"

"At our camp," Little One replied, adding, "Alice said that we are going to run away from Perry. And we are doing it tonight, but you can't tell. It's secret. Alice told me that Perry is going to die."

"What?" Noah was bewildered. "What are you talking about?"

"Perry is hurt real bad," Little One said. Then she pointed behind Noah, and asked, "Who's that over there?"

Looking around, Noah espied Tater peering out of the brush. "He's with me," Noah said, and shook his head. The moment Tater knew he had been discovered he vanished back into the thicket. "His name's Tater. Come on with me, Little One, and you can meet him. Besides, I want to talk to you for a minute."

"Perry never did find out that I have a dollar," Little One divulged as she tagged along with Noah.

"So...what happened to Perry?" Noah queried as he led her back toward the horses.

"He got in a fight with Alice and she hurt him bad," Little One said. She looked like she was about to cry. "Alice is afraid the white law will hang her when they find Perry dead."

"No, they won't," Noah stated as though it were a promise. If anyone really had the right to kill Perry it was Alice. She couldn't have liked what was going on between Little One and that lice infested buffalo hunter. Noah just assumed the fight must have been over that. He tried to imagine Perry all sliced up with a knife, and with gangrene eating away at him.

"Tater, this here's Little One," Noah announced to the boy, who was back keeping the horses company. Little One's presence made Tater nervous in a way that Noah had never witnessed before. Of course, it was hard to ignore the way her little buckskin dress hung on her, and her legs were bare. A deep red color spread up Tater's neck and the best greeting the lad could come up with was a mute nod. Noah couldn't help but notice the way Little One was looking at Tater, and the smile that she flashed him.

"So did Alice stick Perry with a knife?" Noah asked her.

"No," Little One replied, "Alice got him with her war club. And we prayed to Jesus to make Perry die."

"Well, did she crack his skull open?" he pursued.

"No..." Little One said with a coy smile. She was talking to Noah, but she was gazing at Tater. "Alice got Perry right there." And as she spoke, the young Indian girl demonstrated on Tater, acting like she was going to smack him square in the crotch. The boy jerked his hips away, taking a quick step backwards. He was stunned.

Even though Noah's mood was still quite serious, he had to restrain himself from showing any signs of amusement as he watched Tater struggle to regain what little composure he had to begin with. "Oh yeah," Noah said, "and what makes Alice think that Perry might die just from getting cracked down there?"

"'Cause he can't stand up," Little One said. "Perry's leg is all turned black and he can't go piss anymore. Alice threw his guns in the river and..."

"Are you sure?" Noah questioned firmly.

"I saw her," Little One said with a blunt nod.

If that was indeed true, Noah knew Perry must be on his death bed. A leg turning black was an indication of blood poisoning. And that, sure enough, could prove deadly. Was it possible that Alice had already taken care of Perry – in her own way? "Maybe Alice is right," he concluded.

"Alice took his rum away, too," Little One added, "but she didn't throw it in the river."

"Who's Alice?" Tater's curiosity forced him to speak.

"That's Little One's ma," Noah said.

"Well...why do you call your mom Alice?" Tater directed his question at Little One.

"Because that's her name," Little One reasoned.

"Where do you live?" Tater quizzed her.

"Back there," Little One said, looking and pointing down the river.

"Little One, are you sure Alice is really serious about taking off and leaving Perry?" Noah pressed. Everything had changed so sudden that he was still having a hard time trying to determine what he should do now.

"We have to," Little One explained, troubled. "Perry told Alice that when he gets better he is going to drown her in the river. If we go tonight he won't get any better."

"I 'spose that's right," Noah assured her. "Your ma knows what to do. But you tell her that the white man law won't come after her."

"Well, don't you have a house to go to somewhere?" Tater was concerned.

"No," Little One said, somewhat perplexed. "Do you have a house?"

"Of course," Tater declared. "Doesn't everybody."

"Noah?" Little One said.

"What?" Noah said.

"Do you have a house somewhere?" Little One asked.

"No," Noah stated flatly.

"See," Little One smiled. "Everybody don't."

"Well...most people do," Tater argued.

Once Tater got over being bashful he started asking Little One all kinds of questions, and the both of them were giving each other admiring looks. The trouble was Noah needed a little solitude so he could think about his next move. Somehow he had lost the desire to go shoot Burt Perry. It felt like the dark clouds that had been occupying his thoughts were starting to melt away.

"Why don't you two walk on up the river a little bit," Noah suggested, holding out his hand. "And you can leave your pistol here. You won't need it while you're off with Little One."

"Huh?" Tater wasn't sure he had heard right. But he stripped off the gun belt and handed it over to Noah.

"I can't think straight with all that yammering going on," Noah said. "I'll stay here with the horses. Just don't be gone too long."

Little One didn't have to be asked twice. She reached over and grabbed Tater's hand and began leading him toward the river. Tater looked back over his shoulder at Noah with eyes as big and bright as new silver dollars. Still, he was going willingly – and he seemed to have forgotten all about having to get a load of firewood.

Noah stowed Tater's pistol away in his saddlebags and took out the piece of apple cobbler. He found a little stretch of warm sand near the water where he could not only keep an eye on the horses, but he had a clear view up and down the shoreline. He sat with his back up against a pile of driftwood and the sound of the river rushing over nearby rapids filled his ears.

He watched as Tater and Little One made their way up along the river. As far as Noah could tell Little One still had a hold of Tater's hand. It awakened the memory of the last time he ran into Little One and he knew that his son had no idea of what he might be getting himself into. Just the same, Noah thought, that's what a young man Tater's age should be doing – walking with a girl beside the river. They would disappear from time to time behind the bulrushes and willows and it wasn't long until he lost sight of them among the thickets. Noah turned his attention downstream and let his eyes search for any signs of movement, but it was deserted.

It was a day typical of an Indian summer. The early morning dew had burned away and the sun felt warm against him. The white, wispy clouds had long been absorbed by the blue skies, and Noah could smell the river in the gentle breezes that swept in off the water. He ended up staring at the bright silver flashes of sunlight that shimmered along the surface of the river as it tumbled past.

Compassion. That was Bacanaro's word that Noah couldn't think of earlier and now it just popped into his head. Subjects like compassion were what the old Yaqui medicine man used to like to talk about – integrity was another one. In fact, Bacanaro thought it was probably a combination of those two things that made Noah track down and kill the Apache, and ultimately get himself gut shot. Noah would have sworn it was just plain old anger and vengeance, and his own sense of doing what was right.

But regardless of what it was, he knew it was now keeping him from finishing what he had set out to do that morning. What he had set out to do last autumn in Wyoming. Noah could still picture those poor dead Indians hanging from the limb of a tree with their necks stretched out and not get himself worked up enough to walk down the river and shoot Burt. Finding out that the Indian woman had thrown his guns in the river carried the most significance. He simply couldn't find it in him to kill a man who wasn't able to defend himself – even if it happened to be Burt Perry.

It had already occurred to Noah that perhaps justice was finally being served up. If Perry was truly unable to fend for himself and Alice took off and left the scoundrel all alone...it could prove to be a miserable way to die – alone, with the other predators hanging around. The one thing Noah refused to do was let his compassion make him feel sorry for Burt Perry. "I'd only be doing the stinking bastard a good deed by putting him out of his misery," he mumbled under his breath.

In the end, Noah decided that the best thing to do about Perry was to wait until the deputy arrived. Then they could ride out together and perhaps find him dead in his robes, or at least with no means to fight. Either way, he would let the law figure out what to do. As far as Noah could foresee it was no longer his problem. Now he could only hope that at last, one way or another, Perry had met his demise. He overcame the urge to walk down and make sure for himself. Besides, he figured Alice had seen enough misery in her life to know when someone was dying. And there was no reason for Little One to lie.

Noah adjusted a couple pieces of driftwood so that he could settle back and relax in the midday sun. When he began eating the apple cobbler he couldn't help but to think of Rose. Some of the things she had said to him were starting to sink in. What had he expected to find when he came back to the Springwater Valley? What did he expect from Rose? He was the one that had forsaken her – and everyone and everything else he'd ever cared about. His own mother must have worried about him like Rose worries about Tater and his father went to his grave thinking ill of him for abandoning his wife...and even worse...a child. How was Rose supposed to react to him? He wasn't the same person she had known when they were young. And now he realized he wasn't even the same man who rode back into the Springwater Valley just a few short weeks ago. For nearly a year his sole purpose in life was to kill Burt. Something in him had changed.

Dwelling on the past usually left Noah with a hollow feeling. It seemed like the only thing he had been doing for the last few years was just following his nose around like he didn't have any better sense. Living out each day while the sun was shining and somehow making it through each night. There were times that the burdens of thought weighed him down. He suddenly felt worn out and blamed the warmth of the sun and a full belly for making him drowsy and he soon began nodding off.

CHAPTER TWENTY-FOUR

It was Pecos nickering at Tater and Little One coming back down the river that roused Noah from his nap. Tater was leading the way with Little One a few steps behind him and they were both staring down at the ground. The boy looked like he had finally remembered that he was supposed to be getting a load of firewood. Noah had no idea how long he had been dozing, or how long they had been gone. He dragged himself to his feet and yawned and stretched and went over to the edge of the river to wash his hands...they felt sticky from the apple cobbler.

"Good bye, Noah," Little One said as she breezed past him while he was bent over the water with his back to her.

"Well... Bye, Little One," Noah called after her. He stood up shaking the cold water from his hands. "You tell Alice good luck for me." She didn't look back right away, but after a moment without slowing down she turned and gave him a quick wave and an even quicker glance. He walked up from the river to find Tater already straddling the old mare ready to leave.

As usual Noah took the lead and they rode away from the Snake River and started up out of the canyon toward the Springwater Valley. Tater seemed content just to stay back in his own world. It was obvious to Noah that something out of the ordinary must have occurred while Tater and Little One were up the river, and whatever it was had the boy preoccupied to the point that he had forgotten all about asking for his pistol back.

Noah was a little curious about it all, but because of the sensitive nature of the subject he thought it best to take his son's feelings into consideration. And even though Tater was sporting a bit of a smirk and his eyes seemed a little glazed over, it wasn't the same to Noah as kidding around with the young cowboys who were already familiar with girls. He set a pace that would make it easy for the boy to keep up in case he felt like talking.

When Noah reached the crest of the hills that sheltered the Springwater Valley he reined up to wait for Tater. It had been a constant climb since they left the river and he figured the horses could use a rest, especially the old mare. Tater had fallen farther behind and was still coming up along the switchback trail. In the distance below, the Snake River had become a bright ribbon of sky laying at the bottom of the canyon. And another wave of geese came from the north and passed overhead, honking sporadically.

From the promontory Noah gazed out over the Springwater Valley. The golds and greens and browns of the earth basked in the warmth of the midday sun. On a distant knoll the white-washed grange stood out like a beacon. He could see the dark stand of locust trees where Lewis Morrey lived. Then his eyes settled on the white line of fence that ran up into the hills and his thoughts turned to Jared Sowers. Even with Perry out of the mix there was still some unfinished business.

Scattered across the floor of the valley were small herds of grazing cattle. Some were nothing more than dark blotches seemingly lost in the seas of prairie grasses. Maybe Sowers did have a prize seed bull, but the valley had enough grass and water to support a herd as big as most men would want to care for. And there was another million acres of scrubland grazing just across the river. There was so much open range that a man would have to be a moron to keep from getting rich raising beef in the Springwater Valley. Something still didn't make sense.

The old mare came huffing and shuffling along the trail and Tater reined up beside Noah. Not one word had been exchanged between them since they left the river and Tater was still having a hard time looking Noah in the eye.

"Let's spell the horses awhile," Noah said. He took a cheroot from his shirt pocket and broke it in two and gave half of it to his son. Then he struck a match and they sat there on top of the hill quietly blowing out puffs of smoke. Tater turned back so that he was looking down on the Snake. The fact that the boy still didn't feel like talking was fine with Noah – he had already found other things to worry about, anyway.

Noah continued to stare out over the valley and to deliberate on Jared Sowers. He couldn't imagine what it was that Sowers really wanted and began to wonder if there were other things going on that he didn't know about. There wasn't any gold in Springwater Creek. What did the wealthy rancher hope to accomplish by hiring gunmen? Even Dunlavy didn't seem to think that Sowers understood exactly what he had gotten himself into. Maybe Sowers had gone a little crazy sitting up there looking down on everybody.

Over the years Noah had seen the best and the worst in people and Jared Sowers really wasn't all that bad compared to the Burt Perry's out there in the world. As far as Noah could tell, Sowers was just plain lonely, and most likely bitter because of it. Loneliness can drive some men insane. There did seem to be a lack of social events around the Springwater Valley, but Noah had blamed it on the time of year – the grange dances didn't usually start up regular until the end of the harvest season.

Besides, Noah knew the real reason that Sowers had gotten so irate when he showed up at Mixy's place wasn't about losing Mississippi, it was finding out about him and Rose. And when he stopped to think about it, Noah couldn't really blame Sowers for trying to win Rose's favor...she had to be the best looking woman around. At least Noah didn't have to worry about Sowers trying to romance Rose anymore...not after seeing the way she treated him.

It suddenly occurred to Noah; of course Sowers was crazy, the old buzzard was trying to impress a woman. Could all of this be over Rose? That seemed to be the only reasonable explanation for what was going on. And right then, as he fixed his eyes on the far end of the Springwater Valley, Noah swore to himself that the next time he was alone with Rose around the fire he would at least try holding her in his arms again. He always felt like he had missed his opportunity in the barn that stormy day...but it was only a matter of time. Noah knew that time had a way of taking care of things...and time was all he had left these days. What he needed to do now was try and figure out what he was going to do next

– like Rose said. For instance, since he was determined to stay around Springwater, how was he going to make a living?

That presented an entirely new problem. About the only thing Noah was good at other than gunfighting was cowboying, and the only man that he knew who was hiring probably wanted him tarred and feathered and run out of the country on a rail...or dead.

Noah decided that when he found out what Perry's fate was he would ride up and talk to the old coot, be straight with him and see if he was a man that could be reasoned with. And he would let Wally Pomeroy know he was all alone now. If things were different, maybe Noah could do some cowboy work and become a goodwill ambassador between Sowers and the farmers. The thought that he might end up punching cows for Jared Sowers made him shake his head.

The daydreaming came to an end with a deep sigh as Noah looked around for Tater. Noah had given Pecos enough rein to browse around the ground for any fresh shoots of grass. The mare was a few yards away standing on three legs taking a nap with her head hung down. The boy was lying back on the old horse's rump with his hands clasped behind his head...peering into the deep blue sky.

"Are you alright?" Noah spoke up, his voice cut through the quiet.

The only sounds had been that of Pecos chomping at the tufts of grass and the distant honking of the Canada geese. Tater sat up and the mare raised her head and he reined her over toward Noah. The boy seemed to be halfway back to normal with something weighing on his mind. "Noah, do you think they'll really leave?" he pondered.

"I 'spose," Noah answered, looking back down on the river. He knew that Tater was talking about Little One and Alice. "Anyway...it's for the best."

"I just can't picture that girl and her mom riding all that way by themselves," Tater stated.

"I'm sure they'll be just fine," Noah said. "You can bet that Alice knows what to do...she's a tough old gal. Besides, Tater, they're Indians, the whole Earth's like a gosh darn mercantile to them."

"Where will they go?" Tater questioned. "They don't even have a house to go to. Not even a little shack."

"They'll most likely go back to their own people," Noah told him. His son did not understand what Little One's situation had been with Perry, or he would be happy they had a chance to get away. "That's home to them."

The boy seemed to reflect on it all for a minute, then declared, "I'm getting hungry."

"Well...I 'spose we ought to go load that firewood," Noah suggested.

"The sooner we can get on home..." Tater caught Noah's eye and his face was already crimson when he asked, "Is it a sin to kiss a Indian?"

This time Tater didn't wait for Noah to lead the way. The boy must have been able to feel himself turning red because he took off on the old mare kicking her in the sides until she broke into an easy lope.

"I don't think so," Noah yelled after him.

Before going after him, Noah took one last look down on the Snake River. The chance meeting with the Indian girl had altered the course of the day. She had kept him from killing Perry – and had perhaps opened up a whole new dimension of life for Tater. Little One sure seemed to have taken Tater's mind off of the wrecked dam. Noah knew that more than likely he had seen Alice and Little One for the last time and he hoped things would turn out good for them and they would find some happiness along the way.

When he started down out of the hills into the Springwater Valley, Noah wondered if he would ever see Lester Dunlavy again. Maybe Dunlavy had gotten tired of it all and had headed back home to see if he had any family left. Or, maybe he had finally decided that it was time to find an honest job – like he always said he would. Misfit that he was, Dunlavy always knew how to get by. Noah was going to miss Dunlavy.

By the time he reached the valley floor, Noah had caught up with Tater. Behind him, the river canyon and Perry were a good distance away. He felt satisfied with the way things were turning out. This was one of those times that Bacanaro would have told him to look inside his heart and believe that things would work out exactly the way they were supposed to. The medicine man believed that Noah had been given a second chance for a reason. Perhaps this was his chance to try to rescue what life he had left. He swore to himself not to squander it.

In the mean time, he concluded, if Rose could at least tolerate him and it was no better between them than it was...so be it. Still, he wanted to get back to Mixy's and build his fire and see if he could lure her down again.

Later that evening, Noah built his fire in the clearing by the creek, but Rose never came down. He was disappointed and thought of walking up the creek. Instead he left her alone and drank some more of the rotgut whiskey. He knew time was on his side. The embers died down and the night grew cold and he went on to bed. At the dawn of a new day, Noah Conklin was going elk hunting with his son.

Cover Photo by author, Alan Hitchens
Back Cover Photo by Paul Hitchens

Book designed and typeset by
TypeCraft Inc.
Spokane Valley, WA
www.typecraft.net

Printed by Gray Dog Press
Spokane, WA
www.graydogpress.com